D0426378

Douglass' Women

Also by Jewell Parker Rhodes

The African American Guide to Writing and Publishing Nonfiction

Free Within Ourselves: Fiction Lessons for Black Writers

Voodoo Dreams

Magic City

Douglass' Women

A Novel

Jewell Parker Rhodes

ATRIA BOOKS

New York   London   Toronto   Sydney   Singapore

ATRIA BOOKS
1230 Avenue of the Americas
New York, NY 10020

This book is a work of fiction. Names, characters, places and incidents are products of the author's imagination or are used fictitiously. Any resemblance to actual events or locales or persons, living or dead is entirely coincidental.

Copyright © 2002 by Jewell Parker Rhodes

All rights reserved, including the right to reproduce this book or portions thereof in any form whatsoever. For information address Atria Books, 1230 Avenue of the Americas, New York, NY 10020

ISBN: 0-7434-1009-2

First Atria Books hardcover printing October 2002

10 9 8 7 6 5 4 3 2 1

ATRIA BOOKS is a trademark of Simon & Schuster, Inc.

Designed by Nancy Singer Olaguera

For information regarding special discounts for bulk purchases, please contact Simon & Schuster Special Sales at 1-800-456-6798 or business@simonandschuster.com

Printed in the U.S.A.

I dedicate this book to my friends
Pam Walker Williams and Debra Bernstein.

"I am married to an old black log."

—FREDERICK DOUGLASS,
IN A LETTER, 1862

"Who else I got to tell? Who else but my daughter?"

—ANNA DOUGLASS,
TWO DAYS BEFORE HER DEATH, 1882

August 2, 1882

Cedar Hill, Uniontown, D.C.

I used to fill him. I used to. Time once he told me I was the only free he needed. Time when he didn't want to get up from my arms. Time when I filled him. He filled me.

The world loves Frederick Douglass. But I loved Freddy.

I loved him when he had no name excepting "Nigger this, Nigger that." When he looked at me—he was broken then—when he *needed* me, my flesh grew hot, and I opened myself, calling, "Freddy." I thought the two of us would create a world.

I'm dying now. Freddy died long ago. Was that a good thing? No more Freddy. Just the great abolitionist. Was that a good thing?

See Mister Death sitting in the rocker, telling me to "Come on."

I will. Once I speak my mind. Like Freddy did. He told his tale. Left me out.

Begin at the beginning. Tell it true.

Everybody knows Frederick's story. This one here be mine.

Narrative of the Life of

Anna Murray Douglass

A Free Woman of Color

1813–1882

I was born near Tuck's Creek in Carolina County, Maryland. My parents were freed a month before I was born. I be eight of twelve children. Never was a slave. Never had to escape dogs or a bad Massa.

But I seen my share of misery. It come rolling down, searing my back just the same. Come when I least expect it.

Freddy endured much. I appreciate that. I don't appreciate his feeling that hurt makes a person finer. He was "forged," he say, "forged like steel in the fire."

I was forged by love. That's what tore me up. That's what I didn't expect. How can something that causes the sky to be bluer than blue, sends warmth flooding your body, buckles your knees, and opens your soul to music . . . how can what feels *so* good, hurt 'til you want to scratch your skin off? Snatch out the heart that feels so much?

If love be true, you feel more than you felt possible. More everything. More glory. More pain at a touch.

Frederick wanted me prim and proper. Like white women seem to be. But I wonder if they is? Truly? I'm a woman and I feel everything. Even when I don't show it, I feel.

Been feeling since the day I slipped out Mam's body.

Life was good with my parents. Always felt like a smile was growing inside me. A smile wider than a river, deeper than a well.

My name be Anna but I was called "Lil' Bit." Wasn't but four pounds when I was born. Mam had plenty kids but food was scarce. Mam didn't even know she was having me. Didn't know I was growing inside 'til almost the very end. She said her back ache. Low and deep. Not 'til her body say "push," did she think to lay down. No time to get the midwife. Just Mam and me. Pa was in the fields. The other children were finishing chores. Even the youngest was expected to weed the garden and feed chicks. So Mam laid down and I "slipped out," she say. The easiest of all her children. "Slipped out, swimming downstream with the birth water."

Come dinner, Mam told the family she had a surprise. Instead of cake, she brought out me.

"Everybody smile," Mam say, and I did, too. She said a bubble burst beween my lips, "glowing with a rainbow." Everybody laughed when it floated high. Then, Pa held me. Called me "Lil' Bit—lil' black walnut." I was no bigger than that. And I was just that dark.

Pa said I had sense to look like Mam. All the other children were a blend of Pa's brown sugar and Mam's dark coffee. He say, "Rudy and George and all the others turned out a fine colored. Sweet enough to drink." But he say, "Dark coffee be best. Dark coffee be what I married. One day a good man be proud to marry you."

I used to think Freddy be proud because dark coffee covered me. My mistake.

He thirsted for everyone but me. Sweet cream. Buttermilk. Milk-laced tea.

I always thirsted for water. Clear. Cold. Cup after cup.

Mam taught me Water be a spirit. "All things alive," she say. "Earth. Wind. Fire. Water."

The Devil be afeared of Water. Afeared of Water's ghosts.

When they started carrying slaves from Africa, the Devil be delighted. "Good evil," he say. "Plenty good evil." Water be furious white men captured black men, women, and children. First Water thought to smash their boats. But Mister Wind wouldn't go along. Said Water would smash innocents, too—"*What about their bones? The slave childrens's souls?*"

So Water swore any slave that died inside It would find a new kingdom. Not Heaven. Not Hell. But a new world.

Sometimes slaves died in storms. Most times slave catchers chained them, pushed them overboard. When slaves too sick, when pirates chased them, when the British come, Captains shouted, "Dump cargo." And all these women, babies, and men crashed down, drowning in the sea. Lungs exploded. Flesh eaten away. But their bones and souls still live at the sandy bottom. They say there be an army of twenty million. An army that can't be killed. Skeletons, hard and strong. Souls that blend invisible with water.

When Frederick travels by sea, I tell him, "Never fear." Bones be keeping him safe. He don't believe me. But 'tis true and he with all his trips to England, still live.

Frederick probably bury me in dirt. Thinking me a useless, black woman in a casket.

I'd rather be buried in water. Won't go to Heaven or Hell. Don't care. Water good enough. I was born with it. Grew up around it. Swum in it. When I was six, I started making a summer living from it.

June-bug nights the air be crisp, smelling of salt. My brothers played, trying to catch fireflies. Pa would be on the porch stirring lumps of sugar in lemonade. Mam be rocking inside, teaching us girls sewing. Beside her in the cradle, be whatever youngest baby there be. When the baby cried, Mam sang sweet songs. Sang about how *all* her babies made it across Jordan. Nobody a slave no more. They be proud. Mam and Pa. Proud they had a farm which fed us just above starving.

But I got restless staying indoors. Tired of having my sister, Lizbeth, pull my pigtails and Mam complain about my stitches. Tired of Mam singing about crossing the River Jordan when outside my door, there was a bay more beautiful in moonglow than in sunlight.

Free should mean doing things. Not just talking about free!

So, one June-bug night, I built me a trap out of sticks and fishnet. It wasn't too steady. Lopsided on one end. Slats, too wide.

Everybody asked, "What you doin', Lil' Bit?"

"I'm going to catch crabs."

Everybody giggled: "When you become fisherman?" "Where's your boat?"

But Mam said I should be "encouraged." That's her very word: *encouraged*. She learned it from Miz Pullman when she cleaned her house.

I carried my trap to where I liked to play. A small cove with moss, willow trees, and silver fishes. Mosquitoes sucked my blood, but I didn't mind. I pushed my trap into blue-green water and prayed to them bones at the bottom of the sea. I prayed hard for them to bring crabs. Big Blue ones to sell.

First, I didn't hear no sound. Then, I heard what I thought be music. Sweeter than Mam's singing. No words, only sounds. Like children playing, clapping songs, jumping rope or eating sweet potato pie. My soul lit up. I was certain them bones be my friend. They be enjoying this free colored girl. Not jealous, but happy I was alive.

I raced home and asked Mam to make fritters.

Mam say, "Anna, now why? Why I wanna heat my stove tonight?"

I told her, "Them bones gonna bring Big Blues. I'm gonna sell fritters with my crabs. Them bones they promised. Promised me big, blue crabs."

Mam looked at me funny. Her head sideways, her lips puckered. Her eyes squinting at me hard-like. "Did they sing?"

I nodded.

Then, Mam jumped up, scurried to the porch, and shouted for the boys to chop more wood. She sent my sisters to find every bowl we owned. Lu, she told to get the flour. Lizbeth had to collect well water.

Pa complained, "We need sleep. Time for bed. Not listening to Lil' Bit."

Mam say, "Hush. We cook all night. Tomorrow we sell crabs."

Pa puffed his chest, going to complain more when Mam say, "The bones sang. She heard them."

Pa looked at me with respect. He say, "Lil' Bit, I know you special. But just 'cause the bones sing, don't mean they promised. Let's go check that trap."

I was scared. All my family looking at me. Lionel stuck out his tongue; I stuck mine back.

We all followed Pa down the steps, across grass, weaving between lacy willows and blinking fireflies to my special cove. All of us stopped and held our breath as Pa pulled my pitiful trap from the water. We couldn't see. Pa's back covered the trap. A minute. He say nothing. Another minute.

Then, he whistled low and deep. He turned, smiling like Sunday and shouted, "Boys, chop wood for a bonfire. We're frying fritters all night."

So we did. All night, fritters gurgled in the pot. We drained and cooled them on a sheet stripped to rags. We all were hot and weary, but whenever we thought about quitting, Pa checked the trap. It was always full of Big Blues; Pa set them aside and laid my trap again and again.

Come morning, our rooster, Sid, crowed and Mam had six baskets stuffed with fritters. Pa had the buckets stuffed with crabs. In twos, like Noah's Ark (Mam had the baby; Pa took the next youngest), we walked the lane to town.

I be with George and we headed down Charleston Avenue. George carried the ice-cold bucket; me, the basket. Both of us hollering, "*Fresh crabs. Fresh fritters. Crabs live. Fritters cooked. Two pennies.*"

Noontime, nothing left. Everything's gone. We be rich. Mam bought everybody new shoes.

Pa kissed me six times: on my nose, forehead, each eye, then, my lips and chin. Mam bought us licorice sticks. We were happy all summer long.

When September came, Mam say with so much money she could spare some children to school. She say, "Lil' Bit, you go. You learn reading and writing."

I said, "Naw."

If I'd of knowed how much Frederick was going to hold it against me, I would've said different.

Freddy didn't mind my not reading. But it bothered Frederick Bailey Douglass, the ex-slave man. He say reading "freed him." "Reading is the only way to light the corners of the mind."

I be bull-headed. I was good enough when we married, why wasn't I good enough after? And, for the longest time, it was Freddy not Frederick who met me in bed. So, I felt no need to read.

Then, when I wanted to learn reading and writing, there was no

time. Freddy gone most times. Me, alone in a cold house. Left to raise
four children. Bury one. Left to rebuild when the house burnt down.
When those white men burnt it.

After Annie's burial, Freddy didn't touch me no more. But Frederick used me. Like a slop jar to wet.

This be true: I knew my brother and sister would enjoy school
more. I was content by Mam's side. Being her shadow. I dreamed one
day I'd have a baby girl who'd want to shadow me. Hadn't counted on
my daughter being ripped away to boarding school. At seven, no less.
Naw, I surely didn't expect that. Tore me up inside.

My happiest days were spent with Mam. She taught me to crimp pie
crust, braise greens, stuff and lace a hen. She taught me how to clean
sheets by adding a teaspoon of lye, how lemon juice made a window
shine, how turkey feathers dusted finer than cotton. I never liked
sewing much but she taught me when a seam's been tugged too tight,
when a hem has less than ninety stitches.

I loved my days in the house. It was me and Mam's small kingdom.

Seventeen, I started service for the Baldwins. I treated their home like
my own. I took care to make it a place for joy to happen in. But I still
dreamed of my own home. My own clean, good-smelling world for my
children.

Except I was having trouble finding the man to make my dream
real.

When white men treated me with disrespect, I prayed to the Lord.
He kept me safe from bad men. From colored men, too, who wanted my
sugar without marriage.

I be wanting love. Wanting to open like a flower for the right man.

Problem was there weren't enough good men. There were some
kind men. Men who would sell fish, farm for white folks, some even
shoe horses. But I wanted a man who could be more than that, more
than me and inspire my children. I kept pure 'til it seemed like I was

too old to have any choice. My blush of youth blushed itself away.

I almost made peace with lonely days. But lonely nights were harder. My passion didn't bank down like it should. Prayers helped only some. I was needing, needy for love. Needing my own house. My own home.

I figured I'd be like water. Calm, floating, ever still. But them bones taught me about a world beneath water. Bones cried out, singing about desires unfilled. Lives unlived. Lovers untouched. Children unborn.

Just when I thought all hopeless, I got what I wished for. A man to inspire my children. Yet at a price paid. Price dearly paid.

I wonder whether my children—Rosetta, Charles Redmond, Lewis, and Freddy Jr.—be better for it? Whether my dead daughter cared her Daddy was Frederick Bailey Douglass?

Mam never lost a child like I did.

How explain that? Did them bones want Annie? Was that part of the price paid?

Past my prime, I get the man of my dreams. Miracle, don't you think?

Freddy thinks reading and the sight of white-masted ships free him. But I freed him. Me and my bones. We made a harbor. A place to ease his body down.

When I first saw Freddy's face, I saw the sun rise. My promised land. The bones made flesh.

And like flesh, everything dies. Everything goes bye and bye.

*L*ate spring ain't never sweet in Baltimore. Hot, slick. Sticky beyond dreaming.

I was twenty-eight, surviving as best I could. Had me a calico cat. *Lena.* I'd fan both her and me. Put ice chips in her milk. Ice on my head and wrists. May was as hot as July and there'd be no relief 'til November. Breezes didn't cool no sweat.

Legs itching against cotton. Arms damp, staining crinoline. Beads of water draining into my hair, down my cheek. Nights just as bad. Laying in my shift, barely breathing, counting the tiniest stars I could see through the window-top.

I felt drained. Hungry for more water. For something to fill me up.

I'd growed. I wasn't Lil' Bit no more. Wasn't cute no more, either. Just short, round, dark; beyond lonely.

Mam say, "Beauty lives in the heart." But Mam was thirty miles away. Pa now dead, Mam had her own troubles living old. My trouble was forgetting the kind things she said, the words that made me feel special.

Now, I was Anna, Housekeeper. Got servant's wages. Three dollars a month. Half sent to Mam. Got food, which I cooked. Milk for the cat. A room: clean but too small for a chair.

Eleven years, I worked for the Baldwins. A good position. Nobody slapped me. Or cursed. Or expected me to bed them. But there wasn't much room for getting ahead. So I sewed and laundered on my off-day. Thursdays. Anna, Seamstress. Washwoman. Carrying baskets to the docks.

Baltimore, great city then. Harbor for all kinds of goods and people. French and China silk. Spices. Rum. You need a gold cage for a bird? Baltimore. Sugarcane from Haiti? Bananas? Whale oil? All in Baltimore.

Irishmen, New Englanders, Virginia planters, British, Spanish, free colored men, they all passed through that harbor. And women—some dressed fine as queens, some barely dressed, waited for them. Waited for the men to slip them coins. Some folks went off in carriages; some went to the tavern; some got no further than an alley.

Everybody mated, two by two.

Only new slaves—male and female—kept separate. Each had their own cage at the dock's east end. When I could, I slipped bread and meat to the women (some just children). On Sundays, men with great buckets splashed water at the slave holds. Great buckets to wash away the dirt and smell. Nothing washed away the heat. Except when my Mistress ordered it, I kept clear of the docks on the Lord's Sabbath and Slave Auction Days. Kept clear of seeing misery I couldn't fix.

Still. 1841. Baltimore, a great city.

Except for colored folks, everybody a bit rich. Got pennies to spare for colored gals to wash their shirts, pants, and privates. I worked for sailors stitching where a knife sliced, soaking tobacco stains and spit, cleaning where stew crusted on sleeves and collars. I starched jackets for Captains who brung tea, goblets, and Africans across the sea. Some I stitched gold braids for when they got promoted or won slaving treasure. But Captains be the worse. Mean, they say your work not good. Insist you buy brand new shirt. After I lost my profit once, I never worked for any Captain again.

This May that felt like late summer, I was working for Gardner's men. Carpenters with lots of money and no respect. Their clothes, more grease and sawdust than cotton. Mister Gardner had a contract to build two man-of-war brigs for the Mexican government. They say, July, if Gardner be done, he'll win a big bonus. All the carpenters win bonuses, too. So everybody work hard—black and white—building these great ships.

I made my deliveries at dinner break. Men eating be generous. Less likely to complain: "This not clean enough." "This not ironed right." Foolishness. They complained to make me lower my price. Eating men don't talk much. Some even toss an extra penny.

I'd just finished giving William, the mast maker, his clean clothes when I looked up and saw this young man standing at the unfinished bow, the ship still on stilts, looking out across the water. Not more than three feet away. He stood there—legs spaced, solid. Like nothing tip him over. No waves. No wind. He was pitched on the edge of the horizon. Boat beneath his feet. Orange-streaked sky above his head. Endless water fanning out the harbor. Seem like nothing move him from that space he choose to be. He be a colored Captain, watching, waiting for some change to happen. Some sign from the birds flying high. Some new streak of color in the sky. Some sweet odor of free.

His pants weren't fine. Brown burlap. His ankles and shins poked out. Shirt gone. His back was broad, rolling mountains. Copper-colored. Trails crisscrossed his back. I knew then he was a slave or ex-slave. No pattern to the marks. Just rawhide struck, hot and heavy. Enough to know someone had been very angry with him. Once. Twice. Maybe more.

I think I fell in love with his head. He looked up, not down. Tilt of his head told me he not beaten. Not yet. His hair curled in waves, touching his shoulders. Thick, black strands. Made me want to reach out and feel. Made me wonder: what would it be like to bury my face in his hair? Would I smell the sea? Smell the oil they used to shine wood?

His hair made me think of Samson. God's strength upon him. Something else upon me. Some wave of feeling I'd never felt. Made my feet unsteady. My heart race.

"Girl," Pete, the iron maker called. "Hurry your nigger self here."

I scurried like a scared rabbit. This Samson man turned and saw me. Really saw. His eyes were golden, like light overflowing. I knew he saw me as a weak woman. Big. Too fat. Hurrying to this scum of a white man.

I couldn't stop myself. Mam taught me: "Never irritate white folks. Do your work. Collect their money." But this one time I didn't want to scurry. I wanted to move slow, sashay my gown, and have this man I didn't know, think I was pretty. No—*Lovely*. I wanted to be lovely.

Twenty-eight and never had a man look at me with love. *Passion. Desire.* Mam taught me not to say those words. But I learned them as a woman. Learned them watching folks at the wharf. Learned them, too, listening to my Mistress's friends—women promised to one man, yet mad about some other. They were mostly sorrowful. Passionate and sorrowful.

Mam said God made special feelings, 'specially for men and women. She and Pa felt them. I'd never felt one. Never 'til this man, this slave looked at me from the bow of an unfinished ship.

I hadn't enough backbone to tell this white man: "I'm coming. Don't hurry me." I scurried toward him and away from those light-filled eyes.

Head low, I got rid of all those clothes. Quick as possible. Out with the clean, in with the dirty. Collect my money. Just move. Don't think about shame. The colored men were kind. Like they knew my sin. One tried to tell a joke. But it was no use. I hurried to leave that dock. Trembling. Not sure I'd ever come back. Ever hold my head high.

That evening I laid on my bed and cried. Cried 'cause I wasn't lovely. 'Cause this man would never love me. Cried 'cause he *couldn't* love me. Him being slave. I, being free. Him, young. I, old. Him, handsome. Me, ugly.

I cried and bit my pillow to keep from letting my screams out. I'd never have my own home. My own babies. I'd work my days 'til too old to work, 'til crippled and less than nothing, with no children, surviving on what little I'd set by.

*T*ime makes the world fresh. Seven days, the world created. Seven days, my pain eased. Stopped feeling like a horse was sitting on my chest. Sabbath helped. I remembered the Lord loved me. And while I was singing "My Redeemer," I felt Mam, as if she was right beside me, taking my hand.

Got so I could see my reflection again and think I looked respectable. Clear eyes. Thick lashes. Clear skin. I didn't have to worry about freckles like white women. But it was a sore fault not to have Mam's sweet smile or Pa's even nose.

Lizbeth got Mam's smile and four children. Even mean George with his trim features had a family of five. All told, I was aunt to twenty children. Two in the oven. Then, I felt hurt, confused. Thinking about my family, I started thinking about this man. Handsomest man I'd seen.

Between kneading bread, slicing yams, between serving the Baldwins' food, I be thinking: "Why this man off by his self? Where his dinner pail? His food? Why this slave be at the shipyard? Why he not sitting with free coloreds? Where's his Master?"

I thought, "Charity. I can show him Christian charity."

I kept thinking of his hair, too. Light trapped in it. Him standing on the bow, looking like gold glowed about his head.

His Daddy must be white. Most likely his Daddy be his Master. The Dinwidde Street grocer had a daughter who visited a free colored. When her belly rose up, her folks whipped her awful. She lost the babe. The colored man ran to Canada.

I packed a dinner. Miz Baldwin wanted chicken and biscuits. So I cooked extra. Just a few. Then I slipped in a piece of banana pie.

Charity was Jesus' blessing. I'd take that man supper.

I was so nervous. I wore my best dress. It was blue and I always felt small in it. Married women seemed small. Delicate and needful, like Miz Baldwin. If I didn't cook and clean for her, she'd fade away and die, resting on her ottoman.

My blue dress had little buttons down the front and back. Had lace at the wrists. Shouldn't have been wearing my best dress among those coarse men, among that sweat and dust. But I wanted that slave man to see me different.

The trip was all right. Passed out the white carpenters' clothes, then went to the colored men. They ate off to the side. Gaines, a free colored, who trimmed sails, acted shocked. "You almost pretty, Miz Anna." I nearly slapped him. Everybody would've seen me blush if I was less dark. I passed out the clean clothes. Collected new ones. William's shirt had bloodstains from when a saw sliced his fingertip off. Everybody working, too hard. Making mistakes. But now they were having dinner. I had passed out my clothes and if I was gonna meet this slave man, I had to do it now. Had to march myself to the ship edge and holler, "Good day."

I couldn't do it. Too nervous. I stood at the edge of the dry dock looking up. Looking up at this man looking out to sea on a ship on stilts, I started chuckling. Funny. Both of us weren't going nowhere.

He turned, looked down at me. His hand on the rail. He smiled. I did, too. I said, "You eat?" His face twisted, puzzle-like. "You eat supper? You hungry?"

"No. I . . . I didn't eat. I am hungry."

My heart fell 'cause he talked proper. Even so, I said, "Come down, then." I lifted my smaller basket. "Else I'll feed this here to the gulls."

He smiled and it snatched my breath. He moved fast yet smooth, down the bow steps, then ran to where it was safe to leap over the ship's rail. Nimble, swift. He came upon me eager. Widest smile. His beauty nearly undid me. I wondered whether Delilah felt this way when she first see Samson.

But he wasn't Samson. No Egypt black man. Seeing his features straight on, I could see more of the whiteness in him. But the drops of whiteness didn't matter. He still a slave. My life was surely better than his. Not handsome, I knew I'd struggle to make a man love me. Pa said my darkness didn't matter but the world taught me it did. Even colored children called me "Afric."

But a handsome man—mixed black and white—might dream a better life. Might wish for genteel society. A high-yellow wife. Must be hard to have Master be your father. Hard to see white brothers and sisters enjoy privileges not yours.

William catcall, "Better leave that slave alone. Ain't got the sense of a dog."

"Hush," I answered back. "Your sense got cut off with your baby finger."

"That's a fact," said Peter, the nail man.

The colored men laughed and I smiled.

"It's true." This man's eyes were lit fierce. "I don't have a dog's sense." Then, his voice fell to a whisper. "A dog will stay where it's put. Or if it won't, a chain will hold him. I'm a man. I won't be held. Chained or unchained."

I kept real still. I knew he was staring at me. Expecting some response. Maryland was a slave state. Words could get me whipped. But here was this man asking more of me. Asking me to agree that holding a man a slave was wrong. I inhaled, murmured low, "That's proper. Nobody has the right to hold a man."

He smiled sweetly at me.

"Or woman."

He tilted his head back and laughed. Then, he held out his hand. "Frederick Bailey."

I forgot I was wearing my good dress and wiped my hand on my skirt. "Anna Murray."

"Anna," he say. My name sounded like a jewel. He clasped my palm good and solid and made me feel like I'd made a friend. Not just a good-time friend but a forever friend.

And just as quickly, the word "dangerous" flashed through my mind. "A dangerous friend." Don't know where those words came from. They just sprung up. As soon as they did, someone struck a bell and this heavyset-looking man come between us.

"Boy. Hear that bell? Work needs doing. Go on. Get."

"He needs his dinner."

"Don't tell me what he needs," the man turned angrily, causing me to back step and as I did, Mister Bailey moved forward. I held up my hand, not wanting to cause him trouble.

"No, sir," I said. "I understand. I just brung chicken. My Christian deed. It's still warm. You're welcome to some. I be trying to get my spirit right. Do a little something for my fellow man. But, next time, I'll come earlier, so I won't interfere with work. Would that be all right? I can bring you chicken, too. My mistake this time."

This foreman looked at me. His eyes squinting as if figuring if I meant what I said. He had a bushful of hair on his head and face. He smiled crookedly, spoke tickled yet mean:

"You sweet on him? Won't amount to much. Him a slave and all."

"I know," I said as Mister Bailey said, "We're acquaintances."

I felt anger flood me at high tide. But all mixed up 'cause I wasn't sure I was upset at just the foreman. "Acquaintances" sounded cold. Yet that was us. Barely met. Barely knowing each other.

"I'm simply doing my Christian duty. Seem like his Master would want him fed." I knew I was pushing too far.

"I'm his Master as long as he's working for carpenters, learning how to build ships. Go on, now. Get."

"Good-bye, Mister Bailey." I said bowing neatly. Just like at a dance. Suddenly, I felt embarrassed.

"Good-bye, Miss Murray." He looked at me quizzing, like he don't understand me at all. Then, he bowed at the waist like he had all the time in the world.

"Boy. Come here, boy," somebody was already calling. Then there was another cry from the opposite direction. "Boy. Over here. Brace this beam." The foreman was shoving Mister Bailey along. I walked from the place real slow. I still held my baskets. One filled with old clothes. One filled with my best cooking.

I knew I'd return next Thursday. The sky was sheets of orange, yellow, red, piled on top of one another. The clouds had turned slate gray. A storm be rolling in from the Gulf, the Caribbean Sea. I felt happy and shy. Scared and nervous. My world was upside down.

How to be more than "acquaintances"? How to get Mister Bailey to think well of me? Few words exchanged on a year of Thursdays didn't add up to much. And even if it did—a free woman and a slave? Hah! Don't carry much future. I ain't so dumb I didn't know that.

But little things can add up to big. "Be special like you," Mam would always say. I just had to be patient. Take my chance when it come.

That evening I looked for my cat. She came in late, purring. I turned my back and faced the wall.

Thinking of Mister Bailey, it was some time before I finally slept.

$\mathcal{N}$ext week I thought Miz Baldwin gonna throw me out on the street. Everything I touched went wrong. Ended up crosswise. I, who prided myself on knowing everything about a house, top to bottom, did everything wrong.

I starched Miz Baldwins' undergarments. Spilt tallow on the table. Didn't add cornstarch to the pie. Peach juice pooled on the plate. Bread didn't rise. I forgot yeast. Salt. Then, broke a china saucer with gold trim. Even mixed pork fat with chicken grease. Two days, I forgot to clean the grates. Smoke flooded the house. Didn't tie off my knitting so the doll I made unraveled, making baby cry. I even forgot to dust 'tween the banister posts.

I forgot every lesson I learned about domestic comfort. As I came undone, so did the Baldwins' house. Miz and Mister started arguing. Baby be colicky. Beth wouldn't nap. Thomas cut his thumb. Windows got stuck; floorboards creaked; clock ran down. The House Spirit just seemed ornery without my attention.

I felt adrift. Bobbing in a sea with no course. My slave man, Mister Bailey, be filling my spaces. I saw him sitting in the parlor. Everyone knows parlors ain't for coloreds. But Mister Bailey be sitting right there. When he ain't in the parlor, he in the library. I saw the curves of his hair, his fine stature facing those books. Outside with the wash, he be leaning against the tree. At night, when I lit the candles, he lived in the shadows.

Miz Baldwin asked to see me. I worried 'cause I know it be hard to find another position. Baldwins ain't rich. Just have me and a wet nurse. They don't work me hard and I love their three-story house. Narrow but pretty. They just young. Only on their fourth child. And up 'til now, I felt my back and hands be helping them along.

Miz say sit beside her. I be shocked.

She blushed. "Are you in a delicate condition?"

I felt bad, like I wanted to shrink to nothing and wanted to hit her, too.

"Naw. I mean, no, ma'am."

"Are you sure?"

"No. I mean, yes, ma'am."

"I'm so glad. I would've had to dismiss you. I told Mr. Baldwin I wasn't sure I could. You've been such a help. But he said handling the domestic arena and coloreds were my province. My responsibility."

Suddenly, I wanted to slap my Mistress's face. I kept shut and stared at the side of her head.

"Then it must be love," Miz Baldwin chirped.

I pulled into myself. White folks were fools. My feelings were private. Weren't meant for discussing.

"Love can make you utterly distracted. I won't pester you about who it is. Is it that boy, Gates, that delivers our milk? He's a charming colored. Works hard and will make a fine husband, I'm sure. You wouldn't even have to leave me. Only difference would be you'd have your own husband delivering milk."

She laughed silly. High-pitched. I studied the side of her head. I didn't want to look at her. Didn't want her to know how furious I was. Her talking to me like I was some child.

Then, she sighed heavily. Her voice got whispery. "Falling in love is much sweeter than marriage." She blushed some more. Then told me to go.

I got up.

Her voice halted me at the door: "Anna, I'm so relieved. That it isn't the other. You know. Never let it be the other."

"I ain't planning on it."

"That's good. Keep your mind on your work."

I went back to the kitchen confused. Outraged. "Delicate condition," my foot. Yet I wouldn't mind plumping out like Miz Baldwin.

But what she mean—I in love? I can't be in love with Mister Bailey. He don't love me back. Even if he did love me, his Master wouldn't let him marry. No sense thinking.

I started the fire to roast chicken. Sat down to peel taters. Still I see Mister Bailey standing in my kitchen, worrying me.

The Baldwins have a fine marriage. But what Miz mean "falling in love" sweeter than marriage? If "falling in love" mean everything going wrong, almost losing my job . . . what's the sense of that? Embarrassing, too, to have Miz, twenty-five, three years younger, speaking to me about babies! Mam taught me well—"The Bible say wait!"

In the evening, I find it hard to say my prayers. I remembered Pa's favorite story. Samson and Delilah. Pa loved how man overcame, triumphed over woman's lies.

Delilah was paid plenty gold to discover Samson's strength. Three times, Samson lied to her. Each time Delilah called the Philistines, Samson rose up, beat them away, and declared he free. Delilah begged. The fourth time, Samson tell her true. When he sleep, Delilah cut his hair. The Philistines chained him, burnt his eyes, and tossed him in prison.

But why Samson finally tell Delilah true?

Pa say, "Bible don't explain. The point be God's judgment."

God's judgment be to give Samson back his strength, to let him die pulling down the temple pillars. But how Samson judge himself? What he feel when he discovered Delilah cut his hair?

I think Samson knew Delilah's faults. But loved her anyway. He told the truth to give her a chance to be different. To love him back. Delilah failed him and then, I think, she knew she failed herself, too. She hurt this man that loved her true, that gave her his trust after three wrongs. Amazing, Samson loved her that much. Amazing, she don't know 'til too late. She grew cold and bitter like a grave.

If Mister Bailey loved me, I'd know it. I'd hold his feelings safe in my heart. Never betray him like Delilah. I'd bury my face in his pretty hair and whisper, "True. Love be true."

True. Love be true.

The words kept plaguing me. Twice, I'd buried my head beneath my pillow. Huddled under sheets, then kicked them off, disgusted. The moon was disappearing. At dawn, I needed to start baking. Dusting furniture. Washing the cloth panels in the library. But tiredness didn't stop my mind from echoing: *True. Love be true.*

Didn't stop the walls from closing in, making the air heavy, hard to breathe. Making my head hurt. Didn't stop my sense that the bones were laughing. Their voices rising, carrying across the sea. All my high hopes and I'd let it come to this.

Old Auntie. Old Maid.

Samson risked everything. I'd risked nothing.

A man wasn't like catching Big Blues. But at least Lil' Bit got down off the porch. Here I was rocking on a porch owned by somebody else, letting life pass by like heartache didn't matter. Like loneliness didn't matter.

Everything mattered. I threw on my robe, tiptoed outside. There was a small porch off the kitchen. I sat on the steps, scanning the trees. Fireflies lived in Baltimore as well as in Tuck's Creek. But here on Miz Baldwins' back porch, as far as my eye could see, there weren't any trees or ocean. Just cobblestone. White plastered houses and white fences. It was pretty in its own way but not enough lovely green. And while I could smell the sea, I couldn't see it. Couldn't see the water that flowed from Africa to the isles to Baltimore to my cove back home. But water was there nonetheless.

Just like my hope for a husband was there, curled up in the corner of my heart, despite my ignoring it, wishing it away, pretending it wasn't there.

Time for Lil' Bit to teach her grown self a lesson. Can't harvest the sea without thinking about what was needed.

True— no man had ever asked for my hand.

Also true —there'd been no man I'd wanted.

Love be true. Mister Bailey, I wanted.

Him being a slave might be my advantage. I had money saved. Buying him free might be a start.

I might not be what he wanted. But a slave man ain't allowed to have no wants. So, he'd still come out ahead. Him, free. Me loving him with all my might. Him learning to love me. Why not? He'd be free to love. Us, building a family. Soon love be true for both of us.

Tomorrow, I'd find some new customers for doing laundry. I'd work more, sleep less. Save more.

Miz Baldwin could complain about marriage. I still wanted to feel it for myself. No more secondhand, leftover feelings.

I hugged myself and I thought I heard the bones roaring *encouragement*.

Tomorrow, I'd go buy thread, material to begin a wedding quilt. I'd sew two rings locked together.

Tomorrow, I'd aim to be happy. One tomorrow at a time.

That next Thursday I wore my work clothes but felt all dressed up, pretty inside. I truly admired this man and I was going to propose to set him free. Give him room enough to love me.

The day was ordinary. Sweating. Even leaves sweat in Baltimore. Trees just bend their heads low and let moisture leak, drip to the ground.

I took the pony cart to the harbor, then walked a bit past fine ships, rigging ten feet high. Everybody busy, busy. Southeast end be where Gardner's men build. There's a warehouse with one side open to the sea and ships. Men be milling inside and out, going to and fro.

For as long as I could remember, blacks and whites worked alongside each other. Not just slaves, either. Maryland had lots of free coloreds. 1841, good times. Profit made everybody mellower, easier to get along.

This day I didn't see nobody working on the half-done ship. No buzzards worked on its skeleton, hammering, sanding, lashing ties. But I heard a great noise from inside the warehouse. Like thunder. First, I stopped. Not knowing whether to go forward or back. No sense inviting trouble. World won't end if I don't deliver laundry. But I was sure my heart would crack if I didn't see Mister Bailey.

Besides, he might be in that ruckus. Made sense to find out what's going on.

So I started forward again. I heard grunts, shouts, something tumbling, falling down. Then it was: "Niggers. Niggers." Then, "Nigger. Damn fool nigger." Somebody was singled out.

Sometimes my heart tells me what my head don't know. I raced forward, dropping my baskets, sending clothes sailing onto the wharf, some blowing out to sea.

I raced hard, raced to the half-built ship, then turned into the warehouse and pushed through a crowd. Not carpenters, but curious folk—sailors, whores, penny salesmen—hooting and hollering, "Teach him"; "Serves nigger right."

I stopped dead at what I saw. Mister Bailey down on one knee. His hands shielding his head. Three men battering him awful and the coloreds were being held back, punched and slapped. But nothing like Mister Bailey. He be trying to get up, trying to lift off that knee splattered with sawdust and blood.

I cried out to stop them. Nobody paid me any mind. The foreman, off to the side with a wide, wide grin—was enjoying himself like he was at a cockfight with a bottle of whiskey going to the winner.

Mister Bailey gave a great cry. So thundering that everybody step back a bit, even them men hitting him. Mister's Bailey's fist raised beneath the chin of one man. Then, he turned, hit the other. Bailey got hit back, again and again. He clutched his stomach, then fell upon the closest man. Holding on to the man's neck with his right hand, his left fist barreled into the man's stomach. Again and again.

Then, six white men were on Mister Bailey. Pulling him back by his neck, his shirt, beating him down 'til I couldn't see nothing but their legs, fists, heaving backs. Mister Bailey disappeared in that hell.

Seemed like forever . . . maybe it was minutes. When Mister Bailey laid still, the men stopped beating him. They just stepped aside. Sweating, breathing deep and fast like hitting a colored was some of the hardest work they'd ever done.

I got my strength back and rushed forward, wailing, down on my knees over Mister Bailey. "Precious Lord."

"Gal, get outta here. No business here."

I said, "Here's my business. Helping a down man." Foreman considered hitting me I know. I rushed: "His Master won't like him tore up so." That stopped him and he looked at me hard. But the weight of Mister Bailey's head on my lap, the stillness in his body, the blood draining from his nose and mouth made me hold on.

I didn't dare ask: "Why? Why this beating? Why this pain?"

None of the colored men looked at me. Some of them were leaving, quitting the warehouse so I knowed things must've gone real bad. Free coloreds would take a heap of abuse to feed their families.

"Mister Foreman," I said, "Let me clean him up. Take him back to his Master. Just tell me where to go."

"You wouldn't be tricking me, would you?"

"No, sir. You know I Miz Baldwins' maid. Any problem, you find me there."

Some of the carpenters milled, complaining: "Niggers stealing jobs"; "Niggers they don't pay, be worse than those they do"; "Slaves stealing jobs."

I kept shut. Everybody know a slave can't order himself to work. Some white man ordered Mister Bailey here. But these fool carpenters beat Bailey. Hurt a man who has no say over what he does.

Besides, there be plenty work. Bonuses for all. I didn't see no white men crying poor. They made twice as much as a free colored. So why they worried about losing jobs, when plenty work for all?

Foreman shouted, "Go on. Back to work." Then, he tighten his mouth like he was going to spit. "His Master is Auld. Roup Street. Take him. Clean him up. Take him to his Master. Tell him his boy ain't to come back no more."

Don't know how I got Bailey to the Baldwins' kitchen. Me telling him he got to stand. Him stumbling. Moaning low 'cause everything hurt.

"Taught you, nigger," someone crowed.

I kept pulling. Bailey kept straggling. Inching forward 'til we were beyond the ship's shadow and the carpenters' curses.

He laid on the buckboard. Curled up like a baby while I clicked, "Giddy-up," and the old pony did its best trot. Every bump caused him pain. But I was afraid to slow. Maybe some carpenter beat him again. Maybe someone cry, "Lynch him."

I flew as best I could. Streets fairly clear. Everybody at supper. The sun was setting, bleeding red.

I was lucky, this day be my off-day. The Baldwins were at Miz Baldwins' sister's for dinner. The entire house be quiet.

Still I hushed Mister Bailey. Warned him we got to be careful. "Baldwins won't appreciate talk." He nodded and let me guide him to my room off the kitchen.

Inside, even bent, Mister Bailey was big. My room shrinked to nothing. His legs drooped off the edge of my cot. He groaned. Eyes swollen, blood crusted on his face. Shirt, ripped; pants, dirty. His hands were the saddest. Skin torn from the knuckles, blood bubbling up.

I lit the lamp. Poured water in the basin. Not having a chair, I got down on my knees. "Hold still, I'll clean you up."

He swallowed. I touched the cloth to his head. There was a lump. Blood caked in his hair. His curls were heavy and flat. He winced and I knew I had to soak out the blood bit by bit. Then, bind it with a cloth. All over his body there were scrapes, wounds to tend.

"I sorry this hurts, Mister Bailey."

"Why do you call me Mister? I'm just a slave. 'Boy. Nigger. Bailey.' All those names I'm used to. Not Mister."

I shrugged. "Seem like it fit you true—Mister. Man among men."

He laughed harsh. "Here I'm bleeding on your clean bed and you think I'm a man among men. More like a fool among slaves."

"I don't believe that."

"Believe? What does it matter what you believe?"

I drew back, staring at the dark red blooming in the water. "I need a fresh basin."

He murmured, "Please, wait. I'm sorry. My words were uncalled for. Forgive me."

I nodded, repeated, "I need fresh water."

In the kitchen, I caught my breath, tried to soothe my hurt. I tossed the red water outside the door. The moon was rising, drawing the tide high. I turned back into the kitchen. Poured water from the pitcher. My hurt turned to anger. "Young, pretty girls worth believing," I thought spitefully. "Think me an old auntie, like I don't have nothing to say. Humpf. I'll set Mister Bailey on his way. That I will."

He was sitting. A bit shaky, but facing the door, watching for me with his swollen eyes.

"I admire you, Miss Murray. Your words, especially your respect, mean a great deal to me. I'm sorry I'm not more worthy of it."

All my upset faded. "Hush. Lay down. Let me take care of you." I bustled forward.

"All my life," he said, "I've been trying to be a man, trying to be treated as a man. A gentleman like any other. When I forget myself, slavery's won."

He was pale. Blood drained sluggishly from his brow and lips. "Mister Bailey, please lay down. Let me finish my work."

"Only if you call me Frederick."

"Frederick. Freddy. Anything you like as long as you lay down." I lifted his feet and helped him lean backwards onto the cot.

"No one's called me Freddy."

"Then I will. My special name for you since you don't like Mister Bailey."

He gripped my hand and I was surprised by the strength left in him. "I like Mister Bailey. It has a fine ring. But too formal among friends."

His eyes were gold and hazel. Green specks floated inside. I sighed. Even tore up, he was handsome. And I could see he was trying to smile, even though his mouth hurt. "Friends," he said.

I shook his hand.

We were "friends," and I felt happier than I'd ever felt in my whole life. I worked as quickly as I could. Cleaning wounds, pressing ointment, tying on bandages. Friends be a start on the road I picked.

Since being little, Mam said I had a way with healing. I nursed all my brothers and sisters when they got spots, sore throats, gnashes in their limbs. Even nursed Mam when she had her last baby. Next to keeping house, I would've been pleased to heal people. There was that same sense of tidiness, of making things right.

In the kitchen, I drained broth from a chicken, heated the juice with rosemary and a dash of pepper to lift spirits. Then I filled a cup with Mister Baldwin's liquor.

I encouraged Mister Bailey to sip the liquor, finish off the soup. When his lips and cheeks gained color, I felt so happy.

My room smelled good and warm. Rosemary, columbine ointment, and Mister Bailey's—Freddy's—healing body all seemed sweet. Through the window, a touch of sea blew in. The same cooling, comforting smell I remembered from my family's porch.

Freddy just laid still, recovering, his eyes closed.

Feeling close, I imagined this was our house, our home. I touched his hair. He didn't move.

I said, "Let me buy you free. I can do it. Buy you free."

First, I didn't think he heard me. His eyelids fluttered.

Outside, crickets sang. Moonlight made shadows on the wall. Him, on his back. Me, on my knees bending over. His eyes opened but I watched his mouth.

Who can tell what love be? Mam and Pa loved, I think. I saw them talk for hours, saw baby after baby. Was that love? If so, I'd be content.

"Freedom is an illusion," growled Bailey. "Where can a colored man go and live free?"

He sucked in air. I saw bitterness rising in him. He wasn't talking to me. He was lost somewhere inside himself, trying to figure things out. I shivered. Devils tiptoed across his soul.

"Master sent me to a slave-breaker. Not a week went by when I didn't suffer some new cruelty. I was worked so hard until there was nothing left of me but animal. One minute, I'd think 'Oh, God save me.' The next, I'd be praying 'Let me die.' I tried to die. I fought with the slave-breaker, Covey. He wanted to lash me. I said, 'No more.' We wrestled all day. Tired and sore, I thought a feather would push me over.

"Covey was in worse shape. Struck dumb by exertion, heat. I fought and won. I told Covey, 'You'll have to kill me before you ever beat me again.'

"He didn't kill me. But part of me was dead anyway. I worked for him for four more hard years. Covey never tried to beat me again. My service with him ended Christmas Day, 1835. Master hired me out again. But, blessedly, a year gone, my Master sent me here to Baltimore to live with his sister and learn a trade."

I heard his words, but they were about the past. I wanted to live my life forward. Live it entwined with his.

"Until today, shipbuilding was fine. But, today, those carpenters became afraid that slaves, coloreds, were going to undercut their profit and steal their jobs. There had always been mumblings, stirrings of resentment that I was there."

He stopped talking, exhausted. I felt strange. This man had so much learning. I'd none. I wanted to ask how he learned to speak like a gentleman. Did he miss his Mam? His people? Were they left on the plantation? I wanted to know everything about him.

Instead, I blurted, "I have money. Enough maybe to set you free."

He looked at me. Strange, like I was something he didn't expect to see. Like my words were something he didn't expect to hear.

Even tore up, all I could think was he was beautiful. God forgive me, I wanted to lay down beside him and have him hold me. Just hold me.

"My Master won't sell me."

"Even after this beating?"

"It's his point of pride—to keep me."

"What you mean?"

"I'm the trained, educated monkey. If I can't be a carpenter, then, perhaps a blacksmith or a cobbler. I'm teachable. Miss Sophia once started to teach me reading and writing. Her husband forbade her. But the damage was done. I played with white schoolboys and tricked them into teaching me their lessons. That learning has caused me the most pain."

He closed his eyes and already I saw him dead. Not battered on the outside but battered inside.

"Then I'll help you escape."

"Run away?"

"You thought it?"

"Yes. I ran once but was betrayed. Me and—" He sat up, stopping short. "Now I'm not sure it's best. City slavery is far gentler than the plantation. I pay my room and board. Give Master the rest of my wages. In return, I have some freedom to come and go. A fair compromise."

"That's not good enough for you."

"Who are you to say?"

I jerked back. I could see the same fury he'd had at the docks. Wild, his hands balled. Seemed like he wanted to destroy something.

"Have you ever been in the fields? Been whipped? Seen your aunt whipped naked—seen clothes, flesh, sliced from her body—all because she didn't love the Overseer who'd raped her?"

"No. I—"

"Have you seen your grandmother sent off with nothing? Left to die, starving, after Master had no more use for her? Have you known what it was like to have your mother die and not weep because slavery had made her a stranger? Or known that any day someone else could decide your fate—where you live, work, even when you die?"

Great weariness settled upon him. He fell back onto the cot. This wasn't the man I saw standing proudly on the unbuilt ship. This man was low. Of course, he'd every right. Him beaten bad. Him living things

I'd never know about. Maybe education made his feeling finer? But seeing him on my cot reminded me of my own tossing and turning, my own desire not to give up on dreams.

"You once tried to run."

"I was betrayed by a fellow slave. Locked in jail for days. I thought they'd lynch me for certain."

"But you lived. There's a reason. You lived to try the journey one more time." He didn't speak. Kept laying like dead. "I won't betray you. I'll help." Then, boldly, I added, "I'll be waiting for you."

I sat back on my heels.

I could feel him looking me over. Looking at me, counting all the things I had against me. Age. No beauty. But I had will. Some money set aside. I could help. I stared at him straight on.

"You would do this? Help me?"

"Yes."

"I never—"

Never what? I wondered. Had a woman like me? Had someone who wanted to help him, who believed in him? Mister Bailey—Freddy—wasn't meant for quitting. He felt like that now. But that wasn't the best in him.

"I'll help you be free." This time I knew he'd heard me clear. He drew up, looked down into my eyes, my very soul. I tried to show him all my loving. Show him he needn't fear.

"I will think on this." .

Air burst out of me. This felt worse than any other pain. Worse than the time I'd fallen out the tree. Worse than burning my hand in the fire. Worse than the time my Pa laid down and didn't get up. All those times together, still didn't equal my hurt. I'd been fooling myself. Living dreams when the real world had other plans.

I looked at my room. At myself. Me, on my knees, beside this man.

I saw my room clear. Without this man in it, there wasn't much. Even though a small space, by myself, I couldn't fill it.

Family. I couldn't think of anything more worth having.

Gently, I touched my hands to his knees. Looked up, pleading. His arms stayed fast at his sides. But he saw me. He looked hard into my eyes.

I licked my lips, knowing this moment was important. The course of my life was being decided in this room.

"The Africans that never made it to slavery. Them that died or were tossed overboard be at the bottom of the sea. We've got to live the lives they lost. Otherwise no sense for living at all." I sighed. "No sense at all."

He looked bewildered, no, surprised, by what I said. For a moment, I could see him thinking if he really knew me. I think he thought he did, but my words had unsettled him. Then his eyes clouded, like somebody had dropped a veil over them and he wasn't seeing me at all.

"I will think on it."

I didn't see him for months. Lena had a litter of kittens. Two, black. One, calico like her. One, almost entirely white.

Spring turned to summer turned to fall. Maybe all that time Freddy be thinking of a way to be free without me?

Maybe, he, finally, decided he can't be free without my help.

All I know, one day, he knocked loud at the Baldwins' kitchen door. His wounds had healed. He looked fine. Dressed in his best pants and tan shirt. He looked glorious, like the young man once again standing on a ship's prow headed north.

He stepped into my kitchen. Handed me marigolds.

"Good evening," he said.

"Good evening, Freddy."

That night—him sitting across the table, we made plans to escape to New York.

That night I started to breathe again. Without journeying a step, I'd found my promised land.

I couldn't wait to tell Mam and show Mister Bailey, my Freddy, to my family. Soon I'd be building my best home.

After a bit we were both quiet. Freddy stirred his tea and stared at the kitchen fire. Lena settled in my lap. I stared at the only flowers a man had ever given me. When they dried, I'd scatter them to the bones.

Bright orange petals would float, then sink into the sea.

$\mathcal{L}$ove unlocks a woman's heart. I always felt the truth of that. But nothing prepared me for opening like a petal for Freddy.

After dreaming of love, after thinking my dreams would never be true, he filled me. Made me a new kind of whole. I made him whole, too. Baptized him with tears. Tears of love. Happiness.

We met every Thursday in Miz Baldwins' kitchen. I fixed dinner. Fed him my lightest biscuits. My sweetest yams. Poured him lemonade I'd squeezed with my own hands. And though nobody was in the house except us, we whispered plans. Whispered about free papers, the best route, the money needed for trains, the ship to New York. Though we never spoke of it, it would be my money that would ease things. Freddy's Master allowed him to hire his time. But come Saturday, Freddy paid his Master three dollars. He be lucky if he got ten cents back. I had dollars—nearly a hundred—sewed inside my pillow. Dollars from years of sweat, mending my dresses, not buying myself pretty things and from laundering other folks' clothes.

Freddy say he going to be my new half. He say Mam will understand if I send her less. He say, "God helps those who help themselves."

I knew Freddy was right. We had a family to prepare for. Still, my heart was sore. I paid a penny to a man who sent Mam my money and spoke my words of love to her.

Freddy say, "Let me write her."

I duck my head like a baby bird. "Mam can't read. Me either."

The tallow candles burned low, but I could still tell Freddy wasn't pleased. Like some shadow crossed his face, making his features flat, his eyes, without spark. He pushed back the chair, stood, and came round to me. Lifting me from my chair, he caught my hand, pressed it to his chest, swearing, "I'll teach you to read. When we're free, I'll teach you."

It was his holy promise. His vow.

I felt his breath on my face. Sweet breezes. Felt the strength in his hand, the calluses on the palms. I swayed toward him. His arms circled me like silk twine.

It be the first time I felt Freddy's arms about me. My breath came in shallow bursts. I nearly swooned thinking there's no other place I'd rather be. *Love be true.*

Kitchen fell away. Everyday life, just gone. Didn't matter flies buzzed over the leftovers. Didn't matter this wasn't our house. Didn't matter I should be wiping dishes, cleaning, attending to the starter yeast, the stove's fire.

Feeling the fabric of his clothes through mine, I felt new feelings. Special feelings. Things I'd never felt. I didn't stop to think how Freddy felt inside. I only knew I wanted to touch his outside. I'd healed his body once and, God forgive me, I wanted to touch his flesh in a new way. Touch him like I'd never touched anyone before.

I reached up, stroked his cheek. Then, more boldly, caressed his hair. I felt his arms tighten about me. All this time I'd kept my eyes and mind on his chest, on the skin I knew was beneath his shirt.

"Anna—this isn't proper."

His voice sounded far off. Like he wasn't really there at all. I knew he was trying to speak caution. But I didn't care. In this strong man, I could sense a weakness. Weakness for me.

Me? Whoever thought me a shameful Delilah?

I stepped closer, laid my cheek on his chest. I smiled, feeling him breathing with me. Heat burst through me. Standing still, we were breathless, running toward life.

I felt the swelling between his legs. And I thought, just as clear, this man be my husband. For the first time, I felt so much a woman. No man had ever touched me special.

Did Freddy ever touch someone? This upset me so. Imagining

Freddy holding another woman made me cry out. I looked up. His eyes be fixed on me. Staring, piercing my soul. Then, slowly, sweetly, his head came down and we kissed the world away.

Didn't take long to undress, to move to my twilight-lit room. To my small cot. We sealed our union as husband and wife. Without saying so, we agreed to mate. Just jumped over the broom like common slaves. I'd sworn I'd wait for a church wedding. But my body had its own language, its promises to keep.

I could feel his trembling. His desire. His need working from inside his body to inside mine.

Freddy may not have loved me then. But he loved what was happening between us. When he was through, he held still, deep inside me, kissing my face, my throat. He stroked my breasts and suckled them.

My body arched toward his mouth. My babies would suckle here, too. I moaned, cresting a wave, feeling I'd drown, then feeling Freddy holding me tighter, tighter. Then I felt him pushing inside me again. Pushing, pulling out, pushing in, like we were riding the sea together. He cried out that time, and I felt a sweet swoon and thought, "My real life just beginning."

"Soon. We'll be free."

I stroked his back, thinking how nice he link our fates. But I already free. Always been free. Why he not remember that? I shrugged, feeling his ragged breath brushing past my hair and ear.

My fingers smoothed the scars on his back. I kissed the sweat on his neck. He groaned. Shameless, I rejoiced. Rejoiced he wanted to keep touching deep inside me.

Fine, I thought. This loving be just fine.

L ove be true.

Helping a slave escape means death.

I made Freddy a seaman's outfit with my own hands. Sewed it with neat stitches and pressed it fine. Cutting my pillow, I pulled out my money resting between goose down. At the harbor, I bought two tickets for colored passage to New York.

Every step I took, I nearly faltered. *I could be hanged. Hanged.* The words would sing through my mind, unsettling me, making me clumsy, awkward, unable to sleep.

Miz Baldwin lost patience with me. She shouted, "I need you to be responsible. Respectable and responsible." And I hung my head 'cause I knew I wasn't respectable—I allowed Freddy liberties. I enjoyed him touching me. Me touching him.

I was still responsible. Just not to her. What did it matter to keep dusting chairs, scrubbing windows, polishing silver? It was my own house I wanted to keep.

Once Miz Baldwin surprised me, entering my room.

"What's in that bag?"

I'd been folding me and Freddy's escape clothes. I answered, "Laundry. My day-off job."

"You'll have to quit your extra work. You barely have time enough to give proper care here."

"Yes, ma'am."

She was shaking with rage, dressed in a blue muslin, a kerchief in her hand.

"Haven't I been good to you?"

"Yes, ma'am."

"Then why are you upsetting me? Doing less than your best work? I rely on you."

I hung my head.

"If you're in love, then marry. Marry so you may do your work well. Be whole in mind, in heart again."

"I'm trying. I want to be married."

She exhaled. "Then I'll have Mr. Baldwin speak to Gates's employer. He'll make Gates settle down. Gates will be a better worker for it and you will, too."

I felt so guilty. Gates was a good, grown man. Didn't need the Baldwins messing in his affairs. Still, I knew Gates was sweet on a kitchen maid. He'd marry her and I'd be gone soon with my Freddy.

"Thank you, ma'am." I bobbed a curtsy. "You a good Mistress."

She left. I went back to packing.

⁂

Hanged. I could be hanged. Or sold. Kidnapped into slavery.

That Sunday evening, I met Freddy at African Zion Church. There was a church supper and all the women competed to see who could make the best chicken and pie. Normally, I would've entered the contest, but Freddy and our escape was too much on my mind.

In a pew, side by side, Freddy and I listened to "Blessed Be My Savior" and to the Preacher's sermon. "Our Good Lord forgives everything," Preacher say. "There is no wrong that can't be undone. No act that can't be forgiven."

I prayed the Good Lord forgave my sinful urges. I only felt what He made it possible for me to feel.

After service, Freddy and I walked on, away from the talk and good eating. He was so serious. Quiet. I felt a distance between us even though our feet were keeping time, keeping even pace.

We stopped beneath a willow. My back against bark, Freddy kissed me slow and deep. There was a hunger in him and I was glad.

I knew I could feed him, fill him up. I'd plenty love.

Sometimes, Freddy looked at me with wonder. He still didn't quite know me. Except for escape talk, we said little. But we did much and what we did was glorious.

I wasn't coy, simpering like Miz Baldwin. I gave back kiss for kiss. Stroke for stroke. I was shameless. But for Freddy, I was willing to be.

He pulled back, looked at the stars. He was standing like a statue again, looking out beyond the horizon. Wind lifted his hair a bit. He swallowed. Then he say,

"Master Auld threatened to return me to Talbot County. He says my independence in the city is too much. I'm becoming too full of myself, earning wages."

I wanted Freddy to look at me. Master Auld didn't matter.

"I think I should escape immediately. Tomorrow."

My breath came fast. I was scared but said, "I can be ready."

He turned, looked at me over his shoulder. "It would be safer if I left alone. Once in New York, once safe, I can send for you."

I slid down the tree, just crumpled on the earth's ground.

"I should leave without delay."

"Without delay," I repeated, numb.

Looking up at him, looking down on me, I pleaded. "Please don't leave me."

He stooped, his hands cupping my knees.

Thinking my dreams at an end, I cried, "Please."

"I have no way of predicting the future," he said softly. "But I do know, any day, Master Auld will send me back to the Great House. If I'm to have a chance at freedom, the time is now."

"You said we'd visit Mam."

"There's no time."

"Mam must give her blessing."

"No time. Only time enough for me to escort you home. For you to give me the seaman clothes. The ship's passage and funds. I must leave tomorrow. My motto must be: 'Trust No One.' Until I'm safe."

I heard the sense in what he said, still I thought he was hard. A handsome man but hard.

"Why you can't take me?"

He gripped my shoulders. "I want to. But two leaving together is doubly unsafe. Someone will connect us two. We'd both be hunted down."

"Why didn't you say so before?"

"I didn't want to hurt you."

"Or keep me from helping you." I regretted the words soon as I'd said them. Freddy stiffened, wrinkled his face.

He stood. "Believe what you like."

"Please." Folks were singing again, this time about "Johnny Shake Corn." "I don't want to fight. 'Specially if I might not see you again."

"You'll see me. I'll send for you."

"Will you?" I couldn't help my bitterness.

Once free, he had no reason to keep me. No reason at all. Lots of pretty women would be glad to marry him. Now he was asking me to let him go. To trust him when he hadn't trusted me.

I understood his need for freedom. But I needed the whole truth. Not pieces like you'd give a child. Maybe being a man, being a slave, Freddy didn't understand that. Or, maybe, he be lying.

The moon was just above his head. His hands were clasped behind his back. He was a proud man. He could go off and leave me without saying a word.

Maybe this was my test. Letting him go, I'd prove my trust.

I'd let him go 'cause it was best. Best for him. Worse for me. *Ain't that love?*

I stood, threw my arms about him. It didn't matter if he didn't meet Mam, didn't matter if he left ahead of me. Nothing mattered but him loving me—here and now. I held on, pressing close. I felt his resistance, the tightness in his body. I kissed him, kissed him hard, tender, quick, long and deep. I kept on 'til I felt his body responding, felt his desire. Then, I felt happy again.

I stepped aside, letting both our bodies cool down. It wouldn't do to have the Preacher or anyone else find us. But I kept a secret smile, 'cause I believed tonight, when he walked me home, he'd take my hand, lead me into my room and love me good, before saying "bye."

This last night we'd make a memory to keep me warm, 'til he say, "Anna, come," and I'd fly up North, quicker than any bird.

We never made that memory.

•   •   •

Walking home, Freddy got colder. Sullen. Spoke nary a word. And I got colder, too, feeling my job was to give and give. Love was a hard toll. I wanted a breath of kindness from him, a sweet word to soothe my worry.

"I can be hanged," I murmured, turning over the uniform, eighty dollars—the rest of my life's savings, the ship's ticket. "I can be hanged."

He said nothing. Just took everything. Then, kissed me like a father kisses his child and patted my back.

Sweat shone on his skin. He be a giant. Hands locked tight, eyes half-closed, there was a strength and power in him, waiting for release. He was already on his way. Journeying on. He'd already left me.

"Hold me," I begged. He did and I heard his heart drum. But his desire had fled.

"I'll send for you."

"Stay safe," I whispered when I wanted to shout, *"Don't leave me."*

"I'll send for you." He left and I didn't, couldn't move. I heard his boots crossing the kitchen, the screen door opening then clicking shut, heard his footfalls on the steps, then silence as I imagined him walking, then running, speeding swiftly across the yard. A dog howled. I wanted to howl. Howl 'til my heart broke, howl my longing so that no matter how far Freddy went, he could hear me.

But because he was escaping, I kept my mouth shut. Swallowed my pain. I'd cast my lot with Frederick Bailey.

"I'll send for you." Deep inside me, I felt, "Liar, liar."

Lena rubbed against my leg, wanting to be fed. I stooped and buried my face against her fur. "Do you think he loves me, Lena? Will he keep his word?"

Lena's tail flicked; she purred. Her yellow eyes blinked.

"You know, don't you, cat?"

I fell upon the pillow, stuffing my hands into my mouth to quiet my scream. Lena sauntered out the room like she didn't need me, either.

I cried, thinking this loneliness was worse than hanging.

When the stars grew light and the sun started peeking over the horizon, I imagined Freddy already far away, already on the ship north. And I cursed, 'cause at the prayer meeting, Preacher could've married us. I didn't think of it.

Freddy didn't either.

*T*he Penny-letter-man came to call. He had a message from Mam, from over a month ago. Penny-man say, "Can only travel so fast. Got more customers than you."

"Just say what Mam had to say," I said nervous. Mam never wasted a penny unless it was bad news. Somebody hurt. Sick.

"No sense to pay a penny to Penny-man to speak my love," Mam always say. "Penny-man shouldn't have to tell what you already know."

But two months ago, I'd asked Mam a question. I tried not to be embarrassed telling my words to Penny-man. I would've kicked him if he'd laughed. Would've cursed him every Sunday. I'd asked: "How do you know when a man love you?"

I wasn't sure if Mam would spend a penny to answer or not. She might think me silly or, worse, a fool. Ain't a woman supposed to know? But, unlike Pa, I suspected Freddy might never say the words. And if he didn't say them, how would I know?

Penny-man spit, then climbed down from his perch. He patted his horse. He say, "You sure you don't need some soap?" He lifted the flap on his wagon. "I've got good tallow, too. Kerosene."

Penny-man lean and ugly. His face burnt red, he stank of scum and whiskey. He made money carrying messages but colored folks usually had to buy something before he'd give them their folks' words.

"Soap, Penny-man. A bar of soap. Nothing more."

Penny-man chuckled. "Cleanliness, godliness."

"You done gone to the Devil then," I said, giving him a penny. "Well."

He look at me. Toothy-grin. "Little things."

"What?"

"Little things."

"What's that mean?"

"Just saying the words I'm paid."

"There must be something more, Penny-man. Mam must've said something more."

"No more."

I shook my head. "What's it supposed to mean?"

"Give me a penny and I'll ask."

"I'm not giving you any more money. Go on. Get."

"Can't blame me if you don't like the message."

"Get."

He clicked, his horse trotted, pulling his cart. Pans clanging, Penny-man whistling. He grinned, his, toothy-self, and winked.

I sat on the porch step. Mind whirling, I was sorry I'd asked anything.

"Little things."

"Mam, what's that mean? What it mean?" I felt empty. Buried my head in my lap. Damn Freddy. Damn the whole blessed world.

Little things. "Oh, Mam," I moaned. "Oh, Mam." I needed her good sense. But I surely didn't understand her words.

I wanted to be a child again. Wanted her comfort. Wanted her circling her hand on my back, whispering "It's all right."

Little things. Like a hand comforting.

That's what she meant—

Memories rose and I could see Pa courting, loving Mam long after their babies. I could see his hand resting softly on Mam's shoulder. See Pa smiling at her, holding her yarn. See Pa bringing a fish, already cleaned, ready to be fried. Pa, handing Mam a glass of water while she worked in the garden. Watching her drink, then bringing another glass. Pa rubbing Mam's toes. Making her laugh. During fall and spring, he'd bring her the first red leaf or the first flower. Winter, he'd drape a shawl about her shoulders.

Little things.

Wiping my face, I went inside the house, pulled my wedding dress from beneath my bed. Once Freddy brung me flowers. But other than him being inside me, there'd been no little things and I doubted there ever would be.

Two weeks, I'd heard not a word from Freddy. Two weeks, I'd sewed my hopes and dreams into my wedding dress. Cotton, lace, satin ribbons and rows of even stitches were signs of my love.

Now I didn't have any hope or dreams left.

Little things.

The dress was hateful. I snatched it up, shook it, tore the sleeves, ripped the ribbons. Shredded the lace threads. Hateful, hateful dress.

Two weeks had passed and I still didn't know if Bailey made it to New York, if he was walking the streets alive, or dead in some pauper's grave or, sold, being marched south to Mississippi. My heart was chained.

If he was dead, I think I would've felt it. The sun would've dimmed; the sky would've been less blue. Him dead, I could take. But what scared me was him alive, not sending for me.

This my sore. Bailey free and me chained here. All I had to do was look in the mirror to know why Freddy left me.

This isn't how I dreamt it. I needed to leave today. Now. Soon as I started showing Miz Baldwin going to fire me.

I sucked air, letting myself think for the first time, what my body knew to be true. Bailey's seed in me. And I'm chained to a man who doesn't want me—who'd never do little things, *anything*, to show his love.

I wiped my tears. Life goes on. I will, too. I'd better 'cause a baby's on the way and Murrays always take care of their own. Married or not, my family would accept me and mine.

I exhaled. Roads were hard but I could walk.

Next time I see Mam, I'll ask: "What's the best thing Pa ever did?" She'll think I'm silly, maybe a child to feel sorry for. But she'll sit me down and tell me stories, memories to pass on to my child. While my memories, what *didn't* happen for me, be weighing me down.

Two weeks more, two weeks more. Every day I say I'm leaving; every day, I wait one day more. No word from Freddy. I didn't expect it but deep inside I kept a thin sliver of hope. More fool me.

New life was swimming in me like the bones were swimming in the sea. My girl—it must be a girl, I wanted a girl—be raised by the sea. She'd learn gardening, how to make preserves, and how to turn a fine seam. Mam would help me and I would help Mam in her dying days. Mam would love my baby like she loved me.

At the kitchen table, a steel bowl between my knees, I was snapping sugar peas, breaking those poor peas something terrible, snapping away 'cause today I was going to do what every day I couldn't do. I was going to give notice. Tell Miz Baldwin Gates broke my heart. She'll understand this, I think. Tell her Kate Malhew gladly work for her. Kate be Irish but I didn't think Miz Baldwin would mind.

Snapping those peas, a rap came at the door.

"Come in."

No answer.

"You're welcome. Come on in."

Still no answer but a *rat-a-tat-tat* again. Maybe whoever it be, be hard of hearing? I lift myself up.

"I'm coming."

At the screen door, nobody there. I heard, "You Anna?" but didn't see nobody. I stepped outside and, like a thief, there be a young boy, hiding, ducking his head out from under the porch.

"Anna Murray?"

"I'm Anna."

"This yours." He shoved an envelope into my hand, then, took off running.

Amazed, I stared after the stranger who disappeared as quick as lightning. I turned the envelope over:

Anna

My brother George taught me to recognize my name. Two A's bracketing two N's. "*Anna*." But that was all I knew. I opened the envelope and their were marks all over the paper. Made no sense to me.

Then, the paper shook. I thought this be from Freddy. That's why the secret. Why the young man ran away.

Why couldn't Freddy send a Penny-man? Maybe there was no Penny-man to trust? Lord, have mercy. My life was caught up inside those markings and I couldn't read a word. More like chicken scratch to me.

Preacher could read. But I couldn't get to him 'til my chores were done. Lord, six weeks I'd waited, and the truth was in my hands and still I had to wait.

I swore I'd learn reading. I didn't want to feel this way again.

Then, I think this letter must be bad news. Freddy know I can't read. He could've gotten a message to me somehow. He had friends. Even that young colored boy could've said, "Freddy wants you." Maybe Mister Bailey writes to shame me before the Preacher? It be his way of letting the world know he ain't my man. I've got no claim.

Grim, I went back to snapping peas, steaming fish, and mashing potatoes with cream. Damn that Bailey. I kindly let little Thomas have two glasses of lemonade. For dessert, I served strawberries over cake. I cleared the dishes, listened quietly to Miz Baldwin's instructions to sort through the table linens tomorrow, polish her silver. She be planning a party for Mister Baldwin's clerks. She wanted oyster stew, roast beef with carrots, and a butter-rum cake. I say, "Yes, ma'am." Then, bathed little Thomas and Beth while Miz Baldwin settled the baby in the cradle.

I cleaned the kitchen, thinking I might as well wait 'til morning to see the Preacher. But I also knew the sooner I swallowed pride, the sooner I'd be over this love I carried for Mister Bailey.

When the Baldwins slept, I walked to the colored quarters, a quarter mile from town. Feeling the letter, the fine stock paper, I thought Freddy must be doing just fine. Spending my money.

At Preacher's house, the light was still on. I felt relieved. Then, scared. Maybe Preacher called to a meeting, called away 'cause somebody dead? But Preacher answered my knock. Dressed in black, his collar open, his wife behind him in a flannel robe, Preacher look worried, "Miz Anna, you hurt?"

"Here." I shoved the letter at him. "I need you to read this letter."

"Sister Anna," Preacher's wife say, "Come on in. Sit, you look ill."

I didn't move. "Just tell me what's in the letter. Please, before I can't take it."

Preacher must've known I was barely living, holding myself tight. There in the hall, a light hanging low, he read my fate. First, he read silent; I could see surprise on his face. I wet my lips.

"Even if its bad . . . tell me."

He looked at me, smiling. "It's good."

Anna, I am free. I made it safely to New York. My plan is to travel on to New Bedford. Quakers told me I'd find work. Many of our people live productive lives in New Bedford.

I have changed my name to Douglass. It has a fine ring and will confuse my would-be captors. Come to New York as quickly as possible. Don't delay for it is unsafe for me to wait. Come. We will marry.

You will be Anna Murray Douglass.

Frederick

"Love be true."

"Oh, Anna," the Preacher's wife squealed. Preacher put his hand on mine. "If you're ready to leave, I'll take you to the ship tomorrow."

Big, fat tears rolled down my face. "I'll be ready."

"Good girl." Preacher squeezed my hand. His wife say, "What news . . . what news!" By tomorrow noon, everybody in the church and colored town would know my business.

I walked away, then stopped. "Preacher, get word to my Mam. Tell her I'm safe."

"I will."

I walked, stepping softly on the gravel, staring at the beautiful world around me. Smelling salt in the air. I might never be in Baltimore again. Might never see my family again.

But I thought Freddy be Samson. Having faith in me. Faith that my love can make all right. He may not love me now but he will.

My heart soared. I wanted to jump and shout. I free. Free to love as best I knew how.

I'd ride the waves, crooning lullabies, telling my baby her father be a great man. The bones keep us safe 'til the ship arrive in the harbor.

Tomorrow, I'd ask Preacher, "Where's New Bedford?"

Tomorrow, I'd put Lena in a basket, take her with me as my dowry. I'd take my torn wedding dress and mend it as the ship sailed over blue-green waves.

Walking home, walking to my last night in the Baldwin house, my last night before I sailed to my love, I sang to the baby in my belly.

"Love be true. Love frees a woman's heart."

But even as I sang, rejoiced at my future, I felt the pain of it too. Somehow I'd get to a Penny-man and tell him to tell Mam, "You inside me. Inside your grandbaby too." All the way to New York, to New Bedford, I be smiling, thinking what Mam will say to that!

"I be the luckiest woman," I shouted, hugging myself in the middle of the road, beneath milky stars. "Anna Murray Douglass, wife of Frederick Bailey Douglass."

I couldn't find Lena, my cat. That night of all nights, Lena didn't come home. I thought maybe she be making more babies. Taking her chance at a new litter of kittens. But I couldn't wait. If Preacher took me to the ship, Miz Baldwin might try to stop me. If I was going, I needed to go now. Leave like a thief, a runaway.

My heart just broke, leaving Lena. I consoled myself that she'd survive. Miz Baldwin would give her milk, I knew, if she wailed at the kitchen door. 'Sides, Lena had her own magic of caressing, curling about a leg. But she'd only do it if she felt like it. She could be sassy, independent, but when the mood was in her, every step and sound and every curve of her body said, "love me." Somebody just had to stroke her softly and lay down food.

I figured Miz Baldwin would give me nothing if I ever came back. Even if I was starving. I was burning my bridges and nobody was going to take me in—a too-proud colored woman.

Only Mam would always love me. But even Mam's eyes would be wet, her spirits low, 'cause I'd left without saying "good-bye." Mam wouldn't easily get over that. "Family be the only proud you need," she say. And she surely wouldn't get over why after months of waiting for Freddy, I didn't make him wait one week while I got my family's blessings.

Deep down though, I'm ashamed for Mam to see my belly round. Others might not see it but she would. She'd know I'd sinned with my flesh.

"Come. We will marry."

I packed, laid down a whole chicken for Lena, then sneaked out the door into the night. Said no good-byes to the Baldwins, didn't even blow a kiss at the baby, I just ran like fate was snipping at my heels. I ran to the harbor, waited on the wharf 'til the sun rose. I imagined Freddy's face in that sun. His face warming my soul, warming my body and making me forget my lonely waiting. That afternoon I boarded the ship **V-a-l-i-a-n-t.** I didn't know what the marks meant. I only knew if Mister Baldwin tried to drag me off ship, I'd hold steady.

Preacher would make Mam understand.

I'd have Freddy write her, too. Write and send a Penny-man with the longest message of how much I loved her.

She'd understand I had to take my chance at loving. Understand I couldn't expect Fate to give me another chance. With the baby in my womb, I had to fly to Freddy, sail away over the great waves. Sail far north without bittersweet good-byes, no exchanging of kisses or locks of hair. No words of comfort.

Forgive me, Mam. Forgive me, Lena. I gone. I slipped away. Even Jesus say, "God helps those who help themselves."

First hour on board, I wept. Wept for Lena. For her new kittens I'd never see. Wept for my family. My loss of Mam. Mam, who taught me everything—taught me how to sing songs, keep house, even how to be nice to a husband with *encouraging* words, tender looks, and the best yams and dumplings.

I didn't believe the Good Lord meant for me and Mam never to meet again. I said a prayer. Then, I didn't look back. I turned my body north, marched to the prow and watched the open sea.

"Freddy," my heart wept. "Freddy," my heart sang.

"Freddy," I whispered when this officer shouted, "Nigger-gal, you got a ticket?" When a sailor stroked my arm, murmuring, "Me bed needs warming." When everybody white looked at me as if to say, "Don't forget your place."

"Freddy." I be your wife in flesh. Baby flowering in my womb, ready to know her father.

Thinking of him brought me comfort. Even when the wind blew harsh, waves crested, I stood close to the prow, my head back, watching the white sails billow and I thought Freddy saw this. Freddy was on *this* ship. I screamed into the wind, "Free. Free."

Freddy must've thrilled at drawing north. White sails taking him far and far beyond again. Him not a slave no more. I felt my inside self break free, my passion rising. Spray hitting my face, dampening, pressing my gown close to my body, I felt alive. This be the life I was meant for . . . the life I dreamt of.

My inside free and Freddy free. Us, entwined tight together. Forever. He needed me, I thought. I needed him.

For the whole week, skies were seldom blue and clear. The ship rocked, shook, and groaned. I took the storms. When others were sick in their cabins, I just screamed my happiness into the wind. Strife now, calm later.

I dreamed of kissing every part of Freddy's body. He made me a woman and a mother. What a good, great man he be.

What a good, great fool I was!

In that sailing, I imagined only the wonders of his hands upon my body, his lips upon mine. Such glory. His face was in the clouds, stretched across water, his touch was the breeze caressing my face, and the sun was the warmth of his body covering mine. Even the moon, when the currents raged, glowed with his smile.

But the storms were my warning sign, and I didn't witness it. Didn't understand.

Even heard the Captain say, "This weather makes no sense." Heard sailors cry for an albatross, gamblers curse, betting a hundred dollars on the wind's direction. Gentle women whined, fanning themselves, complaining of stifling cabins, vicious, "godforsaken weather."

It was them bones. Bones raging, stumbling, telling me I was going to die. I, too proud, thinking I could face any storm, any struggle with Freddy by my side.

Freddy not even with me. Even then Freddy be a ghost. Freddy Bailey, now named Douglass, wasn't the man I supposed. My sin be I never once felt them bones at the sea's bottom. I was crossing over their pearly grave, over their glistening, moaning bones and I never once thanked them. Never once thought of them. Ungrateful gal.

Valiant landed and I worried I didn't look my best. My clothes were all storm-tossed, salt-stained, and wrinkled. Still I swept back my hair and held my head up proudly. New York. New land. The harbor was larger, busier, noisier than Baltimore's. But I loved the colors—red, yellow, gray, and green. Carriages had pink and purple ribbons. Carts carried rainbow flowers—whites whiter than white, roses redder than red; and orange marigolds. It was the last harvest before winter. Some carts carried silvery fish and black mollusks; some carts shined with shimmering silk and delicate lace. The people, too, were amazing—mainly white, but I saw red Indians, and many brown and black people strolling in fancy clothes. This land—this North—be a miracle.

I walked down the plank into color, into a noisy world. Shouts of homecoming: "Welcome, boy"; "You're home, John"; selling: "Please buy. Two a penny, two a penny"; "Lift anchor. Set sail"; and the screech of masts, sails fluttering to life. Noise was beyond great and in that noise, color. I looked every which way. *Freddy, come get me.*

Brown men dressed in black spats, brown pants and shirt, stepping forward to white folks around me, saying, "Porter? Need Porter, Miss?"

I wondered why none of them came to help me? I shifted my bag's weight onto my hip and stared slowly in every direction. *Where's Freddy? Where's Freddy?* Expecting any minute for him to say, "I'm here."

Instead, a black-frocked man with round hat shading his pink face stepped forward.

"Anna Murray?"

"That's me."

He reached for my bag and I stepped back. He looked up, startled. "I won't harm you." His eyes were pale blue, his lashes almost white. "I am devoted to the colored."

What he mean? Devoted to the colored?

The tiredness of my journey overtook me. I wanted to run.

His nose crinkled like I was some wild thing. Some mare that needed gentling. But I didn't trust myself to strangers. Maybe this a trick? Maybe this white man suspected I was a runaway? Maybe he stole women to be the worst kind of slave?

My heart pulled in my chest. My breath came quick. I stood as tall as I was able and I ignored him. I looked beyond him, sure that Freddy will soon join me. I looked beyond to the only hope I had left.

"I'll take you to our mutual friend."

I blink, confused.

"Our mutual friend is waiting."

What friends we got in common? I thought. I'd never trafficked with white men. I did my work, lived my life with what peace be left a colored woman. This man was mistaken.

"Our friend," he said slow, like I'm dumb, "our mutual friend, of late from Baltimore, is waiting."

I shook my head.

"Your wedding day is here."

My body felt flush and the earth was no longer solid. Legs shook, knees buckled. The world had turned topsy-turvy, worse than the wild sea.

I couldn't keep myself from pleading, "Take me. Take me to him."

He took my bag and I crossed my hands over my baby growing inside me.

I walked away from that harbor, following the black hat of this strange man. I walked away from "Last call. Set sail." Walked away. "Good-bye, good-bye," I heard sons and mothers call. Walked—my legs stiff, shuffling forward to keep pace with this man. And even if them bones had started rising from the sea—hard and lovely, rising like ghostly spirits, stretching their ivory colored fingers, they couldn't have stopped me.

I would've paid them no heed. I was going to Freddy. Frederick Douglass.

My new land of dreams.

I had passion. Courage to walk toward my dream. Step inside it.

I don't know how much time passed. Seemed there be no time, no smell, no sound, no sight, only feeling. This was the last stage of my journey. Riding in a buggy pulled by an ebony horse, my body pressed forward, trying to hurry to Freddy.

This crow man handed me down, lifted my bag, then opened a door to a storied house—smaller than the Baldwins', but elegant, with brass fittings, red brick, and sparkling windows.

A maid opened the door. She waved me and the crow man inside a walnut-paneled hallway, then inside a room that felt too hot, smelled too sweet with hyacinths. A gilt-framed mirror hung over the fireplace.

First, I only saw three white men, a white woman speaking softly by the window to a man with black hair curling to his shoulders.

"They have come."

I knew him by his hair. Thick waves of hair—not quite silk, not quite coarse.

A smile tugged at Freddy's lips, lightening his eyes. His hand stretched toward me.

My breath rushed. Except for his skin, he looked like the other white men. Dressed in a fine, gray suit. A watch chain dangling from a pocket. Lace at his wrists. Proud and handsome. Freddy wasn't a slave no more. He was a man among men, a man among white men. This astonished me. His shoulders back, chin high. Freddy was easy here. Comfortable. Not just clothes, not just good food that made him seem more solid, but something I couldn't figure had changed him. Or maybe made clearer who he was?

I don't know if he called my name or not. But I went to him, hearing, "*Anna.*"

The yellow-haired lady was bubbling, "It's your wedding day." One man spoke to Freddy, false whispering so I'd hear, "She's a beauty. A rare beauty." But I knew that was a lie.

I was sea-stained, dirty all over. Still, I smiled. Freddy's palms clasped mine.

The crow man lifted off his hat. "We should hurry," he say. "Perform the ceremony and leave for New Bedford tonight."

"Freddy—" I began.

"Frederick." He squeezed my hand. "Frederick Douglass."

I wetted my lips, nervous. "Frederick—" Maybe he want me to call him that in front of these strangers? "Freddy," he be with me alone.

"Frederick, I'd like to wash. Change my clothes."

The room dulled like nightfall. I could still see sun on the carpet but it had no glitter, no spark. In the hush quiet, I heard the soft gong of a clock.

The white woman, kindly meant I think, stepped close, soothing, "But of course. We are hurrying like there is no tomorrow. We haven't even introduced ourselves. I am Mrs. Ruggles. These are my friends—yours, too, I hope. Mr. Garrison, my husband, Mr. Ruggles, and Mr. Stevenson." Each, in turn, nodded their heads at me.

"Mister Quincy, you've met." She looked at the black-frocked man. "Oh, John, you didn't. You failed to introduce yourself?" Her face warmed, turning pink. "What barbarians you must think us, Anna. May I call you Anna? I'm Lydia."

"Yes, ma'am," I said, knowing better than to say, "Lydia." Freddy's fingers digged into mine. I sucked air rather than cry out.

"We will marry now," he said. "Promptly. We must get to New Bedford."

The men nodded their heads again. The one named Garrison said, "Very wise."

Miz Ruggles laid her hand on Freddy's arm. "Please reconsider," she said, like a bee touching a flower. Her voice be drawling, not twangy like the men. "A few hours won't undo your haste."

I liked Miz Ruggles. She ain't pretty like Miz Baldwin but there be power in her words. I could tell she got her way sometimes. I felt, too, she understood me some as a woman. Only one wedding day. This be mine and I had no planning. I felt guilty that I'd doubted Freddy.

Felt tiredness, too, coming down hard. Felt tears behind my eyes. Felt ever so lonely.

Oh, Mam. Lost Lena.

Another heartbeat, I prayed Miz Ruggles would gather me and lead me to a room with scented soap and a basin of water. I'd like to press the wrinkles in my dress. I'd like, too, to carry a flower. Just one. One flower to remind me when Freddy gave me marigolds.

"I am an escaped slave. My time is not my own."

There was nothing to say to that.

Strange, being a slave gave Freddy power. For Miz Ruggles's face changed, grew somber. The men nodded again, and Mister Quincy stepped forward, whispering dryly, "Prepare for blessings. You are entering a sanctified union. A holy state deemed by God."

I thought Northerners must truly feel sorry for slavery. It be a revelation to me, a new thought like a Bible miracle. Still, I wished my desires for a wedding were taken into account.

I felt real sorrow but, then, I plucked up. I not my mother's daughter for nothing. This weakness of mine ain't no real trouble. I was still marrying. I still carried a child. I still had good news to tell to Freddy, in private, in our wedding bed. I put my hand in his.

I felt light as water. In the mirror, Freddy and me seemed frozen. Surrounded by strange men. Miz Ruggles, the only one with a smile. Freddy strained to fit my ring. We were married. He kissed me on both cheeks.

Miz Ruggles's maid served wine. My first taste. Bubbles rested on my tongue.

Freddy held up his hands. "Friends, thank you all for your good care of me. These weeks, months, waiting for Anna have been filled with trials and tribulations. But, also, filled with joy knowing that decent people abound in the North. Thank you. From a most grateful heart."

The men clapped and Miz Ruggles beamed.

I took a bite of the pound cake, thinking it ain't as good as I could make it. Later, I thought I'll make another cake. Maybe even send Miz Ruggles my recipe. Freddy could teach me how to write it.

Looking up at my husband, at the men clapping him on the back, wishing him well, I thought, "Amazing." North, way better than Baltimore. In the North, slaves made miracles. I'd been blessed with a good husband.

"We must not tarry here," say Freddy.

With a quick flurry, I was off on another journey. Quincy and Garrison planned to drive us to a place called New Bedford. Miz Ruggles murmured, "There is a cottage. A new home waiting you." I wanted to hug her but I just smiled, and said, "Thank you," as polite as I know how. She be still white; I, still black. African.

In the carriage, Freddy said, "Miss Ruggles likes you. She is a good friend of the Negroes. You did well, Anna." He squeezed my hand.

I closed my eyes and slept. I caught fever. Four days and three nights, I was sick with fever and dreaming. I remember posting houses and Freddy's hands smoothing my brow. I remember seeing tops of trees, some with red and yellow leaves, others just thrusting sticks in the blue sky. At night, I glanced at stars, sparkling in and out like tiny miracles. I dreamed my baby swimming in a wide sea, bones made a net beneath her. She'd not drown.

I dreamed I was in a deep bucket of cool water and a strong, tender arm was cradling me upright while a sponge dripped water down my shoulders, my breasts. Someone wiped my face.

I'm never sick. But I'd be always for this feeling. It reminded me of Mam loving me, yet I knew it wasn't Mam. I was safe in hands strong enough to hold a woman grown.

I pressed my head deeper into the seat cushions. Or maybe it be Freddy's shoulder?

I did not wake 'til we arrived at our new home.

Sleep, Anna. We are in our own home now."

I stirred, waking from heavy sleep. Waking cool, without fever. I felt strangely refreshed. Like my body had renewed itself. Been born again. I remembered little of our travels, yet here I was laying on soft feather down with Freddy's face a breath away from mine, and him saying, "Sleep."

I stretched my hand, stroked his chin, murmuring, "I'd rather be with you."

"We've a hard day ahead of us tomorrow."

"Nothing hard if you here."

Freddy kissed me lightly on the lips. Then he chuckled, and I was surprised, for I'd never heard him laugh. Never heard the richness in his joy.

"Are you well?"

"Yes." I blushed. "Thank you for your care of me."

He felt my brow. "I was worried for you." Then he bent his head lower; I could see his eyes intent. "We need to be strong together. Your strength is what I most admire about you."

"I'm strong. I won't fall ill again. I've always been strong."

"Sssh. Lie awhile. Rest." Freddy's hand stayed me from getting up. "I know you're strong, Anna. Were it not for you, I wouldn't be here. My dreams wouldn't be coming true."

His lips brushed mine and I sighed into the sweetness. "Tell me about your dreams."

He smiled like a child.

"So many have provided me with support. It's amazing. Time and again, men stepped forward to give me clothes, bread, money. But it is the abolitionists . . . Mr. Garrison, who writes a fine paper, *The Liberator*, who've counseled me and invigorated my pride. I feel more free than I've ever felt in my life."

He kissed me again then got up, pacing, pulling off his black cravat, taking off his coat. So handsome. There was a fireplace bright against the fall chill, and tallow? no, beeswax candles brightly flaming on the mantel and dresser. It was a fine room with good comforts and warm light making Freddy's shadow flicker on the wall, making his shadow seem bigger than a giant's.

I nearly laughed with joy and stretched my arms out onto the softest, biggest bed of my life. "This house ours?"

"Not ours. Not yet. Abolitionists have lent it to us. But one day, I'll have a home like this. No, better than this."

"This house be fine."

"You think so, Anna?" He turned and looked at me strangely.

"Well, I haven't seen it all. But, any house you in be just fine." I lifted onto my elbow.

He laughed, his head thrown back, his jaw open. He laughed and I turned my face into the pillow. He sat on the bed beside me.

"Anna, I'm lucky to have you. Lucky to be here. Lucky to have you here. God has answered my prayers. I went from a life with no joy to one where white men listen, respect me, where I have a home of my own—"

"Our own."

"Where I have an opportunity to help others by speaking out against the ills of slavery."

"'Tis a blessing."

"Yes." He got up again, pacing, so much restless energy, I thought. Here be the man I first saw on the prow of the ship, the man looking beyond the horizon, seeing what I couldn't. Well and good. Time for me to help him with what I knew. I'd not shame this man. I'd be stronger than I'd ever been.

"Freddy?"

"Frederick, please, Anna."

"Fred—rick." I tasted the sound. Then rose, wriggling my toes on the bare floor. "Let me have your clothes. I'll fold them so they won't need ironing tomorrow. I should draw water, too, for us to wash. Put away our clothes. Lay out our bedclothes. These my wifely duties. I should start as I mean to go on."

I stood square with my hands firm on my hips.

Freddy's head tilted, his eyes sparkled.

"I should start, too, as I mean to go on."

He blew out the candles and put another log on the fire. "Domestic duties and wifely duties are not to be confused."

If I was less dark, I would've been red. I touched my wedding band.

Freddy took off his shirt and his flesh glowed gold. He took my hands and sat us both down, side by side, on the bed.

"I'm glad to have met you, Anna." Simple as that. Then, he kissed me sweeter, deeper than ever before. My arms reached round and tried to soothe what I couldn't see, the crisscross scars on his back.

"I would've perished were it not for you." His mouth moved down my cheek onto my neck and I felt such yearning, weeks, months, years of yearning banked down, sparking into flames. He undid my many buttons, his big hands so gentle, so quick. Then he stroked my breasts while still kissing me and leaning me deep, backwards onto the bed.

"Thank you, Anna." He kissed me fierce. His hands touching, caressing everywhere. I trembled from the sheer joy of it, from having a lawful husband.

Before I knew it, we were both naked, hot, sweaty, moving our bodies into one. I let myself be shameless and rose up to meet him. I gave him joy as best I could. And when he began to make small moaning noises, when I could feel all the power of him finding a place inside of me, I cried out with him. Shameless, shameful Delilah. But if such pleasure-taking be sin, then God would just have to forgive me.

He talked almost all night. "Abolitionists are a new force." "There will be a war." "The righteous will prevail." "Garrison has his own paper. Devoted to colored people's liberation."

"Mmm," I murmured.

I got up from the bed, stepped into my dress, fallen on the floor, and he followed me, still talking, not caring he was bare. It be cold. I took secret delight 'cause I think maybe all this time, with these new people, these white people, he had nobody just to talk with—to sing out his ideas.

I thought, "It matter that I his woman." I knew him in Baltimore when he slaved on the docks. Our history be deeper than these new acquaintances. Would always be deeper. I his wife.

I went to the kitchen and found a good stock of bread, butter, and apples. A side of smoked ham. Found even a flask of wine. I found two mugs, then a tray and carried the food and wine back to bed. Freddy would surely freeze if we sat at the kitchen table. I pretended that the bed was our shore and spread our food. In between his many words, I fed Freddy a slice of ham, a tuft of bread, a slice of apple. So many words. I watched him eat. Said, "Mmm," when he paused and offered more wine and food. I got giddy seeing him so happy, so alive. My heart was full and my body, warmed from the wine, asked for more of him. I set the tray on the floor, slipped off my dress, and reached for him in the bed.

Later, when we were wrapped in each other's arms, with only embers left in the fire and dawn sneaking in the window, I spoke, "Freddy—"

"Frederick."

"I like Freddy better."

"I'm a new man with a new name. If a wife accords a husband dignity, others will follow. You must understand that, Anna."

"I do," I say. "But when I touch you like this . . ." I touched him low, between his thighs and watched his face change. "Freddy seems the name."

"Anna, please. I must insist. It's how cultured people speak. 'Frederick' is even lenient—most wives call their husbands Mister. Mister Ruggles. Mister Quincy."

"These all white people you speaking about?"

"White people are our model. If colored people propose to advance, we must show all whites, we, too, are cultured, respectable."

"Mam called Pa any name she wished."

"So she should, if your father didn't mind. But, I do mind, Anna."

I didn't want him to talk anymore. I didn't want to argue. I touched between his thighs again.

"In private," I whispered, kissing him. "In private, I must call you Freddy as I wish."

I felt him tense despite my touch, my kiss.

"A mother-to-be should get some respect. Some wishes granted."

That stopped him. He searched my face and, for the first time, I let him hear my laugh. We held fast. And soon it be my head pushing into the pillows and my Freddy, above me, eyes closed, face shining, moving like a man trying to find home inside my body's horizon.

When the cock crowed, Freddy was asleep beside me both like a baby and a man satisfied with life. I told the sunrise, "Thank you. Jesus," I say, "thank you."

I hoped New Bedford had a sea. I could open the window to see if I smelled it. But I didn't want to wake Frederick. My Freddy. There must be a shoreline with clams, starfish, and shells. . . . There must be a world outside that be familiar to me. While the people be new, the town be new, water be as old and as ancient as ever.

I smiled at how far I'd come. Wife. Mother. Anna Douglass. I looked at my husband and thought: *Inside this house there will be much love*. I vow: *My body will never be closed to his*.

*T*wo days we lived private. Much joy in our house. We found water—a colder, rougher Atlantic, with all manner of ships: whalers, fishing junkets, navy ships. The Bedford wharf was a busy place, not as big as Baltimore, but big enough for me to buy new cloth, pins, a candy stick. Freddy bought paper and a small slate to teach me words. He bought a Bible and inside it wrote our names on a family tree, etched in gold. He also bought some "fine vellum," he called it, to write to Mam.

There were many, many colored folk. As we walked the wharf, most nodded at us or smiled. Several spoke with Frederick. Told him about work, all kinds: blacksmithing, welding, caulking. I was proud. Freddy could turn his mind to anything.

Freddy said I should turn my mind to caring for our children. He doesn't want me working for anyone—colored or white. I told him I'd like that just fine. I'd sew, cook, garden, put up preserves, and clean our house so lovely, that everyone would know I be a happy wife.

Colored men said they'd send their wives. Right away. But, then, they say, "In a day or two," when they discover we just married. Suited me fine. I didn't want visitors. I wanted our house quiet, just filled with me, and Freddy and the baby-to-be.

The third day, the Preacher and his wife came. He be fine-boned and thin. She be a big woman—bigger than me. Preacher be quiet. Polite. She chattered and wore a hat with purple feathers which swayed every time she moved. Swayed as she bobbed her head, telling me gossip. She had stories about everyone in the congregation. I said little for I didn't want her to gossip about me. Preacher just say, "Bless you. Bless this house."

Freddy and I both laughed when they were gone. But after the Preacher's visit, there be a flood of people coming to meet us. I was worn out, making seed cakes, serving tea. But I saw how everyone respected and admired Freddy. He'd be a big man among these people, I thought. He might rise to deacon in their church.

My thoughts about our world were too small. The next day a letter came. Freddy, face delighted, told me Garrison has asked him to speak before the Nantucket Anti-Slavery Society. Three days hence at 7:00 P.M. In Mercantile Hall.

"But you still a slave. Won't slave-trackers be there, too?"

"It's something I must do, Anna."

"But the danger? We don't need this house if it means you must speak and be in danger."

"Anna, you don't understand."

"Quakers can take it back."

"They will once I have means to support us. This house is but a way station for slaves with families. We'll be journeying on, Anna."

"And I'll be ready. Long as you safe. Long as no man's hunting my baby's father."

Freddy brushed aside his hair and sighed. His frustration reminded me he be much younger than me. I wanted to stay inside; he wanted to go out into the world.

"Anna, we can't abandon those less fortunate. I did speak once in New York. It was dangerous, I know. Mr. Garrison convinced me to say a few words at a meeting.

"Anna, you'd be surprised at the people who've never heard a slave speak. Some thought slave hardships were fairy tales—"

"What?"

"Stories, lies made up by abolitionists. When they saw me, Anna, they began to believe a little. Believe that not all slaveholders were kindly and good-intentioned. I spoke no more than five minutes, but those five minutes, I felt, meant something. Did good."

I was still frowning.

"Anna, please come here." I walked to Freddy by the back window. "See," he say, "you bought seeds to grow in that little plot of earth."

The yard was a mess but there were old trestles, marking a square where once a thriving garden had been.

"You hope your seeds will take root and grow. So, too, my words." He touched me beneath my chin, urging my head up, to face him, eye to eye. He knew I couldn't help but give in. He be too handsome to refuse.

"Only a few words. Only this time. Then I'll work ever so hard. We'll be rich, for I needn't give any money to Hugh Auld. We'll make a home. I'll even serve in the church."

I smiled.

"You think I don't know your dreams for me? I'll be sober, somber, upright as a Preacher. A Christian man of good sense and learning."

"Will we live here long enough to harvest my garden?"

"I can't promise. But would it matter? You'll plant your seeds anyway. Just as I must plant mine."

That night Freddy asked me to make tea. At the kitchen table, he counted the money he had left from his escape, and he counted the last few coins I had: six dollars and eighty-two cents. Still a small fortune. A dollar a week be good pay.

"We'll spend a dollar on a new dress and shoes for you, Anna."

"Why?"

"You must look well for my speech. Properly clothed. People will want to meet you."

I felt nervous. I didn't want nobody looking at me.

"They'll wish to know you, because you're my wife."

I looked hard at Freddy. "This one time?"

"Yes."

I breathed deep. "Then give me twenty-five cents. I'll buy shoes. The rest we'll save for the future, our babies."

"But, Anna, you must have a fine dress."

"So I don't shame you?" I asked softly.

He shook his head. "Anna, this is important to me."

"It be important to me, too, Mister Douglass." My voice edged high. "I'll wear the dress I didn't wear for my wedding. It be as fine as any dress any woman, white or colored, would wear."

"I believe you, Anna." He handed me a quarter and put the rest of the money inside a sock, which he hid in a drawer.

He kissed me and just as I moved my arms round his neck, he placed them down by my sides.

"Sleep, Mrs. Douglass. I'll be up awhile. I'll write a speech more eloquent than the broken words I gave in New York."

In the morning, he was still writing. But, mainly, crossing out his lines for all I saw. A good two pennies' worth of paper on the floor. He looked a mess. His shirt unbuttoned; his shoes off. His hair tangled from where his fingers pulled. His skin be nearly gray.

"Freddy," I say.

He didn't look up.

"Just speak from your heart. Speak your heart and everybody listen."

I swore I would listen and obey him. *Love be true.*

*J*ust speak from your heart," I whispered when I saw Freddy take the stage. Mr. Garrison be speaking first. "Customary," say Freddy. "It's the custom for a white person 'to vouch' for the colored."

To me, this made no sense. Why have a man say ahead of time that what the other man be going to say be truth? They think colored men lie?

It angered me and, I admit, my anger helped me feel less nervous.

The hall be huge. Almost like a warehouse. Filled with chattering, noisy people. Gentlemen argued about President Tyler, about the Negro character. Ladies talked about souls needing salvation, about the sins of slavery. Some women even be crying. Some men passed out copies of the *Liberator*. Others smoked cigars, slapping each others' backs. Two men fell to fisticuffs and had to be pulled apart like dogs in the road.

A small crowd of free coloreds sat in the back, more quiet and proper than the whites. Freddy made me sit in the front. I didn't like it. The gas lamps smelled awful and I was afraid the smoke would ruin my dress. I looked pretty but I felt sick. Me, never sick in Baltimore, never sick on the sea voyage here. But a month up north, and I'd been ill twice!

Abolition make passions run high. This crowd be rough. Not gen-teel like I expected.

I felt sweat on my lips. I looked at the plain-dressed men, thinking one must be a slave catcher. I wanted to shout, "Run, Freddy. Run far." My mouth made no sound.

Mr. Garrison stood up. There was applause, men whistling, stomp-ing their feet. There were boos too. Each boo came from a catcher ready to steal Freddy, take him south, way deep, beyond Maryland, where I'd never find him.

"Remarkable story, remarkable man." Mister Garrison smiled like a proud papa. I wanted to tell him hush, to stop praising my Freddy. He pointed and Freddy stepped forward proudly.

Someone shouted, "Nigger. No better than a monkey." Others must've lashed out, for I heard a shriek of pain. Freddy acted like he'd heard nothing. He stood at the podium, looking out at the hundred, no, hundreds of people come to hear him.

I trembled. I felt like my dinner wouldn't stay down. But Freddy was calm as folks shouted encouragement, shouted foul words at him.

Then, every one quieted. Freddy's voice, like music, filled the lull.

"Friends," he say, "I was born a slave."

Speak from the heart.

"Slavery separates the child from the mother. So I seldom got to feel her caress, hear her voice, or see her face. Sunup to sundown, my mother worked in the fields. At night, her body tired and sore from work, she walked from the fields to my grandmother's house. My grandmother raised everyone's babies. I guess I was just lucky to have her be my blood relative.

"My mother walked a good hour and lay down beside me as I slept. Sometimes I remember her kissing me, always I remember her holding me, giving me warmth. Most often she was gone before I woke, for she had an hour to make it back to the fields. I thought she was an angel, a ghost I dreamed about. It was my grandmother who told me my mother slept beside me."

Tears streamed down my face. Freddy hadn't ever told me all this.

"My mother was sold south. And like a child, I soon forgot her face. I do not know whether she is even living or dead. But she was sold because, I suspect, my Mistress was jealous of the time my Master spent with my mother."

He didn't have to say: "Master was my father." It was clear to everyone there, I thought. Like a wave had overtaken the crowd, there was silence. They could see Freddy's face. Some, I thought, might wonder if it be the whiteness in him that made him sound so proper and educated. If so, they couldn't mistake the colored in him, too. Colored didn't make him dumb. An animal. Colored made him even finer. His Mam's child. She'd be proud.

I looked right and left. All eyes were on Freddy.

He seemed bigger on stage, not just 'cause he was standing high on a block. He seemed like a giant, with a voice that rung out and said to the world, "See. This be a man." I started rocking my body to and fro, feeling like the Holy Spirit was upon me. Freddy was preaching a sermon about his life.

Freddy be great Samson man, his hands on the pillars of slavery, pushing, shoving, tearing at the walls of injustice.

He spoke for fifteen, twenty minutes and all those people stayed quiet. Like they never heard such words before. Such rich sounds floating from a colored man's mouth. Freddy came to his end:

"I always looked for a way to be free. When Fate offered me a chance, I, took it."

I sat up straight, my hands clasped in my lap.

"I found courage to escape slavery's wretched existence and sail to freedom. I will not tell you of the many that helped me. But the good Lord blesses them all."

Who helped more than me? How come Freddy didn't mention me?

"Though I stand before you, I am not free. Slavery's hand still reaches out to me, ready to snatch me back into its grasp. Good Christians, like you, can reverse this evil. Abolish slavery and you abolish the invisible chains that hold slaves apart and wrest from them feeling, life, and knowledge."

There was thunder, clapping like thunder. Folks rushed forward, surrounding Frederick on stage. Chairs toppled. People pushed and shoved. I cried out. Seemed like everybody was pushing past me. My hem was ripped. "Freddy," I shouted, but he couldn't hear me. I couldn't see him. He be surrounded by dozens of people, waving, trying to shake his hand.

Someone chanted, "Free him, free him." Soon, everyone be screaming it. The sound so loud it made me dizzy again. I struggled back, away from the crowd rushing to the front.

My feelings be confused. I wanted to run from the noise, the shouting, shoving people. Yet, I wanted Freddy to take me by the hand, pull me to the center of the circle, and tell everyone, "This be my helpmate. My true love and wife." I felt shame, too. For I shouldn't need glory. It be Freddy who offered hope to the slaves. Not mentioning me, Freddy be protecting me. I swayed, imagining Freddy caught, sent back to Master Auld, leaving our baby fatherless. I squeezed my mouth to hold back bile. I thought maybe Freddy ain't just Samson. He also be Shadrach stepping into the oven's fire.

Mister Quincy reached me. He seemed so small in his dark suit, his hand clutching his black hat. His eyes were beady like a crow.

"Do not fear, Mrs. Douglass. Do not fear."

How this white man know what I feel? How he know?

"Come. There's a reception line. You must stand with your husband."

I stepped back. "Naw." I didn't have the strength for this. I didn't want to meet people. I wanted my own home.

Pages of the *Liberator*, cigar butts, and tobacco spit stained the floor.

Mister Quincy lightly touched my hand. His eyes be all sympathy.

"Your husband needs you. He is a great man. Let me take you to him."

I thought this Quaker truly be my friend. He married me to Freddy and in his quiet voice (how I hear him over the crowd's roar, I don't know—but I do hear) I heard this man offering to help me.

I tried to pin the strands of my hair, smooth my torn, almost wedding dress. What a fury these abolitionists be!

"I ready." Looking up at the stage, I saw Freddy beside Mr. Garrison. A line of people, bulging and twisting like a snake, waited to meet them. Freddy, at ease, shook hands, smiling, meeting these strangers like it be the easiest thing in the world.

"Let us through. Let us through."

Everybody looked at me, at Mister Quincy pulling me along. My palms sweat and my skin began to itch like I'd fallen into an ivy patch.

Freddy smiled at me, then his smile froze, for I looked a mess. Looked ready to run.

"This is my wife," Freddy said, loud. His hand on my back lent me support. But then he took it away to shake hands with a man shouting, "Fine words. Fine words," and grinning like Christmas had come.

My turn next. I shook this man's hand. His grip nearly broke every bone. But he be looking past me, back at Freddy. I breathed deep, trying to calm myself.

"Wonderful speech." A matron, finely dressed, sang Freddy's

praises. Her husband slapped Freddy on the shoulder, "Good show," and I could feel Freddy getting taller, bigger beside me. These people be giving Freddy new air.

"Charmed," the woman said to me, but I knew she wasn't. I was getting heavier, sweatier by the minute.

Too many faces, hands. Too many strangers. I didn't know my place. Mam said, "Do your work and leave white folks alone."

I wanted to laugh crazy. What would Mam say now?

I kept my eyes low. I couldn't look in these folks' eyes. I was afraid to speak. Afraid they'd hear my stupid tongue. But what I feared most, I already felt—their judgment. Their judgment that I was not the wife for Frederick Douglass—too awkward, too old and fat.

Freddy stood beside me, dignified. He say, "How do you do?" "Thank you." "Thank you kindly."

Another white man bowed, saying, "Mrs. Douglass. You must be proud of your husband."

I stared at his hand. Rough, one finger missing, I did not want to touch it. This hand frightened me. It might grip me and haul me and Freddy both into slavery. This might be the hand that punishes.

I saw down the line more hands. Hairy, thick, thin, rough, soft, big, and small. And I was supposed to press their flesh. Smile and say words of sense. The hand still hung in midair. It scared me awful. I wanted to run, crying out, "Can't stay. Can't stay."

Flee, rush headlong out the door, into the chill night air where there'd be less noise, more peace. Instead, I inhaled. This be a new world for me. But I'm a Murray and a Douglass and I'll make my family—make myself, as best I can, proud.

I clasped the hand. Did my duty.

This be Freddy's last speech. I could live with that.

We stood for hours. Hand sore, feet numb. I heard church bells strike ten. I wanted to go home but if I took the blacksmith's wagon we borrowed, Freddy would have to walk.

I waited but I was fearsome tired.

• • •

Everybody was pretty much gone. Any minute, Freddy would clutch my hand and say, "Home. Let us go home." I felt a lightening of spirit. I'd survived. Hadn't brung shame.

"Frederick, I'd like you to meet Miss Assing."

Freddy's breath caught. Like he'd been startled, surprised anew. His smile be joyful. He bowed before the tall, golden-haired woman, dressed in blue silk. A pretty picture. Fine, straight nose; wide, blue eyes and dark brows that sweep and arch. Truly lovely.

Freddy and this woman speak but I couldn't hear.

Someone threw open the door. Cold rushed in. Time stilled. I be outside the warm, bright circle Freddy and this woman have made. He'd forgotten me. Me, standing beside him. Only colored woman in a white dress. In a big, nearly empty hall. How could he not see me? Feel my love? Feel me?

"Anna." He didn't even glance at me. "Let me introduce Miss Assing."

"A fine man, your Frederick." Her tongue sounded funny. Clipped and strong.

"Miss Assing is from Germany."

I heard the wonder in Freddy's voice. I knew he'd like to go to this place called "Germany."

Curious, Miz Assing's head tilted like a baby bird. She be surprised by me. She smiled and I felt her charm like sun, lifting shadows. "I care very much for the abolitionist cause."

I couldn't speak. I couldn't even nod or smile. I was stone, lacked all grace. Only recently was I, "Miz Douglass." Most my life I'd been "Lil' Bit," "Hey, colored gal," or "Baldwins' maid."

This woman had already stopped looking at me. She admired Freddy. She looked at him like he be special. And so Freddy be. A man unbowed. Reborn.

Miz Assing looked at Freddy a bit like I looked at him. Eyes soft, she leaned slightly toward him. Like she would gladly take his arm.

I saw with my heart that this woman might harm my happiness. I didn't know how I knew this, but I did. Maybe it was my new Delilah's heart, my marriage passion which helped me see. This woman, except for her voice, be soft where I was hard, lean where I was too round. Her lips be thin and rosy, mine be thick and plum. She be at ease like Freddy. Like the two of them fit in a world of stages, speeches, and glory.

"We should go, Miss Assing."

I was happy to hear Garrison's voice.

Miz Assing offered her hand. "I look forward to hearing you speak again, Mr. Douglass. Your eloquence will surely hasten the end of slavery."

Freddy bowed deep. His lips almost touched her hand. "I am honored."

I watched Freddy watch her leave. Her silk rustled. Fur be wrapped warmly about her shoulders. She smiled at something Mr. Garrison said. Then, she looked back, over her shoulder. "Auf Wiedersehen, Herr Douglass."

Freddy bowed again. He swallowed, looked down at me, his eyes bright. His face filled with rapture.

"Let us go, Anna. It has been an important night."

I crossed my hands over my belly. I felt dizzy, sicker than I had all night. *Love be true.*

Somehow Freddy wasn't. Somehow his look denied me. Made me small, "little" in an unkindly way.

I tried to speak on the ride home. The moon hid behind clouds. Trees and ground be frozen. No owl be calling. Like every spirit be dead. Horses just clip-clopped. Clip-clopped.

My eyes filled with water. Freddy's not looking at me. He be looking past the horse's head, far down the road. Beyond where the moon made our path glow.

I heard him murmuring, repeating words from his speech. I thought he was seeing the crowd again, hearing the clapping, hearing the good, kind words from all those good, kind men. Those good, kind women. 'Specially women. Or be it woman?

Freddy needn't tell me. He'd give more speeches. These abolitionists have a big and growing church. I could feel it. See it. Freddy's ready to speak to the world. Never mind every word risked capture. Auld might snatch him back. This wouldn't stop Freddy. He'd found his voice.

I'd found fear.

My mistake. I didn't imagine Freddy big enough when I met him. I remembered seeing him like a ship's captain, standing on the prow of a half-built ship, handsome, bold, even though he a slave. But that's all I really wanted. Him, standing proud. I didn't imagine he'd set sail. Rejoice in the wide, wide world.

Bedroom, garden, parlor, kitchen be all I needed. And when I strolled I wanted to smell the sea, see and feel shells, surf, and imagine my bones stirring on the sandy bottom.

Marrying Freddy, journeying to New Bedford was all the adventure I'd ever need. Babies would be my fruit, and the joy of settling, making a house a home.

But now I also knew something new. Freddy, with no head bowed, no shuffling, could look straight at a pretty, white woman. Eight years younger than me, I knew he might look at pretty women from time to time. Colored women might look back. I just hadn't counted on a white woman too.

Still, there be fight in me. I be carrying his child. I be the best wife, mother. I be the harbor, the safe home for when he grew tired of glory.

Him and me. Always. Love still true.

Diary of

Ottilie Assing

Beloved of Frederick Douglass

1820–1884

"As in all things, love should be color-blind."

—Frederick Douglass,
in a letter, 1863

"Why did I suppose love wouldn't hurt?"

—Ottilie Assing,
prior to her death, 1884

Paris

August 21, 1884

I didn't expect my life to end this way. Me, fifty-eight, sitting like a moonling wrapped in furs, trying to stave off chills. The thought of America makes my heart cold. It didn't always.

I am the Snow Queen. Love's betrayal has frozen my heart, sliver by sliver. Except for one small piece, my heart is ice.

Frederick Bailey Douglass. *Dearest Douglass.* Do I dare say, "You did this to me?" Or was the blame mine all along? I, Ottilie Assing. So smart. Not smart enough.

I'd best hurry. Scribble these words before time disappears, love disappears. Before I'm so cold, so solid, I cannot move except to cross the ocean from which there is no return, no renewal. No gliding across the great Atlantic. No recrossing of seas. Only stillness and death.

Always, I'd wanted to sail to America. "Land of High Purpose and Dreams." Think of it—a bold experiment—to have one's customs, one's culture begin anew. To be reborn! To carve from the landscape a new world. Not a nightmare world but a realm of magical dreams—a land so vast and wide, anything can happen. A land—not chained or closed tight and small like Germany.

I hadn't counted on love's treachery. I'm dying. In Paris. The City of Light. Except there isn't any light.

Douglass isn't here.

Once upon a time . . .

Mama and Papa created an oasis. A house overflowing with much love, books, music, and painting. My parents, elegant and refined, presided over artistic, intellectual salons. Of course, Mama was far more gay and lively. But, on Sunday afternoons, when it seemed all of smart, creative Hamburg was in our parlor, even Papa, less dour, hugged me close. I delighted in smelling his tobacco, feeling the itch of his beard.

At two, I sat on Feodor Wehl's knee. Herr Steinheim introduced me to chess. And Fräulein Orff commented on my early paintings of bold suns floating in purple skies. "Lots of color but little technique." But, at five, it didn't much matter. Both Mama and Papa exclaimed "how smart," "how beautiful" I was! And even when my sister was born, their attentions, rather than lessening, redoubled.

What pleasures of childhood! Two enlightened parents who didn't believe a girl was only fit for sewing and bearing babies. Two parents who thought love was worth all sacrifice. Indeed, worth any scorn. Papa, the gifted physician; Mama, ex-governess, now painter. Both poets celebrating their passion. Creating a cocoon for their daughters to fly!

Outside our home, there was far less light. Like a Grimm's tale, a world dulled by a witch's spell. Odors were less of sweet bread and more the rank of hard toil. Sunlight rarely pierced the maze of brick. Linen, drying on clotheslines, collected the air's dust.

Hamburg's Jews were well-educated, prosperous. Nonetheless, prejudice had blunted opportunities like unleavened bread. Dark men in prayer shawls whisked silently through lanes; little boys and girls wrapped in thin cloaks, played, kicking cans. Mothers bartered in the market for coal and candles to shelter against the long, winter nights. Of course, because they were Jews, some found it even harder. Women whose husbands and sons had gone missing. Orphans who'd lost entire families. Strange disappearances afflicted the ghetto like plague.

Once I gave my gloves to the butcher's daughter, a little girl who was shivering in a shop with no warmth other than a black kettle-stove which instead of being steaming hot, was warm enough for me to touch. Mama was buying a roast hen. Our maid was sick, and I'd pleaded with Mama to let me help with chores. For me, it was a grand adventure.

The little girl's black eyes seemed to sink inside her head. Blue veins were visible on her forehead and wrists. Her dark hair reminded me of my sister and it might have been merely that resemblance that encouraged me to move toward her. I couldn't have been more than seven. Mama was supervising the weighing and plucking of the hen. The girl was as tall as me. But she looked like a scrawny chick in her shift and shawl, whereas I was plump and warm in my coat with fur cuffs and collar. She sniffed, wiping her nose with her palm. I offered her a handkerchief, embroidered with my initials: *Q. A.*

"Are you a princess?"

I giggled.

Butcher Stein spoke sharply in Yiddish. In secret, my grandparents taught me Yiddish. Butcher Stein told his daughter not to bother me, to leave me alone. He told her I had no heart. I was no more a princess than the dead hen in his hand. Then, he looked at me, a fierce, intent stare and I felt shame. Mama sensed it, too. Some shift in the sawdust, the blood-scented air. "Let us go. Deliver the hen." She motioned for me to go. Impulsively, I pulled off my gloves, stuffed them into a little ball into the girl's hands. "Auf Wiedersehen."

The girl, her nose running, stared at the floor.

"Stubborn people," Mama kept repeating all the way home. "Stubborn people."

I looked at Mama, her cheeks red from the cold, her blond curls wild beneath her hat. In the coach glass, I could see both our images. We did indeed look like a queen and princess from a fairy tale—all golden and prosperous. But, even as a child, I knew from dreams that darkness overtook the beautiful.

"No enlightenment without suffering," Papa would say.

That afternoon, going up my house's steps, I realized keenly the differences between outside, inside. I stepped into the vestibule and Nanny was immediately upon me, clucking about the cold, asking where I'd lost my gloves. Even when she'd hung my coat, I felt, compared to the butcher shop, our home was an oven. I smelled sauerkraut and sausages.

Inside was a riot of colors: red, gold, blue, not just weathered wood, black caulking, and dulled brick. Portraits of our family hung on the wall in gilt frames. And Papa was at home that late afternoon, for I remember him playing his favorite melody—Beethoven's *Piano Sonata No. 14 in C-sharp minor*. (Herr Rellstab renamed it "Moonlight

Sonata," because it reminded him of moonlight over Lake Lucerne. But I always thought of it as Papa's song. Sad and dreamy.) Mama rushed forward, kissing Papa, and he kissed her all about the face while Nanny took me upstairs to biscuits and tea.

Jews lived outside. Christians, like us, lived inside. Surrounded by Jews. Yet, my grandparents were Jewish; Mama's and Papa's friends were Jews. "I converted to Christianity to marry Mama," explained Papa. "But I refuse to pass." He was Jewish by culture; Christian, in religion. "But none of this really matters, little one. Individualism is beyond culture."

I didn't understand him then. I don't understand him now. Even the choices that I thought were all about me—were they? Or were they merely reflections of sweeping social change, of my own self-delusions, of Frederick? *Abolitionist. Suffragette. Shadow wife.*

I do remember the next morning, packing my clothes, my books, my favorite doll. I wanted to give them to the butcher's girl. Mama hugged me and Papa called me his dear little girl.

Mama consented to a few clothes but took away the books. "The child can't read."

I was shocked. All afternoon I cried. Not reading stories was great poverty to me.

At ten, I asked directly, forthrightly: "Why don't people like Jews?"

It was Mama who kissed my fingertips in turn. "Religious differences. Belief in an Aryan superiority. Nationalism without compassion. If each German could love one neighbor as I love your father, there'd be no room for hate." Then, she pretended to bite my thumb. I laughed and squeezed her tight.

1830. Pogroms had begun.

Only inside our house could you escape violence. But sometimes it'd come right up to our door.

Of the four of us, Papa and Ludmilla looked the most Jewish. Ashkenazi heritage. Both tall, dark, thin. Ludmilla would sometimes have eggs splattered on her. Papa would come home, suit torn, hat missing. Bruises on his face and arms. Mother and I could roam unmolested throughout Germany. Only our Jewish neighbors knew us, and many would mutter "half-breed," as I passed by. This was nothing compared to Papa's and Sister's trials. Ludmilla felt resentful. Sometimes, she'd pinch me. Or cut my best gown. I never told.

"Germany is a great nation," Papa believed fervently. "In time, it will give up these cultural prejudices and realize Jews are as patriotic as anyone."

1835. Pogroms again. For weeks, months, dark clouds would consume Papa. He'd barely eat or sleep. Even pretty Mama, whom he loved more than anything, couldn't cajole him with her kisses.

"You children are our experiment," Papa said. "Our proof that enlightenment is a moral, not cultural choice. Everyone is equal." But even as he said the words, a stain of sadness would rest upon his face and mouth. He'd drink another glass of schnapps.

It was Papa's choice to convert for Mama. Papa's choice to change our name from Assur to Assing. Papa's choice to live in a Jewish community. Yet, as I grew older, I wondered what choices Papa would've made if he looked blond and blue-eyed like me? I dared not speak these thoughts aloud.

Just as Ludmilla and I dared not go to school and endure endless taunts. Mama taught us things no conservative German would condone: "Life is for the senses"; "Passion over propriety"; "Great literature instead of morality tales"; "Nature is the heart of a woman."

Summers, we traveled abroad. We met George Sand (how I adored her). Visited Keats's grave in Italy. Weeping, Mama made us recite *The Eve of St. Agnes:*

Awake! arise! my love, and fearless be
For o'er the southern moors I have a home for thee.

Traveling abroad, we were always happy. No questions about identity, religion, or morality. All of us equally free to follow our hearts' desire.

For my fourteenth birthday, Mama gave me an ink drawing of America. How I laughed! Germany could fit inside New York. America had grown acres and acres—a living, vital thing, pushing farther into the vast wilderness. Right up to the Mississippi River. Amazing.

I painted landscapes. Me, inside America: atop the Appalachians, peering out the window of a Delaware train, or paddling the Erie Canal in a canoe. Sometimes I was in an elegant city parlor—New York, Philadelphia, Boston—expounding on the nature of freedom.

Like Columbus crossing the sea, I never doubted I'd find myself in America. Not Jew, half-breed. Nor German. Just Ottilie. Me. My best self.

How näive I was!

One afternoon, when Papa should've been seeing patients, he burst into the parlor, surprising me and Mama. "Don't apologize for who you are. Never apologize." He was red-faced, furious.

Mama shooed me from the room. I could hear Papa ranting first about Rabbi Shel. "What does it matter if Jesus is a Jewish prophet or a martyred Christian? European faith can hold both. We live in Germany, not Palestine." Next, he ranted about the politicians. "Bourgeois bureaucrats. Idiots. Fools. Aryans were not the first to settle Germany!"

Mama soothed Papa's storm. She took him upstairs, closed the bedroom door. This was the pattern. No matter the time of day. A closed bedroom and hours later, Papa would emerge optimistic, elated. When Ludmilla and I were young, Nanny pulled us away to play with blocks and dolls. Later, I painted or read in the library. I learned to accept there'd always be hours when Mama and Papa were both inaccessible. So close. Behind a slight, wooden door, never to be disturbed. No matter the sounds: the shouts, the creaking springs, weeping, or thundering silences. The maid would leave dinner outside their door. Sometimes breakfast too.

Mama tried to explain love to me.

"Passion is fierce sometimes. You desperately want, need each other."

"Why do you cry? I hear you crying."

She shrugged like a lost bird. "Sometimes feelings are too much."

For Mama, the best literature was all about love eternal. Ms.

Browning's *Sonnets from the Portuguese* enthralled her: *How do I love thee? Let me count the ways. . . .*

"Paint emotion instead of America, Ottilie, and the world would be at your feet."

I'd reply, "Yes, Mama," and she'd scribble new poems in her journal. She raved about Dante's *Vita Nuovo*, his "new life" inspired by his unrequited passion for Beatrice.

"Your Mama is a romantic," Papa would tease.

"No more than you," she answered. "Marrying a Christian. Believing in true love."

"I'll be like you, Mama. An artist. A governess."

"We shall see," said Mama, teaching me mathematics and geography as if I were a boy. But declaring, "You'll have a dowry fine enough for any man."

Except no man would take me. The men, so pompous, so assured of their superiority, preferred me docile, silent. Slow and dull like a milk cow.

I called each one of them pigs. Swore I'd never fall in love, never marry.

Alas, childhood gave way to more complicated learning—Jean Baptiste Basion.

He was the persona of Mama's poetry. On stage, with a glance, he could make audiences weep. Speak eloquently in meter. And when he dueled, my heart raced at even the thought of a pretend hurt. Seventeen, how could I not have become infatuated?

Mama took us backstage to meet him. Everyone in Hamburg, it seemed, was crowding in! But I was proud, for it was Mama he hailed. "Rosa Maria, Rosa Maria." Jean Baptiste flourished a bow. Mama blushed as lovely as an angel.

"These are my daughters, Ottilie. Ludmilla." He offered us roses. Red for Ludmilla, yellow for me; then, he hesitated, picking white instead. "An uncommon color for an uncommon beauty."

Giddy, I inhaled the roses' perfume.

All summer, I painted Jean Baptiste instead of America's horizons.

In love with an actor? How scandalous, my grandparents, our neighbors thought! But Mama and Papa approved. "Independent thinking. Independent heart."

Jean Baptiste Basion. A made-up name for a self-made man. He told parlor stories, making light of his childhood poverty, the drunken father who beat him. He made us laugh with his tale of being abandoned to Jesuits. "Bad food. Straw beds. Jesuits loved me. To them, I was Original Sin." Years, he endured their catechisms, their repressive scorn. "Until I could read and write well enough to run away. An actor's life for me. If I'd been a priest, I would've missed the pleasures of the Assings." Then, he winked at me.

Imagine, an artist's soul locked in a cleric's robe! The thought of his suffering made me cry. Ludmilla was exasperated with me. Mama murmured, "Awakening love." Papa accorded me respect.

All summer, I fed my passion with poetry and romances.

Only once, in the garden, with pine yielding its lush scent, did Jean Baptiste kiss me. Light. The touch of a butterfly.

I wrapped my arms about his neck. "Marry me."

He laughed.

"Please." (Such young earnestness I had.)

"I thank you for the honor."

If he'd said nothing more, all would've been well. A noble knight deflecting praise.

"But you are an indulged, spoiled girl. Whatever would we have in common?"

"I'm going to do great things," I insisted.

"Beyond bearing a dozen children?"

I hit him. Hard. In his chest.

He laughed, gripping my hands. "A farce? How sentimental. I've misjudged my part. Forgive me, Fräulein."

"I *am* going to do great things. Travel to America. Become a great artist. A painter. Essayist. Journalist."

"Why not free the slaves, too?"

"I will."

Jean Baptiste laughed. He was still laughing when he skipped up the steps, into the house, and bid my parents farewell. Still laughing as his carriage clip-clopped down the road. What a tale he'd tell! He'd dine on it for months. Amused by the Assing girl.

All night I cried, curled beside Mama (the only time Papa had the bedroom door closed to him). By dawn, my face was puffy, swollen from tears. Mama promised me, "You will be loved beyond reason. Like Isolde, you'll want to die for this true, great love."

How prophetic it all seems!

Yet, by dawn, I hurt not so much from Jean's rejection. Rather, I ached that he'd found fault with my America. Slaves were servants, weren't they? Indentured bondsmen? But from one's station, one could rise. Egalitarianism would rule. Jean Baptiste was proof of that.

I was on the edge of a precipice: *How could Americans not be free?*

Winter 1839, Mama collapsed. Papa called in a consulting doctor. But neither man knew what made Mama take to her bed, wither, and fade. Her belly swelled. "Love's fruit," Mama said, convinced she was pregnant, that true love and the seeds of passion had defied age.

Next, her arms, legs, and ankles swelled. Tumors rested against her veins. Mama wailed: "How can I be dying?"

Hard, rocky masses choked off color (turning her skin yellow, then blue). Choked off breath. Mama accepted her fate. In her journal, she wrote:

Hail to me, the happy one! I call out in joy at the end of my life,
For I have not lived in vain, for I have known love!

Brave Mama! Her last entry:

You, Amor, I served always.
Of all the gods you reigned supreme.

For Mama, dying was another art. She quit life with more grace and peace than I've yet to know. How I've missed her!

✣

Mama was buried in a Christian plot with priests and hymns.

"Why have You forsaken me?" Papa cried over and over again when dirt was thrown atop the casket. Papa fancied himself as Job. But no one thought to ask Papa which God. The resurrected Christ or the Old Testament Jehovah?

I didn't cry for Mama. Papa was furious. But how could I mourn the beauty of her life and passing?

Papa mourned. Weeping, flailing. Sick like a girl. Only Ludmilla could care for him. Ludmilla, the good girl, like Rachel in the Bible. Or was it Rebecca?

Papa acted as if he were the one whom God had lain waste.

He repented. He ordered Ludmilla and me to cook, cover our heads, and sit in the women's corner. He mourned his firstborn. The son who would've become a great physician. Become the ideal who could move fluidly throughout society, valued as both German and Jew.

Useless daughters should be banished to conformity!

Worst of all, Papa counseled me to set aside my paints. He said there was no art to be made that hadn't already been made.

Suffering had made Papa bitter.

He became gaunt, then skeletal. A slight cough, a cold in Papa's lungs. Nothing from which he couldn't recover. But he stopped eating. Only Ludmilla could get him to swallow broth. Then, that no longer.

I wept outside the door. Ludmilla said Papa refused to see me. I reminded him of Mama.

How I begged to comfort Papa. Pleaded. But those last days, Ludmilla insisted I stay beyond the door. When I became adamant, she locked it.

I heard Papa draw his last breath. I heard one wild burst of energy and passion: "Rosa Maria. Rosa Maria."

Poor Papa. Dead within a year of Mama's death.

Nothing held me. Even Ludmilla was eager to see me go: "You're no longer the favorite, Ottilie. There's no one here to show off to."

So I left. Within a month, I was sitting on deck, feeling wind whirling my hair, snapping my dress about my ankles and my knees. I was on ship, completely in awe of the miles of deep, blue sea with white-tipped waves.

Nothing seemed impossible to me.

Like Mama, I'd rejoice in living. But I'd love a man who was his own anchor. Someone who wouldn't end his life sad and torn. And I did love such a man—and I found out just how difficult it was to hold him.

I remember, vividly, believing my journey across the sea would be all pleasantness. An honorable adventure. I tried hard to be good. The proper heroine.

On the third night, the Captain invited his first-class passengers to dinner. I felt guilty knowing others were less well fed. It wasn't polite to know our ship, the *Indian Queen*, carried people in its belly. Immigrants. Poor people following dreams. Stowed in warrens meant for rats.

I digress. I agreed to dine at the Captain's table. But I shocked everyone. A young woman traveling alone. They thought me wanton but dared not say so. *But how to explain my best companion, my Mama, was dead?*

Five gentlemen rose: plump, Herr Leider, a banker with interests in American cotton; Rolfe Stangelberger, a student, with his leering tutor, Herr Schmidt (I suspected he terrorized house maids); Herr and Frau Mueller, she was a mouse, and he, a petulant bear, an owner of a factory that made sturdy shoes for German schoolchildren. (His wife was upset because he'd risen for me. Silly woman.) Lastly was Mr. Newcombe, a planter, from America. "Vir-gin-nee-yah," he says. A lovely word.

I was delighted to meet Mr. Newcombe, believing all Americans must be courageous and of good sense. Divine Providence, was it not? Would not the best and brightest of humanity—men and women with dreams, visions—be called upon to tame a new land?

"How do, Ma'am?" His tones were sweet, dulcet in comparison with my awkward English.

"Good. I am good."

His eyes twinkled and I could not help that my heart raced. So dignified, so handsome, Mr. Newcombe. No more than thirty. Young for a man. For the first time, I thought, perhaps without my background haunting me, I might find love in America.

"Miss Assing," the Captain said, "I would be honored if you sit here, on my right."

"If Mr. Newcombe sits to *my* right."

Frau Mueller squealed, fluttering her fat hands. The men, decorously, glanced away. Herr Schmidt coughed into his hand. I couldn't resist. Only one American and I wanted to know everything about him and my soon-to-be-adopted land. I didn't want to be squeezed between two disapproving Germans.

The Captain, his color heightened, clicked his heels. "As you wish."

Mr. Newcombe pulled out my chair. "I like rebels," he whispered, so soft, I could barely hear. Then, loudly, "Miss Assing, you delight me."

"Thank you, sir."

Dinner began with blood-red borscht. Were it not for Mr. Newcombe's stories, dinner would've been interminable. Instead, he delighted us with tales.

"My family built a plantation as rich and as civilized as any could claim in a wild land. My Papa and his Papa before worked sunup to sundown to make paths, roads, sheds, barns, and houses. We made our own paradise."

"What about the women?" I asked.

"They worked hard, too—"

I liked that answer.

"—worked until we were successful enough that they need not work. Southern beauties, belles, we call them. The pride of Virginia."

"Do they get bored?"

"My, no. There are dances, teas, weddings, church socials. A host of things."

"What about education?"

"They oversee the domestic arts, of course. The raising of children. But we encourage them to take advantage of all social graces."

I became sadly disappointed in Virginia. How cruel to encourage women to work, then end up prizing leisure.

After dinner, I gathered my gloves, fan. I curtsied and went on deck. The sea calmed me. There isn't anything more beautiful than a night sea. Water, black as velvet. Overhead, a sky filled with bright, glittering stars.

"Have I offended you?"

I swung around, startled. "No, Mr. Newcombe. But your stories became less interesting as the women became more dull. God gave women minds to use."

"Not all women are unhappy with their lot. Whereas you . . . ?" His fingers grazed mine.

"You think I'm wealthy?"

"Wealth makes you all the more beautiful. Virginia could still use a woman like you."

"Scoundrel."

"A charming word from your lips."

He meant to kiss me. But as his hands gripped my shoulders, I turned aside.

"Forgive me. I've acted less the gentleman."

"I learned long ago that the words 'gentle' and 'man' do not usually go together."

"So harsh, Miss Assing."

"Merely a realist."

Mr. Newcombe guided me toward the bow. Sailors were watching us with interest.

"I would like to issue an invitation. Please say you'll come to my home. You remind me of my mother. Nothing diminished her strength. Until her death, she carried on as well as my father. Tilling, laying seed, strangling hens when needed.

"True, my sisters are soft. And my nieces are as silly and delightful as sugarplums. But what is civilization without softness? Without kindness and good-hearted women? A woman's duty is to lend charm, pleasantness to the household."

"Then, I wonder how you ever could've loved your mother? If she was indeed as strong as you say."

Mr. Newcombe flushed.

"Forgive my manners." I clutched the railing and stared at the moon's watery trail. I was indeed becoming too bold.

"No, do not apologize. It ruins the effect. I'm almost tempted to offer you tobacco." Mr. Newcombe chuckled and sauntered away.

I was left blushing.

Sailors guffawed. Mr. Newcombe had neatly put me in my place.

Chagrined, I felt vulnerable. Childish and seventeen again.

I do not know what awakened me. I tremble as I write this, for it was indeed too terrible, what I heard and what I saw.

At first I thought it was the wind howling, shrieking like a banshee of ghosts. There were sounds, too, of a weight being thrown or dropped, then, yawning silence. The noises as much as the unnatural quiet made me want to investigate. How I wish I had not.

I threw on my wrap, not caring that my hair was unbound, and flung open my cabin's door. The wind was fierce and, for a moment, I thought how it would knock me overboard. Calm seas had turned restless. My resolve lessened and I thought to return to my cabin. The sounds were probably the wind lashing the sails, the wood straining under pressure, the ship creaking, shuddering at its rough progress.

But a scream—a woman's scream—held me.

There were women, I knew—thin, pale women down below—who were only allowed on deck between the hours of eight and ten and four and six. In first class, there was only myself and Frau Mueller. No honest woman would be out in this early morning with the moon still high, the wet spray stinging, and darkness shielding. The scream, more piteous, echoed again. I stepped gingerly, clutching the rail.

Just around the bend, I saw Mr. Newcombe, no longer neat, elegant. His hair, wind-swept, his shirt wrinkled, open at the neck, his pants hastily drawn over bare feet. He looked distraught, wild-eyed.

I looked to where he was looking. One leg over the rail, was a woman, stark naked. So black she almost blended into the velvet night. Had she kept still, I might not have seen her. Or else thought she was a mirage come out of the ocean's depths to haunt. Or, perhaps, some forlorn spirit invisibly riding the Arctic wind. But the cold sent tremors through her body; her entire body contracted to provide less surface for the wind's kiss. And were that not enough, the silver chains about her wrists glinted almost like diamonds and proved this was no apparition. How I wished that it wasn't so.

Our eyes met. Hers, brimming, luminous with tears; mine, mirroring hers.

"You are my slave, Hessie," Mr. Newcombe shouted. "You'll do as I say."

The black woman answered. Her words were foreign, but her meaning clear. "No more. No more," she seemed to say. "I will take no more."

The Captain, Herr Schmidt, the quarterdeck master, and rough sailors maneuvered forward, enclosing her, trapping her body against the sea.

"Let me help," I pleaded. "Let me help."

"No place for a woman." "Go back to your stateroom." "Have you no sense?"

"You've no right," I shouted back. "No right." But the men paid no further attention to me. All eyes watched Hessie.

Hessie tilted her head. Her eyes blinked, tears overflowed, and like someone dousing a candle, her eyes lost their light and were as dull as Mama's had been. She looked straight through me as though I, no, everyone on the deck were invisible.

I placed my fist into my mouth to keep from screaming.

"Come on, Hessie. It's a misunderstanding. You don't need to do anything you fear."

I blushed and even one of the sailors looked away. Were she not black, not a slave, not naked in the frigid air, one might have suspected this was a lovers' quarrel. Perhaps a virgin bride introduced to abhorrent wifely duties? But Hessie *was* a slave and she'd been chained. How long? We'd been at sea for a month and I'd never until this cursed night seen her. How could it be that I didn't see her or at least not hear her? Did I mistake her voice for wind howling, sea churning, spray lashing against wooden boughs? How many sounds were hers that my ears, no, my mind, mistook for a ship's course across the rough Atlantic?

"The sea has upset you. We'll soon be home in Virginia."

Hessie looked down into the thunderous sea.

"We must be done with this," shouted the Captain. "A storm will have us all overboard."

"Hessie," I breathed. She looked up. I think she heard my soul crying out to her. "Hessie," I said louder, my arm outstretched as though I could reach over and through the men's shoulders and backs.

"Oluwand."

I spoke back her name. *"Oluwand."*

"Mine, Hessie. You are mine," barked Mr. Newcombe, thumping his chest like some wild beast. "Mine to do with as I will."

"Grab her, men," ordered the Captain, and they rushed forward, reaching, grabbing for her dark skin. Hessie—no, Oluwand—without a sound, twisted beyond their grasp (a graceful, arcing movement), and let herself fall, no, dive, into the choppy, velvet-ink sea.

Gone, without a whisper. Without a trace. Like a seal submerged, refusing to surface. Gone as if she had been nothing more or less than a ghost.

Everyone was silent. Still. Quiet, I thought, out of respect. Waves still lapped against the stern. Sails whistled in the wind. And stars, overhead, blinked, as if they were crying tears.

"Fifteen hundred dollars lost," Mr. Newcombe whispered, peering over the rail, into the sea. "A dozen children she might have birthed. A fortune. A small fortune overboard."

Banker Leider solemnly nodded, Herr Schmidt puffed his fat cheeks, and the Captain patted Mr. Newcombe's back in sympathy. The sailors, some grinning at the excitement, some somber as priests, went back to their posts.

I was shocked. There was no rush to rescue. No "Man Overboard" for a slave. For a woman.

I screamed, "God shall punish you. God shall punish you."

Mr. Newcombe, the Captain, Herr Schmidt stared at me. They thought me crazy. A witless woman.

Not witless enough. *I will carry Oluwand's pain to my grave.*

9 thanked God to be off that foul ship.

We landed in New Bedford. I planned to rest for two, maybe three days, then travel south to New York.

I remember thinking: "I can make this journey. I can find my dream in America. I must have the strength." I kept repeating these words, in my head, like a singsong, a child's nursery rhyme.

Mr. Newcombe refused to tip his hat to me. As though it were I who pushed Oluwand into the sea.

Herr Captain denied my request for funeral rites. "Slaves haven't souls."

No words could convince him otherwise.

Frau Mueller taunted me daily until, weary of her harping, I kept to my cabin. *Invisible like Oluwand.* Feeling, almost beyond hope, that the voyage would never end. Feeling in danger of losing my mind. I kept painting canvases of hands reaching out of the sea.

I'd hadn't thought of slaveholders as handsome young men. Hadn't thought of slavery forcing a woman to choose death.

Papa would've said: "Through the desire for freedom, all men shall rise." But how could Oluwand have risen, chained to a bed?

If Mama was alive, she'd cry with me. Perverted lust. A greater sin than all other sins.

Mama and Papa both drilled in me there was a God. As a woman grown, I'd taken God's name in vain; but the child in me had always believed deeply. Papa's God, so fierce, insisting on sacrifice; Mama's God, so forgiving, insisting all was redeemed. After Oluwand's sacrifice,

I began to doubt either existed. Did Oluwand have a God? At the moment of her death, she didn't call His name but proclaimed her own.

Oluwand.

Ottilie. I had much to think about. Much to reconcile.

I saw things differently in New Bedford. Instead of landscape—arching trees, solid rock, plains caressing the horizon—I saw people. All manner, but the colored in particular: some, barefoot, dressed in rags, some in elegantly cut coats with polished boots. Most were dressed simply like the workers in Germany. Plain, good, cotton fare.

A charcoal man, his callused hands holding the reins of a job horse, waited at the far end of the wharf. I hurried up to him, bypassing fine, private carriages, job horses and carriages driven by white men. Colored men were last in line.

"Are you a slave?" I demanded. I could no longer keep my emotions in check.

"No, ma'am. Free. In the North, most coloreds be free."

I started crying, balling my fists against my eyes to stop my tears. I hadn't cried before and now I cried for Oluwand and for every one I ever loved. I cried for all the injustices I'd seen. The attacks on Jews, the poverty of a butcher's child, Mama's agonizing death, the despair that leeched into Papa's soul.

The driver took pity on me, for he checked his startled horse. I leaned against his cart.

In my mind's eye, I saw Oluwand diving into the sea.

My knees buckled, and the driver, leaning forward, his hand cloaked in rough leather, clutched my elbow and steadied me.

"Do you want Mr. Garrison, ma'am?"

"Who?"

"Mr. Garrison. The Abolitionist Society. They fight against slavery."

"Yes. You will take me to this Mr. Garrison?"

He looked at me quizzical. He must've thought me a crazed, wild-eyed woman.

"You should rest first. You look tired, ma'am."

"As do you." I was feeling more myself. Ottilie Assing. I smiled at him.

"Me and my horse work all the days and all the nights."

I exhaled and smiled again. "What is your name?"

"Moses."

I laughed. "You are my sign, Herr Moses."

"Just Moses."

"No, Herr Moses, as they would say in my country. I insist. A mark of respect. Will you help me? Lift my bags? Carry me to a hotel?"

"My pleasure. My work, too. To carry things."

"Good. You'll carry me. I'll change clothes. Then, you'll take me to Herr Garrison."

"And eat, ma'am? You look like you could use warm food."

"Yes, eat." I smiled at the kindness of the man. The first real kindness anyone had shown me in a long while.

He jumped down and lifted my bags into the wagon bed. Not a big man, but strong. A workingman. He laid a blanket in the wagon crib and motioned for me to sit.

"No, Herr Moses. If you please, I'll ride beside you."

"Where you from?"

"Germany. A cold place. Far away. Weeks by carriage. Months at sea."

"They all like you? In this Germany?" He scuttled onto the seat, then held out his hand to help lift me up. He smelled of soap and sweet hay.

"I think there is no one else quite like me. That is why I left."

He chuckled. "None like me either, I expect."

"Yes, that's true. Not in Germany."

We laughed.

Sitting on the wagon perch, this was the closest I'd been to a colored man. I thought this was the closest Herr Moses has been to a German woman. I felt excited about new possibilities. America was still my land of dreams. Moses, like God's gift, had started me on a new stage of my journey. For a moment, I felt lighthearted again. I was found in the promised land.

Moses clicked his tongue, snapped his whip, and the horse jerked forward.

Oluwand was sitting in the wagon beside me. I nearly screamed. The wagon moved steadily. I knew Moses couldn't see her. *My hand moves through her, touches air.*

One day in America and I was seeing ghosts. Bones rose from the sea, walked on land.

Oluwand and I had become fast friends.

$\mathcal{G}$ went to see Mr. Garrison. He was a fierce man—bushy hair, mustache, his nails stained black with ink. He was of fair height with a lean nose and a gaze that sweeps judgmentally over everything. I imagined him taking seconds to decide if the day was too cold, the clouds were too low, and if his sole visitor was a waste of his hard-earned time.

"Work. I need workers. I don't need another society matron who weeps but will not work."

I thought of nothing to say except "Guten Morgen."

His brows rose. "Fräulein?"

"Assing."

"Excuse me. I thought you were one of our local matrons here to interrupt my work with needless weeping. Or worse yet, one of Griffiths' disciples."

"Griffiths?"

"*Humanity, Rights, and Reason.*"

"I don't know this name."

"You will." He displaced reams of papers, books, quills, and asked me to sit in a chair long used for storage. "What can I do for you?"

"It is I who wish to do for you. Help your cause."

"You've read my paper, the *Liberator.*" It was more statement than question.

"No."

Garrison sighed heavily and leaned back in his chair. It creaked with his weight. "I don't have time for this. Lives are at stake. There are things I must do, Miss," he raised his brows, "Assing."

I sat up straighter. "Yes, Miss. Fräulein." I saw him weighing my absence of an abigail, a companion. There was no man to lend me countenance. No wedding ring to bespeak respectability.

"Well, good day to you, Fräulein." His hand swept through his hair, and once again he was busily searching through his papers, upsetting a flurry of quills. "I have much to do."

"I've just left the *Indian Queen*. A slave—a woman—committed suicide rather than remain in her Master's care."

Mr. Garrison said nothing. He studied me. I didn't flinch.

His eyes shifted to newsprint, his hands shuffled broadsides. "Of course, perhaps you could help distribute papers. Or hold a tea to raise monies? We are always short of money."

"I am independent."

"Are you now?" he inquired softly. And I saw him deciding that I was wealthy. Saw him change his opinion, his use for me.

"Neither father nor husband rules me. I wish to give my heart to a cause."

"Abolition is an uphill struggle. Tumultuous. Dangerous. Not for the fainthearted."

"Nor is traveling the ocean. Nor being a woman. Nor being a German Jew." I regretted my words as soon as I spoke them. I didn't trust Herr Garrison. Still, I went on: "None of these things are for the fainthearted."

"I'm surprised, Fräulein. With your blond locks and blue eyes, I would've guessed you for a German but never a Jew."

"Half Jew. My mother was Christian."

"How interesting."

Garrison moved from around his desk and studied me like I was some rare creature, a butterfly, perhaps, caught, then dissected under a microscope.

"Your family has been persecuted?"

I nodded. But my answer was only partly true. Mama and I had never suffered. Yet, perhaps this was the link to the new promised land.

"Herr Garrison, being Jewish, even half, as much as being a woman makes me eager to help end slavery. Any curtailment of freedom is wrong."

"I know little of Jewish fate. Nothing of the trials women claim.

Though I do find you quite interesting. Have you heard of miscegenation, Fräulein?"

I shook my head.

"You should," he said, returning to sit behind his desk. "A most interesting concept. Nonetheless, there is but one battle I care to wage. Were you colored, I would be more interested in your thoughts, your speech." Fists propping his head, he bent over his desk, his pen scratching out lines in an article. "In a few months, if you haven't gone home, come see me. I'll put you to work."

"Are you always this arrogant?" I stood, trembling.

"Fräulein Assing, I don't have time for anyone—male or female, who seeks to fill their empty lives with the colored cause. I don't know what dream you're pursuing, but either give me your money and leave or come back when you know something more of what I do, what I'm trying to do, and what it means to be an abolitionist in America."

"What about what it means to be black in America? Do you claim to know that too?"

"Touché, Fräulein. You have a mind. Come back when you fill it with America's history. Not Germany's. Not Jews'. Not women's. But fill your mind with white cotton and black hands. Good day, Fräulein. Come back, if you dare. I have work to do."

I turned, hastening away from his patronizing face.

"Aren't you forgetting something, Fräulein Assing?"

I looked back. In his outstretched hand, Mr. Garrison held his paper. The *Liberator*.

I wanted to rip the paper and throw it at him. But the word "liberator" held me. *Liberation*. Mr. Garrison was perhaps right. I couldn't free others without freeing my own mind. I didn't like this Mr. Garrison. But he was right, there was little in my head about American slavery. Much in my heart, but little in my head.

I took his paper. "Good day."

"Guten Nacht," he called out, chuckling.

As I stepped out of the building, I realized how cramped and ill-smelling both his office and Mr. Garrison were. Printer's ink made a poor perfume.

A light snow braced me, uplifted my spirits. A man in a cape was lighting streetlamps with a rod of flame. Candles glowed behind curtains. Smoke streamed out of brick chimneys and mingled with the moist air. Part of me recognized how beautiful the world was . . . how, in some places, the heart was warmed by a fire's glow. But my heart was coldly furious with Garrison. Furious with myself for accomplishing so little. Furious I'd given Garrison information that might hurt me.

Evening approached. The sun set orange over the horizon and I could see the watery expanse where Oluwand rests. A few months before, I'd left Germany. A few hours before, I'd left ship. A few minutes before, I'd spoken to a man who thought me frivolous. Now evening. My first night in America begins. Old life versus new. And I'd already faltered.

"Ma'am, ma'am." Across the street, Moses waved his scarf at me. Even his dusty mare neighed, flicked her tail. Courage. I knew someone kind in America.

Tomorrow, I'd begin anew.

$\mathcal{I}$ surprised Garrison and returned.

"I've read your *Liberator*. Every issue. Fräulein Griffiths' essays. *The Narrative of Gusta Vasa*, America's *Declaration of Independence*, John Adams's musings on the rights of man, and much, much more. Unless your cause has been won, you still need my money, my help, and my offer to work."

Garrison laughed and as though he'd never offended me, said, "Fräulein Assing, how delightful to see you. Just the woman I need. We have a new slave who's just escaped. Splendid man. Exceptional, I'd almost say. The Anti-Slavery Society is sponsoring him. Him and his new wife. Would you care to help?"

I spent my days and nights hand-lettering posters announcing the Society's meeting and its speaker, Frederick Douglass. Garrison wanted hundreds of posters, thousands of flyers. Herr Moses and I traveled throughout the town and countryside. I nailed with my own hands dozens of leaflets on trees, on solicitors' and government doors. It was thrilling. So many goodly Americans. Upholding the cause of freedom. I was part of it. Even proofing Garrison's paper, staining nearly every one of my gowns with ink, made me happy. I worked harder than I ever had in my life and Garrison came to depend upon me. I read his correspondence and gave him summaries. Brought him food when he forgot to eat. Sometimes deliveries were made and Garrison would disappear. There a minute ago, then gone. I'd be forced to pay the supplier. I let Garrison play his cat and mouse. I had a trust—a small one. Papa's grief had prevented him from working. So, I was careful. I saved on oils; I was so busy working for abolition, I rarely had time to paint. All day and late into the night, I wrote letters, posters, headlines proclaiming, "Frederick Douglass, A Slave, Is Here." Then, finally,

TONIGHT HE SPEAKS.

I dressed with care, wanting to look my best. I wore no jewels, swept my hair into a chignon after the French, and wore my best black silk. When I looked into the mirror (a long cheval glass) I thought perhaps I was too pale. My days of reading had worn creases and dark shadows beneath my eyes. With my tongue, I wetted my dry lips. Excitement high, I felt my heart thundering, my breath inhaling shallowly. Now I'd live. I'd step inside my dreams.

Almost six o'clock. I'd told Mr. Garrison I'd meet him in the hotel lobby.

I gathered up my fur, for New Bedford had its chills like Germany, and turned to go. Out of the corner of my eye, I saw a flicker of motion, some shadow dart across my room. *Oluwand.* I don't know why I spoke her name. It expelled from me like an unbidden prayer.

I shuddered. The clock chimed six. I rushed from the room.

The meeting hall was impressive. It overflowed with passionate people, and the din was almost deafening. Shouts about "Freedom," "Fighting for the Negro soul," "Southern greed and corruption" exploded from conversations. No one questioned my place here as a woman. Nor was I segregated. Mr. Garrison had found me a chair in the first row, slightly right of center stage. I was in the thick of pandemonium and from time to time, I could see Mr. Garrison brushing his hair back, talking to one person then the next, issuing orders about proper placement of chairs upon the stage. There were to be several speakers, but Mr. Garrison's new protégé was to be last. Garrison was clearly nervous. I could tell by how often his fingers combed his hair. I saw him shake hands with each speaker—white and black. But it was the last, a man sitting in the far-thest row, in the last chair, that he stayed with the longest. I could

barely see this man. Mr. Garrison blocked my view. And the man himself kept his head bowed, as if in prayer or contemplation. His dark
locks fanned forward and his features were indiscernible.

Garrison stepped up to the podium. The program began. I pitched
forward on the edge of my seat.

Oh, the speeches. My head was filled with so many remarkable
ideas and my heart was wrung hard by so many desperate stories about
the colored people's plight. Nothing in my reading prepared me for the
moment of hearing about hardships in slaves' own voices. The power of
the word was extraordinary. I thought, "Hearing one slave speak, how
could anyone not be moved? How could anyone wish to hold a being
with intelligence and soul?"

Again, Mr. Garrison took to the podium and announced, "Now for
our last speaker of the night, an escaped slave, a man most worthy of
belief." The excitement in the hall had become almost unbearable.
Men stomped their feet, catcalling, clapping their hands. Mr. Garrison
raised his arms high.

"Good friends, allow me to present the fugitive slave, the self-
educated man, the remarkable Mr. Frederick Douglass."

Everyone was on their feet clapping with abandon. I was, too. People chanted, "Douglass, Douglass," and I called out the name as well. I
was flushed, so taken by the energy around me, I glanced away from the
stage, and missed when Mr. Douglass stepped to the podium. But the
people to the back, right, and left of me, grew quiet. Somber. They
grew still, everyone holding their breath, waiting for something
extraordinary.

I looked up on the stage. I grew quiet too.

Herr Douglass was the most striking man I'd ever seen. His skin was
burnished copper, as though the sun had lightly and continually kissed
him. Just standing there, speaking no words, he seemed larger than life,
as though he could command an army. Beautiful. This man was truly
beautiful. Douglass' hair caressed his shoulders and the head, which
had been bowed during all the prior speeches, now seemed incapable of
any shyness, false humility, or reticence. He'd been merely waiting,
harnessing his energy for this moment.

We all sat in our chairs and when the shuffling feet stilled, the mur-
murs and coughs died down, and every eye was fixed upon the stage.

Herr Douglass, Mister Frederick Douglass, an escaped American slave, began to speak.

"I was born a slave." His voice was melodious, strong. "I seldom got to see my mother. Feel her caress, hear her voice, or see her face. She would walk miles to sleep beside me for a few hours. I thought she was an angel, a ghost I dreamed about. But she was my mother, trying to give the gift of a mother's love."

The strategy was brilliant. Even taken by him, I could understand the intelligence crafting his speech. What person could not identify with wanting a mother's love?

"Slavery demeans familial ties. I do not know my birthday. White children know their birthday, but I never did. No less important, I did not know my last name except for that of my Master's. I will not say his name here. For even as I stand here, a search party, hound dogs, are hunting me. Slavery will give me no rest. The Fugitive Slave Act continues to strip me of rights, of my ability as a man to shape my own fate." He went on, his cadences moving through me, upsetting the world as I knew it.

Fate. It was here, before me. This was why I had crossed the Atlantic. To hear Mr. Douglass. To hear how my dream of freedom was but an echo of an entire race.

It humbled me.

I couldn't take my eyes off Douglass. He was majestic, proud as the audience leapt to their feet, shouting, clapping, stomping his praises. I heard the wonder expressed: "Never has a slave spoken more eloquently"; "God has sent a deliverer"; "How can anyone believe this man has no soul?"; "What ape speaks thus?" Indeed.

I'd witnessed magic. A slave convincing fellow Americans of his humanity. He'd the "gift of tongues"—the words, the timbre, the tone to move women to weep and men to herald him.

I kept seated in my chair as pandemonium about me increased. The receiving line was long and from my vantage point, if I remained seated, I could better study the lines and planes of Mr. Douglass' face. I would've been content to do so for hours.

"Fräulein Assing?"

"Mr. Garrison, this has been wonderful. The most exciting night of my life."

"Then let me make it more so." Courtly, he offered his arm and I rose, letting my hand rest gently on his arm . . . and all the while I felt such breathlessness, such thrills as Mr. Garrison guided me toward Mr. Douglass upon the stage. People seemed to fall away, part like the sea before Moses. Bantering, exclamations, laughter were muted. Color seemed to drain from the room—red and yellow silks became gray, white faces paled, and the rich wood of walls and chairs lost their luster.

Like walking through a tunnel, dulled, without life, I was moving toward a burning warmth, toward a man of color and passion, intelligence and conviction.

Mr. Garrison introduced us. I offered my hand and Mr. Douglass clasped it, then bent over it like a distinguished European. I was charmed.

"Your speech was wonderful. Exhilarating."

"Thank you."

"Miss Assing is thinking of financing our cause," said Garrison.

"If you would allow me."

"I'd allow much for anyone who helped in the abolition of slavery."

I smiled at Herr Douglass. Up close his brows were thick; his eyes, flecked gold and green; but his hair most reminded me of unbridled energy, strength without measure. Waves of black velvet strands shielding the mind of a brilliant man. A mind inside a body owned by a Southerner. Probably one who was less intelligent. Certainly less noble and kind. It made me feel more vehement on Herr Douglass' behalf. No one should own this man. Or any man. But especially this man.

"May I introduce you to my wife?"

"By all means, Douglass," exclaimed Garrison.

"Miss Assing." Douglass nodded his head and I gracefully curtsied.

Garrison surely spoke, but I've no notion of what he said. No notion of anything other than watching Douglass turn toward his right. Seconds seemed like minutes, minutes seemed like hours, and then I heard my name again and saw Douglass gently pressing a woman forward. I saw the stark contrast between black skin and white silk. I was disappointed. Frau Douglass was short, thick in stature. She reminded me of a butcher's wife. Contrite, I offered my hand.

"A fine man, your Mr. Douglass."

She didn't speak but trembled as if I frightened her. I felt sympathy for her. She looked a woman bowed, overlooked, and overshadowed.

"My wife is free," said Mr. Douglass. "She has but recently come north."

I gave her my best smile. They did not fit. Looking at her, my eyes settling on him, I could see the incongruity. Herr and Frau Douglass. They were not a good pair. No more than one would mate a dog to a cat, pair china with crockery, or sweet wine with sour borscht. Him, tall; her, short; him, glowing with color and life; her, dark and dull. Douglass was triumphant; yet his wife seemed to be grieving.

Who was I to question?

I was here to help abolition and so I would. Help Mr. Garrison. Free Mr. Douglass. These were good causes. German Marks would be put to good use.

I laughed.

I told Herr Douglass I hoped to see him again soon.

He bowed, never once allowing his gaze to break with mine. "And you, Frau Douglass. Good-bye. I hope to see you soon."

My breath quickened.

I felt a new story was being written and I was a part of it.

Anna

"I will speak boldly against any evil.
My voice shall carry far and wide."

—FREDERICK DOUGLASS,
ABOLITIONIST CONVENTION, 1853

"I only thought of doing, not speaking. Of sewing,
cooking, caring for my children. Showing my love
with my hands."

—ANNA DOUGLASS,
SPEAKING TO ROSETTA, 1882

*C*ould I have turned away Freddy's loving? Naw, I couldn't. I didn't have the heart.

How strange to return home. Our borrowed home. I dragged my feet; Freddy walked on air. I'd barely lit the kitchen candles when Freddy began tugging at my clothes, kissing my cheeks, neck, and mouth. There was a fire in him as if his speech unleashed a new passion. Nothing I could do to bank it down.

Strange. Me, who loved Freddy with all my heart, slowing my feet when it came to loving. This wasn't me. Not the me I wanted to be. So I wrapped my arms about him, hugged him with all my might, and kissed him fiercely.

Freddy breathed harder. His hands roamed over my body, touching my breasts, thighs, touching my stomach where our baby lived.

I almost tripped as Freddy bent me back onto the bed. He moved rough, shoving my dress up, his knees spreading my thighs, and him entering quick and hard.

Everything quick and hard.

"Freddy, Freddy," I say, but he didn't hear. He be lost in his pleasure.

I tried, but I didn't feel anything. This loving was too fast. I couldn't help thinking: my best dress getting wrinkled, my lace torn; his suit would need pressing in the morn; we be on top the quilt, not under it, not warm together with flesh touching flesh.

I stared at the shadows on the ceiling. This be my husband. Let him take what he needs. "Take"—it be that. And 'cause he wasn't giving, I didn't. Shame on me.

I buried my mouth against his throat, tasted beads of sweat on his skin, and murmured, "You my true love." But he didn't hear. He cried out as I spoke. His body arched back and away from me. Then, released, he fell onto me. Breathing hard, his face buried deep in the pillow. My face turned toward the window and the fading moon.

Freddy got up. His face hidden by shadows; he said he'd get his nightshirt. He didn't offer me a hand. Or a caress. Or a word of love.

I sat up, feeling the room sway. As Freddy undressed, I undid my buttons, one by one, and slipped out of my best dress. I let it fall to the floor. So unlike me not to hang it neatly. So unlike me not to take each of Freddy's clothes and smooth them with my hands, hang them on pegs, or fold them within the drawer. I put on my shift, crawled into bed, and tucked myself beneath the quilt with the wedding ring pattern I'd stitched with love. When I was full under and turned on my side, Freddy slipped into bed. We laid back to back.

I bit my lip. This was the first time we be ashamed to let the other see our nakedness. First time we loved without looking into each other's eyes. Head averted, clothes on, Freddy rode me like a mare.

What had Freddy seen that he didn't want me to see? Why didn't he let our joining be more sweet, warmed by our bodies clasped together?

Darkness be good for lying. Be good for hiding faces and true feelings.

His breathing slowed. Freddy slept. I stayed awake.

$\mathcal{H}$e is not here." "He is not here." That's what I got used to saying. Folks all the time be knocking at my door asking for Frederick Douglass. "The great Frederick Douglass."

"He is not here," I say. Freddy strongly told me not to say "ain't."

"He *ain't* here, isn't good English," Freddy said. But whether I say "ain't" or "is not," didn't change the truth. Freddy be gone and I was left with white folks, colored folks, Quakers in black, abolitionist ladies with white gloves and fur hats knocking on my door, looking sorrowful when I answered.

Some got angry. Some suspected I lied. Some thought I was the maid! Foolishness.

My one comfort was if a slave catcher called, I could tell the same truth: *Freddy is not here.*

After a month, I stopped answering the door.

Five months married and I barely saw Freddy. He be off speechifying, preaching the evils of slavery. What about the good of marriage? The good of getting ready to raise a child? Our baby—almost due, kicked inside me, hollering for her Papa.

I may have been selfish, but I hadn't seen Freddy more than two days in a month. I was more lonely in New Bedford than I'd been anywhere. Church folks invited me to Sunday dinner. They praised Freddy, told me how proud I must be that the Anti-Slavery Society be promoting his speeches. They said he be the most famous colored man in America. I nodded my head. But I also saw that many of them pitied me—a new wife left all alone. Maybe it was 'cause I wasn't a *young,* new wife. Maybe Freddy thought an old hen could take care of herself. And I *could* take care of myself. I could take care of the whole world if I had to—but it didn't mean that I wasn't hurting inside. It didn't mean I wasn't afraid of birthing my—*our*—first child.

Sundays, I was given pieces of pie left uneaten. Given cold biscuits, ham, and anything else not eaten at dinner. I took these offerings with shame. Neighbors, church folks, knew I was poor. They didn't know their food sometimes stuck in my throat. Still—I thanked them for their kindness and ate gratefully, 'cause the baby needed more than the slim choices in my larder.

Weather had turned cold, and rocking in my chair, I sometimes thought of Lena. I wondered whether she came back to the Baldwins' kitchen hunting for me. Or maybe she died? Drowned? Fought with another cat? Maybe she found a new home to raise her kittens?

Sometimes I couldn't help taking to bed. I thought Freddy had found a new home too. Sleeping in abolitionist houses. Living, eating, speaking with Mr. Garrison, the Quakers, and those who packed great halls to hear him speak. I stopped myself from thinking of Miss Assing. I didn't have a good way to think about her. But I wondered if she be at home too? in New Bedford? doing whatever white women do without a husband, without a child, or parent to care for? What was there to hold her? Even Miz Baldwin had babies and household matters to keep her busy. Miss Assing could do anything without a care for nobody. I wondered if she be at Freddy's side in all those cities and small towns where he spoke?

Our baby weighed me down. Nobody would ask me to speak. And if they did, what would I have to say? I'd say, "Life be precious. Babies, gardening, a home be special." That be what Mam and Pa taught me. Nobody in this world would pay to hear what I knew.

I made circles on my belly. I sang to my baby, hoping it'd be a girl who wouldn't grow up to leave me. Like I left Mam.

Freddy said he sent a Penny-man, but I wondered. I'd not heard back. But then, it be a long way to Maryland. Maybe just now the Penny-man be pulling up to Mam's house, smiling, saying, "Anna fine. Baby fine. You fine?"

Maybe Mam didn't have a penny to answer? When Freddy came home, I'd ask him for another penny. This time I'd speak the message myself. Maybe Mam would answer.

I only needed to wait.

And wait and wait some more for Freddy to come. I stared at the small stack of letters he'd sent. I was too ashamed to ask anyone in the town to read them to me. So I cried over the black ink.

When me and the baby napped, I dreamed Freddy was with us, whispering his words, his letters, into my ears.

I woke, feeling a pain rip across my belly. Like someone had taken a knife and stabbed it deep within me. It be dark—sometime past midnight, I thought, but not quite dawn. Demon hours.

The pain came again and I balled my fist into my mouth. My other hand held my belly to keep it from breaking apart, wrenching open.

My time be here. Freddy was not home.

Light snow outside and I thought I must get help. Get up, get out of bed. Get a midwife. Get someone to help me birth my baby live and kicking into this world.

I dragged my legs over the bed, and I stumbled forward, holding on to the bedpost. Pain rocked me again and I breathed deep, telling myself, "Girl, get going. Get help."

I shuffled forward one step, another, then one more. I made it to the bedroom door, then my water broke like an ocean undammed. Water poured down my legs, ankles, onto the wood floor. My flannel gown be soaked and though grown, I felt like a child again.

"Mam," I hollered. "Mam."

Even though the window was barely cracked open, wind snapped through and curled around my damp legs. The cold air braced me. *"I'm here, baby,"* I heard Mam say, *"I'm here."*

My heart calmed. I no longer gulped air like a fish. I thought: "What would Mam do?" Mam who gave birth to me when no one was at home—Pa and the children were clearing fields. *"You slipped out the easiest of all my children,"* she said. My baby be easy, too, and, if not, I'd manage as if Mam, Pa, and all my family were beside me, speaking their love.

I pulled off my night shift and pulled a second quilt from the dresser and wrapped myself in it like an Indian. I snatched my sewing kit and brought it into the bed beside me.

Pain roared, wave after wave after wave. Sometimes I thought I'd get towed under; other times, I thought I'd float; still other times, I saw myself a beached, black whale, flopping on land without enough air.

I grunted. I groaned. And when the urge came to push, I raised my knees and clutched the sheets. The blood scared me. So much of it. Too much of it. And I began calling my baby's name: *Rosetta*. Praying. Calling my little baby to come out and be just fine.

I screamed. Toward the end, I screamed. I thought Freddy could hear me anywhere in Massachusetts. But no one came. If anyone heard me, they probably thought I was a haint roaming Bedford's streets. It be two days past Sunday and no one thought to check on Miz Douglass. Part of this be my fault. I found more peace being alone. Part of it be the abolitionists' fault too.

Abolitionists told everybody when Freddy married. These white folks were truly excited to help a slave find love. (Acted like they had some hand in it!) So even though I'd been big for months, my neighbors counted well enough to know the baby wasn't due. Not yet. Not yet.

Not when I was only six months married. Not if I went to my marriage unspoiled.

My baby didn't know anything about polite time. Secret time. The pains grew stronger.

In my mind, bones be rising from the ocean. Bones be mocking me, scattering my family, shooing them away. Wind rattled the window. And Mr. Death be rocking slowly in the corner chair. Old two-horned, hoof-footed devil.

I'd die from this pain. And if I died, who'd come to care for my baby? Who would know that I was gone? It might be days, weeks, a month before my baby's Daddy came home.

One last, low, howling scream and out came my baby's head, face up, curious about the world. I cried, laughed. Then pushed some more and the babe slithered out like a fish. But, too quiet, she scared me. I cut the cord connecting us and lifted my baby to my breast. Milk was running down my chest. Her lips found me and suckled hard. A new kind of pain. My baby's hand curled against my bosom; her other hand, curled against her cheek. Drawing down milk, I knew she'd be all right. "Sickly babies don't milk," Mam always said.

One last push and the afterbirth whooshed out—all purple, red, and glittering like silver. I wrapped the afterbirth in a sheet. I wrapped my baby in a blanket I'd knitted from the finest yarn. I cleaned myself with rags, then put on a clean shift. I folded the stained and bloodied blanket and laid it upon the floor. Then, I climbed into bed beside my baby.

She slept peaceful. Warm brown like her Daddy. Smelling like new earth. Her lips, red like a bright rose. Inside her mouth, all pink and sweet. Everything about my baby be delicate. Light, soft, tender, matching the blanket I wove. *Like a rose—Rosetta.* My little girl. My answer to loneliness. My answer for who I be: I was proud to be Miz Douglass, but I was Rosetta's Mam and always would be.

Rosetta would get my truest love. And I'd raise her as Mam raised me. I'd show her my bay where I caught Big Blues. Then I'd whisper my news that the bones had promised to bring her sweet, blue crabs every time she dunked her trap into warm waters. The bones would provide for her just as they did for me. The bones be happy she alive.

I counted Rosetta's toes. I counted her fingers. I kissed the soft spot on her head, the cord, already drying, already cracked red on her belly. I smelled her hair.

Before I fell asleep, before I let myself rest, I thanked my Mam. Thanked the bones too. I smiled as the sun rose so sweetly on a new day. There be no turning back. I was now Mam. I thought: Poor Freddy. He has missed this. Missed this new and special wonder.

*A*nna. Can you wake, Anna?"

I thought I was dreaming. Freddy's voice be in my ear.

"Anna, the child is beautiful."

I opened my eyes. A beautiful face be in front of mine. "Freddy?"

"I'm home, Anna."

"Home." I threw my arms about Freddy, hugged him tight. "Let me get up, fix you some food."

"No, Anna, I think you must be ill. You're still abed at noon."

I pushed myself deeper beneath the sheet. I hadn't the heart to tell Freddy nothing be wrong with me. I slept when the baby slept. With the ground still hard with ice, my garden wouldn't grow. If I slept, my time waiting for Freddy flew.

"Was the delivery hard?"

"Naw. I did just fine."

"Why didn't you have the midwife in? Pastor Wells's wife to help?"

I heard the scold in Freddy's voice. Neighbors talked to him before he could talk to me. "It be too fast," I answered, "too late to ask for help."

"You don't want people thinking—"

"What? That I be strong?"

"That you don't require the same care a white woman expects."

I was shocked. Mam sometimes had a midwife. Sometimes not. But Miz Baldwin had the whole world watching when she gave birth. There'd be the doctor, the nurse, the baby-to-be's nurse, and oftentimes a woman friend. I was asked to stand outside the door, in case Miz Bald-

win needed anything. That always made me laugh. What was I supposed to do? Cook her a stew? Bring her a cup of hot milk when she be
screaming beyond the door, calling upon Jesus one minute, then shouting for everybody to go away the next?

"Let me show you Rosetta. Show you that she's fine, growing
strong. She didn't need any help coming into this world."

"Rosetta?"

"Yes. You don't mind? She's fine like a garden rose." I went to the
dresser drawer that I'd made into a cradle. Rosetta be sleeping, but I
pulled back the blanket and showed the pink soles of her feet, the pink
undersides of her hands.

"She's not so dark."

"Naw. She's warm-colored like you. Like you, she'll have black,
silky hair."

For the first time in a long time, there be joy on Freddy's face.

"Come, sit with her in the rocker."

"Her eyes," he murmured, awed. "She opened her eyes."

It be love, deep and true. Freddy rocked in the chair, sang, cooed,
and told his daughter she was free and nobody was going to chain her.

He clutched my hand, "Thank you, Anna." I was right pleased. My
body warmed.

I looked into Freddy's face and I saw the strain on him. Not from
the baby but from long days on the road, long nights giving speeches.
And I was proud of him, proud for him. He worked for something bigger than himself. I saw he worked for our baby's future. I leaned forward
and kissed his brow.

Freddy reached out and stroked one of my breasts. They were both
heavy and full with milk. Almost hard. A trickle of milk drained from
my teat.

"Does it hurt?"

"Naw." I smiled as if he be my baby too. "Rosetta just needs to be
fed." I gathered her in my arms and held her to my left breast. Though
sleepy still, my baby fed hungrily and dearest Freddy, my husband, was
amazed at what my body could do. Then, he was up, saying, "What
chores need doing?" "Let me feed you." "Bring in more wood." "Anything you need, just let me know, Anna."

I laughed. He be acting like the new, proud Papa. It made me feel special. He be on his knees, watching me feed Baby, and from time to time, he be stroking Baby, then gently stroking me.

"When was she born?"

"A month Tuesday." I realized my mistake.

"Why didn't you write me? Have someone write me?"

"I didn't need no one."

"You offended the folks of this town?"

"That's not what I said. Folks came Sundays. Some offered to stay. But I kept telling them I was all right—"

"And they left you alone."

"Yes."

He stood, pacing before me. "Anna, Anna. You have offended them. Don't you know who I am? Don't you know what folks will say about me?"

I started getting tight, angry. Baby started crying. Freddy didn't care for the noise, didn't care for a child's wailing and me, talking back.

"Freddy, I'm sorry," I said, wanting our good feelings back. "But I didn't need them people. Didn't need them asking about when I was due. Asking: 'Did a fright cause the baby to come too early?'

"Pastor Wells's wife was the worst: 'When did you say you married, dear?' I didn't want no one looking crosswise at Rosetta. Didn't want folks whispering behind their hands."

"If you'd acted graciously, no one would've questioned you."

"You mean no one would've said you jumped the broom too late."

"Anna!"

I kept my head tucked down, looking at Rosetta. "I'm sorry. I don't feel at home here."

"You feel more at home in a room off a white person's kitchen?"

"You felt home enough there to make Rosetta," I shouted back.

Freddy be furious. "She is the last child to be made in a bed not my own."

I didn't remind Freddy that the New Bedford house wasn't his. The sheets and quilts, I'd made with my hands. But except for books and words, nothing in this house be his.

I reached out my hand. "Freddy, let me take care of you. You must be tired. I can fry some fatback. There's some cornbread left."

But Freddy didn't look at me. Rosetta was still wailing 'cause I stopped feeding. Then, I looked down at myself. I be a mess. Heavier. Hair undone. Shift stained with milk.

"I'll dress, Freddy, and bring you some food."

"See to the child, Anna."

That's it. That's all he say. Then he left me, shutting the door ever so softly, yet ever so sure, for I heard the click-click when the latch took. And I looked at the sunshine flooding our room making my shadow look like it was lying on the floor.

$\mathcal{I}$ could've explained to Freddy I'd wanted to tell him about the baby myself. (Seemed like good neighbors would let a wife share her joy first!) Could've told him though I felt well, having a baby takes its toll. Could've told him how I sometimes feared the cold, not having enough to eat. Could've told him how I missed him, missed Mam. Told him I was afraid he'd stopped loving me.

I could've given a hundred reasons for acting so uncivil. But Freddy didn't want to hear them. He be cold, formal. I thought he believed his sense of right applied to both him and me. He didn't think I might *feel* different. *Believe* different.

Loneliness came stealing over me again. Silence stretched between us.

After an hour, both Mam and Pa would've been saying "Sorry," "My mistake," "My fault," "No one's fault," and been hugging before all us children. During dinner, they'd be serving each other bread, greens, slices of ham. Offering a glass of water. Sweet buttermilk. Feeding each other like babies. We children would giggle as Pa spooned Mam some greens, as Mam lifted a glass to Pa's mouth, and we would know all was right in the world.

But, during dinner, Freddy said not a word. Said no kindness, said nothing except, "On the road, the food was plentiful. Quakers cook simply, but abundantly."

Humpf. I looked at the table. My pickings were slim indeed. A bit of rice mixed with collards. A squash mashed into soup. Lard biscuits. A cup of tea. I didn't tell Freddy I'd saved the rice for his homecoming. Or that he'd used the last grain of sugar for his tea.

"Tell me about your journey," I said.

His head tilted up and in the between space where the wall met the ceiling, he fixed his gaze. I looked to see what he be seeing but I saw only dust, cracks, and a spider weaving a sac around its babies. But Freddy saw packed halls, people applauding him. He saw the glory of the road. Saw Garrison's flushed, excited face, the respect Quakers have for him, and maybe Miss Assing's admiring gaze too.

"There is great joy in speaking for a cause. It soothes me greatly."

"What you mean?"

"Slave memories disturb my rest. Each day slave owners are inflicting such hurt, such injustice. But, when I speak in these great halls, I imagine I am talking to slaveholders."

"Anna, if I can convince one slaveholder that not only is it evil to hold a slave, but that the slaveholder risks great evil to himself for owning the slave, then there is real hope for the antislavery cause."

"How do owners get hurt? Seems everything already be their way."

"Yes, that's it, Anna. Why should a Master give up slaves if he gains money, gains property, gains workers, gains leisure?"

I was touched he called me Anna. I could feel his passion, his words taking wing.

"The slave owner must be convinced that slavery is as injurious to him as it is to the slave."

"In-jur-i-ous?"

"That it hurts him, Anna. Hurts his wife, his children. The moral fiber of his family. Don't you see? Slavery corrupts. Turns the kind-hearted owner into a demon, the sweet angel of a mistress into a devil. When one human owns another, the power corrupts. Owning even one soul, the slaveholder risks losing his own."

"You should be preaching the Bible, Freddy. The word of God be upon you."

"It's not the word of God. It is an argument, Anna. A logical argument."

"It be hard for a rich man to enter the Kingdom of Heaven, so it be hard for a slaveholder too. That your argument?"

"Yes, Anna, but—"

"That be in the Bible. I remember that from church. Pastor's words." I was excited. I thought I understood what Freddy meant.

"You preaching Gospel, Freddy. You preaching the word of God. This be the way for your learning to make a living. Helping folks come to God."

He stood up, tossed his napkin on the table. "I'll never preach the Bible."

I shocked. "You godless?"

"No. Of course not." His voice be strained like bark. "But I disrespect religious men who say the Bible allows for slavery. They tell white men it is their *duty* to baptize savages. Then those same preachers counsel slaves to be happy, compliant, for their reward is in Heaven. Suffering under the white man's care, slaves can reach the great hereafter, cross the great River Jordan beyond the sky. Paradise is in death."

"Freddy—"

"Frederick."

It felt like he slapped me in the face.

I stood straighter, my hands clasped. I wanted to be clear. I wanted him to hear me.

"Frederick, you speak fine words. I don't understand everything you say. Your mind be quicker than mine. But I understand there be a baby in the room beyond, and if you keep preaching abolition, then I need to take in laundry. If you preach Gospel, I know you can make a living. But if you preach abolition, I'll end up carrying my baby on my back and cleaning some white woman's house."

"No." He moved quick, grabbed my hand. Then, he wrapped his arms about me. "Anna, I'm sorry. I've not been fair. Leaving you to handle so much on your own."

"I can manage, Frederick."

"Freddy," he said. "I like that better."

"I can manage." I touched my hand to his cheek. "I know you have important work to do. I see that now. But we be a family. Rosetta needs us both. She needs her father."

"It's because you've never been a slave."

It was softly said, and though I heard it, I questioned I'd heard it. "What? What you say?"

"You've never been a slave."

"You think I don't be feeling other people's pain?"

"I didn't say that, Anna."

I know he didn't. But I felt this be what he mean. How could I explain that? *You said it without saying it.* How did I say that without angering him again?

Rosetta began crying. Time for her feeding. With great relief, I left the small parlor. How good it felt to have my baby taking from me what she needed. How good it felt to have something that somebody needed.

Truest love. Love be true. I be failing myself, failing my daughter if I didn't try to understand this new man in my house. *Frederick Douglass.*

Where Douglass come from? Did he pull the name from air? Where'd he get it from? My name, Anna Murray, be real. Douglass, not so real. But my vows be true. I made them as real as I could speak. As real as my own breath. My own blood.

I buttoned my gown. Laid my baby in the pine drawer that was her cradle. I went back into the parlor. The food was uneaten and Frederick was by the window, looking at the horizon like the first time I saw him on the ship being built, dry-docked, sailing to nowhere.

"You don't have to preach. Water here be just like the water in Maryland. I'll ask for the bones to help."

"Superstition, Anna."

I frowned.

"Garrison thinks I could write a book. It might pay."

"That be fine."

"A book should sell fine, I think. It'll help promote the cause. More towns will want me to visit. That'll suit me well."

"So you be going again?"

"Yes. Maybe with the baby here, I can ask abolitionists for more support."

"Pay?"

"Yes, for my speeches. They'll recognize I have a family. Yes," he say, as if to himself, "I will ask for more support."

"So you going?"

"Not for a while yet."

"When?"

"When they call for me."

"Tomorrow?"

"Anna, you're being stubborn. I can't just stay here because you would have it so. People, the cause, need me. I am doing great good."

He be so handsome. So mightily handsome. He'll bring down the walls of the temple, I thought. I only hoped he wouldn't die doing it like Samson did.

"Then teach me letters."

"Yes. I'll teach you, so you can teach Rosetta."

If you ain't here. The words hung in the air.

We worked for hours. My mind twisted around those scratch marks. *Anna*—I knew. Frederick taught me to see—*Rosetta.*

Rosetta

"You like the name?" I asked.

"Yes. Our next child should be called Frederick Junior."

If you ain't here. He was telling me so I know. If he ain't here. He was telling me a baby boy be better.

My tears made all the letters swim. My head ached. Rosetta cried. She needed feeding again. This time Freddy came into the bedroom with me, watching me feed her.

Freddy looked hungry, too. He said, "Time to let the letters be."

ABC's tomorrow.

We made peace in the bed today.

*T*here be lulls before storms. I couldn't have lived my whole life next to water and not have known that. Clear skies, sunshine, quiet waters fool. Wind and water be raging down the coast. Deep in their watery grave, bones be clattering. Biggest fish be eating the smallest.

Still—there was a short good time.

Me, Freddy, and the baby, took pleasure in each other. Freddy loved me many times while baby Rosetta slept in her drawer. I tried hard to keep myself open. To be a good and giving wife. If there were fewer words of tenderness, fewer caresses, I told myself it didn't much matter. My baby be proof of loving. She was the "littlest thing" Freddy had ever given me. A "little thing" that grew hold of my heart and became my world. When Freddy held the baby, he was holding me. Holding our world together. God bless.

One day Garrison came and brought Rosetta a rattle. My hands shook, splattered tea, dropped the pie. That's how certain I was he'd come to take Freddy away from us.

Mr. Garrison said, "No need for speeches yet, Douglass. It's a false spring. Ice will return soon."

"Do you think slaves care that it is winter up here?"

"Patience, man. All things in good time."

In good time. I rejoiced; Freddy grew sad.

He grew restless. He'd been on a big stage and our house be so, so small. Sometimes I thought he'd burst. So much energy and no place to put it. Without abolitionist work, he was adrift. Only so much energy to be used in tending to a wife and an itty-bitty child. Only so much energy needed for chopping wood, hauling tinder, and tossing grain at our one chick. Though I praised him, I couldn't compare to a stomping, clapping crowd.

Freddy never complained. He saw how much money was needed for candles, cotton, and thread. How much money was needed for flour, ham, black-eyed peas, and rice.

He tried welding. He was good at it. So good, white workers complained.

For two weeks, Freddy straggled home tired. Sore in spirit.

"Coloreds might not be slaves, Anna. But it doesn't mean we aren't resented. Prejudice has well-tended roots in the North."

I didn't say a colored church be more welcoming. I didn't say that with his learning, a great Pastor he'd make. Mam always told me "deeds, not words" speak the truth of a loving heart.

I wanted to ease Freddy's burden. I guess, too, I wanted the big man who thought great things and fought to free the slaves. Tired out, this new, quieter man slept soundly in bed. Less time for us touching. Less time for playing with his baby before the fire. Less time for learning ABC's.

There was only one bright spot: as days became weeks, my heart grew full; Miz Assing didn't knock at our door. I hadn't actually seen her for a good long while. But Freddy came back full of smiles after visiting Mr. Garrison in town. I figured Miz Assing must've been at some of them meetings. I figured Freddy, too, must've told her not to come. Not to his house.

I still hadn't found a way to *think* good about Miz Assing; but I knew the way to *do* good for Freddy.

I carried my baby on my back and went to town.

Love, love be true.

Chill was creeping in the air again. Squirrels who poked their noses out early, scurried back to rest. Even birds flew south again. Wind blew white kisses across the waves.

Still I knew where to go.

Salt Hill was where rich white folks lived. In Baltimore and in other cities and towns, too, I imagine, there be Salt Hill places. Streets where folks lived better than most. Where white folks could pay others to do their work.

I walked the half mile, trudged up the hill with a view of the harbor, ships and flapping masts, and knocked on the first kitchen door I came to.

"Laundry," I said to the colored kitchen maid. "No one does it finer."

She nodded and left me standing on the steps, in the cold, my baby curled against my breast. I kept my head up; my face smooth. No frowns. No false smile. When the woman of the house came to see me, I spoke quietly:

"I'm Anna Douglass. Honest. Clean. Not afraid of hard work. I wash, iron, sew better than anyone."

The colored maid whispered in her Mistress' ear.

I thought: in Baltimore, I would've been invited in. Told to wait in the kitchen, then escorted to the parlor. Northerners had shabby manners. But I kept my face ever still, my eyes cool. The woman studied me; her faded brown hair pulled tight beneath a white cap.

"Fine lace. Can you clean and sew that?"

"Yes, ma'am. Most anything. I worked for a fine lady in Baltimore."

"Twenty cents a week. On trial. Come back Tuesday."

I bobbed a curtsy and turned to step down.

"You're Mr. Douglass' wife? The escaped slave?"

I nodded.

"And that's his child?"

"Yes, ma'am."

She cracked a wide grin. "Come back Tuesday. I'll have a fine load for you then."

At first, I didn't understand. What matter who my husband be? My husband won't be turning his hand to cleaning. I knocked on houses, door-to-door, and those ladies that hesitated, didn't hesitate to hire me once I said, "Anna Douglass. Wife of Frederick Bailey Douglass." Some would say, "I heard him speak." Others would say, "Time for him to lead a quieter life. Abolition has no meaning here. We've always been enlightened this far north."

Mercy me. Foolishness. These women cared more about the one cleaning their clothes, than the cleaning. Cared more, for better or worse, that it would be in Frederick Douglass' house and be Frederick Douglass' wife that boiled water, starched, and pressed their clothes. Fine with me as long as I received my due.

And I did. Eight households gave me their wash. Eight basket loads Rosetta played in while her Daddy worked at the shipyards, twisting metal.

At the end of a week, I fixed a fine dinner for Freddy. Even baked a cake as good as Mam could make.

"What's this, Anna? Has the North taught you wastefulness?"

He'd come home bone-tired, I could tell. Stinking of fire, soot, and metal.

"Wash up, Freddy. I have a surprise."

"Not before you tell me the meaning of this. Do you think I work for niceties, Anna? Survival, Anna. I work for our survival."

I blinked back tears. I took his hand and pulled him into the parlor. There I'd cleared the table and made a desk. I had a candle, a quill, an inkwell, and vellum I'd purchased at the feed and sundries store.

"You big, Freddy. Too big for shipyards. I think I tell you that before. In Baltimore."

"What does this mean, Anna?"

"Write. Your book. Your story should be written down. I'll work."

"Anna, no—"

"All my life, I work. I be proud of what my hands and back can do."

"You have work, Anna. You have a child to raise."

"If Mam can raise five kids, I can surely raise one and do a little laundry on the side."

He squeezed my hand. His hands touched the quill and paper like he was a blind man. He feel every fiber, every wrinkle, every feather.

Then he dipped the quill in black ink:

The Narrative of Frederick Douglass,
An American Slave

He paused, looked at the words, then added more scratches:

Written by Himself
1845

I brought food to him. He worked all night. Such pleasure on his face, I be almost jealous. He here. In our house. Home. My husband. Daddy to my child.

I thought another babe be on the way. Rising inside my oven. Rising because of the warmth inside me. Mam said nursing kept another baby from coming too soon. I wasn't done nursing Rosetta, but I didn't mind. I thought how strong Freddy's seed be. I thought even though I was older than him, my body knew woman's work.

❧

Six weeks of heaven. Days grew colder, a snowstorm blanketed roads and frosted all the windows. I heard the *Bedford Mary* was lost at sea.

Freddy wrote, said little; but I was content. Mr. Garrison, once he found out about the book, gave us a drudge horse to carry me to and from my white women's houses. While it helped, it was another mouth to feed. Mr. Garrison didn't think about that.

He thought about Freddy's "tract," he said. "All the time. All the time." Said he'd pen the introduction. Wendell Phillips might pen another. He was so excited, he couldn't sit still. Eyes wide, cheeks bright, his lips cracking from all his licking, like he think a slave story be a piece of pie.

Mr. Garrison lifted one of Freddy's many pages. "Have you read your husband's words, Mrs. Douglass?"

I shook my head. (I thought Garrison be trying to shame me on purpose.)

He cleared his throat; a picture flies out of his mouth:

"Mr. Gore then, without consultation or deliberation with anyone, not even giving Demby an additional call, raised his musket to his face, taking deadly aim at his standing victim, and in an instant poor Demby was no more. His mangled body sank out of sight, and blood and brains marked the water where he stood.

"A thrill of horror flashed through every soul upon the plantation, excepting Mr. Gore. He alone seemed cool and collected."

So much I didn't know. These markings were a window. My fingers touched the sanded and dried ink.

Freddy buried his head in his hands.

"Success. This is to be a big success," Mr. Garrison chortled.

And so it was. So it was.

$\mathcal{F}$reddy be the biggest man. Everybody wanted to hear the man who wrote so fine a book. Telegrams, letters came every day, inviting Freddy to speak. Sometimes money was folded into envelopes.

"Abolition has no finer champion than Frederick Bailey Douglass," wrote Mr. Garrison in the *Liberator*. Everybody be happy: abolitionists, for printing the book; Freddy, for doing such noble work.

I be happy, too. Freddy didn't travel further than a half day from me. I was clumsy, filled with a new child. Rosetta still tugged at my breasts. Freddy forbid me working. I could make lots of money. More money than I did trapping Big Blues. All the white women in town wanted me to clean their sheets. Freddy said, "No." He said, "Dignity." Still, I wished there was extra to send to Mam.

On Sabbath, Freddy be home. His hands waved when he talked. He practiced his speech about his battle with Covey:

"My long crushed spirit rose, cowardice departed, bold defiance, took its place; and I now resolved that however long I might remain a slave in form, the day has passed forever when I could be a slave in fact. I did not hesitate to let it be known of me, that the white man who expected to succeed in whipping, must also succeed in killing me."

I clapped my hands.

Having babies gave me good excuses not to go to meetings. I didn't miss the cigar smoke, the loud noise, the people pressing tighter than a school of fish. Freddy, though, enjoyed being noticed. He be more joyful than Christmas.

Sabbath evening, he said, "Today, Anna, we begin again. Frederick Junior is inside you. My son must read and write."

"I'll send him to Pastor's school."

"And how will you know if Pastor teaches him right? What about that, Anna?"

I had no time for letters, I thought. There be laundry to do. Cooking, cleaning. The new baby be draining much from me. Sometimes I just wanted to lay in bed. Not even get up for Rosetta's call. But I did. I found the strength. Maybe this be why having a second baby too soon caused grief?

I bit my lip. It wouldn't be right to ruin Freddy's vow. I nodded and smiled. Freddy's fingers caressed my lips.

On a small chalkboard, Freddy made me draw uppercase, "*I*," and lowercase, "*i.*" I frustrated him because I asked, too many questions, like why have upper and lower? Words would always say the same thing. He said, "It's grammar." But I thought a word be a word . . . be a word. Whether it be tall or small. He'd just finished sighing at me when the knock, no, the pounding, came at the door.

Both of us looked up, startled by the sound. I didn't move, 'cause the sound was too big and loud, too frightening. None of the neighbors would knock so.

Freddy moved quick, like all along he'd been waiting for the sign. Been waiting for this sharp crack on wood to call him, make him jump from the chair, and swing open the door without putting on his coat.

"Garrison," he said. "Miss Assing." My heart froze. Freddy bowed. I lost my breath.

Something made me get up and move, though—get up, get baby Rosetta from the bedroom, and come back into the parlor, cradling the baby just as Mr. Garrison and Miz Assing come in.

It be raining. Miz Assing's worried her cloak be dripping water on the floor. All this time, I'd let myself forget about her. But here she be like a ghost in my parlor.

"Not to worry," I said, taking her wrap.

Garrison, slicking back his hair, say, "Plenty to worry about. There's word, Frederick, a slave catcher's on the hunt for you."

Freddy stumbled back like someone had hit him a strong blow. Funny, I felt next to nothing. None of this was a surprise. All along, I expected the slave catcher to come. In Maryland, the children sang: "Run, nigger, run. The paterrollers come." Slave and slave catchers be common. What's not so common be a catcher traveling this far north. Staying on the trail for months. This catcher must be stubborn. He meant to have Freddy or die trying.

Freddy looked at me. "I am the trained, educated monkey."

"We'll buy you free," said Miz Assing.

Freddy shook his head. "Auld won't sell."

"Then you must be gone, man. Gone to escape this fate. Enslaved again, you cannot help the cause."

"You mean I'd be worthless to you?" Freddy said bitter, his words sharp.

"No, that isn't what Garrison means," said Miz Assing, placing her palm in his. "You are worth much, dear friend. So much so, I commit all my resources to keep you free from slavery."

"Europe," said Garrison.

"England," said Miz Assing. "London is the place."

I moved forward. "What you mean? We can't travel that far with a baby. Not in this cold."

Then all three turned—two white faces, one black; two men, one woman. The outline of the door framed them. Miz Assing be in the middle, Garrison be beside her on the left and Frederick be on the right. The two men be looking at the floor but Miz Assing be looking directly at me and the baby. Hand outstretched, she stepped forward. One step, two. Three. She stopped, shrugged. Her hands fell to her sides.

"Naw," I said. "Naw. Not without me. He not going without me."

"Mrs. Douglass, be reasonable—" "You must see—" "Anna—" All three spoke at once. But Freddy, he come take my hand.

"It's like before, Anna. I need to go ahead. I'll send for you. The baby, too."

I didn't want to fight in front of these people. I tried to keep my voice calm; I spoke softly, but I knew these strangers could still hear. "Freddy . . . Frederick, I do not want you gone so far from me. Please." I murmured again, "Please."

"He'll become a slave again."

I didn't want Miz Assing speaking to me. Her voice grated; it be too harsh. I kept my eyes fixed on Freddy. His two hands cupped my face and, though wordless, he be speaking to me. Telling me to stay strong.

"Frederick, my friend." Garrison cleared his throat and spoke, soft and serious. "It's true that you are worth much to the abolitionist cause. But I couldn't bear knowing you were enslaved. Were your soul not known to me, I'd still dread and fight against your enslavement. But knowing your spirit and soul, I think I'd lose my mind if you were enslaved and I'd done nothing to help you."

"Thank you, Garrison." Freddy never turned around; he spoke his words to me. Cupping my face, looking at me, he gave his solemn thanks to this white man. All the while suggesting it was my turn to be generous.

I bowed my head. "My fault."

"No one's fault."

"But the book—"

"I would've written it without you."

But not so soon, I think. I stared at the chalkboard and cursed the letters. White marks on black slates. I shook my head. There be no hope but to give in. "I'll fix tea."

"We'll make plans," said Miz Assing, curt and sharp. I imagined spilling scalding tea on her skirt. Foolishness for me to feel so spiteful.

While I worked in the kitchen, I heard their voices. Freddy's voice, like a sweet melody; Garrison's deep, like a smooth drum; but it was Miz Assing's voice that ruined the music, making it flat.

More fool me. Being mad at Miz Assing 'cause Freddy was leaving. Why did I expect his journey to be over? Eyes open, I knew I married a slave. What right had I to complain? But, Lord, it hurt. Until Pa died, he never left Mam for even a night. Now Freddy would be so far gone, I couldn't pretend he'd be home any day. Far as England be, it would be months of travel there and back. Months of living in this place called London. The tea canister crashed to the floor.

"Anna, are you all right?"

"Yes," I called back. Tears filled my eyes; I silently pleaded, "Come see for yourself, Freddy. Come see for yourself if I be all right." Talk from the parlor kept on and I shivered. "Don't be scared," I tell myself. "Don't fear."

Freddy's fleeing was my children's only hope to know their Daddy one day. What a funny truth. Freddy's leaving meant I still had hope. Meant he'd still have a chance to come back. Meant he might return to my side.

Mercy, this side of Heaven, my marriage would still abide.

I looked at Rosetta sleeping in the box on the kitchen table. She only knew her Daddy weeks and he was gone. I'd known him for almost two years but only for a few months had I kept him by my side.

Ottilie

"Sometimes the journey from slavery never ends."

—FREDERICK DOUGLASS,
IN A LETTER TO W. L. GARRISON, 1859

"I learned to whisper love in his ear.
While he slept, I spoke my heart."

—OTTILIE ASSING,
DIARY ENTRY, 1862

New Bedford

I felt sorry for Anna. Standing with her baby clutched to her breast, she looked so vulnerable. Fierce too. How can a woman be both?

Frau Douglass didn't want to be left behind. How could I blame her? I, too, would've wanted to stay with my husband.

When Douglass touched her arm, Anna grew hard. Like Medusa's victims.

Douglass shifted his weight and, over his shoulder, I glimpsed her eyes. Such naked emotion. Such power. She was pleading with him. Saying nary a word. Yet, even from a distance, I felt her yearning. Not visible in the rest of her body but visible in her eyes. Brown like a doe's.

I thought: How can Frederick refuse? He'll have to take her with him. What kind of heart could leave such love behind?

I felt inexplicably sad. I turned. Garrison was looking at me, speculative. Inquiring. How dared he watch me! I spoke sharply.

"Why does no one ever call you Lloyd? It's a more interesting name than Garrison."

"Fräulein Assing, you of all people should know that actions are more interesting than mere words."

I flushed. "What are you implying?"

"For the moment, nothing." Then, his lips thinned with perverse satisfaction. "We have a slave to protect. Do we not?"

Douglass was coming toward us. It was like I saw him anew: handsome, certainly; resolute, of course. But such sadness rested upon his shoulders. I wanted to care for him. Hold him close and give him comfort. Anna was gone, disappeared into the kitchen. But I understood her need of him. I felt my own desire like some tidal wave, pulling me into its undertow and rendering me breathless. Douglass was like some hybrid god. More beautiful than plain African, more beautiful than plain American.

The current had been there all along, pulling, shaping me toward new shorelines. First, America, then New Bedford. But geography was nothing compared to my heart—compared to the heat stirring in my blood.

Mama taught me to praise feelings: "*The idea of love has its own beauty.*"

But what was the source? Was it the man Douglass who stirred me? Or the *idea* of his enslavement that made him so appealing?

As in the best art, the man Douglass revealed himself in his *Narrative*. Emotions ironed into words didn't lie. Sometimes, I had to stop reading and cry. Sometimes, I pressed my lips to paper wanting to soothe his hurts. Such injustice that such a gifted man should be a slave. How could I separate intellect from the concrete, the tangible Douglass? How could I separate my love of his ideas, from my response to his body? Sinew, blood, flesh. If Mama was a heroine of her own life, then Douglass, surely, must be his own hero. I am his companion-in-arms as he meets a new trial. A new test of courage.

Douglass drew ever closer, despair etched on his brow, and I responded with trembling and dampened palms. I mustn't be a school-girl. I was an intelligent woman committed to the cause of uplifting colored men and women from slavery. I exhaled. Clasped my hands.

Abstract and physical. Spiritual and carnal. All one.

"Let us sit down and plan," said Garrison.

At some point, tea appeared. But I was lost exploring new sensations within me. I was conscious of little things. A scar on Douglass' hand. His blunt fingertips. His lips parting as he spoke to Garrison.

Plain table, plain room. Serviceable. The candles had a strong odor and made much smoke. Not more than a peasant's cottage in Germany.

I remembered Douglass striding the stage. This room wasn't good enough for him. I remembered him moving gracefully, forcefully, abandoning the podium, bellowing his rage, then sweetening his prose with reason. The totality of him moved me.

"So, this is it," said Douglass.

"Yes," answered Garrison. "I can provide letters of introduction. As for funds, Miss Assing has been generous."

I heard my name from a great distance. A spider illuminated by flame.

"London it is," said Douglass, his voice muted, dry like paper.

"You can still speak to the cause. Excite our European allies," said Garrison.

"Yes, and I will write. Articles. Essays. Dispatches." His tone was firm.

"Good man." Garrison shook Douglass' hand. But when he would've released it, Douglass didn't let it go.

"Will you care for my family? I do not want my wife taking in laundry."

"Yes. I'll see to her," Garrison said quickly.

Too quickly, I thought.

"Tonight, Frederick, you must see to yourself," urged Garrison. "Get to the ship at the farthest end of the wharf. The *Marie-Therese*. Do not sleep here tonight. Too dangerous."

"Yes," I agreed. "Leave now. This instant, if you can manage it."

"You cannot mean it?"

The haste was troubling. It was now becoming real to him—he was once again escaping. A runaway.

"I do mean it. Unless you wish to be recaptured."

"I'd rather die."

I covered his hand with mine. "It'll not come to that."

(God help me. I almost rested my cheek atop his palm.)

Once the decision was made, things happened quickly.

Garrison began writing letters of introduction. Douglass began selecting papers, books, stowing them into his black portmanteau. His energy was focused, but watching his hands, I could see the slight tremors. At times, he paused briefly and stared. Arrested by some private vision. So his fear subtly presented itself. His vulnerability made him all the more appealing.

I spoke impulsively. "I'll come with you. You can pretend to be my servant, if need be. My slave, if questioned. No one would doubt my word. No one would dare take from me what's mine."

"Yours?" mocked Garrison.

"A figure of speech, Garrison. I have funds. Plenty enough to bribe and smooth the way. Funds, too, in banks in Germany, Europe." I was lying. I had money. But not unlimited.

"I had no idea, Ottilie. Such largesse."

I ignored Garrison. "I speak several languages. Douglass, you may need an interpreter if the abolitionist cause expands. The French, are they not already sympathetic? And, in Germany, I can assure you of a warm welcome. I can translate your *Narrative*, translate your story for the European community to understand." My words came fast as though they'd been stored inside me, waiting to spill forth. Waiting to signify that I, too, could be useful.

"Pack lightly, Douglass. Let's be on our way."

He looked at me, his bushy brows arched high. "As you wish, Miss Assing. I appreciate your efforts on my behalf, your good sense."

I felt as though the room were spinning. Garrison steadied me by locking hold of my elbow. I could barely settle my breathing.

Douglass went into the bedroom. The door still open, I saw him pulling clothes from the dresser, stuffing them into a bag on the bed. I thought: Black; White; German Jew; Christian Mulatto; European; African and American. Male, female. What a pair we make!

Anna came from the kitchen and gave a great cry when she saw Douglass packing. She rushed into the room, threw one arm about him while her other held their baby. Douglass removed her hand from his neck. I couldn't hear his words, but I saw Anna collapse, fold like a rag doll, slouched on the bed. Douglass kept packing.

A clock ticked. Days seemed to have passed but the clock told it was only a half hour. A half hour of terror in a slave's life. A colored family home.

Douglass grabbed his bag and marched from the room.

"Freddy," Anna moaned. But she didn't move from her stooped posture on the bed and Douglass didn't stop walking.

Garrison patted Douglass on the back. "Good man." He opened the front door and the two, having thrown on their coats, walked out into the rain. I found my wrap on the hall peg, but I couldn't yet leave. The silhouette of Anna on the bed, her head bowed over her child, struck me. Mother held me so. I felt as though I were a child swept back in time.

Then, Anna lifted her head and notes rose from her throat that almost had me weeping. Lullaby, spiritual, I don't know which. It was a soulful music that made me shudder.

"Fräulein, hurry."

In the darkened rain, from inside the transom, Garrison was calling me and still I rushed forward into Anna's and Douglass' bedroom. It was so simple, so small. Few adornments, bare walls. The bed quilt, I could tell, had been stitched with care.

Neither the baby nor Anna moved. A still life like in one of my paintings. I could see Anna's stout form well enough, her belly curving with another child.

"Here," I said. And laid beside her a miniature I'd painted of Douglass. Her fingers, like claws, gathered it up.

I left a pouch, too, on the bed beside her.

"A gift for you."

Her brows raised. And I was certain I saw . . . jealousy—no, hatred. Raw feeling such as I'd had for those who tormented, placed obstacles before me.

"For the baby, then."

I left quickly, swinging on my wrap, walking into the rain, onto the porch step. Douglass and Garrison were in the carriage. The driver tipped his hat and the horses neighed impatiently.

I looked back. Anna, her baby, were as I'd left them. Like a narrowing of a telescope, I could see them at a seemingly great distance. Far, far away, mother and child, alone on the bed, in a home not theirs, with few possessions, the stink of tallow, and a parlor table scattered with the mess of half-finished tea, paper and ink, a chalkboard with lessons halted in midstream. . . .

I felt sorry for them.

No, I felt sorry for her.

I thought: How could a fair God have it so? Douglass leaving her and going with me?

Shame on me, for if there was a God, I was glad. Glad to be the one going. Glad, at this moment, to be more useful to Herr Douglass than his wife could ever be.

Quietly, I shut the cottage door.

*O*f anyone spoke of how "odd" it was for a colored to have a first-class cabin, to have meals brought in, and chamber pots changed by cabin boys, I gave them a haughty look, replying: "My servants are my business." The crew thought me eccentric. And if eccentric meant buoying and sustaining the freedom of another man, then so be it. Garrison was to make overtures to Auld to secure Douglass' freedom. My promise was to keep Douglass safe and in good spirits. But while I rejoiced, Douglass' misery was palpable. Being hunted, being on the run again, enslaved him as surely as steel.

Once I felt compelled to go to Douglass' room. I hadn't seen him for days and I became obsessed that some harm had come to him.

"Herr Douglass. Herr Douglass." When he didn't answer, I became alarmed. Since all thought Douglass my servant, I had an extra key. I unlocked the door. All was dark, but as I pushed the door farther, I saw Douglass slumped over his desk, his arm dangling, his pen on the floor. I rushed forward, anxious to assure myself that he was all right. I wildly thought: he's dead. Ironic to escape slavery, only to die crossing the sea.

The lamp was askew, but there was enough light to confirm Douglass was alive. His chest rose. He'd fallen asleep, exhausted. I leaned over him, eager to see his new writing. Like a truant schoolboy, he'd written *Anna* . . . *Anna* . . . *Anna* . . . *Anna* . . .

I felt wicked. An unwanted intruder.

I didn't sleep all night. I worried when Douglass awoke, he might guess I'd been near. Might guess I'd seen his private longing.

In the morning, he seemed to have shaken his malaise. Like he knew we'd crossed into international waters. Knew he was beyond bounty hunters.

He was an impressive man. Much admired, striding on the deck for his morning and evening constitutional. Mannerly, he tipped his hat but initiated no conversations. He kept his dress somber, his hands deep in his pockets or else clasped behind his back. Indeed, no one could say he wasn't a gentleman. After a time, even the sailors gave him their respect. Begging his pardon, asking if he required anything.

He was like some king.

I enjoyed those days. Strange, at sea, in a confined landscape, I felt freer than I'd ever felt in my life.

Watching Douglass relaxed me. Such a figure he was, blocking the horizon. Hope, which had allowed him to survive slavery, reasserted herself. When Douglass smiled, I felt there was no finer pleasure. I stretched myself to be my most charming, most witty self.

Sometimes we sat in deck chairs, side by side, saying nothing. Yet, how companionable we were! Douglass watched gulls swoop to fish, then rise high into the sky blending with thick, swirling clouds and sunlight. I preferred the sea: the foam, the crests of waves, the changeable currents. Such mysteries in the deep. Mysteries in my own heart.

One dawn, after a restless night, I wrapped myself snugly in my shawl and stood at the rail, staring into the water. Slivers of silver darted just beneath the waves.

A woman's body rose and fell with the waves. Oluwand? But I thought it could be Mama, too. Reborn as a mermaid, celebrating her daughter's love.

Shivering in dawn's chill air, I was the happiest I'd ever been.

ℵ

I'd tried to keep away from Douglass. Particularly, once his daughter was born. I'd left New Bedford and found an apartment in Hoboken. "The best of Germany away from Germany," or so I was told. I'd rather have lived in New York, but it was too expensive.

I secured an agent and painted. Wrote articles for *Morgenblatt.* And spent my evenings debating with German radicals. It was pleasant. But time and again, my heart betrayed me. I felt compelled to return to New Bedford. Or else travel to conventions, abolitionists' meetings, wherever Douglass would be speaking. And I felt compelled to paint his face. Huge canvases with his riot of shoulder-length hair, his bushy brows, and amber-colored lips. His gaze was never quite right. Too piercing. Too dull. Flat, not alive with intelligence enough. I tried to imagine his eyes alive with love. *Had I seen him look at anyone with love?* I tried hard to paint him looking at me.

The Greeks believed the moon exerts a pull on the waves, altering the tides. So, too, Douglass' pull over me. Black and brown had always been sparse on my palette. But in my apartment, before the bay window, I mixed new oils—darkened shades to capture his warmth.

Douglass was the Greek slave the Romans would've ennobled.

In my stateroom, we discussed nearly everything. While the ocean swept by, outside my porthole, we spoke of the injustice of the Fugitive Slave Act. We spoke of Goethe, Shakespeare (I promised to take him to his first play), and the U.S. constitutional amendment that counted a slave as three-fifths a man. Often, Douglass became morose. It was my job to rally him.

"I should've stayed in New Bedford."

"And be caught? Think of the cause."

"While Anna bears the burden?"

"Gladly, I would think."

Douglass stared into his port. "Colored women have always carried a large burden."

"Being free, Anna's load is lighter than yours."

"Are you betraying your fair sex?"

"No. But an honorable life is lived by principles. You, yourself, have said this."

"'All men are created equal.' So fighting for freedom means that I abandon Anna? My child?"

"But all men aren't equal. All men should be free, yes. But few are equal to you, Douglass."

"You are my defender?"

"Always."

"At what cost?"

I lowered my eyes. "When did anything worthwhile not require sacrifice?"

How prophetic! I should've climbed over the ship's rail. Traveling with another woman's husband. Feeling not the least guilty. I should've remembered some penance would have to be paid. When had anything worthwhile not come at a price?

I was drowning in his company. Both readers and thinkers, I thought us fast friends. Two people joined in a common cause. Isolated for three months, on a ship, in the middle of the sea, we were both foreign—outside ourselves, our cultures.

Two weeks before docking in Portsmouth, I invited Douglass to dinner. We'd had a fine evening despite the lack of fresh food. We enjoyed our dried beef and potatoes as though it were pheasant with mushroom and wine sauce.

"How did you choose the name Douglass?"

He laughed. "An accident, really. I thought to use the name Johnson. But, in New Bedford, everybody colored seemed to be named Johnson. A friend was reading Scott's *Lady of the Lake*. A character was named Douglass. Seemed as good a name as any. Better than most."

"Why not Graeme? He was the lover?"

"But Douglass was the statesman. Graeme languished in prison."

"But he weds the lady in the end."

"Still, I'd rather be the noble Douglass."

"The brave, strong leader."

"Of course."

For dessert, we shared crackers, cheese, and port. Though I must admit, we drank far more than we ate.

"I admired your 'Parody' at the end of the *Narrative*." Castaway, I stood and recited:

*"Come, saints and sinners, hear me tell
How pious priests whip Jack and Nell
And women buy and children sell
And preach all sinners down to hell."*

"I'm flattered. You memorized it."

"How could a just God allow your enslavement?"

"If Anna was here, she'd say—"

"What?"

He looked down, swirled his port. "She'd say, 'God works miracles in His own time.'"

"Do you believe in miracles?"

"Of my own making."

"You don't believe in God?"

"I didn't say that. I just don't believe in slaveholding gods."

"If anything, I think love will be my salvation."

"Ah, like the good shepherd." Douglass laughed. "'Come live with me and—'"

"'—be my love.'" I laughed with him. "You, too, admire the good shepherd's wooing?"

"Indeed." It was Douglass' turn to stand:

*"Come live with me and be my love
And we will all the pleasures prove. . . ."*

"Exactly." I giggled. He was flirting with me. I wanted to shout, celebrate. Douglass was flirting with me.

He relaxed into his chair.

Jean Baptiste had taught me how passion could darken a man's eyes, make his eyelids heavy, half-closed. Douglass seemed to uncover me, render me bare.

The ship's bells sounded midnight.

"I should leave." Douglass stood, bowed formally. "Good night, Miss Assing."

Miss Assing. I stretched out my hand. "Please. Ottilie. I call you Douglass. By all rights, you should call me Ottilie."

"It's not the same."

"What do you mean?"

"It's not the same, Miss Assing," he said, fiercely. "You know that it is so."

"No. I do not know it is so."

His smile was a mockery. "I have no leave to forbid a white woman what she may or may not do." He tilted his head. "Good night, Miss Assing."

I felt shaken. Weren't we friends? Companions? Tonight, I thought I saw that we—I—meant something more.

Did he think it wrong of me to call him Douglass rather than Mr. or Herr Douglass? Why didn't he say so? Or was he complying with society's notions that a white woman could call him what she liked? Yet he, a colored man, must stick to proprieties. Were we not beyond that? Was he patronizing me? Or was he trying to make me feel guilty?

True, for nearly a year, I'd called him Douglass and never once, until tonight, offered my common name. But it wasn't quite the same. I didn't call him Frederick. Always Douglass. Like I called Garrison, Garrison. No difference. I treated both men the same.

I felt frustrated, restless. Nonetheless, I prepared for bed. I didn't trust my expressions or actions to the common ship. Indeed, part of me wanted to climb to the crow's nest and scream.

Enough people whispered about me already. Like a good girl, I lay in bed. It was small, uncomfortable, save for the rocking of the ship.

I heard Douglass in the next cabin. Many nights he stayed up late. Many nights I heard him pacing. Many nights I timed my breaths to his stride—back and forth, back and forth. His stride and the rocking sweep of the ship lulled me. But tonight I imagined him pacing and not thinking great thoughts, but pacing with annoyance.

I who had tried to do right was in the wrong. I had *not* thought matters through.

Had nothing he'd done or said been authentic to him and me? How sad. When all my thoughts and actions toward him were as natural as breathing.

I pressed my fist tight against my mouth and cried.

I must've fallen asleep. For I dreamed Oluwand and Anna were in my room. Both were standing by my bed, staring down at me.

"Go away, ghosts," I murmured, fearful they would pounce. But neither woman moved.

Moonlight glinted through the porthole. I focused on the light, hopeful it was a beacon.

*D*ouglass. Herr Douglass, I must speak with you."

All morning, I'd lain in wait for him. Waited until I heard him open his cabin door, then I quickly opened mine, confronting him before he moved on deck.

"Please, I must speak with you."

He stepped back into his cabin and bowed me inside.

His cabin was not as large as mine but the furnishings were similar. What was dissimilar was the smell of him—some sweet spice he used in his shaving lather or pomade. His desk was cluttered with papers. His script was sloping, elegant. Perfect penmanship. All the more amazing for a self-taught slave. I stopped, appalled by my thoughts. How patronizing. No wonder Herr Douglass didn't trust me.

Trust—that was it. A white woman need only cry out to have a colored man hanged. Why should he have such trust? I hadn't earned it.

He watched me. Not saying anything.

"Accept my apologies, Herr Douglass. I didn't mean to condescend."

"No apology needed, Miss Assing."

"Please. Ottilie. In the truest sense, I wish to be your friend."

"I'm not sure that's possible."

"In America, perhaps not. But we're on a ship, between two continents, in a space that no country rules. No law abides other than Nature's. Surely, here, we can be friends. Human to human. Man to woman."

"Not colored? Or white?"

"What does it matter? We share human nature."

"When you look at me, don't you see my color?"

We were inches apart and I thought: *He has offered me a test.* Answer rightly, and we may be friends. Answer wrongly, and a wall will rise between us.

I turned his hand over and back. I cradled his palm. "I see color. As much as I see colors in the sky, the sea, in the plumage of birds. Your hand, light tan on one side and burnished copper on the other. As an artist, a painter, how could I fail to see beauty in these colors? I can't lie and call myself blind."

His eyes clouded. His hand closed in a fist about mine.

"I think," he spoke slowly, "the world should be color-blind. Not see brown, black, tan, or white. Actions comprise character. Character is how each man should be judged."

I'd failed the test. But I was furious. "Judge, yes. By actions, deeds. Judge as you wish. But thoughts and heart matter, too. You mustn't be blind to these. In the world, there is the physical. Shape, color, and form. When you look, do you not *see* me?" My sharp tone had become a gentle pleading.

"Yes."

"What do you see?"

"White skin, smooth as porcelain. Red lips. Brows of gold."

"Then close your eyes. Touch me like a blind man." I pressed his fingertips to my lips. I felt his trembling. Felt the tips of his fingers caress my brow, my cheek. Touch my hair. "Do you really want to be blind to how I look?"

"You're too smart for me, Miss Assing."

"Now it is you who condescends to me."

"I must ask you to leave."

"Your color is what makes you beautiful to me. I *will* see. I'll not give that up."

He pulled away, bent, his palms flat on his desk. His chin resting on his chest.

Douglass desired me. I must make him admit it. I bent over him, my cheek against his back. My arms about his waist. "I am not nor will I ever be a Southern Mistress. I will not be an angel turned into a devil like your old Mistress. I will be, if you'll allow it, someone more." Whispering, my breath caressed his ear. "I'm a German woman—half Jew, half Christian. I, too, have been an outcast."

He spun around; I stumbled back.

"Your parents chose. My mother was raped by my father. A father who owned me as he owned his horses, his house, and fields. Half black, half white, I am still the nigger. Had I but one drop of my mother's blood, I would still be a slave."

"My parents chose. But I didn't."

"You can hide." He gripped my wrist. I cried out. He was standing over me, my arm bent awkwardly. His tone, low. "Behind that pretty white skin, you can hide. Behind nationality, you can hide. You can be German with no coloring to indicate your Jewishness. I'm not even entitled to be called an American. I'm a thing. A piece of property, Miss Assing."

He could break my arm with no more care than he'd give a stick of wood. I was terrified. But if I screamed, everything would change.

I told myself: it is Douglass' pain that gives him his persuasive power. It's his rage that makes him the greatest abolitionist of all time.

"You're a man." I spoke softly. "A beautiful man. I'll not allow myself to be blinded to your beauty both inside and out."

He let me go. He stared beyond me at private demons.

I smoothed my dress. Swayed with the rocking ship. Without thinking, I stroked his hair, soft waves of indigo. He inhaled sharply.

"You should go, Miss Assing."

"Ottilie."

He gripped my hand, stopping my caress. "You should go."

Midnight, another restless night. Another new day. Ocean and horizon stretching endlessly. All day, I possessed a secret joy. Though he was loath to admit it, Douglass desired me. Why shouldn't he? Emotions can't be chained. I remembered Mother saying, "Paint emotion, Ottilie. And the world will be at your feet."

All day, in the cabin, I painted (my room was rank with fumes, but I didn't care). I was painting my desire. My need of him. There were no shapes in my art, only color. A riot of warm blacks and browns. Dramatic. Engaged. Passionate.

Sweating, light-headed, I fell back across my bed. The swelling waves made the colors move. And in my mind, each brush stroke, each splash of paint shimmered and took new form. But it was always Douglass. Douglass speaking. Reading. Thinking. Desiring me.

Amour—love—was the essence of freedom.

He desired me. I held on to this talisman. Imagined no one else was on board ship except for me and the lion in the cabin next door. I heard him pacing, quick strides in a confined room. I imagined his hair lifting ever so slightly, haloing his head like a mane. I smelled him— oak and cinnamon. I saw him. His shadow captured by unsteady candle- light; his white shirt unbuttoned against the musty heat. Brown fingers held a gray quill; he stopped, dipped it into ink and scratched marks across a thick, ivory page. Brown table, brown-paneled walls, brown man; behind him, a wood bed dressed in white linens. I waited and waited until I heard nothing more. No movement. Stillness. Quiet as a dormouse.

I hoped he hadn't locked his door. If the door was unlocked, surely it meant something. Meant something had passed between us.

I unbraided my hair, threw on my robe with its silk ribbons and lace. I was amazed by myself. Yet like the moon pulling waves, this man pulled me toward him.

The wind on deck nearly knocked me over. In the darkness, I felt for his door's handle. I turned; the cold metal gave way. I darted inside—a ghost blowing in from the sea. I closed the door and held my breath. Moonlight guided me to Douglass sleeping, his arms thrown back over his head. I looked down upon him, wondering what he dreamed.

I meant only to have a look at him. He wore no night rail and though the white sheet covered his waist and below, I could tell by how the cotton molded against him, he was bare entirely. I needed him. Wanted my flesh to cover his. White skin for white cotton.

I untied my robe. Lifted my night rail above my head. He'd left his door open. How could I have not offered myself to him? Made him believe he could love me without fear.

I bent over him. My breasts hardened as they brushed against his

chest. I pressed my lips against his. His eyes opened. He saw me—
Ottilie. As real as I'd ever been.

I stroked his manhood and felt it rise within my hand. Heat filled
me. I lay beside him, one leg across his thigh, my chest atop his, my
face buried in his throat. My breath and body had their own rhythm. I
wanted him to hold me, press himself close inside me.

His fingers combed my hair. "Spun gold. Like Rapunzel's."

I kissed him and this time, he kissed back.

He cupped my face. I pulled back. Just a little.

Even in dim moonlight, I knew my skin, my blue eyes were clear.
Douglass knew well enough whom he was choosing.

His hands stroked my breasts. Then, his tongue reached up to flick
my pink tip. I moaned. Douglass watched me. Just for a moment. Judging my passion. His mouth reached for my breast and I pushed my flesh
inside his wet mouth. Still, he watched me. I couldn't help squirming
against him, feeling desire, feeling his body was a new reality for me. I
straddled him. Guided his brown shaft into my whiteness. I whimpered.
Frederick tried to lift me away. "Please." I stroked where our bodies
met, his black hair, coarse against my blond curls. I rocked against him,
feeling his manhood stiffen again inside me. "You are my first and only
love."

He sighed and closed his eyes. An invisible barrier fell away. His
hands reached for my buttocks and I arched against him.

His darkness was intoxicating. My hair fell forward, curtaining us. I
touched a nipple to his lips. He sucked and as he did, I rocked against
him.

"Be blind," I murmured. "Deaf, too, if need be. Be blind and love
me."

$\mathcal{H}$ow hard it was to sneak back to my cabin. I wanted to stroll the deck, shouting my love to the stars. Douglass' soul, flesh, and seed had entered me.

Giddy, I embraced myself. I didn't wash. I wanted to keep his lingering scent, his fluid on my thighs.

I curled in bed, marveling that I understood a new language. Understood the heaven when two bodies became one. Intimate, engaging, and engaged. The Romantics hadn't prepared me for this rough and marvelous passion.

My fingers pressed into the flesh between my thighs. A poor substitute for Douglass' body riding mine. He kissed me everywhere. My tongue licked the scars on his back. I wept for every lash he'd ever received, every hardship he endured. Then, he rode me. Deep, hard, until I exulted with pleasure. "I'm not a slave, Ottilie. No one's slave." His shaft moved slowly, maddeningly, in and out of me. "I'm no one's slave. Say it." I could barely see or speak. My hands clasped his back, trying to press him deep inside. "Say it." My stomach pressed his. Still, his body moved slowly in and out of me. "You're no one's slave," I whispered, desperate. "I'm the equal of any man." He plunged deep. "Beyond equal."

Sweet memory. Muscles contracted about my fingers. I exhaled with pleasure, feeling new dampness releasing from me. I knew I should sleep. But love had given me another gift—memories—and if I touched myself just so . . . if I imagined my dark lover stroking, caressing within me, my body would respond, shuddering, delighted. Yes, a poor substitute for Douglass. But greedy for loving, rocked and lulled by ocean waves, I touched myself again. Ah, just so.

❧

I woke to knocking. "Are you all right, Miss? It's past noon. Captain wanted to make sure you were all right."

"I'm fine. Tell your Captain I'm fine." I stretched like a cat. Blood-stains were on my gown; I folded it carefully and put it deep inside my trunk. Surely, Douglass understands my gift to him. He felt the barrier to my womb and broke through.

He loved me. Each caress told me so. I sponged my body. The memory of him aroused me.

Sail on, great ship! The European community will welcome us. British royalty bespeaks a mingling of bloods—French, German, Span-ish. Why not American? Why not Douglass and me?

I saw him. My heart quickened. I smoothed the blanket over my legs. On deck, the wind was biting. Spray lifted over the rail as the sun set, blood-red, in the wide sea.

Douglass sat in the chaise beside me. Like mine, his torso was inclined. If our chaises were closer, we could lie, propped as if by bed pillows. Shoulders touching shoulders. Arms touching arms. Hands entwined.

I'm embarrassed by my wanton thoughts. "Guten Abend."

"Good evening."

The wind snatched his words away from me, drowning them in the sea.

"Douglass." I leaned forward. "I miss you."

He nodded. "Miss Assing—"

"Ottilie."

"Miss Assing. I'm aware of the great honor you've done me."

"This is about love, not honor."

"Please."

Two sailors passed by and I hushed. My fingers were balled tight beneath my blanket.

"You cannot disregard what happened between us."

"Miss Assing, I can do as I please. Isn't that what you've been telling me? If I'm free, particularly on this blue, watery expanse without apparent boundaries, then I may choose. Choose to do as *I* please."

"I don't please you?"

Eyes cloaked, he leaned back. Long, taut legs stretched before him. His chin touched his chest. Such calm reserve belied the passion he showed last night. Or was it morning? Yesterday? The day before?

Time stretched like the sea as though I'd always been on this ship. Always and forever. Rocking, sailing with no clear boundaries, no clear notion about how to be the woman I dreamed of being. Mama dead. Oluwand slipping effortlessly into the sea.

I admit: my dream of being loved was bigger than my dream of America. This dream was the one hidden inside me, catching me off guard. Douglass was not like Papa.

"Is it true your wife cannot read?"

Douglass stiffened.

"Is she interested in anything other than domestic arts—cooking, cleaning, canning? Tell me, Douglass, is this the woman you dreamed of sharing your life? A peasant, is she not? Not well-bred at all."

"Whereas you?"

"Very well-bred. The daughter of a physician and a teacher. I paint. I read. I write. Speak many languages. Read Greek. I understand the world of ideas."

"You understand nothing."

He got up and left me. I made myself small. Cried tears into the blanket. And if any passengers or crew saw me, I didn't care.

For several days, I painted. All of it bad. I supposed he wrote. Successfully? I didn't know. But we both grew tired of our own company and as though he'd never touched me in my most intimate places, I coolly invited him to dinner. "To talk of ideas," I said.

We talked. He wanted to revise his *Narrative*. I offered to translate his first effort, to write articles for *Morgenblatt*. Germans will be very interested in you. The British too. Maybe I'll be more successful at journalism than at painting."

He laughed. "Will you show me your paintings?"

"No. I can't get the colors right in this dark hole."

"Will you paint Rosetta?"

I remembered her only as a bundle in her mother's arms. "Of course," I said, refilling his port. "Do you miss them?"

"Yes," he replied, then moved on to Jefferson's hypocrisy. "Jefferson was too selfish to free his slaves. George Washington too."

"John Adams was truer to his principles."

As we talked, I felt communion with Douglass. "This will be enough," I thought. "Ideas are enough. I'll be content."

Then, both of us quieted. We sat, drinking port. I once got up to add new oil to the hurricane lamp. Resting in the chair, I let my head fall back, feeling the lull of the ocean, the quiet happiness of having Douglass again in a room with me. He rose and I watched him come toward me. He touched my arm.

I clasped the chair's arms. I didn't want to touch him. If I did, I wouldn't be able to let him go.

"You still see me as mulatto."

"Your color pleases me."

"I want a woman who only sees me as I am. Beyond color to character."

"What does Anna see?"

He turned away.

"Douglass, please. Aren't you asking the impossible? Doesn't your wife see your black skin?"

"Don't speak of Anna."

"Why? Are we both invisible to you?"

He was angry again. His fist pounded into his palm. "I'm the equal of any man."

"Superior." I wanted to touch him. Could I seduce him with passion? Probably. But if Douglass was to be won, it would be with the mind.

"Douglass, a free man is free to choose his desires. But you're not free to choose how I see you. My desires are my own."

He poured more wine.

"I think I loved you from the beginning. Desired you."

"I've been taught not to want you."

"Why shouldn't you? I'm no white American."

"In my mind, I'm free. Free to do as I please."

"In your heart, too."

"There's Anna."

"Only you can answer, 'who is my wife?' In a free world, acting like a free man, I believe you'd choose me."

His fingers traced the lace at my bodice. "We should live in a world that is color-blind."

"We're beautiful together."

"Ottilie?" Barely a whisper. His hands slid up my skirt, stroking my hips. His lips pressed against my neck. "I claim you because I allow myself to claim you."

"I'm the wife of your spirit." I kissed his brows, his rough skin where his beard begins. His soft lips.

He took my hand, guiding me to the bed, his hands undoing my buttons. "I'm the equal of any man."

"More so."

Flesh straining toward flesh, I gave myself up to his passion. I reveled in my own. I rode him. His member inside me, I rocked and moaned. I was riding to a new country. I wanted to cry out. Instead, I bit at his chest, his lips, and tasted the blood in his mouth. He turned me over, my face and breasts pushed deep into the pillow. He entered me. Over and over. I was satiated by his glory. But still he rode, his thighs rubbing against mine. His abdomen against my buttocks. I turned my head and saw us in my dresser mirror, his copper skin stretched high above my bright, white skin.

He lay flat upon me. Moving, thrusting. His black hair mingling with my blond tresses. Heat washed over me again. The two of us—such color, form, and symmetry. How I wished I could paint us lying together. Exhibit it for the world to see. His face buried in my skin; my eyes, wide, dilated, swimming in joyous tears.

"What's the matter?" Douglass asked, pulling out of me.

We were face-to-face. Our bodies slick, sticky. I clasped his manhood. "Have you bruised me, Douglass? Have you left bruises?" I felt his member elongating, growing harder. "Love me. Love me hard. Leave bruises."

I thought he would tear me apart and swallow me but I gave him good measure. Matched his fire with my own. Oh, how he rode me. And when he tired, I did the riding. We loved until dawn. We made a new world of dreams.

I was who I was. Half Jew. Half Christian. Loving both the blackness and whiteness in this man. Can Anna do that?

Anna

"Anna, I trust you will find someone to read my words."
—FREDERICK DOUGLASS,
1841

"I did what needed to be done. I depended
upon me. Why that be so terrible?"
—ANNA DOUGLASS,
A YEAR BEFORE DYING, 1881

I forgot to tell him about the bones. Forgot to tell Freddy that the bones would keep him safe as he crossed the water.

My trip north had brought me some joy, but much pain. But I never forgot those bones that sang to me as a child. Freddy say, "You don't understand. You've never been a slave." Don't I have a heart? Living on the seacoast, I saw bones get washed ashore. Slaves killed, pushed, shoved, dropped overboard. "Been going on for a hundred years," Mam taught me.

Well, I lived. Even in those hard times. Even though in a long time, I hadn't heard the bones sing, I believed they wanted *me* to sing. Wanted me to take as much joy as I could from this cold, sometimes heartless world.

I took Miss Assing's money. But I couldn't take the portrait she'd left—a small cameo with black ribbon and a picture of Freddy's face. She must've painted it and worn it around her neck, beneath her shift, warm against her bosom. I tossed her gift into the fire. I didn't need paint to see Freddy's face.

Early morning, I wrapped Rosetta well and went to the harbor. Not too close to Freddy's ship. But I stayed on a rough hill, waiting, watching 'til his ship sailed.

When it was gone, I thought I should be gone. I never liked New Bedford. Neither white folks nor colored folks treated me natural. I'd go where no one knew I be Miz Frederick Douglass. I'd go where I could find honest work. Where I could raise my children in peace. Who knows when Freddy be home?

I sat and cried. I overstayed too long, for both me and Rosetta got chilled. My fingers and feet be numb when I get home. Rosetta's nose be bright pink. I should've known better. I wasn't "Lil' Bit." I was a woman grown. A mother like Mam.

I fixed tea and grits and took both the food and Rosetta into bed with me. "This be our party," I say. "Farewell party." Rosetta gurgled at my nonsense. I wiggled her toes, sang songs. I whispered about Baby Jesus and spirits in the sea. The wind be howling outside my window. The storm done come fierce and without mercy.

Garrison could write Freddy a letter. Tell him where I be. Where me, Rosetta, and baby growing inside me be.

We be building a new home until Freddy comes home.

Lynn, Massachusetts

*M*oving day everybody be my friend. Nobody wanted me to move. But I was tired of living in somebody else's house. I'd make my own home. Make my own friends too.

Garrison let me keep the horse and cart. I was grateful and told him so.

It didn't take long to get to Lynn. I picked it because it had a woman's name—Lynn. It was another small town with plenty of hard-working colored folk. They made shoes. Drying and curing skin into leather all day. But the women I met were as friendly as pie. Soon as I arrived with my baby in a basket, my belly puffed up, women came out eager to help. Fluttering around me. Cradling Rosetta. Tethering my horse. Didn't care who I was. Just cared that I needed a hand.

A woman with a mole on the side of her nose, shouted, "Girl, you going to need me. I'm the midwife." She shook my hand, helped me down from the wagon. "I'm Miz Beasely. Just that. Miz Beasley."

"I'm Anna. This be Rosetta."

Miz Beasely squinted at me but said nothing about a husband. Her finger touched my wedding ring. Looking me in my eye, she said, "I know a sweet little house you can rent. A doll's house."

I gave her a big smile.

The house be small all right. Maybe too small for Freddy. But the gray cottage suited me and Rosetta just fine. It wasn't grand. Just simple. It had a kitchen, a parlor, and two bedrooms. Space for a garden and all within spitting distance of the sea. I baked Miz Beasley a "thank-you" pie. Cherry with as much sugar as I dared.

The very next day, I sent a Penny-man to Mam. Told her I loved her. Told her she was soon to be a grandmother, twice over. I had one girl and be hoping for a boy. I watched the tin salesman go, hoping he be honest. Hoping he'd pass the message, like a bird, to another Penny-man headed further south. My words might tumble for several mouths before a Penny-man finally spoke them to Mam. But I'd be patient. It'd been nearly three years since I'd spoken to Mam, but I felt it in my bones that she be alive.

Freddy be alive, too. But I couldn't send a Penny-man to him, so I sent my love by wishing on the stars. "Be safe." "Come home soon." "Rosetta and I miss you."

Day and night, I thought of Freddy. I thought of him holding me, touching me. Sometimes my mind conjured him so real, I shivered, remembering him loving me.

Not a day went by when I didn't think of him. Not a day went by I didn't think of her. White women always had more freedom than a colored gal.

When I prayed on the North Star, I told Freddy what thoughts be falling out of my mind. How Miz Greene tried to cheat me; how I'd planted my garden with tomatoes, lettuce, and snap beans; how I bought two chickens; how Rosetta crawled faster than a bug; how the new baby (I didn't get to tell him about) be growing bigger each day. How I be making a home for us. How I scraped enough money to buy a desk for him, a table to eat. Right now, me and Rosetta be sleeping on quilts. But I be saving for a bed big enough to hold me and my husband twice over. I blushed. I thought the North Star be winking back at me.

I knew Freddy, wherever he be, be seeing the same stars as me.

Days turned to weeks, to months. I began to doubt. Happiness be hard when nobody be beside you to say "good night" when shadows fall or "good morning" when the sun rise.

Laying on my pile of quilts, feeling the wet summer breezes, I thought as much as I loved him, I was not, in Freddy's mind, the woman for him.

By fall, I thought, if Freddy truly loved me, he would've taken me with him. True, a sea trip would've been hard. True, the new baby made my stomach weak. But I would've done it. I did it before.

Come winter, ice crusting over everything, I wondered: why Freddy not think of Canada? Still north. But not so far. If Canada be good enough for Miz Tubman and the Underground Railroad, why ain't it good enough for him?

Would Miz Assing have gone to Canada? Naw, I answer. Miz Assing knew I surely would've followed.

Mercy. I started to cry. I mustn't think of her. Mustn't doubt what be in my heart.

I promised to love, honor, and obey. I would. He vowed to love and honor me. So he would.

Love be true.

In the meantime, I took in laundry. I did a good job. Earned good money. I took Rosetta everywhere. Folks gave me an extra penny because of her. Rosetta liked playing in the soap when I did laundry. She be the cleanest, sweetest baby.

Our home be our small kingdom. I left it only for work. Or church.

I learned new hymns. Songs that sweeped my spirit into the sky. Preacher wasn't Holy Roller. He talked plain, good sense. Didn't have as much book-learning as Freddy. But he knew one book well enough.

Local abolitionists asked me to speak. Garrison must've told them who and where I be. I said, "No speeches. Raising my babies be enough." I didn't know if they ever saw such a determined black woman as me. But I wasn't going to change my mind. I was afraid, too, if my friends found out who my husband be, everything good in Lynn would change. Like the Bedford folks, people might start thinking: "Why'd he marry her?" "How'd this fat, dark woman get picked?" "What she got to offer famous Mister Douglass, the runaway, ex-slave man?"

Always, I kept praying for Freddy's safety. For my own. For Rosetta's. For the baby's-to-be.

• • •

One spring Sabbath, I be kneading bread when the Penny-man comes. I had to buy a quarter pound of tea before he'd speak my message! Such a cheat! All the while, I excited, jumping up and down like a child. Penny-man cleared his throat: "Dear Anna, I was sick for a while but each day I grow stronger. I be happy you married. Kiss the baby for me. Kiss the new one when he come due. Mam."

"That all?"

Penny-man tipped his hat. "Want to send a message back?"

"I don't have money to spare," I shouted, angry 'cause I'd bought too much tea. I rubbed my belly, feeling guilty and sad Mam had been ill. Was it her heart? Her head?

Penny-man climbed onto his wagon.

"Come back next time," I hollered. "Try me next time." But what could I ever say to change the fact of my leaving . . . change Mam's sickness, change the fact that I was thousands of miles away? Unlikely to see her before she died.

I crossed my hands over my face. I didn't want Rosetta to see me cry.

Next time, I wouldn't let Penny-man force me to buy tea. Next time, I'd save money to send to Mam. A whole dollar. Wherever Freddy be, he didn't need my money. No message had come. No Penny-man. No money wrapped in oil paper. No marks upon a page. I thought he didn't need me.

❧

My•baby was coming. Miz Beasely rubbed my belly with chamomile. She pressed hard against my aching back. Rosetta, while I labored, stayed with the Pastor's wife.

"Can I send for the father?" Miz Beasley asked.

I laughed. Then, gasped at my pain.

"A man's needed."

"He can't help birth."

"Naw. But you're gonna need looking after. Two babies plus taking in laundry be hard."

"I'll survive." I shut up as pains started rocking me off the bed.

"Sweet Jesus," I murmured. "This be worse than Rosetta." I couldn't help thinking I did something wrong to have so much pain.

Pain visited me for three days, two nights. It stole my breath and ran like fire along my spine, across my belly, and down my legs. Sometimes I felt like rolling up and dying. But I didn't 'cause of Rosetta. She needed me.

Miz Beasley pushed on my stomach. Next, she pulled and pulled. Later, she put lard on her hands, saying, "It's got to be done, Anna. Bite hard on this."

I bit on a piece of rope. Still my screams escaped, sliding out the sides of my mouth. I must've fainted.

But, at first, I thought I died. I woke and the room was quiet and dark. No more waves of pain, no Miz Beasley, and my stomach be empty. *I be floating in a dark sea, floating, following after Freddy. I see his ship just out of reach. Bones rise up, two by two, singing, "Better day if you believe in Jesus."*

I did. I did believe. Freddy be Samson-man sent to pull down the pillars of my heart. Even in Heaven, in the sweet hereafter, way over yonder, I be loving Freddy. Telling him to love our children. Even the ones he didn't see. The ones he needed to see.

"Anna."

"Freddy?"

"Naw, Miz Beasely. You need some water, child?"

"Where's the baby?"

"Sleeping."

"Ain't dead?"

"Mercy, no. You had a rough trip, but the baby's born."

"Rosetta?"

"At Pastor's house. Just fine. She already been in to see you. I told her you be sleeping. She sleeps now, too."

I licked my lips, squeezed Miz Beasely's hand. "Thank you. Thank you so much."

"Hush. You did all the work."

She left for a minute, then came back carrying a bundle in a blue blanket. "He's hungry."

Oh, how handsome my son be. Thick curls like his Daddy. As perfect as a child can be.

The baby bit hard on my breast. I welcomed the pain for I knew both me and my baby be alive.

"What you going to name him?"

"Frederick Bailey Douglass, Junior."

"My word," gasped Miz Beasely.

"My word, too. This be his son." Then, I let myself cry—with relief, joy, sorrow, pain—all my feelings tender. Now everybody knew I was not just me. I was an abolitionist's wife.

I cried and cried while Freddy Junior took his Mam's milk mixed with salty tears. Miz Beasley went to fix me broth. I kissed my son's head. I wondered whether in this world he'd get to see his Papa.

Ottilie

"Freedom has the sweetest taste."

—Frederick Douglass,
in a letter to Julia Griffiths, 1846

"He was always free with me. Wasn't he?"

—Ottilie Assing,
diary entry, 1865

*E*ngland! We arrived triumphantly as lovers. Garrison's letters opened doors. Douglass' brilliance opened hearts.

The *Narrative* was extremely popular. People from all walks of life clamor for Douglass' autograph. Whether it's a coal miner, a duke, a don at Cambridge, or a sheep farmer, all seem enamored of an intelligent slave. Douglass' words, too, touch Englishmen's cold hearts and, without question, they can feel superior to their one-time colonists.

Douglass was generous and gracious to all.

He dressed like a gentleman now—silk cravats, perfectly tailored evening suits, leather boots, a walking stick, and tweed jacket. I gave him a gold watch and chain to wear inside his vest. I dared to place a lock of my hair in it, dared to have it engraved: *Ottilie to Douglass. With Love.*

Sometimes I caught Douglass standing before the cheval glass, fingering his pocket watch, admiring his new form. He was truly altered from the humble slave.

He visited the finest houses, currying favor with politicians, lords and ladies. During summer parties, it was nothing to serve champagne and lobster patties, dance the quadrille, and then listen to Douglass' fire and thunder. The newest rage.

Douglass performed an open letter to his Master. He spoke as if Auld were present, conjuring the spirit of this evil man, bringing slavery right into aristocratic homes.

His voice filling with pathos, Douglass struck a noble pose: "Why am I a slave?"

Voices hushed; china cups and saucers quieted; and the musicians laid down their violins and bows.

"When I saw the slave driver whip a slave-woman, cut the blood out of her neck, and heard her piteous cries, I went away into the corner of the fence, wept and pondered over the mystery. I had, through some medium, I know not what, got some idea that God, the creator of all mankind had made the blacks to serve the whites as slaves. How He could do this and be *good*, I could not tell.

"One night, sitting in the kitchen, I heard some of the old slaves talking of their parents having been stolen from Africa by white men, and were sold here as slaves. The whole mystery was solved at once. From that time, I resolved that I would someday run away."

"Hear, hear," guests would shout. Ladies applauded with soft gloves. Douglass fixed his eyes on a point just above his audience's heads.

"Mr. Auld, the morality of running away, escaping your cruel legacy, I dispose of as follows: I am myself; you are yourself; we are two distinct persons, equal persons. What you are, I am. You are a man and so am I. God created both, and made us separate beings. I am not nature-bound to you, or you to me. Nature does not make your existence depend upon me, or mine to depend upon yours. I cannot walk upon your legs, or you upon mine. I cannot breathe for you, or you for me; I must breathe for myself, and you for yourself. We are distinct persons, and are each equally provided with faculties necessary to our individual existence. In leaving you, I took nothing but what belonged to me, and in no way lessened your means of obtaining an *honest* living."

Then Douglass would bow, ready to answer questions. But there weren't any. Women were too moved to tears; men stretched out their arms to welcome him in brotherhood. Everyone was committed to ending America's slavery.

Lord Devers, one evening, even dressed as he suspected a slave owner dressed. Coarse cotton, thick boots, a straw hat. A corncob pipe. He pretended to be Auld while Douglass made his speech. He sneered and stomped (a twisted parody, I thought), and the aristocrats loved it. Douglass didn't find it offensive, so I kept quiet. Just as I kept quiet that Douglass' speech was a rewrite of the *Narrative*'s Chapter I. Except, he'd made himself more precocious. Without a doubt, Douglass was a rhetorician par excellence.

Each evening, flushed with his success, Douglass made love to me. I had no complaints. Except for Douglass' strict instructions that I couldn't touch him in public, or smile, or look at him too long, or give any indication of my affection. Nor could any of my paintings of him be exhibited.

To maintain appearances, we kept separate rooms at the Park Royale. Sometimes, on purpose, I refused to sleep in my bed. I curled up on the sofa, knowing, in the morning, the hotel maids would suspect I'd spent the night on the other side of the connecting door. I didn't do it often. Douglass would've been furious if he found out. Nonetheless, refusing to mess my sheets was my own small rebellion.

Garrison wrote that Auld wanted Douglass to return. He promised better keeping, a chance for Douglass to earn more money as a slave.

In the meantime, we're seen together in all the best places. Having ices at Gunter's. Visiting Lord Elgin's marbles, the British Museum, Piccadilly. Riding in Hyde Park. Douglass even had an audience with the Queen.

*E*venings when there weren't any speeches, Douglass and I went to the theater. Douglass was charmed by Shakespeare. The intricacies of *Henry IV*, Parts I and II, *Richard II*, and *Julius Caesar* spoke to him beyond measure. But he'd no patience for *Hamlet*.

"No man would be haunted by such indecision," he insisted.

Romances he disdained. *As You Like It* and *Romeo and Juliet* were useless to him. Even *Othello* gave little pause. "A weak man corrupted by emotions," said Douglass.

"What of Desdemona?"

"She should've held true to her own course. Othello was irrational. Not worthy."

"Romance defies logic."

"Why should it?"

"I thought you loved the Romantic poets."

"I do. But that's poetry, Ottilie. Not life."

Sometimes I wondered how much Douglass did feel. Of course, he was passionate about the antislavery cause but he relied, too, on clearheaded logic to argue his case. I told him he was wiser than Aristotle! But, late at night, when he came to me, his hands caressing my body, his lips brushing against mine, I wished, oh, how I wished, he'd speak sweet words.

• • •

I tried not to think of Anna. She was unworthy of him. She should've been the slave. Whereas Douglass was never meant for field work, for manual labor of any kind. It wasn't fair.

I trembled. For I had such coarse thoughts! Anyone enslaved was wrong.

I shouldn't think of Anna. Yet, I did think of her. My thoughts were spiteful beyond bearing. It's all jealousy.

How angry I'd become at the women—the silk-gowned women swarming to Douglass like bees to golden honey. How I wanted to pinch the arms of those fair-headed beauties. I was fair-headed, too, but at Lord Montcrief's salon, I overheard one of the women say, "But she's a Jew." The other replied, "A Black and a Jew—can you imagine?" How I wanted to destroy them both. Scratch their eyes out, screech at them.

Still, I was enormously happy. I was with Douglass constantly. But I wasn't his by law. Nor he, mine.

I wondered: Was Douglass' union legal? Could a slave marry? Or, once free, could he remarry?

How hard to keep my desires in check!

When Douglass loved me, I felt as though I could soar well beyond the moon and stars. But when he left me, I still felt breathless, hungry for him. Hungry for his presence, his touch, his body inside mine. I never wanted him to leave.

When he mounted me, my mind turned inward on those points of contact: sweat and blood. Dante's distant love of Beatrice didn't compare with a union of mind and body. I needed his loving as I needed to live. Without it, what would I have?

"Douglass, I don't want to leave," I once pleaded after he'd fulfilled himself.

"My reading will keep you awake."

"I'll read with you."

"I have writing to do."

"Let me help."

He patted my head as if I were a child. "You can't learn for me," he said. "Nor can you write of bondage you haven't lived."

"I'll be your secretary. We can work day, night, anytime you wish it. Don't make me go." I circled my arms tightly about his neck. I kissed his cheeks, his mouth. "You write the new book, I'll translate the old. It'll be good, Douglass. The whole world shall know of you."

He looked at me, his head tilted, like he was seeing me anew.

"You're a beautiful woman, Ottilie. A pleasure in all ways."

"Then let me stay." I kissed him. "Please."

We loved once again. And, for the first time, Frederick Douglass fell asleep, cradled in my arms. I felt as though I could keep the world at bay, and while he slept, I stroked the scars on his back. Stroked and wished them well away.

At dawn, when Douglass woke, he was irate. "I missed a night's work."

"You needed rest."

His back to me, tying his dressing gown, he spoke simply. "This will never happen again, Ottilie."

"What do you mean?"

He looked down upon me and I felt vulnerable, like he was the Master and I, the slave.

"You believe you have influence over me."

"No, Douglass. By no means. I only want to help as best I can."

"I think we should focus on the work, the writing, the cause. That should be enough for both of us."

"I don't understand."

"I won't have you criticizing my behavior—"

"I'm not."

"—you think I don't understand your ploy to tie me?" His hand slapped the bedpost. "You think if discovered in my bed, it'll prove to the world I'm your lover."

"Why can't we announce to the world you're mine?"

"Because I'm not yours."

He was breathing hard; his expression, implacable. I felt as though I'd been doused in cold waters.

"You've been seeing someone."

"I want you to leave."

"You're seeing someone else."

"Quiet."

"Of course, you never come to my room. Here, in the hotel, you humble me, making me come to you. While you go into aristocrats' bedrooms. I assume you've been with ladies, not whores."

"Quiet." He was on his knees, his face even with mine. "Quiet, Ottilie."

Fear flickered across his face. Did a white woman's screams have the same power in England as in America?

"Douglass, I'm sorry."

I reached for him. He stood, tightening his gown closer about his body. He walked to the sideboard and poured himself a glass of water.

"Leave."

"Please, don't make me."

"Leave."

I squatted on the bed, naked, crying. "I didn't mean what I said. I'm lonely. Jealous. I love you, Douglass. Anything you want. Anything I can do to help. Only please let me stay. Say you forgive me."

"I think we should focus on the work." He handed me my night rail and robe. "This is my room. I'd like you to leave."

❧

Like a truant child, I was punished. Sweet loving was forbidden to me.

I told myself he is free. Our love is free.

Every place we went, women stalked him. Women in French fashion, silk, and satin. Suffragettes in their plain, black garb. I kept my emotions in check. I was his secretary, his helpmate.

Side by side, at desks, our heads bowed, our fingers busily scribbling a pen across the page. Douglass revisited his *Narrative*. I translated. So be it. I'm his loyal worker.

I organized his schedule, deciding where he would and would not speak. As his fame grew, there were many demands on his time. So I protected him. Funny, if he wasn't here, I could give his speeches. I knew them by heart. I could dress as a man, black my skin. There'd be two Douglasses. Two slaves promoting abolition.

For surely, I was his slave—willing to be his friend despite the pain it caused. I cursed at parties, when he sat down to dinner with another woman. I was driven crazy when I couldn't hear their words. I imagined the women seducing him, telling him how wonderful he was. Married women and widows were the worst. Debutantes only sighed and fluttered like giddy hens. But those who'd known the marriage bed speculated about the pleasures of Douglass' warm body covering theirs. The aesthetic, the contrast of colors appealed.

Douglass had no counterpart in Britain. Englishmen spent hours gambling, deciding which cravat to wear, whether to hunt fox this weekend or the next. They'd no notion of the meaning of survival.

I, too, was tempted by Douglass' life force. But I'd not flirt. I'd show him my love was for all seasons. Steadfast and strong.

Still, I understood Papa's agony now. How terrible to have your love die. How terrible to have your love live and keep you at arm's length.

But one must follow the logic: men and women were free to love, free to give their hearts where they will. If I disallowed this, then I enslaved Douglass as much as Master Auld.

How I wished Mama was here. She would've understood. Held and comforted me.

Nights, in my lone bed, I touched myself. I'd become very good at imagining the pillow as my lover's head. My fingers became his. Sometimes I kissed the air, believing he's atop me, riding, loving me with passionate wonder.

Each time I was done, I was dissatisfied. I sat by the fire, drank cognac, and in the dance and play of firelight, I couldn't help thinking: Did Douglass *ever* love anyone? Did he take a slave girl to his bed? Or was he now (this minute!) rustling, playing among silk sheets? Miss Hayward touched his arm, fluttered her fan and, without words, continually offered herself to him. I drank more cognac, trying to blot these images from my mind.

I thought Frederick must've pursued Miss Hayward's offer. His body had the same needs as mine. Yet I couldn't imagine him rubbing himself like I did.

I'd bide my time. Patience was not my virtue. I drank and drank some more. My flesh grew thinner; my skin, more pale. No friends. No family. No ghost. Each night, I stumbled into dreamless sleep. If I was senseless, I didn't imagine Douglass, naked, beyond the connecting door.

Seasons changed. A small bird darted among the bushes outside my window. Ants favored the window ledge. Everywhere, along with London's grime and foul air, I inhaled the scent of blooming roses. Days became weeks became months. Seasons changed again and again.

I was running out of money. How mundane. Not romantic at all. I needed to find some employ. But my commitment to abolition must also remain pure.

I was still lonely. I only attended lectures. I was in the grip of an enchantment.

❧

Douglass was going out. He had a meeting with the publisher of the *London Daily Mail*. He dreamed of starting his own newspaper in America.

"Garrison won't approve."

"I'm my own man."

"You shouldn't antagonize him."

"You contradict yourself."

"Why? Because I think you should keep allies?"

"I make my own decisions. Those who are my friends will respect that."

"But it isn't smart."

"Why?" he demanded. "Because I don't agree with you?"

I held my tongue. He opened the door. I called out, "Will you be back for dinner?"

"I won't."

I spent the afternoon translating; when I became bored, I straightened Douglass' desk, which didn't reflect, in the least, the orderly quality of his mind.

There was a letter from Mr. Garrison. Three months it'd taken to arrive. My heart constricted. Perhaps Douglass' freedom had been purchased? Perhaps even now he was making plans to leave me?

I slipped the thin sheet out of the envelope.

Dear Douglass,

You're a father once again. A son. Douglass Junior. Your wife and child are doing well. They

*live in Lynn, Massachusetts. I tried to discourage
your wife but she proved persistent. Your
abolitionist work in England has not gone
unremarked. The Society is pleased with you.*

Yours Truly,

W. L. Garrison

The letter aroused such conflicting feelings. A child. Now two by Anna. And I didn't like the condescension of Garrison's tone. "Yours truly," indeed! The Society was pleased as though Douglass were a child. "Good boy, Douglass." "Job well done."

Then, I felt joy, for Douglass wouldn't be leaving. We'd need money. Perhaps I could convince him to travel to Germany. Switzerland. To anyplace where anyone might wish to hear him and pay for the privilege. Douglass was old news in England. But a European tour? A triumph. Douglass, too, away from London's pleasures, might have more time to write. And write . . . and write . . . and look to me again. Look to me for remembered pleasures.

I collapsed into the chair. My hand, of its own accord, stroked my abdomen. How lovely a child of mine and Douglass' would be—what a blending of race, nationality, and religion. Though Douglass believed in God, he practiced no faith. For me, Jewishness and Christianity didn't matter. Sometimes I was furious to think God could twist so freakishly my fate with Douglass'. But, of all the faiths, being Jewish aligned me closer to Douglass and his ill-fate as a slave. "Go down, Moses." So be it. I'd never lay our babe in the bushes. I'd raise our baby—blond hair? hazel eyes?—our outcast and special baby. Like Mary raised Christ.

For the first time in a long while, I felt a desire to take up my paints. If I envisioned a portrait of our son-to-be, maybe Douglass would be convinced to lay his hands upon me, to touch me with his ever fulsome grace?

I was ashamed. Weaving fairy tales. And yet . . . and yet . . . was it wrong to love as deeply as Mama? To want to be loved deeply in return?

Mama and Oluwand. One loved willingly; the other, unwillingly.

I was my mother's daughter. I'd renew Douglass' love.

He never mentioned the new baby. Never mentioned being a father twice over.

Did he ever write to Anna?

Suffering before enlightenment. Why shouldn't I fight for what I want?

I'd make Douglass love me as he's loved no other.

I'd pray to God as I'd never prayed before.

I began my campaign. In the hotel, I allowed my hair to hang wantonly about my shoulders. Except for bedtime, I left the connecting door open, so Douglass could glimpse me, smell the heady scent of roses on my dressing table. I always looked my smartest; I even took to carrying a fan like Miss Hayward.

I sometimes caught Douglass staring at me as I translated his words, wrote articles for the German papers. Muslins easily exposed my figure, the arc of my neck, the length of arm between elbow and fingertips. There were many lovely women. But I'd been, all the while, admiring; helpful, never forward. I was his companion of the mind. I was the one who managed the money, the bills . . . that added grace to our lives.

Days and some nights, we worked. Either his room or mine. He was revising his autobiography.

"I'll call it *My Bondage and My Freedom*. Less the tale of the runaway slave. More the tale of how my mind liberated me."

"Brilliant," I answered, biding my time.

And if I stroked Douglass' fingertips when I passed a sheet of paper, or bent over him, my hair tickling his cheek as he sat, reading the latest article in the morning's paper . . . or if I brushed my bosom against him when he helped me from the carriage, or smiled sweetly when he spoke . . . Who was to say this was wrong?

Some would say, "Such a fallen state love has brought her." But desiring union with a beloved could never be wrong. I'd be crafty. Smart.

 ℋ

Another summer, another fall, another winter. We got a letter from
Garrison: Auld won't sell.

"Damn him. I hate his blasted arrogance."

"All in good time, Douglass." I massaged his shoulders. "Live your
fullest. In England, Auld can't deny you that." I pressed my lips to his
hair. Douglass stiffened.

I murmured, "Good night."

At the connecting door, I paused. "Ireland, Douglass. Let's visit the
heather. See if we can't find shamrock green, the fairy people."

He laughed bitterly. "I'm visiting the Irish while fellow slaves are
suffering."

"Don't you think they hear of your travels? Don't you think they're
happy for you?"

"When you're a slave, Ottilie, survival is all that matters," he chastised.

One step back. Another forward.

He agreed to travel through Ireland. We were both overcome by the
heather, the craggy rocks, and endless dales. Sensual nature: lush greens,
moist fog, and endless streams. We rented a cottage and propriety be
damned, I hired only a cook and kitchen tweeny to help with chores.
Douglass and I lived alone like man and wife. We went for wild rides, shot
quail, and feasted on trout we'd caught. Evenings, we drank whiskey and
read before a roaring fire. Debated monetary policy, the English rule of
Ireland. Though he didn't touch me, we made love with our minds.

The way to Douglass' heart was through subtlety. He must freely
desire and love me.

He began writing poetry. I painted a miniature of a baby. Lighter
than any child could be from Anna's body. I knew he kept the portrait
on his desk.

I encouraged Douglass to take up the violin. Strings were the music
of the heart. And the instrument did seem to soothe and inspire him all
at once. He had a talent for it.

I taught him the waltz. In the cottage, he embraced me and twirled
me about the floor. His arms were reluctant to release me.

Small victories.

Douglass was a passionate man. But for all his control, I knew he thought of me. When I'd earned his bed again, I'd see to it that I never left it.

Garrison wrote again: *Auld will not sell.*

We returned to England. Douglass had been asked to debate two touring Southerners. The British wanted to see America's civil discord in the flesh.

"Douglass, it's a trap. What if they try to kidnap you?"

"Scotland Yard has assured me it won't happen."

"These men are beneath you. Not worth your time."

"It's my decision, not yours."

I was glad I didn't overrule him. Maybe it was hearing the Southern tongue or that the debate was two against one? But Douglass was inspired.

"Slavery is as injurious to me as it is to you." And step-by-step, he got the slaveholders to admit their laziness, their drunken moments, their boredom. Made them admit that slavery had blunted their life's purpose. Blunted their passion for self-advancement. It was like Douglass was converting them all to the Abolitionist Church. Even when one of the fellows, so furious, threatened to kill Douglass, the British gasped with certainty that it was slavery that had made him a would-be murderer.

For Douglass, it was a significant triumph. It infused him with new energy.

"Ottilie, I bested them. Reduced all their arguments to nonsense."

"Champagne. This calls for champagne."

Then, he kissed me. Maybe from sheer happiness, I don't know. But I took full advantage of that kiss. "I've missed you."

"I, you." Still clothed, we lay beside each other. He held me in his arms. We talked as candles burned low, the fire died down. And though we grew chilled, neither of us gave way from our embrace on the bed. The night grew blacker. I could hear the pounding of his heart. Feel the tension radiating from his body.

Then, I heard a sigh. Mournful and poignant. His voice rose like a whisper, a disembodied spirit. "I've been trying to decide how to live my life."

"Devoted to slavery's abolition."

"Of course. But beyond that. Am I always to be a black man, the runaway slave, living within and without the strictures of a corrupt society? Sometimes I think what a coward I am, hiding here abroad."

"Never."

"Even now Master Auld is determining my life."

"You're doing much good."

"Am I?"

"Champagne has made you morose."

"Have I stopped one slave from being beaten, raped, sold from his family?"

"Policies change."

"A war will come."

"It may be the only way."

"Yes." He stroked my hair. "How beautiful you are. These months I've wrestled with my passion. I kept from you because of all the lessons I've learned about white women and black men. Breaking that taboo, at first, thrilled me. But it was unfair to you. And the weight of it came to unnerve me. I could be killed twice over—as a runaway and as someone who loved you."

"Do you love me, Frederick?"

There. In the darkness. Hung my words. I heard his breathing. Felt his hand clutch my waist and pull me tightly, ever close to him.

"In my fashion, Ottilie. In my fashion."

We kissed, our hands roaming as though we both had to be reminded of so much—of the curves, lines, and shapes of each other's bodies.

"If love is to be real, it should be color-blind. Your whiteness should be as nothing to me. Only our spirits should matter."

"Yes, yes, I understand." I would've said anything to soothe him.

He stroked my face, as if, in the darkness, he could see me. Our mouths, breath to breath; our lips, almost touching. "If I take you now, it's because you mean more to me than taboos, laws forbidding our pleasure."

"Yes." my lips lingered on his throat.

"If my people are to be equal, we must ensure a color-blind society. The best sight is to be blind."

His arguments had come full circle. But I didn't care. Not seeing my color was the same as seeing it. I would've much preferred him to say, "I missed your body." But say what he would, Douglass had convinced himself to return to me.

I undid his cravat; for a time, he lay passive, yielding to me. Then, as he grew more and more aroused, he took me fiercely, thrusting inside me like a man searching for water in a desert.

"Take, Frederick," I murmured. "I'll give."

Simple as that.

*H*ome," he shouted. "I can go home. Ottilie, look."

He waved the letter before me like a flag. He was thrilled, almost giddy.

"Here. Friends have bought my freedom. Auld has consented to sell."

I read Garrison's loping scrawl and felt as though I'd been handed a sentence. Condemned to losing Douglass.

I smiled for him. He moved about the room, unable to keep still, his hands and mouth moving in concert. I heard not a word. Yet how could I say I loved Frederick if I couldn't be happy for him? Yet, I felt as though my life's blood was draining, as though a wicked witch had cast a spell over me.

Garrison's letter fell from my fingers. I stared at my desk, at my busy translations. Tears welled. Glimmering as if in a pool of water were Douglass' words:

> *"Oh, would that I was ever born to this*
> *misery! To be a slave."*

"Ottilie." He was moving, his arms grasping, reaching as if at stars. "All my life I've wanted to be free. Not just *act* free, but *be* it. Now the dream is real."

"This is some trick?"

"Never. Garrison would've made certain all was right."

"But your freedom papers aren't here."

He paused. Happiness drained from his eyes. "Garrison probably didn't want to entrust them to a sea voyage. America to here, anything could've happened. Yes, that's it." His voice grew more vibrant. "I'm certain that's it."

"Yes. That's it," I said, knowing I shouldn't steal his joy. But what of mine? "Promise you'll stay, my love." I didn't like the tenor of my voice. Too much like those women who have no education other than what a man allows or gives them. I was Ottilie Assing. How had I come to this?

Weeping, I laid my head on the desk, not caring whether I smeared ink script. Not caring for anything, except my own lost heart.

His hand touched my shoulder. I grasped his hand, kissed his palm. He gathered me up, carried, and laid me on the bed. "Frederick," I exhaled.

"Your loving made me feel I was already a free man."

He loved me then—more gently than ever before. He loved me thoroughly and well.

≫

Crossing the Atlantic again was like death. Douglass rarely came to my bed. He was a celebrity. The ship's captain invited him to dinner.

When I pressed, no, begged him, he answered, "Puritan stock. Americans lack European sophistication. They know me as a married man, Ottilie. Know me as a father to a son and daughter."

Douglass only came to me when his need was most great. He'd enter my cabin like a specter, say nothing, but, nonetheless, devour me. All but a handful of nights, I slept alone or, should I say, tried to sleep, tossing and turning in my flat, sailor's bed.

Anna

"He came home a free man. Maybe too free."

—ANNA DOUGLASS,
SPEAKING TO ROSETTA, 1881

"Mama, look. That white lady's so beautiful."

—ROSETTA DOUGLASS,
SPEAKING TO HER MOTHER, 1846

I knew Freddy was coming but I didn't know exactly when.

"Ships at sea don't keep good time," said Mr. Garrison. "Plus, he's got to travel to Lynn. Much farther than New Bedford."

Humpf. Mr. Garrison had his own pride. Thought everybody ought to do as he say!

Mam taught me only I can live my life. No matter what Mr. Garrison said, I liked living in Lynn. I liked my neighbors and church friends. They liked me because I be me. Nobody was beholden to Mr. Garrison. Thank goodness! Nobody was nice just because of abolition. 'Cause I was Freddy's wife.

Still, I should be charitable. Mr. Garrison worked hard for Freddy's freedom. For that, me and my children will always be grateful. I surprised "puffed-up" Garrison and kissed him on his cheek. "Thank you, thank you. For all you've done."

He turned fire-red and left me so fast I couldn't believe it. I laughed and laughed.

When Garrison left, I declared a holiday. I was tired of washing. My back ached, my fingers felt gnarled. I took my first holiday in over two years. I played with my babies all afternoon.

Rosetta just be four and Freddy Junior be walking, babbling nonsense, saying, "Waaaater." I taught both my babies about water and crabs. About bones littering the sea. About their Daddy, a strong Samson-man who was coming home a free man.

All afternoon, me and my children sang songs about crossing the River Jordan, about itty-bitty spiders climbing the water spout. I told tales about the bravery of "High John the Conqueror," about their Daddy being the first slave to write his own book.

Oh, it was a fine, warm time waiting for Freddy to come home. Nothing upset me. It was like a different season, a time out of mind. A time when life seemed all the more precious and trees glowed vibrant, the sky shimmered with rainbows, and clouds seemed like pillows to rest a weary head.

And if I worried some that Freddy would be angry at me, I kept it to myself.

If I worried Freddy would dislike the life I'd built, I kept that, too, to myself. I kept all kinds of frightening worries to myself, burying them deep in my heart. I'd gotten used to my life. I liked it. As much as I wanted Freddy to come home, I didn't want my life to change.

It was Sunday. We be playing, "Ain't That Good News." Each child be telling me about something good. Each be trying to find a newer, better, good thing. Rosetta shouted about "cotton ribbons," "dandelions," and "hearing the church choir sing." Freddy Junior hollered about "bugs," "squishy bugs," and screamed, "tall"—he mean growing tall like his Daddy.

My children surely lifted my spirits. And, strange, they needed lifting. This Sunday, for no reason, I woke feeling my bread dough wouldn't rise, my sheets wouldn't dry, and my food would sour. Strange. The day was balmy, yet overcast. Storm soon to set in, I thought. I quivered as I saw a flock of birds swoop over the yard, blocking rays of sun. Then, just as quickly, disappearing.

I heard the low rumbling of a cart. My hands shaded my eyes.

"Mam, look," Rosetta called.

A speck, at first, just coming over the horizon. But as the cart got closer, I could make out the shape of two men. Both wearing black hats like they going to prayer. My heart raced and I began to murmur, "Freddy." I step forward. "Freddy." I step again, then I was running with the children running after me. Freddy Junior, with his fat, wobbly legs. Rosetta, swift like a colt. All of us be shouting, "Freddy, Freddy, Freddy."

We stopped short—children jumping up and down, my breast heaving, fingers clasped together. "Dear Lord, let it be—"

The driver was Mister George, a colored hand who did odd jobs. The other man lifted his head. The shadow of his hat's brim cleared and I screamed, "Freddy!"

He leapt down and gathered me in his arms. The children clutched his coattails.

"Who's this? Who's this?" Freddy picked up Rosetta and swung her around. "My, you've grown." Rosetta giggled, covering her mouth with her hand.

Then, Freddy dropped down on his knees. He's got a fine suit on, real wool, and I almost told him to "stop, you'll get dirty," but I kept quiet. He be on his knees before Freddy Junior. This be the child he'd never seen. The child looked like him—all brave and strong and handsome. Just small. Looking like his Daddy might've looked when he was a child.

Freddy Junior be shy, but he didn't cling to my skirts. He held out his hand. "How do, sir?"

Freddy gasped and clutched his son to his chest. Freddy be crying. Then, he reached his hand out to Rosetta and hugged her, too. Freddy and the children, all in the dirt, holding on to each other for dear life.

I wiped my eyes. Blessed day. I whispered a prayer to the bones.

Freddy looked up at me and say, "You've done well, Anna. You've done well."

༄

My children did me, themselves proud. I'd done a good job. Feeding them, dressing them, loving them, making them strong.

All of us sat down to eat, talking before the fire like a family again. Happiest day of my life. If neighbors were curious, they'd the good sense not to show it. Nobody visited. Nobody asked about the stranger.

We had time alone. Time for Freddy to put both children to bed. To kiss them hundreds of times, catch them up and squeeze them, and swear he'd never go away. He'd leave their room, only to be called back, to kiss and hug some more. It, took quite a while before the children fell asleep with smiles and dreams of their Daddy made flesh.

Whole. No more stories. Their Daddy be real. He'd never be a ghost no more.

Freddy loved me before the fire. Kissed me until I felt I'd surely suffocate or drown. All the aches in my bones and joints eased. I gave myself with fierce pride because I'd been a woman strong.

Freddy weeped when he released himself inside me. He rested his head on my bosom and said, "Home. How I've missed my home."

And I believed home meant Lynn. This new town I'd found. Later, I thought Freddy meant my body. My body be home to him. That be all right.

I didn't know my body would become, for him, like an old bed. An old chair.

But, for that one night, laying on rugs before the fire, Freddy covered my body like new land—he explored, stroked, tasted, and smelled my sweat. Knowing the children were breathing in the next room, I inhaled their Daddy deep.

And I knew, once again, a baby be swimming inside me.

*G*arrison be furious. Freddy wouldn't back down.

"I want my own employment, Garrison. My own business." The two of them were arguing in the parlor, right off the kitchen.

"Have you no loyalty? No sense of fair play?"

"I can't be your man forever. Have I been freed just to be another kind of slave?"

"A united front, man. We must show a united front."

"We are united. In the cause of freedom. Freedom means I can do what *I* choose. Not what you choose."

"Damn you, Douglass."

"A colored man should be free to speak to his people."

"But you don't punish your supporters."

They argued worse than children. This storm wasn't going to roll away. There'd be lasting bitterness. What a shame.

Still, it'd be special for Freddy to publish his own paper. A paper about coloreds' and slaves' rights written by a colored. What a wondrous thing! Freddy may not be a preacher, but still he'd be doing good things. Spreading grace through his words.

I be plump again. Sometimes I just sat and smiled. I don't know why I didn't tell Freddy about the baby. Maybe only so much joy could be felt at once. Maybe I was saving up good news for when times were bad. I don't know.

Miz Beasley knew. She cared for me so special, I like to die. Always she brought me treats. Spun sugar. Carrot cake. A lotion for my swelling legs.

Miz Beasley said she came to see me, but I thought she really came to see Freddy. She liked seeing such a handsome, colored man doing so good. Other folks came, too, and Freddy was always polite, thanking the whole colored town for its care of me and his children. People asked him to sign his name in his book. He did. Everyone went away with a smile.

I thought Freddy be happy. Just like me. Our house be small and Freddy and his newspaper filled it, 'til it overflowed. The parlor be his main office—stack upon stack of letters, papers, books, and more books. Overflowing with words. The kitchen table be where he "edit." I wasn't clear what "edit" meant, but it seemed like writing to me. Only he crossed and recrossed hundreds of words.

Freddy fussed about me working. Since he didn't want my money, I set it aside for the children. I said, "When your paper's a success, I'll quit laundry."

"I have money, Anna. From speaking fees."

"What's harm in extra?"

Working be the only thing we argued about. I liked working. Being independent. When Freddy fussed, his eyes glaring, hands crossed behind his back, I fed him.

"In London, nothing like your stew and cobbler, Anna."

Feeding Freddy was the only thing that calmed both him and me. Whenever he be in a bad mood, whenever he be reading or writing, whenever silence reigned, too long between us, I fed him. Like me, Freddy grew plump. But no babe inside him.

I fed him apples and biscuits when he stayed up late and didn't come to bed. I felt lonely in the bed. But Freddy didn't want Rosetta or Freddy Junior to be curled up with me. "It isn't proper," he said. The children didn't understand.

I fed Freddy. Tried to sleep as best I could.

※

"We're leaving for Rochester, Anna."

"When?" I asked, excited. Me and the children ain't been nowhere. I thought this be a pleasure trip. Maybe, one day, we could visit Mam. This year we go north; next year, south to Baltimore.

"Everything needs to be packed by the end of the month."

"What you mean?"

"What I say, Anna. What don't you understand?"

I flushed. He looked at me like I was a stupid, ignorant, old woman. Freddy didn't do that much before he left for England. Now he did it all the time. I stood as tall as I was able.

"Why I need to take everything just for a trip?"

"It *is* a trip. To our new home."

He turned his back, arranging his papers like everything's been said.

I was struck dumb. I didn't move. After a while, Freddy looked up, surprised I was still there.

"Surely you see this house is too small, Anna."

"Yes. But Lynn's home now. These good folks helped me weather storms."

"I'm here. I'll help you weather your storms." He smiled. "Squalls in a teapot."

"I don't want to go, Freddy."

"Newspaper prospects are good in Rochester. Friends have found a house for us."

"You seen this house?"

"Only drawings." He looked down. I couldn't see his eyes. "It'll be fine, Anna."

"Who draw?"

"Drew. You mean drew."

"Who drew?"

"Miss Assing was kind enough."

"I don't want to go, Freddy."

"You don't want?" Freddy looked up, his voice harsh. I shivered. "What right have you to want or not?"

"I'm home here."

"You'll go or stay here—"

"Fine," I say.

"—without the children."

"Naw, Freddy. What you mean?"

"Court of law. Public opinion. The children belong with me."

"Like they your slaves?"

"Stop it."

"You just run off with them?"

"You're not being sensible."

I started weeping and thanked God the children didn't see me cry.

"A man is responsible for his family."

"These past years, I've been caring for the children. You not here, we do fine. You here, we do even better. What if I've said when you'd come home—'go away. You're not needed?'"

"It's not the same."

"'Tis so, You saying you'd leave me. Like I'm not needed. Like the children don't need me."

"I'll not allow the children to be taken from me. They're my precious possessions."

I swallowed.

On his desk, Freddy had set, side by side, four bottles of ink. Rosetta liked playing with them bottles. One day, she was going to drop one. I told Freddy he should move his ink, but he wouldn't listen.

In England, Freddy forgot the noise of children. Forgot how even one tiny baby can create a big mess. It was like Freddy grew rigid as he came into himself, a free man. Like his *self* became the center of all things. He be saying he don't need me. He didn't care about my feelings. He forgot I helped him to escape.

"Anna, didn't you swear to love, honor, and obey me?"

I looked at Freddy hard, letting tears run down my face. I wanted him to see my hurt. See how he'd beaten me. Rosetta and Freddy Junior needed me. And as long as I breathed, I'd be beside them, loving them as Mam and Pa loved me.

I packed and packed some more. Freddy wrote. I cleaned and cleaned some more. Freddy wrote. I soothed the children's falls, made them supper. Freddy Junior always wanted bread and jam. Big Freddy wrote.

My bones ached. At times, I felt sick, like the baby be uncomfortable inside me. I didn't sleep. Freddy didn't, either. He wrote.

Sometimes, when the evening was warm enough, I sat on the porch. Fireflies blinked all over and, if I was quiet, I could hear the soft roar of the sea and the rustle of small animals in the brush. I say my prayers. I promised next year I was going to see Mam. Or die trying. Mostly, I stared at the stars and wondered how I got in my fix. I loved Freddy. I did. I do. He was my last—only—hope for marriage. I was his hope for freedom. Funny, how that made all the difference in the world.

❧

Leaving, Miz Beasley hugged me tight. "You haven't told him about the baby?"

I didn't answer.

"I'm going to miss you."

"I, you."

"Make sure you find a good midwife."

"None as good as you."

She squeezed my shoulder. Looking at her face, I saw wrinkles, long life lines I hadn't seen before. "What's your name? Your Christian name?"

"Effie."

"If I have a girl, I'll call her that."

"Naw, child." Miz Beasley wept over me like I was her own daughter. "You need a proper name. Effie sounds like a bit of nothing."

I hugged Miz Beasely. "You something. Special."

We all left Lynn. It was rough traveling from Massachusetts to New York. Hard to keep children from crying, hour after hour, as we bumped along in the wagon. Me and the growing baby be so sick. I told myself, if Freddy loved me, he'd notice the baby poking out my belly. If he loved me, he'd know a child be due.

Freddy never guessed. All the way to Rochester. Four hundred miles. One hundred and twenty days. Sometimes we left the wagon and stayed in colored folks' homes. All the women cared for me like I was glass instead of flesh. They fed me the best bits of meat. The biggest piece of pie. Freddy never guessed.

At Quakers' and abolitionists' homes, Freddy was fussed over. Fed first, given the first glass of water. Everybody wanted to please him. Me and the children were given a wash bowl, blankets, and expected to lay down and sleep while, downstairs, Freddy talked about books and freedom. Guests dropped by to see the important man. Me and the children slept, grateful not to be rocking in the wagon.

Freddy never guessed.

I gasped. The Rochester house be lovely. Big, with two floors, white shutters and a wide porch. Much nicer than the Baldwins' house. Nicer than any home I've known. The children clamored off the wagon. Play. Squealing like fools. I told them to stay close. "Don't stray too far from the grass."

I clasped Freddy's hand. "We got enough money for this?"

"The newspaper will pay."

I looked about in wonder. I could make a garden. Lots of space for pole beans, tomatoes. Corn. This be another chance. I could make all well here. Make a home, warm and close. Writing the paper, Freddy not travel so much. Maybe he'd come to know me better. Maybe he'd guess the baby be due in four months. Maybe, in our own bed, he'd touch me again and feel the hard rise of my belly, the fullness of my breasts.

I stepped across the lawn, marched up the steps. I unlocked the door with the key Freddy had given me. I sighed, overcome by the loveliness of this house so full of light. I began sweeping the wood floors, dusting corners, wiping down the oven. I worked all day. Children played. Freddy unloaded the wagon. There wasn't much. Mainly Freddy's desk, two bed frames, and a dresser. Freddy claimed his office then, he was gone like a ghost. In my mind, I made lists about what we'd need. I needed to sew curtains. Find a carpenter to make beds. Go to town for supplies: flour, sugar, meal, fatback.

That night, I woke from the deepest, tired sleep. Startled by crickets. By silence. By pine and oak smells.

Startled, because this be the first time I didn't live near the sea.

Freddy guessed. Not because he touched or stroked me in bed. Not because he watched my dress grow tight. Or saw me breathe heavy doing my housekeeping. Or even heard the children arguing about whether it be a brother or a sister.

Some, I could understand why Freddy didn't notice me. He'd bought a print press and taught himself how to set letters. Nonsense marks to me. But I could recognize *A*'s, *N*'s, *E*'s, *D*'s, and *L*'s now. Others I could guess at.

Freddy was writing, printing, trying to find folks to buy his paper. A ton of work. All day, all night, he worked. His eyes grew darker and sometimes, I caught him rubbing his neck or half-asleep in his chair. Other times I heard him working himself into a fever, muttering, "Garrison."

No doubt, my children's father be a hardworking man. I was proud of him. Proud for him. But I wanted him to guess. Wanted him to say, "This is my child." Wanted him to hold me tight.

• • •

Freddy guessed when he saw *her* looking at me. Ain't that a shame. When he saw me through Miz Assing's eyes, he saw me and the baby.

Freddy had insisted I make all kinds of tea cakes for Miz Assing, and I did. Lemon tarts. Carrot bread. Currant biscuits. I wasn't happy about her coming. But Freddy hadn't asked me.

I cooked for two days making that fancy platter for Miz Assing. Showing her, I thought, through my baking, that I could make Freddy happy.

Freddy *be* happy. He had to be. Since everything he asked for, I gave. I was a good wife.

Miz Assing looked at me with scorn. Something else flickered in her eyes, but she pulled a shade down on her feelings. I did that, too. Though I wanted to shout and hit. Still, I kept my dignity. Even when Freddy squinted at me. Like I'd embarrassed him.

I said sweetly, "More tea?" Going back into the kitchen, I turned and saw Miz Assing's blond head next to Freddy's. She laid her hand on his knee. She let him cover her hand with his.

Love be true. I knew then, Freddy hadn't been true.

I went outside and threw up into the bushes.

Ottilie

"I shouldn't have hated her. She loved him just like me."

—OTTILIE ASSING,
1874

"Miss Assing wasn't a Delilah. I see that now.
Freddy laid himself waste. Just as he raised
himself high."

—ANNA DOUGLASS,
1882

New Jersey

Douglass went home to Anna and I went home to empty rooms in Hoboken. For three years, I was Douglass' constant companion; now, his absence was like an open wound. I felt out of joint, out of time. Even a little frightened that my life would become days of empty pursuits, nights of unfulfilled desires.

It seemed to me that Oluwand pitied me. *She'd appear in my bedroom, on the edge of my bed. Her black eyes blinking like an owl's.*

Some days I didn't bother getting out of bed. Curtains closed, I lay in bed dreaming. *Only then did Oluwand disappear to God knows where.* But whenever I tried to get up, to do something, to be productive, she was there. Haunting, hovering. Whenever I moved through my apartments, she shadowed me. Watching me dress, eat, even cleanse myself with a sponge. When I tried to paint, she mixed up all my colors. When I wrote articles about Douglass for the German press, she caused ink to blot his name. I'd start over. And over.

Once I shouted: "Leave me alone."

Oluwand pressed her fingers to her lips. Then, like a mirage, she was on the ship's rail. One leg already flung over, her body arcing backward. Diving, diving toward death.

Winter was harsh in New York. Seemed so much colder than Germany. In my sleep, I must have wept. In the morning, my lashes were frozen, tangled shut.

Dear Ottilie,

*Come to Rochester. I could use your help with the
North Star.*

Yours,

Frederick

I crumbled the letter, tossed it into the fire. My help, he could use
my help! Nothing about love, about whether he missed me. Not "I *need*
your help." Instead: "*Use*." "*Use* your help." I felt like a person let out
to hire. A secretary without feelings.

Still, I packed my luggage on the weight of one word: "*Yours*."

The train ride seemed endless. The constant clacking, the swaying made
me uneasy. Twice, I swallowed bile. Twice, I used all my willpower to
remain on the train. I counted to ten to keep from pulling the emer-
gency cord, which would've sent everyone tumbling to the floor.

Strange. I was going to meet my lover. I was frightened. I couldn't
believe it. Me, frightened? More frightened than I'd ever been in my
life.

Across the aisle, I saw a wife with a husband. How companionable
the two were! Her hand laced in his. Two heads tilted together.

Douglass sent a carriage for me. I felt insulted. But, then, if he came
for me, his wife might suspect that I loved him beyond imagining. That
he loved me. So, I stepped inside the bleak carriage, lowered the
shades, and recited, "*Your love is sweeter than an angel's repose. Sweeter
than all the wonders in heaven and earth. In heaven and earth. Your love is
sweeter than an angel's repose.*"

He was on the porch, waiting for me. A bit plumper, filled out by his
wife's cooking. He was down the porch steps before the carriage came
to a halt. His smile reassured me.

"Douglass."

His arms were like steel rods, holding us apart. "We must be cir-cumspect."

Over his shoulder, I saw the upstairs curtains flutter.

"Here's for your trouble," Douglass said, paying the driver, lifting my portmanteau. "Come, Ottilie. A room is prepared."

"The one with the back bay windows?"

"I thought it might be your favorite." Then, he stopped, his hand gripping my arm. "I never thanked you for finding this home for me. Us."

Then, Douglass, I'm certain of it, for the first time blushed. "Us"—him and Anna, not him and me.

Yes, I found the home. It was I who approved the study, the parlor, the bedrooms. I, who drew the portrait. I, who for a few hours, pre-tended the fairy-tale house belonged to me—all white, windows gleam-ing, a fortress against reality. Against the American prejudice that said a white woman couldn't love a black man.

"Come in, come in."

I stepped inside the vestibule. My spirits lifted. It was a beautiful home. Warm and inviting. Maple floors waxed beyond gleaming; sconces glittering, free of dust. A floorboard creaked. I looked up. Anna was descending the stairs. Dark, unlovely Anna, I thought; then reproached myself for jealousy. She was different. These past two years had given her a hard-earned dignity. A natural grace. She looked directly at me, her gown swaying, slapping against the stairs. She was brave. Mistress in her own house.

Had it not been for her hands, I wouldn't have noticed. At least not right away. Anna was broad. Her hands seemed disproportionate, thick, short. One hand held to the railing, firmly; the other hand was palm flat against her abdomen. Protective.

My throat swelled, choking off air. It would take little to turn around and run. What a fool I'd been. Sacrificing, suffering, while all the while Douglass suffered not. Like a greedy man, he'd fulfilled him-self. Enjoyed his wife's bed.

How could he bring another child into the world? Another child that wasn't mine. Emotions moved through me like a tidal wave. Worse, I could see him: his limbs entwined with hers, his lips pressing against hers. I wanted to cry out. But I held fast.

"Good afternoon, Anna."

She nodded.

"Bring us tea, please, Anna. Some of your cakes, too."

Then, I saw it. Her hands fell to her sides and she looked at Douglass. Waiting for some sign, some recognition that her abdomen swelled her gown.

"Currant? Is currant cake still left?"

She looked heartstruck and I rejoiced. Was my joy always to be at her expense? I felt an overwhelming sadness. Then, anger at Douglass. He was so smart, yet ignorant of a woman's heart. It probably never occurred to him how a child would seem between his wife and mistress. Just as it never occurred to me that seeing his child growing inside Anna, I'd wonder what was wrong with me. Years, and we'd had no issue.

Papa, with his notions of German and Jew, would be startled by the yield of German, Jew, black, and white. Such a child would rule the world. Yet, Douglass was fertile. I, not. I wanted to sit upon the stairs and laugh. No issue from my body. No child to call my own.

I exclaimed over Anna's tea cakes, though they tasted like dust in my mouth. She poured graciously while Douglass, excited like a boy, recounted his argument with Garrison and his plans for the *North Star*. His hands were flailing, his mouth moved rapidly. All I needed to do was to say, "Yes, Douglass"; "Very interesting, Herr Douglass"; and he talked as the sun lengthened shadows across the parlor. The journey from the city to Rochester was exhausting. But Douglass kept talking as I sat in my dust, thinking, I'd rather be back in my rooms. Settling in bed with Oluwand watching.

Eventually, Anna left. Went into the kitchen. I heard children's voices. A little boy babbling, and even with his nonsense words, sounding like Douglass at his imperious best. The girl's voice was more musical. It floated up and down the scales, sometimes a tinkling, laughing soprano, sometimes a somber alto admonishing her brother.

I never heard Anna's voice. It was like she'd disappeared.

Just as I'd disappeared while Douglass talked on.

Anna cleared the dinner table and said she'd retire. She wasn't feeling well. The children had been put to bed hours ago. "I've no strength," she said, "for talk and drinks."

Douglass didn't look up once from the fire. "Very well, Anna. I'll show Miss Assing to her room. We must discuss what she's to do in the days ahead."

Anna and I looked at each other. Both of us embarrassed by the glance. But she bristled and left with an energy that belied exhaustion. I wanted to say, "Take me with you." I, too, wanted to retire, but I kept hoping Douglass would notice my own tiredness, notice how I was still dressed in my stained traveling clothes. But why should I expect such consideration when he couldn't recognize his wife's breeding?

Lassitude crept over me and I listened, without interest, to the editing and writing plans he'd made for me. I listened for the tolling of the hall chimes as hours slipped away.

Finally, I stood. "Douglass, I'm tired."

"Forgive me, I didn't mean to be so thoughtless."

He smiled, all charm, but I offered no platitudes. I was exhausted. I wanted to go home.

I undressed slowly. I'd not unpack. I'd leave tomorrow. I took out my folded night rail and slipped it over my body. I shivered. Goose bumps rose on my arms. Spring's air was too cool. Still I kept the window open, for I enjoyed how the wind lifted the sheer cotton, exposing the half moon, the twinkling stars. Life, I thought, wasn't meant to give you everything.

I must've slept. For I stirred feeling a touch, an insistent warmth. My lips had already parted for a kiss when I realized Douglass' arms were encircling my waist, his legs lying against mine.

Pleasure seems to be a male right.

Yet, I felt it—*pleasure*, a shuddering beyond this world to some nameless land. I was drunk with feeling. And I knew this pleasure would make it hard to leave Douglass.

Anna

"When I was most angry,
I reminded myself Freddy fathered my children."
—Anna Douglass,
speaking to Rosetta, 1882

"When I was most lonely, words failed to comfort
me. Ideas can never be children."
—Ottilie Assing,
diary entry, 1874

Rochester

Sunrise

$\mathcal{I}$ be furious. The whore of Babylon be in my house. Jesus say, "Forgive." But I couldn't.

I went outside, thinking I'd find some peace in gardening. But I kept tearing roots of healthy plants, missing them weeds like I be blind. And I was. Blind with tears.

Freddy said, "I worked all night."

"Hunh," I say back. And I stared at him like I'm no fool.

But Freddy didn't budge. He shuffled his papers. Sat and read his book. Clothes mussed, shadows beneath his eyes. I picked up the vase on the mantel. Clasped it with two hands and held it high. Then, I let go. Left his study not caring where the glass, the water, them flowers flew.

This much I knew. Freddy didn't ever believe he was in the wrong. Or if he did, he didn't show it. Having been a slave made free, I think he believed there be new rules made just for him. Like he could cause hurt, 'cause he'd suffered so much pain. Or, maybe, 'cause he'd suffered so much pain, he'd a right to take pleasure as he found it.

I stared at the tomato in my hand. A worm done made a hole. I poked my finger. All the seeds, juice broke down. I smashed the tomato into the dirt. Wiped my blood-red hands on my skirt.

I looked up. The sky was bright, bright blue. Like an upside-down ocean.

I had children in my house. I needed to tell Miz Assing she got to go.

❧

I didn't even knock; I barged right in. I stopped short at the vision. She be all white, dressed in a robe of white lace and silk ribbons. She be sitting at the vanity, combing her hair, threads falling like spun gold. I sucked in air. She looked at me caught inside her mirror. I saw myself, all musty, dirty, and stained.

I didn't back down. "You should be 'shamed."

Her brows lifted; she turned and faced me. "Shame? So bourgeoise."

I blinked. I didn't know what she meant. "Leave," I say, quiet yet hard.

"You'll have to speak with Douglass."

I wanted to charge forward, knock her off her chair. "I'm speaking to you. This between us."

"Is it?"

"Stop it," I say. "You so smart, you can speak. Not hide behind questions. This be my house. My home. I don't want you here."

She sighed, a soft, fluttering sound. Made me want to wring her neck. Snap it like chickens. I stepped closer. I saw her soft flesh rising above her gown. I wanted to scratch and draw blood.

"Get out my house. Leave. Go. I don't want you here."

Her blue eyes reflected sunlight. "He has to ask me. Not you."

"You his slave? You got your own mind." Something flickered across her face. Couldn't tell what it was: sorrow, anger, fear? That be funny, I thought. Fear. She should fear me. I filled with the wrath of God.

"You just got to say no. You can do that, can't you? Speak your mind and say this is wrong."

"I don't believe it is."

"Didn't your Mam teach you right from wrong?"

"She did, Anna." She stood, taller than me. I thought she was going to clutch my hand. But her hands fluttered like fans at her side. "She taught me love was worth any sacrifice."

"Sacrifice. If anybody's doing it, it's me."

"And me. Don't you think I miss him too?"

"You're evil." I pushed forward, making her step back. "Plain evil.

White woman think everything by right be theirs. Thinking you better than anyone else."

"Not so."

"Yes, 'tis so. All my life white people been trying to take what's mine. You a slave catcher, too. Catching Freddy right up from under me."

"Anna, you don't understand."

"I do."

"No, you don't." Her hand clasped my wrist. "I'm the wife of his spirit."

Then, God help me, I threw her off. Everything Mam taught me about staying out of white people's way, went out the window. I shoved her, pushed her back, 'til she clung to the bedpost. No screams. Or pleas for help.

I couldn't catch my breath. "You are—You are—"

"What?"

Tears were in her eyes. I got angry at myself for feeling sorry for her.

"You are not a good woman. God shall punish you." Her brow touched the post. "Leave my house."

No words. Just hush. I could hear morning robin birds starting to sing. I could even hear the old house creaking, someone was going down the stairs. Rosetta? The curtains flapped. I could smell my jasmine wafting up from the garden. Poor Miz Assing. She knew I be right. Her own hair a curtain as she held on to the bedpost for dear life.

Then Freddy called from downstairs. "Anna, Anna." Both our heads turned toward the door. "Rosetta's hungry. Time to be doing. I'd like some tea." Silence. Then, "Anna, Anna," more insistent.

Miz Assing looked at me. Her body straightened. "I'm not giving up Douglass."

Stubborn like a spoiled child. I'd have to make Freddy change. Choose. Tell him he's got to choose.

But what if Freddy didn't pick me? Such a hard place. Me, believing in my marriage vows. Me, still loving him. Me, believing it be better to raise my children with him than without him.

I swayed; I was falling down a well. I couldn't catch hold of the sides. I was falling and falling, deeper and deeper. I'd hit bottom and drown.

"Anna," she said, all sympathy.

I bristled. Felt rage, fury at being so trapped. "The children are not to know."

She nodded.

"You are not to enter my kitchen. My sewing room."

She nodded again.

"Or my children's rooms." I looked at the bed, sheets scattered like wind. I imagined her and him, twisting, tossing beneath them. "Change your own linens. They kept in the hall. Keep your own mess. I won't."

"That's fair."

"Fair ain't nothing. Means nothing. You still ought to be 'shamed."

I opened the door, headed down the stairs. Pain settled in my joints. I heard another shout. "Anna."

I put my face on for the brand new day.

Ottilie

"Mistresses are cheap. I understand that now."
—OTTILIE ASSING,
DIARY ENTRY, 1882

"Human heart be a miracle. Can withstand all kinds of hurt and still not break."
—ANNA DOUGLASS,
SPEAKING TO ROSETTA, 1882

$\mathcal{M}$y life was split between two worlds: my boardinghouse in Hoboken; Douglass' home during the summer.

It isn't true that I didn't live when I was away from him. I did. I painted. Had dinner with friends. I stayed away from abolition meetings. There was too much talk about me and Douglass. Too much talk about Douglass and any white woman, for that matter. Some were scandalized by his friendship with Julia Griffiths. But I knew beyond abolition and women's rights, Douglass had no interest in Julia. Their relationship was innocent.

While ours adapted to the seasons. Confined to the times I worked side by side with Douglass. Confined to three months when I lived more intensely than many did during their entire lives!

Birthdays arrived in regular fashion. My sister wrote me of her marriage. Later, the birth of her children. I imagined her a regular hausfrau. And though I didn't think Ludmilla really wanted to see me, I missed her.

I did have companionship. There was Emma, who discussed music with me. She was a fine violinist. Then, there was William, *Wilhelm*. Very sweet. Filled with Old World courtesy. He did nothing more than kiss my hand and cheek. Delighted to have my attention. He was a grocer (that bothered me, at first), but he was very smart. Cultured and well-read. He loved to cook, too. "You are, too thin, Ottilie. Scrawny like a baby chick." Often his meals kept me from starving.

Once, so poor, I took a job as a seamstress. Sitting in neat rows with immigrants. Little ventilation. The women wouldn't let me organize them. We were little more than slaves. My back, fingers, ached constantly. I coughed. My only thought was that this was one-tenth the pain of Douglass' experiences.

I was a poor seamstress. I was fired. Told to go home.

I could've written Douglass of my need. His paper was turning a profit. But I didn't want to jeopardize our relationship. What would it mean if I asked for help?

William took care of me all winter. Feeding me soup, buying coal for my small stove. Once he brought the warmest winter coat. He was good to me.

I was terrible to him. For, when spring came, I grew impatient with his kindness. His avowals of love. Spring meant summer was coming and I'd sojourn in Rochester. Color started returning to my cheeks, my curiosity was aroused. I devoured papers, political essays. I painted again in earnest.

After three seasons, William had it out with me. It was one of those thick days, overcast with the scent of rain that never came.

The train was preparing to leave. Clearing its steam valves, blowing its horn. William had seen to my bags, tucked a blanket about my legs. All that was left was "good-bye." Instead, he said, "Ottilie, stay. Marry me."

"I must go. I must."

"Why? You correspond with this Douglass all the time. You can continue to do so. You needn't be his unpaid worker during the summers."

"I enjoy the work."

"Then stay and do it here."

The train whistle squealed.

"William." I stroked his cheek. "I must go. My heart has no choice."

"It's true, then. What they say."

"I don't abide rumors." I looked at him, coldly, direct.

"But you don't deny it?"

I saw then that William was petty, small-minded like all the others. Conformist. His teeth bit into his chapped lip. Head cocked, he stared at me. Like he was looking for some nuance, some new discovery in me. Of course, I said nothing. He didn't want to hear what I had to say.

I think if William had been more at ease, more flexible, I might've married him. Might have been content to let him hold me. If he would've allowed me the freedom to love elsewhere, I think I might've allowed myself to love him. Just a little. Maybe more. My heart was big enough.

Strange, I didn't realize William was my last chance for a normal life. He was kind, smart. We found much to talk about. Young, I'd thought I'd be content to be Douglass' paramour forever. I failed to weigh how lonely days would far outnumber time spent with Douglass. I was too young. Young enough to believe permanence and true love were both real. Real and within the realm of possibility.

Summer. Anna and I kept our uneasy truce. I stayed in Douglass' office, the guest bedroom or in the walled garden. Anna had the kitchen, the vegetable garden off the back and the rest of the house where the children roamed. If I decided to take my meals in my room, I sometimes didn't see Anna for days. It was the children who rambled back and forth between rooms, between worlds.

I didn't have much to do with them. I thought Anna preferred it that way. I told a fairy tale or two. Brought them candy. Kites. Twine balls. Douglass' family had grown—one, two, three. Another child soon due.

Without a doubt, I must be barren. Though sometimes I thought if I lived with Douglass year-round . . . if he held me not just during midsummer nights, a child would root in my womb. Still, I must be content. We'd found a compromise that saved Douglass' reputation (I don't care about mine!) and one that Anna tolerates. Maybe she felt she had the better bargain: house and children.

But she didn't have the nights of passion.

July. Our pattern was familiar. Most mornings, I stayed late abed. Douglass would love me past midnight and still rise at dawn. I slept in, stretching like a cat, recalling his touch, caress. The angle of his body in relation to mine. The spaces where his lips pressed.

Each summer night was carefully preserved in memory. Come winter, I'd retrieve, savor, mimic Douglass making love to me.

"Who's there?" I heard scraping. Thought I saw a blue flash from the corner of my eye. If it was Anna, I was going to scream. Though decent, the bed was mussed for two rather than one. Both pillows had impressions, strands of blond and black hair. When the fire had died and the room had chilled, Douglass held me close. I refused to let him go. I talked and talked about our longings, our love, until I fell asleep. While I slept, he must've left, gone to his room. The one with the connecting door to Anna.

"Who disturbs me?"

I saw children's shoes at the bottom of the curtain.

"Come out. Or I shall tell Douglass. Have him put you in jail."

"No, please. Don't." Rosetta stepped forward.

"You're a pretty thing." And she was, too. Darker-skinned like her mother. But her eyes were intelligent like her father's. Her hair, though coarser than Douglass', fell in great waves, framing her face and thin nose.

"You're pretty, too." The girl puckered her lips.

"You think so?"

She nodded solemnly.

"Does your mother know you're here?"

She shook her head.

"What are you doing, then?"

"I wanted to see if you were as pretty as I remembered."

I laughed. "Am I?"

"Yes. I like your hair." She scrambled onto the bed, her knees tucked under her blue checkered dress. She stroked my hair, rubbing it together in patches in her hands.

"Would you help me brush it?"

"Oh, yes." Her eyes brightened and I laughed again.

"There on the dressing table. Bring my brush."

She moved like a young colt, finding the brush, then skipping back toward me. She shoved the pillows aside and commenced to work.

"Do you go to school?"

"No, ma'am."

"A smart girl like you should be at school. Or do you have a governess? No, of course not. Douglass is not yet rich." Her small hands running through my hair felt glorious. Everything she did was soft and gentle. She smelled of soap.

"My mother was a governess," I murmured, happily remembering. "She believed in learning."

"Did she teach you?"

"Yes, she did."

"In Lynn, the Pastor teached me."

"Taught."

"The Pastor taught me."

"No one here?"

"No." She pulled the strands of my hair from my brush. "We should burn these."

"Why?"

"Mam say, 'If a bird makes a nest with your hair, your hair will fall right out.'" Her head bobbed; she was serious. I felt angry that such superstition filled her head.

"Can you write?" She bobbed again. "Show me." I gathered my writing case and opened it to quill, paper and ink. "Write."

Biting her lip, her fingers gripping the pen, she wrote:

ROSETTA

"How old are you?"

SEVEN

"What do you like most?"

FATHER'S BOOKS

I laughed. "You can't even read his books."

"I try."

What a charming child. I had to rescue her. Her life would surely be blunted if her head was filled with nonsense, old wives' tales. What must it be like to live in a house with her mother all day, day after day? I wondered if Anna even followed suffrage.

Douglass had spoken on women's behalf. Not as enthusiastically as I would have liked. He didn't think you could argue abolition and the vote at the same time. "Once slavery is ended, then women's concerns can be more forcibly addressed," he said, and we argued all night. "America is not ready for both."

I knew, eventually, I'd change Douglass' mind. Pride was almost a sin with him. How nice then that his daughter should set an example. How awful to think she might know little more than a few written words and domestic trivia.

I bent, whispering. "Would you like to go to school?"

"Couldn't you teach me?"

"I could. Painting. Reading. Writing. Even German, if you wish. I could teach you about all the great thoughts men have had. Some women, too. I could teach you more than many a tutor. A new world dawns, Rosetta. We need intelligent minds. Intelligent women."

"Start now, please."

I liked this girl. Sweet and beyond sweet. I could paint her. This time not the infant, but a full-grown child. I'd paint her hair a bit more gold. Her eyes, more hazel. She'd be my child with Douglass. In oil; if not in fact. I lay back, closing my eyes to hold back tears.

"Give me a kiss," I murmured.

Trustingly, she put her arms about my neck and kissed my lips. Her breath smelled of strawberries. Her hands felt so comforting and delicate. I'd never played with dolls but I liked her trust in me. She curled up on the bed beside me. Lying in the space her father had so recently been.

"Are you a good girl?" I asked.

"A very good girl."

I laughed again. "My darling girl. Then we shall have to see what can be done. What we must do to make you as smart and as famous as your father."

Anna

"For me, Anna? Why didn't you try to read for me?"

—Frederick Douglass,
1882

"It ain't all about you."

—Anna Douglass,
1882

Rochester

𝒴ou can't do this. You can't."

"I can and will."

"Freddy, please. Rosetta's my baby girl. I couldn't feel joy without her. We be happy here in Rochester."

"So I'd best believe. But Rosetta deserves a fine education."

"As fine as Miz Assing's?" I stood as tall as I could muster and dared him to look me in the eye.

His eyes cast down, he used his big boom voice, the one he saved for speeches. "The future for the colored race lies in being as prepared as any educated white."

"As prepared as Miz Assing?" I demanded.

He looked straight at me. "Yes. As fine, as prepared as Miss Assing."

Trembling, I moved toward the window and looked out over my garden. Freddy's study was the nicest room in the house. He had southern light, the horizon, and a view of roses. His office was big enough to hold all his papers and books. He even had a nice fire though the day had only the slightest chill. Seeing his reflection in the glass, my heart raced. Even though my soul and body ached.

His clothes were the finest; I laundered them with great care. Everything I did for Freddy, I did with great care. I saved the finest tea for him, cooked sweetbreads and puddings. I wove lace for his handkerchiefs and polished his boots and walking stick. When Freddy left this house, he looked as well and as well-fed as any white man.

His watch chain caught the sunlight and glittered from his vest pocket. I pressed my lips together. I didn't give him the pocket watch. He came back with it from England. But it was a fine piece and one day, I hoped to hold it in my fingers. Hold it and stare at the letters that I see him reading inside.

I watched the sunlight cut across the tall sunflowers and strawberry vines. Winter would come again and all my handiwork would die. Seemed no one cared about the vegetables I grew. Bean poles, kale, cucumbers. Or the flowers I nourished alongside the food. Pale, tender azaleas. Strong-headed marigolds. More roses. The garden Frederick visited with Miz Assing was far off from the house, just a clearing with shrubs and bushes. An iron-wrought bench. I don't know what they all did in there—staying well beyond twilight. Dark, manicured, not alive with the flow of color or of growing things. My garden had all anybody would ever need—food and beauty. It be my garden I see from the kitchen. My garden Frederick sees when he writes. When he works with Miz Assing.

I speak softly, promising myself not to cry.

"Frederick. Seem like this family done give you everything you want. The world, too, waits at your feet. Abolitionists be charmed by you. Why can't you allow me Rosetta?"

"She's not only your daughter."

I moved forward, swift, slammed my fist on his desk. "She be my daughter more than yours. I birthed her. You weren't there. You didn't see her swimming out of my body. You didn't see her take her first breath. You saw nothing. When she first walked, first talked, you weren't here. I raised her. Me. You went off to England."

"I had to leave, Anna. You know that."

"Just as I know you had to take Miz Assing with you. Just as I know you had to have her in this house."

"I won't discuss Miss Assing."

"Why not? I'm certain the two of you discuss me. Whisper, carry tales behind my back: 'When will Anna leave?' 'Too bad you had to marry her.' 'Yes, too bad.' 'A young man's mistake.'" I swallowed. "You think I'm blind, Frederick?"

"I'll not discuss this with you."

"You think I'm stupid. Stupid and blind both."

"You're ignoring the subject of Rosetta's education."

"I'm not. I taught her, be teaching her all the wonders Mam taught me. She can sew, cook, garden. She be doing right well."

"Have you taught her Plato, the text of my books, how to write a letter?"

He was towering over me, making me step back, give way, inch by inch. "Have you given her anything to think about other than your small domestic arts? Have you given her wisdom and ideas to think and dream about?"

Freddy be bullying me like my brothers used to do. Pushing me back with his size and strength. If I didn't stop, he'd roll all over me. Roll me down 'til I was flat out, smashed down to nothing. I struck his face.

Freddy caught my wrist. But I didn't flinch.

"I be teaching—"

"*Be* teaching? What kind of English is that?"

"I be teaching—"

"Who are you to teach anyone?"

I twisted my wrist from his grasp. "I *be* teaching Rosetta to be a good, God-fearing woman. At seven, she be smarter than Miz Assing. At seven, she know it be wrong to lust after another woman's husband. To commit adultery. To sin against the Bible."

"Shut up. Stop this talk."

"You think I'm too black to know anything. Like you believe the only thing good in you be white. Be having a white woman like Miz Assing. I know what goes on under my roof. I know it as I know I be carrying another of your sons in my womb. I know it as I know you, the honorable Frederick Bailey Douglass, be a liar."

He struck me then. His rage fierce. I wiped a trickle of blood from my mouth.

"This be what learning gets you? Hitting a woman?"

He slumped in his chair. "Get out of here."

I despised him then. "You should know better than to treat me like your slave."

"I didn't mean to hit you, Anna."

"Naw. You be telling lies again, Freddy." I dropped down on my knees before him. Head bowed, Freddy looked young and needy. I touched his hair, crooning as I would to Freddy Junior.

"I still love you. I love the man in you, intent on making good. I just don't understand how you forgot your vows to me."

There be silence. Then, the clock chimed loud and clear.

"Look at you, Anna," he said softly, his voice drawn out to a hoarse whisper. "Look at Miss Assing."

I clutched my belly, feeling pain rush through me. I pounded my fists on his thighs. "Did you think I be ugly when you made this child? Or Freddy Junior? Rosetta? Did you think me ugly when I offered to buy you free? Was I ugly then? When I gave you all my money to run free?"

"No." He stood, glaring at me. "You looked well enough. It's the ugliness of your mind that punished me. You're an embarrassment, Anna. Barely more educated than when I found you."

"Whose fault? When you been here to teach me?"

"You could've continued on your own."

"When? When I needed to provide food, money, and warmth for our children? When I needed to take your role as father and head? Even now you travel from home. Here, then gone. Here, then gone."

"It's easier to go than stay."

"Go then. You should've let me stay in Lynn, rather than bring me to this God-forsaken Rochester."

"Rochester offered a new beginning."

"For who? Not me. I didn't need one. Naw, 'a new beginning' be another lie. You wanted a place to bring Miz Assing."

"Rosetta will go to boarding school."

"Go to Miz Assing. Leave Rosetta here."

"She'll go to boarding school."

"Book-smart mean nothing. You write books, and still don't care you breaking God's law."

"There's more to God's law than interpreted by man. Miss Assing is a companion of the mind and soul. If you offered more, I would gladly take it, Anna. But you don't."

Both of us breathed hard. I closed my eyes, wishing I could undo what I was hearing, feeling and seeing.

"Why'd you marry me?"

"Loyalty."

"I wish you hadn't."

"So do I."

I pulled myself up, tears running down my face like a baby. I swore this be the last time I'd cry over Frederick Bailey Douglass.

"I found you," I said, stopping before I closed the door.

"What?"

"You forget. I found you. You didn't find me, Mr. Douglass, ex-slave man." I closed the door softly on my dreams. Poor, woeful dreams.

Love ain't true.

$\mathcal{F}$reddy thought he won. He thought I gave in to him. I was ready, though, to fight for my baby girl. Once I birthed the new baby, I figured I'd go to Mam. Freddy owed me a trip. I'd say, "Let me take the children to Mam this one time. Then, Rosetta go to school." How could he say no? And once I was with Mam, in Baltimore, I'd stay. Just say "no" to returning, regardless of how he frighten me. He'd have to call the law and oh, how embarrassing that would be for ex-slave man. 'Specially in the same state his old Master live.

But I never got to win. Never got my choice.

I took to bed for several days. Freddy called in a woman to do the work I did. I didn't care. I was worn out, tired in spirit. This baby had me feeling poorly too. How could I let Freddy love—no, use me again? He'd have to call on Miz Assing.

The children, bless their hearts, tiptoed softly. Tried not to shout. I laid in bed, thinking about how everything about me was slowing down. Thinking I'd die before Freddy. Knowing Mam would die before me. Eight years since I'd seen her. No more than a couple Penny-men carrying news. Sometimes I heard from brothers and sisters. But they in awe of me. Think it be all good news to be Miz Douglass. Mam would know the story from one look at me.

My room was cold. Fire dead. Only a single candle flickered its light. Freddy didn't come to see me, to see if I was all right. He, took to sleeping in his office. I didn't have the energy to move. Like a great big baby, I let myself, finally, cry. Not since I was Lil' Bit did tears sting so. Nothing like a good, wallowing cry.

"Mam," Rosetta whispered, barefoot in her night rail. "Mam?"

I quieted and sat up. I didn't want her to see me crying.

"How's my baby girl?"

"Fine, Mam. I couldn't sleep."

"Snuggle down beside me and I'll tell you stories about my Mam and my Mam's Mam. Come on. Under the quilt. I don't think your Father will mind this evening."

Rosetta laid warm and soft against me. No longer smelling like a new baby but like a girl on the verge of womanhood. Like a colt. All legs and all sweaty, warm, smelling like grass. I hugged her tight. I couldn't let her go. I kissed the top of her forehead.

"My Mam's Mam told stories. Did I tell you that?"

"No, ma'am."

"She told how long, long ago, Africans could fly."

"Folks can't fly."

"That be your Father talking. This tale Mam told me and as her Mam told her and how I'm telling you. You got to believe. Just as I believe in them slave spirits scattered in the sea. They help you. Never fear."

"There's no sea in Rochester."

"No, there ain't."

"Isn't."

I wanted to fuss: that's your Father speaking. 'Stead, I tickled her. "My word, Rosetta. Only seven and telling me how to speak proper!"

"You don't mind?"

"Naw. You my bright, shining girl."

"I want to go to school."

I be glad Rosetta staring at the ceiling, not at my face. "Why you say that?"

"'Cause I do."

"We can find a Pastor to teach you, like in Lynn."

"Miss Assing says I need the best learning. Everybody in the world knows me as Frederick Douglass' girl." She lifted onto her elbows, her face, sweet and beautiful. "Can I go to school?"

I shuddered. "That what you want?"

"Yes, ma'am."

"You don't want to help with your new baby brother?"

"He won't be a baby long. And I'm growing up."

"So you be."

"Can I, Mam? Can I go to school?"

I couldn't speak. I held her, squeezing so hard it hurt. She squirmed in my arms. But Rosetta let me hold her. Didn't say anything when I cried and cried. But, in my fierce hug, my kisses, my caress of her back and hair, I knew she could feel my body saying what my mouth couldn't. "Yes."

Go to school. Learn everything. Build your own kingdom. No matter where you go, your Mam be loving you true.

Ottilie

"Book learning doesn't replace everything.
I should've told Rosetta about love."
　　　　　—OTTILIE ASSING,
　　　　　DIARY ENTRY, 1872

"You were another kind of mother
locked inside my head. Mam had my heart."
　　　　　—ROSETTA DOUGLASS,
　　　　　IN A LETTER TO OTTILIE, 1883

*B*e careful what you wish for. What you desire. I'd learned that phrase in America. But no one told me how awful it could be. How things could turn out right but still be wrong.

I desired a child. Rosetta was my experiment. Elizabeth Stanton's *Declaration of Sentiments* had circulated, declaring the "duty of women of this country to secure to themselves their sacred right to the elective franchise." Though I wasn't American, it was thrilling to fight for women's equality! For abolition, I was a liability. But the right to vote movement was spreading like a wildfire and I could wholeheartedly be part of it.

Rosetta, with her father's charm and bright mind—how could I not rescue her? Be the mother I suspected Douglass wanted me to be.

The summer before school began, I researched the academies. No institution preparing ladies for marriage was good enough. I wanted a curriculum with substance. As rich an approach to learning as my mother gave me. Miss Seward's Academy in Albany seemed appropriate (though I did have my doubts about the schoolmistress even then), but Miss Seward's was the best school to fit Douglass' admonition that Rosetta be no more than three days' drive from Rochester. I suspected Anna put him up to this! No fine institution in a New York City school or Quaker school in Philadelphia. Upstate New York had its limitations.

"Call me Miss A."

"Truly?"

"Yes. Each afternoon, I want you to meet me in the garden. We'll do lessons. Fun things to prepare you for Miss Seward's. Would you like that?"

"Oh, yes."

I kissed her cheek. Sweet child. "We will begin now."

"I've got to ask Mam."

"Your father has given his approval."

She dug her toe at the dirt, twisting her torso back and forth. I patted the stack of books beside me. "All right. Go ask your mother."

She ran, fleet like a deer, her dark pigtails flapping at the back of her knees. I heard the kitchen screen door slam. Then, silence.

I imagined Anna in her kitchen, her arms dusted white with flour, listening to a breathless Rosetta. Knowing Anna, she'd keep kneading her dough. Then, when Rosetta fell silent, she'd wipe her hands, look at her child, then cross to the window as though she could see me behind the hedges. Her eyes would cloud like they were seeing beyond to something else. She'd say "Yes."

I'd seen Anna reach decisions about her children before. She never failed to do what's best. I give her that. Even when Freddy Junior had fallen and Douglass thought it wasteful to send for a doctor, she did. Douglass hadn't ridden more than an hour before his son spiked a terrible fever. Anna would say "yes" to Rosetta. Even though it cost her her own pride. She'd say "yes."

How many other mistresses taught their lover's daughter? Taught her in her mother's garden? Taught her in daylight, midafternoon, while loving her father by moonlight, the night before?

"Miss A. Miss A." Rosetta was tugging my arm. "Mam says you can teach me."

"You mean your mother said, 'yes.'"

Rosetta nodded. "Long as I finish my chores."

"Good. Let us review the ABC's. Numbers. How well do you add? Subtract? Do you know your geography? Where's England? Germany?"

Rosetta knew most things and what she didn't know she learned quickly.

So, all summer, we spent pleasant afternoons in the garden. In the evenings, I told Douglass of her progress and I knew he was pleased.

I bought Rosetta several dresses. Poplin. Checkered cottons. A yellow muslin. Even a night rail with a lace cap.

I invited Rosetta to take tea with me and Douglass in his office. Anna had filled the teapot, jam pot, and baked delicious pastries. Rosetta was so delighted! Her first grown-up tea. When she'd prettily eaten a slice of lemon cake, I set a box beside her. She looked to her father.

"Open it," he encouraged.

Rosetta squealed with delight. She lifted the dresses as though they were precious gold. "My first store-bought clothes. Store-bought dresses."

She held a dress in front of her and curtsied.

"You look good enough to eat," said Douglass. He winked at me. I felt joyous, basking in his approval.

Anna came to clear the tea. I saw her dismay before she veiled her expression.

I should've known Anna would make Rosetta's new gowns. Wasn't she always cutting patterns, sewing as June gave way to July, then August? Some nights, she practically hurried dinner so she could put out her basket, thread a needle and stitch. How thoughtless I'd been.

Rosetta was bubbling with laughter. "Aren't they pretty?" Anna hugged her. "Yes, they pretty," she said, then looked at me.

I stood, nearly upsetting the tea cart. "I'm sorry, Anna."

"For what?" asked Douglass. "Your gifts are lovely and generous."

Anna and I looked at each other. My gaze fell first.

Anna didn't travel to Miss Seward's Academy for Ladies in Albany. She said she was too sick: "The new baby, almost due."

Rosetta said, "Have a sister. I'll watch over her at Christmas."

Anna did look ill. I'd never seen her so sad. Not even when Douglass first left for England. Face puffy, I suspected she'd spent the entire night crying. Rosetta, with all the goodness of a child, understood her mother's grief. She held her tightly, kissed her sweetly good-bye. Douglass tipped his hat. Then gathered each of his children into his arms and kissed them soundly.

I waved from the carriage. Blew kisses at the boys, now crying, hanging on to their mother's skirt. Douglass and Rosetta climbed into the carriage. Anna just watched, stone-faced.

I shouted as the carriage jolted forward: "Safe passage with the baby." The horses clip-clopped onward.

Anna didn't blink. Rosetta waved and waved until there was nothing left to see but a road of dust. She threw herself against my bosom and cried.

Douglass opened a book, Hawthorne's *Scarlet Letter*. I much preferred Washington Irving's tales and sketches.

I'd begged Douglass for time together. Away from Anna's house. He'd agreed to travel onward to New York. I was thrilled. He'd have a chance to talk with new investors for his paper. Money always flowed in fits and starts. And once Rosetta was safely stowed, I'd imagined the two of us on holiday. Yet, holding the weeping child, I felt hesitant to give her up.

Rosetta wasn't a strong traveler. The swaying motion upset her stomach. We stopped by the side of the road more than twice. I pressed compresses to her head. Pleaded with Douglass for an early evening. "What does it matter to arrive a day late?"

When Rosetta vomited again, spoiling the carriage, he ordered the driver to find the first inn.

Two rooms, Douglass thought more than enough. A bed for him; Rosetta, on a cot. A bed for me across the hall.

I didn't expect Douglass to come to me. But he did.

"You should go. It isn't proper with Rosetta here." But Douglass insisted it was all right; and, God forgive me, I let myself be convinced.

Maybe it was my fear of discovery or the long years we'd known each other, but I felt less than satisfied. Romance wasn't triggered deep inside me. I kissed without passion. Stroked out of duty rather than desire. Douglass seemed satiated as usual.

He lay, eyes closed, legs spread-eagled atop me. He'd said nothing.

Went about his business. Inhaling, exhaling. Pushing, pulling. In and out.

Moon waning, there was a soft tap at the door and Rosetta wiping away sleep, shuffled in, calling, "Miss A. Where's Father? I'm scared."

Her eyes widened; lashes fluttered, then blinked once. Like one of those new daguerreotypes, she'd taken a memory picture.

"Leave, Rosetta. I'll be there shortly." Douglass sat, his chest exposed. "Go, Rosetta."

She turned, closed the door softly.

She knew. Of course, she knew. Douglass would hear none of it. He dressed, went back to his room. Did he tuck Rosetta in? Speak to her? Or did he merely say "good night" before crawling into his bed?

℘

"Mam say, 'Don't get lost in the wilderness. Don't get lost. Don't get lost in the wilderness.'" She was staring up at her new school.

"Rosetta, stop that at once. You're to make a good impression."

"Yes, Father."

Rosetta quieted but I noticed her lips still moved. "Don't get lost. Don't get lost."

I bent before her. "Miss Seward's Academy isn't a wilderness."

"Mam says anyplace can be a wilderness."

"Nonsense," said Douglass.

"What does your mother say you should do? To keep from getting lost?"

"Remember I'm loved."

"That's good advice. Your mother is a wise woman. Remember you're loved."

Rosetta flung herself into my arms. I hugged her and we followed, hands clasped, behind Douglass.

The new school was impressive—a towering brownstone with lace curtains. Douglass hurried up the steps; Rosetta held back. I tugged her along. The sky was missing the sun; the air felt too thick to breathe. Perhaps I should've insisted Anna be schooled in New York City. I could've kept an eye on her through the long winter. But Anna wouldn't have approved. A thin maid with red marks on her face opened the door.

The hallway was marble with a huge chandelier. How rich, I thought. To think such luxury existed inside a school! But while it was lovely, it felt cold. Harsh. Rosetta pinched my hand. I felt anxious. Girls, with wide, mocking eyes, peeked down at me through the wooden banisters. An old woman with a white lace cap shooed them away.

We were escorted into the parlor. The headmistress was in black bombazine, looking withered, I thought. Like one of the stepmothers in a Grimm's fairy tale. But I calmed myself. This was a good American school. Not a German forest. Not a land of make-believe.

Sitting in the headmistress' parlor, I felt unbearably old. Rosetta was a good girl. She didn't fidget. Didn't break the teacup though her knees shook so. I offered her another cake.

Douglass was busy, telling the headmistress about his escape from slavery, his travels in Europe, his newspaper. The headmistress said she was "sincerely delighted" to have such a famous abolitionist in her room. She was "delighted," too, by me. "A continental woman of such intelligence and learning."

But I didn't think she was delighted by Rosetta. She spoke not a word to her. In between smiles toward me and Douglass, she looked blankly at the girl. The dullness of her stare unnerved me. I wanted to grab Rosetta, run from the room.

"She's to be treated as all the others," said Douglass. "Color-blind. I want her education to be color-blind."

Miss Seward smiled thinly. "She's not as fair as you."

Douglass simply tilted his head. "She favors her mother."

Rosetta's shoulders slumped. I wanted to hold her. Instead, I said, "Douglass, I wish to speak with you."

And he misinterpreted me—purposefully, I don't know. But he rose, saying, "Yes, it's time for us to go. Time for Rosetta to become familiar with her new school."

"Douglass, we should talk—"

He bent before Rosetta. Kissed her check, murmured softly. I was close enough to hear. "Don't embarrass me," he said. "Don't embarrass me."

Rosetta squared her small shoulders. I wrapped her in my arms. Trying to convey my deep affection, trying to undo my growing alarm that

Miss Seward's Academy was the wrong place for her. I whispered, "Don't get lost in the wilderness."

Her lips puckered. I kissed her tiny rosebud mouth. As gently, fervently, as I imagined Anna would.

Douglass was shaking the headmistress' hand.

"Remember your Mam loves you." I gave her my handkerchief to dry the tears brimming in her eyes. "Write to me. Be strong."

"Don't embarrass Father."

"No," I lifted her chin. "Don't embarrass Rosetta." One last fierce hug. "Who loves you?"

We were soon out the door. Douglass, when he made up his mind to go, rarely lingered. Behind me, I heard the headmistress: "How coarse your hair is. Make sure it doesn't tangle. Else we'll have to cut it."

Douglass helped me into the carriage. He opened his book again. I peered out the carriage window. There was a hard glint in Miss Seward's eyes. Rosetta was waving. Then, Miss Seward spoke to her and Rosetta bobbed a curtsy like a maid. I was furious. But I knew Douglass wouldn't tell the coachman to stop. Rosetta, her father's daughter, would survive.

The main door shut. Rosetta was lost deep inside.

John Coachman cracked his whip. "Aie-yah," he shouted.

I looked up at the many curtained windows. In the far right, on the tallest floor, I saw one curtain lift.

Oluwand, like a sentinel, stared at me from behind the glass.

I waved and waved. Irritable, petulant, Douglass asked, "Ottilie, what's the matter with you?"

John Coachman rounded the corner.

"Who loves you? Who loves you?" I repeated.

Douglass stroked the back of my neck. "We're to have a fine time," he said. "A fine time."

Anna

"We raise children only to say good-bye.
Don't seem fair."

—Anna Douglass,
at Annie's birth, 1847

"War is justified for a righteous cause."

—Frederick Douglass,
1851

Rochester

 $\mathcal{T}$ wilight crisscrossed the sky. Penny-man didn't even need to get off the wagon. He come like a great shadow. Like Mister Death himself. Yelling, "Whoa." He looked at me, shook his head. My knees buckled. He made to get down from the wagon and I just shouted, "Naw." His head jerked up then, he cracked his whip, and went on. *Mam's dead.*

I clasped my belly. Charles Redmond was deciding to come.

Freddy Junior and Lewis come flying out the house. "Candy," they hollered. "Penny-man bring candy?"

I clasped Freddy Junior's hand. He just five. Still a babe.

"Mam needs to lie down," I say. "You and Lewis play in the house. In the kitchen, there be a jar of cookies and candy."

"Wheee," he squealed, pulling Lewis, running back inside the house. I took my time. Pausing to breathe. To bend over when Charles Redmond kicked rough inside. I knew it was a boy. Just as I knew Freddy wouldn't be home to see our fourth child born.

Just as I knew I'd failed Mam. I broke my promise. Landlocked. Not near no kind of water. *How long my Mam been dead?* Shame on me. I didn't feel it. Surely the earth knew. Ground must've shook. Flowers must've faded. Wind whistled it through trees.

I crawled into the bed, hoping this baby be quick. Nobody here but me and the children. *How come Mam's spirit not come to me?* The pain made me roar.

I hurt too bad to light a candle, to light the fire. I writhed, twisting in the bedsheets. Everything going to get bloody. In the darkness, I whispered, "Oh, Mam."

From far, far away I hear, "Oh, Mam." Rosetta calling. I hoped she'd keep her promises better'n me.

Charles's head pushed its way out. Tearing me like a dozen knives.

Everything dark. I couldn't see my child's face. *But in my mind's eye, I see Mam.*

"Sorry, sorry, sorry," I said.

Moon raised herself high. Charles Redmond wailed. *Curtains flared and a breeze rushed over me.* Holding my bloodied babe to my breast, I heard a song: *"Here. Here. I'm here."* Heard Rosetta cooing, *"Mam. I love you."*

Dear Father,

We are reading the Revolutionary War.

The new Americans were very brave.

I am well. Please write.

Tell Mam I miss her. Tell the boys to draw pictures.

Love,
Rosetta

I stared at the words. Freddy read them to me and I memorized them. Rosetta didn't know she had a new brother. I should draw pictures too. Of me and the baby. I thought about how little she said. Almost nothing.

Christmas. School holiday. Rosetta was home. I was happy.

All Freddy did was talk politics: "War will come one day. See if it won't. The North can't ride the fence forever."

His words scared me. But he was jubilant. "War for the rights of slaves," he exclaimed. "Freedom for everyone."

All I wanted was home. Christmas feast. Hymns. Prayers to the good Lord. My children's safety.

I wanted, too, not to be so tired. Everything tired me. Rosetta was a big help. She fed Lewis and Freddy Junior. Helped clean the kicthen. Washed clothes. She didn't talk much about school. Freddy talked all the time. He be leaving again. To speak in New England. He practiced:

"I changed my paper's name from the *North Star* to *Frederick Douglass' Paper* . . . to distinguish it from the many papers with 'Stars' in their titles. There were 'North Stars,' 'Morning Stars,' 'Evening Stars,' and I know not how many in the firmament. . . ."

I didn't think his speech too interesting. Only when he say: "There were those who regarded the publication of a Negro paper, in the beautiful city of Rochester, as a blemish and a misfortune" did he perk my interest. Though I never thought Rochester beautiful.

In time, Freddy's voice became noise. His babble mingled with the boys' rough games.

I watched Rosetta. She be moody, be staring at herself in the mirror.

In the New Year, Freddy would be gone traveling. Rosetta would leave after. Freddy had planned to take her early to school. But Deacon Thomas offered to take her. Offered 'cause he knew I didn't want to lose a moment of me and Rosetta's time. Freddy didn't think of that.

Christmas Eve. Me and the children strung popcorn. Rosetta mixed cranberries with orange rind. We sang carols. Charles Redmond gurgled. We ate fine roast beef. Freddy even kissed me before the children. It be a fine night. We gathered in the parlor to exchange presents. Our tree be lit with candles and decorated with bows. Freddy Junior liked his wood whistle. Lewis, his ball. We saved extra to give Rosetta a doll. But when she unwraped the white china doll, she burst into tears and ran from the room.

Freddy be right angry. I told him, "Please, put the children to bed." He shrugged. I knew he'd only say, "Children. Go to bed." Then, hide in his office and preach abolition to the walls.

Fine. I laid my sleeping baby in his cradle. I found Rosetta on the front porch. Facedown, bent over her knees, crying her heart out. "I'm ugly. Always going to be ugly."

Then, I understood her dislike for the doll. Girls at school must've tried to dull her shine. I sat beside her on the step. "Did I ever tell you about how your granddad, my Papa, wooed your grandma, my Mam?"

"Naw. I mean, no."

"Naw be all right. My Mam said 'Naw.' She was the prettiest colored girl in all of Maryland. She said 'naw' to all her beaus. It be your granddad who got her to say, 'Yeah.' Not yes. Just 'Yeah, I do.' Didn't need proper speech to make a happy marriage."

Rosetta giggled.

"Didn't need no cream in her coffee, either." I held out my hand. "Darker than me. Pa was proud to marry Mam. She be a beautiful Egypt queen."

"Am I an Egypt queen?"

"No. Still a princess. Lovely, though, like Mam. You understand?"

She nodded.

"It be cold out here. Should we get our coats? Or get some hot chocolate and snuggle in Mam's bed?"

We talked all night. Talked until neither one of us could keep our eyes open. Freddy never came. Which was fine. Rosetta drifted to sleep, snuggling beneath quilts, soft against my bosom.

I whispered, "You beautiful. Just like Mam. Inside and out. Better than a china doll."

Half-wake, half-sleep, lids heavy, Rosetta sighed, "I won't forget again."

Them words made my best Christmas.

$\mathcal{L}$ate spring, my garden was in full bloom. All my children be home.

Rosetta cut and arranged dahlias. I taught her how to make corn relish.

Freddy Junior be six; Lewis, five; and Charles Redmond, almost one. Freddy had been gone for forever. I felt guilty 'cause I was glad he wasn't home, glad Miz Assing wasn't in the back bedroom.

My bones be hurting. I felt like I was "making memories." Like my whole life be passing by a lot faster than I wished. I felt Death coming. Not quite near but coming just the same. So, I let my children make mud pies, build campfires in the backyard, and sleep beneath the stars. I told them stories about the sea bones and the taste of crabs.

Some days, Rosetta played the pianoforte. Freddy Junior and Lewis made up songs. Nonsense tunes. I sang, too. They laughed since my notes be flat. Children didn't mind. They happier than they'd ever been. Even Rosetta didn't mind when Lewis ripped her paper dolls. Or when Charles Redmond sucked their heads off like sugar candy.

One evening, we all sat on the porch. Freddy Junior tried to catch fireflies in his Mason jar. Lewis giggled at the flickering lights leaping across the lawn. Charles was sleeping, open-mouthed, atop a quilt. I felt I'd gone back in time to Talbot County. Any minute, Mam gonna come out. Any minute, Pa gonna light his pipe and make his face shine in a halo.

I rocked. Content.

"See the patterns, Mam? In the stars?"

"Where you learn that from?"

"Teachers at school. See. There's the Big Dipper. The Little Dipper is right beside it. And there's Aquarius, the Water Bearer. Leo, the starry-eyed lion."

"My, God makes wonders."

"Won-der," said Lewis, tasting the big sound in his little mouth.

"School done taught you good things."

"Yes, ma'am." She scrunched her lips. Then leaned and kissed sleeping Charles.

Lewis was jumping off the steps, pretending he could fly. "Whee," flapped his arms. And he did it over and over again, even though I said "hush." But Charles was a good baby. Hardly a sound ever startled him. So I said nothing when Rosetta moved down the steps and said, "Fly. Fly to me." She caught Lewis and twirled him around 'til they both fell down dizzy.

"Mam! Mam!" Freddy Junior was almost to the gate, whooshing his jar through the air. "Mam!" he hollered shrill. "Mam!"

I stood. There were horsemen with torches, a wagonload of others. Some wore white hoods, covering their heads. Horses were neighing, snorting, breathing hard like they'd run many a mile. But the men made no sound. Like a passel of ghosts, dead and dumb, carrying the flames of hell.

Lewis began wailing. I snatched him up, yelled, "Freddy Junior, come, be a good man. Look after your sister and brothers."

Rosetta looked up at me.

"You the oldest. I rely on you. Let Freddy Junior help. You understand?"

She nodded. "Good girl," I thought. "My sweet, good girl."

Freddy Junior grabbed Lewis's hand. Rosetta, took the baby. "Out the back. Out the kitchen door. Into the fields."

"What about you?" Rosetta asked.

"I'll be there." I kept focused on the men. Must be about twenty. "Once I know you all safe, out the house. Hidden in the fields."

"Come on," said Freddy Junior.

"Go, Rosetta."

The screen door slammed shut. I heard its echo: the back screen door banged hard open. The children must be running across the field.

I let myself breathe. The moonlit night stank from burning oil. Fireflies gone. Not even a cricket sawing his legs.

Not one of those men said anything. I preferred the ones with hoods. The few without looked like rock. Stone-hatred. Like nothing could ever be said. Nothing could ever stop them from burning Frederick Douglass' house.

I didn't move. Stared just as cold at them. Stood my ground 'cause each minute I kept them focused on me, my children had one more minute to be gone.

Out the corner of my eye, I saw a man on the left move. Him, high on his horse, moved forward. Then, I heard a big *whoosh*. A torch was on the porch just behind me. I didn't flinch. Held steady. Then, someone else threw fire. Then, another. Flames started licking up the posts and I felt like an oven was opening around me.

I imagined the children, running, crazy, full out. Charles might be crying. Rosetta would be leading them to a good place. A torch hit the window; air cried out, and the glass shattered like rain. Splinters licked my arms.

I prayed, "God deliver us." Inhaled, exhaled. Twice. I wouldn't cry over things lost inside the house, my treasures were safe. Felt it in my heart and bones. Charles be sucking Rosetta's finger, quieting himself. Freddy Junior be telling Lewis, "You a good soldier." And, Rosetta, wide-eyed, watching left and right, forward and behind, would make certain no one saw them hiding, belly-low, in the wild.

Content, I stepped down off the porch. Walked like I was going for a Sunday stroll. My moving seemed to release their throats. They whooped and screamed like they was in a war fighting an army. They fired pistols. Bullets in the air, bullets at the windows. Bullets into the lattice trim. The big, white house was their enemy, fighting back something fierce.

I walked dignified, right down the middle, made those men part their horses. Not a one called my name. Though they all knew me. Some I might've purchased supplies from: flour, sugar; some I might've bought seed from: kale, collards. Or bartered eggs. Or did sewing for their wives. These white-hooded ghosts seemed like no one I knew. But I knew they knew me; and, in the sunshine, I would know them.

I walked without looking back. Hummed in my throat.

Later, I'd double back. Zigzag through the woods. Find the children. Watch the house burn to ash. Kiss them, saying, "What brave children you be." Pat Lewis's head; shake Freddy Junior's hand and pretend I didn't see him cry. Smile my widest smile for Rosetta. Tell her, "Thank you." Let Charles feed at my breast. When they all slept, huddled about me, arms and legs tumbled all over each other. When we were all as close as close could be—I'd—what? Think of Freddy? I didn't know. He ain't here. He never here.

Naw. I wouldn't let myself think that. I'd think I'd tell Mister Death to fight me if he want. But I ain't leaving this earth 'til my children be grown.

My church found ways to feed us. House us. Somebody rode and told Freddy. It took him a week to get home.

But he nearly flew from his horse and he hugged the children, played with them all afternoon 'til they all were worn out from the excitement. Even Rosetta yawned. We all sat down to supper.

Freddy thanked Pastor and Pastor's wife for their good care of us. Let Pastor praise God without minding that the food was getting cold. Even said, "Thank you for that heartfelt prayer."

All day, me and Freddy didn't say much. Freddy kept drinking in the children, like they water for a dying man. Every second he be kissing them. Every second, he be gracious, shouting his appreciation to the whole, wide world that his family was safe.

When the moon was quarter-high, we tucked the children in bed. Ready for a deep, satisfying sleep.

Freddy offered his hand. Together, we harnessed the horses to the wagon. Then, drove to the crusted, black mound that used to be home.

Moonlight made the house seem haunted. Like a haint going to rise up. Pale, white streaks cut across the scorched, black land. No marigolds. No green beans. Only twisted wires.

Freddy stepped over charred beams, kicked at shards of glass. He lingered in the far west corner, lifting his lantern high. His papers, books, all gone. Printing press gone. He set the kerosene lamp down and didn't move. I kept still, respectful of his mourning.

"Were you scared, Anna?"

"Some."

"Have I ever told you how proud I am of you?"

He wasn't looking at me. He was staring out across the horizon. Like I'd first seen him. His hair still long. Only a few gray strands. He, like me, be getting older.

"Thank you for keeping our children safe."

He turned, his arms wide open. I felt such love. I ran to him. He hugged me fierce. Soon I was crying. Freddy be kissing me all over.

"It's all right, Anna. It's all right. I'm here."

I sobbed for my lost Mam. Sobbed for my lost home. Rosetta's first blanket. My wedding dress. Sobbed for the times when I was mean, spiteful. Furious at Freddy. Sobbed 'cause my marriage seemed to have more rough than smooth.

Freddy pulled me onto the grass. Where it still grew green, it was soft. He kissed me with the same hunger as the first time. Shameless, he undressed me; I, him.

Beneath moon and stars, we loved on the grass. I cried out, "Freddy," digging my nails into his back, never wanting him to leave me. Leave my body. He must've felt this need too. For he stayed inside me for the longest time. His head buried in my neck. His tongue licking away my joyful tears.

We made Annie that night. My last child, second girl.

He helped me dress. I buttoned his shirt. I plucked grass from my hair and twisted a new bun. We be presentable. Holding hands like children, young lovers, we walked back to the wagon. The horse was stubborn when Freddy say, "Giddy-up." Freddy had to snap the whip to make him trot. I looked back at my lost home. Only later did I realize we'd made love in the garden where summer nights, Freddy and Miz Assing kept company.

*T*ime flew. Wasn't long before Freddy had the house rebuilt.

"I won't run, Anna. This is our home."

So be it. "You going to be here when they burn it again?" I wanted to ask. But that be water over the bridge. No sense asking him to stay.

The house rose like a white dream. I would've painted it blue. Would've built it cheaper, too. Freddy always gone to pay for it. Speeches, speeches, and more speeches.

As far as I was concerned they could've torched the house again. Freddy built it with an extra room (never mind extra cost) and I knew, come summer, Miz Assing be living in my house like a second wife. I didn't count how many summers. Ten, twelve. What's the use? Seemed like they just rolled into one, my long trial by fire. Most days, if I'm lucky, I just smelled her. Lilac was her scent. That sickly, sweet smell haunted my house; I threw open the windows even when it stormed.

Bible said man, like God, be head of his house. All right. Though, Freddy thought he lived in biblical times. Having many wives.

Sometimes I heard things. I wondered if Miz Assing did too. Julia Griffiths' sister, Amy Post, lived in town; Miz Post boasted, "Julia's a dear, dear friend to Mr. Douglass." Humpf. White women could sure lack dignity. Colored women too. In church, sanctified women sat in the pew behind me. Before the children came in from Sunday school, they talked, whispering, but wanting me to hear every word. They read all the colored papers and what they couldn't read, they heard as good gossip from the Pullman porters. They always managed to say, "She white." Like that be the bigger insult. I rarely shopped in town.

Couldn't stand the false "how-dos," then, the tittering behind gloves. I almost quit church. But before I knew it, Pastor would be on my door wanting to know why. I couldn't lie to him.

"Thou shalt not covet thy neighbor's wife." How come it don't say husband? Covet thy neighbor's husband? Maybe God knew married women be more faithful. Obeyed their vows.

Miz Assing don't go to church any more than Freddy. But Freddy went on special days: Easter, Christmas. He knew colored folks wouldn't stand for him being godless. Even now, after all these years, I don't know how deep his faith be.

Mine be deep. But I never expected God to make life perfect. Didn't get angry at Him even when I hurt the most. Even when I was awake, knowing Freddy be inside Miz Assing, down the hall. *Lord, have mercy.*

I drew strength from my children. My garden. As Miz Sojourner Truth say, "Ain't I a woman?" I'd feelings. I'd survived by fighting back in "little ways" where and when I could. Small battles. Still.

I'd survived by being me. Anna.

Ottilie

"I waited, wasted my life away."

—OTTILIE ASSING,
DIARY ENTRY, 1857

*"Miz Stowe's book, Uncle Tom's Cabin, made me
wish I could read. Well and good. Like you."*

—ANNA DOUGLASS,
SPEAKING TO ROSETTA, 1857

I was in a cheap boardinghouse in the nation's capital. Douglass wanted his speech transcribed, translated into German for publication:

"Gratitude to Benefactors is a well recognized virtue. . . ."

I'd heard Douglass give this speech numerous times and each time, I'd felt outrage. He'd never thanked me. Never mentioned me.

"When the true history of the antislavery cause shall be written, women will occupy a large space in its pages, for the cause of the slave has been peculiarly woman's cause. Her heart and her conscience have supplied in large degree its motive and mainspring. Her skill, industry, patience, and perseverance have been wonderfully manifest in every trial hour."

For eighteen years, I'd served Douglass to the best of my ability. A true companion. Lover. Strategist.

There was only one thing I was certain about: Douglass hadn't lost interest in the fair sex. Nor they in him.

"Foremost among these noble American women . . ."

American. Not German.

"Foremost among these noble American women, in point of clearness of vision, breadth of understanding, fullness of knowledge, catholicity of spirit, weight of character, and widespread influence, was Lucretia Mott of Philadelphia."

Old witch.

"Kindred in spirit with Mrs. Mott was Lydia Marie Child."

I appreciated these women. Truly. But they were sanctimonious in the extreme. They held their teas and never invited me. Each passing year, I grew lonelier and lonelier.

"For solid, persistent, indefatigable work for the slave, Abby Kelley was without rival."

Miss Kelley survived more egg peltings than anyone.

"Nor must I omit to name the daughter of the excellent Myron Holly, who in her youth and beauty espoused the cause of the slave. . . ."

But what of *your* daughter? The summer your house burned, Miss Seward sent a letter kindly asking Rosetta not to return. Poor Rosetta. She endured much for our fine principles. Now nearly a lady grown, she hasn't stopped struggling to please you. Off to Oberlin College to be educated, of course; but, particularly, because she'd thought you'd approve. Have you told her? That you admire her? That you're grateful? I can still hear her saying, "Don't embarrass Father." Her vision of life.

When I felt downcast, I reminded myself that Rosetta and Anna have less of you than I do.

"Recognizing not sex nor physical strength, but moral intelligence and the ability to discern right from wrong, good from evil . . . I was not long in reaching the conclusion that there was no foundation in reason or justice for woman's exclusion from the vote."

No, it didn't take you long to herald the cause of women. I'd a hand in this. For wasn't I the first woman to argue with you as an equal? To challenge your interest with my mind? Long before the body. Confessions of love. Remember, Douglass?

"Mrs. Elizabeth Cady Stanton, when she was yet a young lady and an earnest abolitionist, she was at the pains of setting before me in a very strong light the wrong and injustice of this exclusion."

Youth, beauty, and intelligence. I'd grown less youthful, less beautiful. My mind remains. Unfortunately, in America, in this world, time blunts the appeal of a woman's thoughts. Why does intellect seem sharper when one's face is unlined?

"What can be said of the gifted authoress of Uncle Tom's Cabin, Harriet Beecher Stowe? Happy woman must she be that to her was given the power in such unstinted measure to touch and move the popular heart! More than to reason or religion are we indebted to the influence which this wonderful delineation of slavery produced on the public mind."

"More than to reason or religion . . ." Douglass didn't really care about religious hypocrites. But, oh, how it bothered him that emotion, not reason, won the day! "To touch and move the popular heart . . ." Didn't anyone but me understand the condescension?

> *"Nor were all my influential friends all of the Caucasian race. While many of my own people thought me unwise and somewhat fanatical in announcing myself a fugitive slave, there were brave and intelligent men of color all over the United States who gave me their cordial sympathy and support.*
>
>   *"I need not name my colored friends to whom I am thus indebted. They do not desire such mention. . . ."*

Why was Douglass so sure? Would it have hurt to speak gratitude? Or, maybe, he didn't speak it, because there'd be no gain. White women opened their purses.

I ought to go home. But where to?

> *"In a word, I have never yet been able to find one consideration, one argument, or suggestion in favor of man's right to participate in civil government which did not equally apply to the right of woman."*

Frederick Douglass was indeed a great man. How sorry I was to love him.

Anna

"Who will remember me?"

—Anna Douglass,
on her deathbed, 1882

*"My brothers and I. Our children
and our children's children."*

—Rosetta Douglass,
answering her mother, 1882

*M*ister Death be playing hide and seek with me. Some days I could barely stand. Barely get out of a chair once I sat down. I was growing older with the children. Except life be new for them; for me, it be just Time. Time be Mister Death's cousin. Liked to play tricks. When everything happy, Time flew fast. But with me, Time made a minute seem an hour, an hour seem a day. Telling the same tale. Same story. Not a bad story, just the same one. Caring and tending to life. Be it the children, the garden, or my chickens out back. As my body slowed, Time slowed, seemed like life needed me less. Or wanted me less. My garden, on its own, bloomed fine. My chicks ran wild.

Rosetta had already gone to Oberlin. The boys were ready for trades. Fine, educated boys. "But they must learn a trade," I'd say. I worried they were too proud. Too proud to take off their coats and chop wood. Too proud to get dirty, work among laborers. They kept saying they be Frederick Douglass' sons. As though that made life easier. "They still colored," I say.

Rosetta say, "I want to teach." That be fine. She could teach colored children. Teach her babies book-learning. Unlike me.

I'd like to read *Uncle Tom's Cabin*.

Annie reads it to me. She be my dream child. If it weren't for her, I'd tell Cousin Time, "Stop fooling. Tell Mister Death to come on." But Annie, by her own self, could make Time fly with happiness.

I told Freddy he could do what he wanted with the other children. But Annie, my late-in-life child, I'd school as Mam schooled me. I insisted Pastor teach her letters. Freddy thought I didn't understand the importance of learning. But I did. My children lived in a different world.

With Rosetta gone, the boys at school, making mischief like boys

do, me and Annie made a pair. We sang spirituals. She read me the
Bible. We cooked. Gardened. Told each other tales. Sometimes I felt
scared at how happy I be. Eleven years, Annie'd been in my life. Eleven
years, she'd never left home. Never wanted to go. Yet, that didn't mean
she wasn't interested in *doing,* in living life full.

Annie was always up under me. Curious. Wanting to know how to
make fancy cakes, not plain cakes, how to snip flowers and feed them
syrup-water to make them last longer. How to starch curtains so they
flapped like angel's wings. How to make a seed ball for birds to eat in winter. *"How do you? How do you?"* Questions until my head tired. It be
Annie who kissed my brow, brought a blanket when I was cold. Annie—
young enough not to be embarrassed saying, "I love you, Mam."

It be Annie who brought life home from the wild forest. A twig
with a spider's web. A leaf with a cocoon attached. Ants in a box, bur-
rowing in dirt.

It be Annie who wanted to know the old tales: horn-footed devil,
skeletons in the sea, spirits of the dead. Even though Mam's dead, she
ain't dead. I pointed out the star I thought she'd be. The breeze that
flapped the curtain when we were stirring grits. "Sometimes," I told
Annie, "Mam be the ladybug, pausing on the porch step."

In the afternoon, me and Annie rocked in our chairs. Content not to
say nothing. Just enjoy the day. After a while, all the animals came visiting.
Butterflies hovered. A buck and doe wandered onto the grass. An eagle
glided past the roof; we could see its blinking eye. Annie liked ladybugs best.
I told her they be good luck if they landed on you. Never told her the old
rhyme: "Ladybug, ladybug, fly away home. Your house is on fire, your children are gone." Seem like we went through that. Before Annie was born.

Annie be the good luck child. No sorrow in her. The promise of a
summer morn.

Annie reminded me of me. Before I became a housekeeper. Before I
Miz Frederick Douglass.

Freddy didn't argue when I insisted Annie stay home. Maybe he
afraid another white woman schoolteacher send his second girl home
too! Maybe he tired from supporting five children and a wife. Cheaper
for Annie to stay home. Maybe he knew I wouldn't back down. Maybe
he knew he owed me for years and years of lonely days.

Whatever the reason, I'm glad Annie stayed. I needed her more
than she needed me.

Ottilie

"Douglass was going to lose all because of one unthinking white man."

—OTTILIE ASSING
DIARY ENTRY, 1859

"John Brown was a martyr."

—FREDERICK DOUGLASS,
NEWSPAPER EDITORIAL, 1861

ohn Brown will get you killed," I told Douglass. "He'll get you killed."

The two had been meeting regularly. Sometimes in Boston, sometimes in Rochester. I distrusted Brown from the start. Ascetic, thin beyond pleasing, rangy and tall. Some say he looks like the politician Lincoln. Except Lincoln has warmth in his eyes. Brown's eyes are ice. Stone cold.

"Don't you see how Brown is using you?"

"I'm a grown man of intelligence, Ottilie."

"I'm not questioning your intelligence. I'm questioning Brown's." Indeed, I shuddered when Brown raised his Bible high into the air, proclaiming, "God's will. Killing to free the slaves is God's will. Look to the Israelites."

If Papa was alive, he'd argue history shouldn't dictate present actions. Papa and Mama both believed in the healing power of love. But what offended me most was Brown's proclamation, "I am the black people's Moses." Such arrogance. Moses, the black driver I first met in America, was more special than this lunatic Brown.

I caressed Douglass' arm. "Don't you see? Militancy will make it harder for the slaves."

"How long, Ottilie? How long? Over twenty years, I've been working to free the slaves. Over a hundred years, black bodies have been sold, bartered, and exchanged. Violence may be necessary."

"This isn't like you."

"How do you know? This *is* me. Angry. Irate. Disgusted by the slow pace. Politics, appealing to whites' better nature has no effect."

"Come, Douglass. Let me soothe you."

He looked at me so angrily, I stepped back.

I'd risked the journey to see Douglass in winter, because my body missed him. I'd risked the journey because I'd heard Brown was in New England enlisting supporters and their money for his "holy war." I'd risked the journey because only a few months ago, Douglass (foolishly!) let Brown stay in his home and write a new constitution for a free slave territory. I'd risked the journey because I needed him. Needed Douglass to keep himself safe.

"Don't you see? Anti-Brown supporters have already burnt your home, threatened your children. Don't you see? Violence begets violence."

"Wouldn't you be as militant for the suffragette cause?"

"Picketing isn't the same as raising a gun."

"Brown understands the pain of black people."

"Nonsense."

Douglass' sigh was a moan. The sound was wrenched from him. "It makes sense to me."

"What?"

"It makes sense to me. Just as I fought Covey, Brown is encouraging the race to rise up."

"Douglass—"

"Sssh, Ottilie." He kissed me tenderly.

"You're tired. You look tired," I said.

"Yes. Bone-weary. Heartsore. Every breath I take as a free man is borne on the backs of slaves. How can I enjoy freedom? Twenty years. I've talked myself hoarse. Twenty years. No change. I think Miss Tubman does more with her Underground Railroad than I've ever done."

"Not true."

He clasped me in his arms. I could feel his strength, almost crushing me, taking my breath away. I caressed his hair. "Douglass, Douglass," I said.

He pulled back. Tears were in his eyes. "War, Ottilie. There'll be war."

"If there is, let the president be the one to start it. Not Brown. He only wants to be a martyr."

"Don't we all."

"What are you saying?" I shuddered. "You're not planning anything foolish?"

"No more foolish than a white man capturing slaves. No more foolish than another white man believing he's their savior."

He blinked like a curtain drawn, a scene shift in a play. He blinked. Firelight shone in his eyes. He blinked and became a shadow of himself.

He picked up his coat and gloves. "I must go. Anna isn't well."

I bit the inside of my cheek. Tasted blood. I wanted to shout, "Stay!" Instead I said, "Give her my regards."

Head cocked, face blank, he replied, "I'll do that." Then, he opened the door and left.

I stood, shocked and still, in a hotel room. Snow fell outside and I could imagine Douglass, ever proud, walking to his carriage. Only later did I find the money he'd left beneath the tea service. It made me feel like an unused whore.

✢

John Brown. Such a simple name. Anything but a simple man.

John Brown built a shack in the Carolinas. Whispered to free black men, whispered to slaves, "Armageddon is here." Oh, what an uprising he planned. Nothing less than the murder of every slave owner. Including their wives and children. *"Everyone who participates in slavery is a sinner. Wrath to all of them."*

Wrath. John Brown thought he was God's wrath. The sin of pride he had.

"Hills will keep us safe. A single man can hold off a hundred in the hills." So, the slaves believed. Some equipped with picks, shovels. Some with guns.

This was the story as I'd heard it:

John Brown led a raid on Harpers Ferry, Virginia. But before that, there'd been warnings. In Kansas, bloody Kansas, the ground ran red. He fought to keep slavery out of the territory.

In Kansas, John Brown shot a man to death. With a broadsword, he hacked to bits two others. They say, "Pieces were licked and chewed by the dogs." Cruel. Barbaric beyond measure.

Brown said he was establishing a black utopia in the hills. Another Underground Railroad for fugitives. But his grand design was reduced to war. Brown's small army was on the move. Hiding, ducking, and skirting capture in the South. They disguised their real plan: an attack on the military arsenal in Harpers Ferry, Virginia. "We'll arm every slave. They'll be a rise of swarming bees," declared Brown, who crazily argued that Douglass should join him, become "queen bee" to control the swarming blacks.

Douglass said, "No." For the record, he refused Brown's call to arms. Refused to follow the words of a man he'd lost faith in.

October 16, 1859

Brown and a group of twenty-two seized the arsenal. Two men were sent out to rally the slaves to revolt. Revolt never came. The army surrounded the arsenal. All Brown's troops were either killed or captured. Brown was bound, cursing slave owners to Hell, raging like the Devil himself.

And, oh, what hell he wrought.

For days, weeks, months, all throughout the South, whites were in the grip of insanity. Slaves found life much, much harder than before. For the German papers, I told of the vicious attacks on helpless people. Told of heartrending screams. Beatings. The rash of hangings. Every slave, age six to eighty-six, was capable of revolt. Every girl child or old woman was capable of mixing poison. So, no male was left unmarked, no woman untouched by suspicion.

"John Brown will get you killed."

Douglass was in danger. A note from him was found in Brown's papers:

> *"My dear Cpt. Brown, I am very busy at home. Will you please, come up with my son Fred and take a mouthful with me?"*

The note was published in the nation's papers. Virginia, Philadelphia, New York. Never mind that it had been written two years before. Virginia's Governor Wise insisted that President Buchanan send soldiers to arrest Douglass. The charge: "Inciting Servile Insurrection." To my mind, this was payment for all the times Douglass stood proudly as a man.

History repeats.

"Flee, flee!" I shouted at Douglass. "Flee. Flee," said abolitionists. Even Garrison begged Douglass to "Flee. They'll hang you for certain."

Run for your life.

No time for long good-byes. Run, Douglass. I'll run with you.

He was in New York when the headlines of his presumed betrayal hit. He stole away to my rooms in Hoboken and spent an anxious, waiting time. How I tried to comfort him. He was the fugitive again. He'd done nothing to help Brown's raid, but here he was tormented. Blamed.

In the morning, I, took a carriage with him as far as Paterson, New Jersey. Douglass, took the train with a connection to Rochester. But he wasn't safe. It was only a matter of days before the Rochester papers printed his letter.

Amy Post carried a letter from William Still, a colored, famous for his Underground Railroad work, warning Douglass to get out. *Flee*, it said. *Run, nigger, run.* Douglass left his house. Kissed his family good-bye. Took a boat to Canada.

I never got a good-bye. Not a word. Never got to say good-bye as weeks later, from Canada, he sailed across the Atlantic.

And whom should he meet in England? Julia Griffiths. A "kind" friend, the type who left notes unsigned, wrote and told me.

Julia, now married to Reverend Crofts. But that didn't matter. Pastor, so liberal in his thinking, would graciously tolerate his wife's wonderfully famous paramour. So jealous I was. Julia and Frederick! I told myself: "Love is free." This was the principle my mother and the Romantics taught me. Still I fumed, reading that Douglass was the Crofts' guest through Christmas and all through January. I wondered if Anna's illiteracy meant she experienced less pain than I? After all, how would she know of the insinuations, the gossip written in the two-faced spirit of friendship? The lingering touches, the kiss witnessed by a serving girl. The rumors of doors flying open at night . . . of ghosts ever so tangible, moving from bedroom to bedroom.

I, so smart (not smart enough!), had long known I was not the only (nor even the first) mistress of Frederick Douglass.

Mother married Father and they both loved true. Wasn't that the Romantic Ideal? Anna never had it. Neither did I.

Or am I just becoming proletarian? I should've married William. Been a grocer's wife.

December 2, 1859, John Brown was hanged.

In Britain's Mechanic's Hall, Douglass gave a speech, reaffirming himself as a self-made man: "I decide my own course."

I crumbled the paper and burnt it in my fireplace.

I waited a year.

Then I went looking for him.

Anna

"He ain't here."

—Anna Douglass,
1859

"I should have been there to support your mother."

—Frederick Douglass,
writing to Rosetta, 1860

*H*e ain't here." "He ain't here." When the militia came. When curious neighbors came. When church gossips came. I said what I got used to saying the last twenty years: *"He ain't here."*

I was glad Freddy was gone. *He could be hanged. Limbs loose. Tongue black. Freddy could be hanged, side by side, with John Brown.*

I never cared for Brown. He came in my house like he was God or an angel at least. He gonna free the slaves with war. Hallelujah! Why he think slaves gonna follow him? A colored man gets hit twice for each lash given to a white. Sometimes the white man don't even get punished. Just hang the colored man. Liked they were trying to hang Freddy, saying he was a traitor.

Give America its due: John Brown was hanged. Good riddance, I say. But Rosetta say some papers now called Freddy a "cowardly runaway." Abolitionists had been swayed to violence. Brown be a martyr. A hero. Freddy, a weak link for the cause. I be so angry. Freddy been speaking all his life against slavery.

Rosetta say, "Mr. Henry Thoreau gave a speech: *A Plea for John Brown.*"

Everybody North weeped, then rallied to fight. Brown dead, they could now destroy the colored man.

I told Rosetta to write Freddy and tell him to stay safe, law-abiding. To keep quiet 'til he was sure who his friends be. Abolitionists couldn't be trusted no more.

Lewis came home bloodied one day. Said he fought to prove "Father wasn't a coward."

Mercy. My boys too eager to fight. Feeling shame when their Daddy be a good, upright man. Strange world—when abolitionists called the one who felt slavery's lash a "no-account" weakling. Coward. They would've loved him better if he was hung?

I thought Freddy was smart to survive.

I was pleased to say, "He ain't here."

"He ain't here. Ain't here."

"*Isn't. Isn't* here." Rosetta kept correcting me. The words became a sore: "Freddy ain't here."

All winter, my mind was on Freddy. I worried sick even though he wrote Rosetta saying he was safe in England at the Croftses, with Julia (born Griffiths) and her Reverend husband. Good Christian people. They had opened their home and I was grateful. The scent of war in the air and my boys, tall as oaks, be sniffing the breeze like hounds on a hunt. I wanted Freddy to tell Freddy Junior to stop shooting cans in the yard. Wanted him to scold Charles and Lewis for battling with sticks instead of doing their chores. Many a time, Annie cleaned a grate for Charles, laid down clean straw when the boys were deciding how best to stab a man. Like John Brown, my boys say, "When the first shot is fired, all the slaves are going to rise up."

"Ain't that simple," I told them. "Otherwise would've happened."

The boys roll their eyes. I'm a woman, don't understand much, but I understood keeping my family alive.

But still. I was blind.

I was so busy fretting, I didn't see him. Didn't see Mister Death sliding in the back door (pretending he Father Christmas). He took a good long look at Annie.

It was a cold. A simple cold. Annie, hazel-eyed, curly-haired, my sweet baby girl, one day couldn't rise from her bed. Couldn't even rise to eat her Christmas orange or sing carols with the boys. Rosetta calmed me. Told me, "Never fear." For a while, I didn't.

Rosetta read stories of Sir Gawain, blessed with purity of heart. "Goodness never died," read Rosetta. "Goodness brings great strength."

I watched as Annie smiled. Just ten. She be all that's bright and ever-sweet.

In January, the fever and chills came. The boys tiptoed about the house, ever quiet. Brought in firewood. Icy well water. Extra blankets from the attic. Whatever was needed. They set aside war talk. Made up stories. Whittled dolls.

I stayed by Annie's side. Made me a cot. I swore Death wasn't going to find me sleeping. Wasn't going to steal my namesake child.

I wiped her body down. Changed her gown. Sheets. Held compresses to her brow. Brushed the dirt from her hair. Massaged her feet. I did everything a mother could.

I sang as Mam sang to me.

I prayed, "Take me, spare her." I stood at the window, imagining water, the ocean, bay, rivers, imagining the bones I'd long lost and no longer saw. "Please. Please. Let me be the one."

Mid-February, Annie sat up. She'd eat if I placed small, soft bites in her mouth. Or spooned her fresh water.

"Mam," she once say to me. "I seen your Mam."

"Naw," I cried.

"All of us going to be fine, she said."

"Naw, naw." I howled for Mam, myself, my marriage . . . my children grown, bursting to get out the door and leave home. 'Cept Annie. My youngest child.

"She said an angel will come and carry me."

I hoped Annie was dreaming. Or crazed from fever.

Come March, when crocus and daffodils started to push through the earth, Annie was much better. Even laughed when Freddy Junior made a coin disappear in her ear.

I breathed a great sigh. Made a fine dinner. Roast beef. Potatoes. Yellow cake. Everyone in Annie's room, like this our new parlor. I knitted a bed cloak. Rosetta stitched *A. D.* on six handkerchiefs. She kept her back to Annie so she couldn't see her birthday surprise.

"Nine more days you be eleven. What you want?"

Annie just smiled. Rosetta teased: "You want a beau? How about a chariot? Or Sir Gawain slaying a dragon?" Charles Redmond say, "Pick. You got to pick something you want." Lewis, who never had any money, said, "I'll buy you a doll." Freddy Junior say, "Kisses. I'll give you eleven kisses."

Annie just smiled some more.

Candles burned low and, one by one, the boys said good night. Rosetta opened *Knights of the Round Table*.

"No more," said Annie. "Thank you all."

Rosetta saw first what I didn't. "You all right, Annie?" she asked, her tone sharp.

Annie just nodded and said, "Cover me. I'm cold."

Rosetta gave her a big hug, then tucked in the blankets. "I'll heat a brick. It'll warm you."

"Yes," I said. Then: "Rosetta, why you cry?" Her eyes glistened. She just shook her head and ran from the room.

"Mam?" Ever soft.

I turned and saw a girl, mostly bones, lost in a big bed. I wailed: "Annie?" And before I could gather her into my arms, Mister Death done snatched her soul and gone.

Ottilie

"Poor Annie. Poor Anna."

—OTTILIE ASSING
DIARY ENTRY, 1877

"I could not help but wonder whether
Annie's death was part of my burden of guilt."

—FREDERICK DOUGLASS,
IN A LETTER TO ROSETTA, 1860

Glasgow

I found him in Scotland. I sold my mother's pearls, booked passage across the Atlantic, traveled by carriage and by rail, and caught up with him in a Glasgow lecture hall.

How hearty and hale he looked! In the midst of people, he was the center of attention. No John Brown critics here, calling him "traitor." Or "pacifist." Only Scots held breathless by his every word.

I stood off to the side, waiting for him to recognize me. I'd bought a new dress—with a clan shawl striped in red and green. My hair was less severe and I'd bought red paint for my mouth.

I watched him and my desire grew strong. He was still my lion, bronzed and vibrant. Scotsmen were utterly unappealing. They seemed too dour, effeminate, with their kilts and pale white skin.

The women, on the other hand, were glorious. Red- and golden-haired. Blue- and green-eyed. Staggeringly lovely. I was alert. There were no stolen glances, no pressed fingers. No languishing glance from across the room.

He must've felt my presence, for he looked up.

"Ottilie." He came to me with arms outstretched. We clasped hands and Douglass gave a tug that pulled me close. "I've missed you," he whispered into my ear. Then he introduced me all around:

"Famous German reporter. Painter. My translator, Ottilie Assing."

A few clapped. Most shook hands. Ladies politely nodded.

Side by side with Douglass, I felt at home again. Absence had intensified my emotions. I felt his comforting hand on my back and felt safer, more cared for than I had in years.

We were hurried off to a castle, a great, crumbling pile, it seemed to me. But Douglass was honored. Honored by the great party. The almost orgy of excess: lamb, potatoes, and stewed beets. Bagpipes filled the air, managing to sound both mournful and lustful.

Everyone drank whiskey, danced reels. The men seemed to compete for whose kilt could rise the highest, who could best show their bare bottom to good effect. Unlike the English, the Scots were affectionate. Hugs and kisses all around. Douglass laughed when men kissed my cheek or hailed me with effusive compliments. Douglass didn't try to steal a kiss. But as I danced, I felt he watched me. Among swirling bodies, capes, kilts, and clan scarves, we were aware of each other's presence. The party seemed intended only for us.

A few hours short of dawn, Douglass offered to take me to my hotel.

"The Claymore," I responded.

"How industrious, Ottilie. How neatly you discovered my whereabouts." His voice low, he kissed my hand and we were away, leaving revelry behind.

In the closed carriage, Douglass couldn't help himself. Nor could I. We came together as two lost at sea, now found. Hot, close, quick. I shuddered against him. He held me on his lap, caressing, murmuring, "Ottilie. My dear Ottilie." As the carriage slowed, I lifted myself from him, smoothed my dress and hair.

Across from him, in the soft darkness, in the swaying carriage, I said bluntly, "I want to share your room."

"Circumspection, Ottilie."

"As you were with Julia Griffiths?"

"If you've come to criticize, you can go."

"Where?"

"Home."

"America?"

"Where you please."

"You used to enjoy my banter."

"Peace, please, Ottilie. Tell me the news of America."

I heard the tiredness, irritation in his voice. I stared at the window with its blackened screen pulled down. I didn't want him to be angry with me.

"Brown's dead. Abolitionists, more militant. It isn't safe for you to return."

"Tell me what I don't know."

"Fury is still heating up over the Kansas-Nebraska Act," I said.

"It completely undoes the Missouri Compromise."

"Yes. It allows slavery to enter the territories."

"War will come," Douglass said, his voice calm.

"Will you take part in it?" I asked.

"If I must. Though I dreamt of constitutional change."

We sat silent for a few moments.

"The Scots love you."

"A runaway? Why not? A uniquely American tragedy. They can feel both sorry for and superior to me."

"You exaggerate."

"Do I?"

The carriage made a sharp turn. I lifted the screen. It was snowing. Hotel lights blinked like snowdrops. Shoulders hunched, chin bowed, Douglass' face seemed all crevices and shadows.

"Why didn't you write? Ease my worry?" I touched my fingers to his lips. "No, you needn't answer. I've traveled thousands of miles to see you. I love you, Douglass. I don't believe I'll ever stop."

Hooves quieted on cobblestone. "Claymore Hotel," hailed the driver. Douglass got out first, then helped me down. Just barely, a streak of yellow lit the horizon. My hands trembled, for I'd risked all. How many years did it take to speak my heart so forthrightly?

Purposefully, I thought, Douglass kept his eyes averted. He paid the driver. Tipped the doorman who opened the hotel's great, wood doors.

My room was on a different floor than Douglass'. I walked the hallway with Douglass beside me, feeling condemned.

"Good night, Herr Douglass."

"Fräulein." He lifted my hands, kissed my left palm, then the right. With his eyes, he seemed to be searching my face. For what? I don't know. But he must've been satisfied. For he murmured, insistently and sweetly, "Come live with me and be my love."

"And we will all the pleasures prove."

Like the good shepherd and his lover, we made each other whole again.

How best to describe those Scottish days and nights? I felt young again. A girl embarking upon a new love. A new adventure. Douglass felt it, too, I'm certain. We walked the heather and the hills in snowshoes. Visited the castles of Lochmere. Afternoons we sipped tea laced with whiskey and Douglass wrote. I sent an article to *Morgenblatt*. A plea for less haste in judging John Brown a saint.

I took up my paints again. Trying to capture the Glasgow port, the tall-ship masts against the splendor of mountains and gray foam waves.

Nights, Douglass slipped into my room. All my hurts slipped away, all my loneliness.

Six weeks we had. Six weeks to rival our first sojourn in London. Six weeks before Rosetta's letter.

March 13, 1860

Dearest Father,

Annie is now an angel. She is gone to Him whose love is the same for the black as for the white.

Mother sends her love and wants to know when you'll come home.

Mother, desolate, is not well now. She is quite feeble about the house.

Your Affectionate Daughter,

Rosetta

With no thought to his safety, Douglass headed back to America. To evade his captors, he went by ship to Portland, Maine, then by train to Montreal, then he headed southwest, down to America, to his home.

I, who'd long since given up God, prayed. Prayed, yes, to keep Douglass safe. Prayed for Annie's soul. Of all Douglass' children, I had known her the least.

Sometimes, late at night, I stared out the window at the Scottish hills. Bagpipes sounded like laments. Like children, animals wailing. Like my own heart about to burst. How fickle I was. Christian. Jew. No matter. I'd prized intellect over faith. Yet how quick I'd run to God if it meant another day with Douglass.

I remained in Glasgow for a few weeks, then headed east to Germany.

I made a pilgrimage to my parents' graves.

I stopped praying. I was well aware the world could call me many things. But not, I hoped, "hypocrite."

Anna

"She be the daughter you let me keep.
I must've sinned good for God to take her."

— ANNA DOUGLASS,
1859

"With Annie dead, I thought
our marriage, too, was dead."

— FREDERICK DOUGLASS,
1860

*F*reddy came home. Comforted the children. Tried to comfort me. He didn't give no speeches for four months. A good long time for him. He stayed home, tried to feed me peaches. Get me to water my garden. Tried to get me to sew myself a pretty dress. But with Annie gone, no life was left in me. At least, not for this world.

Annie, six months dead, and I still couldn't believe it. I loved all my children. But the boys went their own way quick; Rosetta, once she got a taste of school, had no patience for housekeeping; while sweet Annie was always content by my side. She reminded me of myself and Mam. Maybe that's why my heart broke down so. Past and present mixed liked sugar and water. Now all that's left be memories.

Annie was the only baby Freddy got to see born. He acted like I was dying, but when the midwife didn't arrive, he held out his strong hands and caught Annie, bloodied and brown, and already wailing.

"She's beautiful, Anna."

I cradled her. She was beautiful: eyelashes, thick and black; her head, full of curls.

"Annie," Freddy whispered. "Let's name her Annie, after you."

Freddy's kindness touched me. I knew this child be my last. I clasped his hand. "Don't send her away. Ever."

Annie burped and I laughed. Freddy laughed. Soon, we be hugging, laughing, our eyes full of tears. Our other children came running, expecting sorrow. But barely a minute old, Annie brought happiness. Everyone giggled. Each day she lived, she graced my life with joy. I remembered:

Annie, at two, learning her first word: "Pie." Apple, peach, cherry, pumpkin, sweet potato—she loved all pies. Couldn't help sticking her fingers in, tearing off the crust.

Annie, four, crawling into bed with me, asking for stories about Big Blues, endless ocean, and spirit bones. "Tell me again. Like the first time." And I did, over and over, told her tales of the happiness of catching crabs, chasing fireflies, and summer nights when Mam and Pa and all us children sat, played, and told stories on the porch like we owned the whole world.

Annie, six, coming out to the garden, seeing me sweating, my hands gnarled from pain. "Rest, Mama," she said, and taking the seeds from my hands, made holes in the black soil, planted the seeds, covered them gently and sprinkled water. Those plants bore more vegetables than we could ever eat. Fine, fat tomatoes. Tender greens. Bright cucumbers and squash. Every planting thereafter, Annie was humming a song beside me.

Eight, Annie helped with all my chores. Took real pleasure from it. I'd say, "Go play," but while her brothers romped, Annie basted a roast and made the sweetest breads.

Ten, her womanhood was starting to flower. "You a pretty girl," I said. She hugged me tight and murmured, "I love you, Mam."

I love you, Mam. Annie was me at ten years old. I felt Mam's presence cloak us in love. Felt Annie's fingers, my fingers, Mam's fingers squeezing, holding tight, promising never to let go.

𝔛

All those, wet spring months—March, April, May, all summer, all fall—memories haunted. No matter the weather: hot, sticky beyond dreaming; leaves turning yellow and dying; frost lining the windows. Annie's spirit shadowed my every thought, my every word.

Annie was good. Kinder than me. She was Freddy's dream child. Soon as he walked in the door, tired from journeying, he'd call, "Annie," and she'd come sliding down the banister and throw herself into his arms. Freddy never chastised her like he did the others. Never insisted she be an example for colored society. Be better than anyone else because her name was "Douglass." Freddy never did anything but love her.

And when he laughed, tickled, hugged my namesake, I felt as though Freddy was loving me.

Loving the girl, the Baldwins' maid. Loving the girl I used to be.

Freddy came home from Scotland. I'd worried he'd blame me for Annie dying. But all he did was hold me and cry. Wailed like he, himself, was a little-bitty baby. I rocked him and let him stroke me until my body was afire with more than fever.

In the morning, though, he seemed embarrassed. Like loving wasn't true to Annie's memory. He didn't say that but I felt it. He said, "I'll sleep in my office, Anna. So you can rest better." I was hurt. But I was often racked with fever, hauntings. I flailed, tangled myself in sheets.

Each evening, Freddy spent an hour with me after dinner and just talked and talked. His hands moved like fans, and from time to time, he slapped his thigh to make a point. I liked watching his face, seeing the fire was still in him.

Some nights, my bedroom be like a parlor. Freddy and the children crowded in, talking about the day's news. Most times I stared out the window, watching whatever life swept by. Sometimes a bird. A rabbit. A baby doe. Sometimes I listened. Or, at least, well enough to know Lincoln be running for president.

"Lincoln's not an abolitionist," Freddy said, "But he's antislavery."

"Don't antislavery and abolition be the same?"

"Lincoln would return runaways." A shadow crossed Freddy's face. Fists clenched, pounding his thigh, he remembered his time on the run. "I hope to change his mind."

"War," I exhaled.

"Yes. It's coming."

"Truly. This time."

Freddy Junior hollered, "Praise the Lord."

Lewis and Charles pretended to fire guns from behind my rocker. Freddy Junior clutched his heart like he's hurt. Just like children. 'Cept they grown men with no more sense than chickens. War, when it comes, will make rivers run red. Plenty of bones buried in dirt. I started to cry.

Freddy shooed everybody out. Rosetta offered to make me tea.

Seasons came and went. *I dreamt Mam and Annie be waiting for me.*

•   •   •

My spring garden be a tangled mess. First time in a good while, I felt like I should get up. Put my house in order. Annie's been dead a year now.

I was still ill, light-headed. My heart raced, then slowed. I thought I was going to die. But Mister Death didn't come. Shame on him.

I felt sorrow that Annie never met Mam, never saw the ocean. She be buried in a plot under an oak, well beyond my garden. I didn't visit it. Rosetta kept it nice with polished rocks and flowers. But I didn't visit because I knew, like Mam, Annie's spirit be elsewhere and everywhere. I told Rosetta I saw Annie. Rosetta was so alarmed, she sent for the doctor. He gave me a draught. I slept for three days. Now I don't tell anyone that Annie's waiting for me.

I abided. But, finally, there came a time to be doing. Time to get up. My feet touched the floor. Time to set grief aside. Be the Mam and wife of my house. Annie would know I still carried her in the center of my heart.

I heard a great whoop. Freddy opened the door, grinning, waving a telegraph. "Lincoln's won, Anna. He's won."

"I'm right pleased, Freddy. Hand me my wrap."

"I mean to have great influence, Anna. Time's come to dismantle slavery once and for all."

"You'll do it, Freddy. If anybody can, you can. Please hand me my shawl."

"I've been dreaming of this day."

"Praise the Lord."

"Praise the Republicans who had sense enough to nominate Lincoln. Praise the men who voted."

"God had a hand in it, too." I gathered up my wrap. Freddy would be talking politics all day.

He sat beside me, put his arm about my shoulder. I thought he might kiss me.

"We're moving to Washington, Anna. I've already found our new home."

"I don't understand."

"Our new home."

"This my home."

"Cedar Hill. You'll like it, Anna. I promise you. Right in the heart of our government. I'll make headway with representatives and senators. Match my wits with them and win."

He sat beside me, squeezed me quick, then he was up again, couldn't keep still, pacing like a soldier journeying to high adventure. Never once did he think to admire and say, "Anna, you're up. You must be feeling better." All Freddy's thoughts be big: changing the world, ending slavery, talking to the president. This be good. But I wished he'd stay focused on the small. Take into account I'd raised my children in Rochester, buried one.

"It's near Baltimore. Talbot County. You can visit your Mam."

"She's dead. I told you so." He looked away, flushed.

"Yes, I'm sorry." He stooped, both hands on my knees. "You'll be nearer to the shore. Nearer those bones you've told me about."

I clasped his hands. I wasn't sure I'd the spirit to start over. I was comfortable *here*. In Rochester. Ain't perfect. But good enough. I had my house. My garden. But I didn't say any of this. With Annie dead, what did it matter where I be?

I say, "Fine, Freddy. Just fine."

He stood tall, proud as ever. A little more stout. Grayer. Still, he was Samson-man, standing, perched on the edge of his horizon.

I touched his back. Now clothed in fine wool rather than burlap. But I knew if I pressed hard enough, I'd feel the scars on his back. "Freddy." I wanted to tell him how much I admired and loved him. Wanted to say it in a way that meant something. That he'd hear. Say it lovely like his speeches.

"Freddy." I tugged his sleeve but he didn't turn. "Freddy," I say again.

"This is a fine time in history, Anna. Fine time to be colored in America. This time next year, slaves are going to be free."

My face felt hot. I wanted him to acknowledge we'd done some good together. Raised a fine family.

"In a month, Anna," he said. "Be ready to move in a month."

Words bubbled out my throat. "How big this house? Big enough for Miz Assing?" I wanted to call them back, instead I fell into a fit of coughing.

Freddy handed me a glass of water.

Twelve summers she'd visited my house like a haint.

"No," he said, surprising me. "No room for Miss Assing."

And I surprised myself by feeling almost sorry for Miz Assing. Freddy done said good-bye. Flat. Done gone. She'd a taste of my bitter medicine.

Then, he turned sharply, walked to the door, and ever so gently, closed it while whispering, "Rest, Anna. Annie would want you to rest."

I exhaled, let myself fall back upon the pillow, feeling tension lift off me like a cloud. Like Freddy said, Annie would've wanted me to rest. So I did. More contented than I'd ever felt in a good long while.

Rochester

"*Fort Sumter's been fired upon. War's here! War's here!*"

Lewis and his friends hollered like Christ had risen. My sons—
Freddy Junior, Charles, Lewis—dashed off to Washington. Didn't know
if there'd be a colored troop. But they wanted to beg enlistment.
Wanted to beg their chance to die. "Bless me, Mother"; "Give me a
kiss"; "It'll be finished by Christmas"; and they were gone. Rosetta left,
too. She planned to nurse the wounded, to "take care of Father" at
Cedar Hill until I came. She was a good girl. A good help. Freddy
insisted he'd have Lincoln's ear. "Colored dignity demands it." If he was
younger, I know he'd pick up the sword. But he was going to slay the
world with words. Bend justice to his will. "Bye," I said. "Bye." And I
didn't once let them see me cry.

Each morning, I sniffed the air, sensing blood. Mister Death going
to be busy, busy. He'd have no time for me. "Make time," I prayed, "if
it'll save Freddy's life. Save the lives of my children." But Death didn't
answer; so, I sang songs to the bones. Spoke prayers to God. Sunup.
Midday. Twilight.

I rambled about the house and fields. Everyone was gone. And I
was glad. *Sometimes I saw Annie drawing quick, bright pictures of the gar-*
den. Or Mam poking about the kitchen. I nodded, Mam nodded back. Annie
always waved with a wide smile.

I went about my business, glad I didn't have to explain myself,
muster the strength to be polite. I could be me. Alone with my
thoughts and feelings. Alone with my ghosts.

Alone, pretending America was at peace. My children, visiting friends. My husband, giving a speech.

Some days, seemed like nothing in the world mattered. Other days, everything mattered. One minute, I felt cheery. Next, I was crying. Everything, a sign.

Outside my kitchen window, a baby crow fell from its nest. It didn't die. Just lay in the dirt 'til I picked it up. Though I held it warm by the fire, fed it worms, it still died. A calico showed up on my doorstep, looking for all the world like Lena. I cooed, "Kitty, kitty." She stayed for two days, warming my feet at night in bed. Then, she just sauntered away. And yesterday, I saw a man slip in the market and I felt like I'd caused it. Like I'd pushed him with my two hands when I knew I hadn't.

I studied myself in the mirror, wearing black, which didn't flatter me. But Annie's death was still raw. Seeing the old woman in the mirror made me wonder, "Where's Lil' Bit? Where'd she go?" A blink of time. My young world gone.

I cleaned the house from top to bottom. Whoever bought it, I wanted them to know, colored folks had pride. I scrubbed and scrubbed even though my hands and back ached. I cleaned out the pantry, collected the children's toys, books and gave them to the church. I dried flowers and herbs from my garden. I took those dried plants and scented me and Freddy's bedroom with them. Sprinkled dried roses on the bed. Rosemary in the drawers. Jonquils on the window ledge. It'd been a long time since I'd been held. A long time of me laying in bed, longing for a touch.

I hadn't forgotten what loving once meant between me and Freddie. What loving meant for my body, my heart.

I said my prayers into my pillow and cried for my old, shriveled-up body. Stark as midnight, I realized nobody was ever going to touch me no more. I be a woman with a woman's feelings. Freddy showed me the way, but it was me who did the feeling. Me who allowed passion to claim my body. Like drowning.

Something I never admitted before—I was born for loving. How else explain why I let Freddy take me before marriage? Take me all those years even when I knew about his unfaithfulness? Over fifty now and I know the passion still be inside me. My body.

I was meant for loving and Freddy never enjoyed all I had to give.

I never betrayed Freddy. He betrayed me.

Freddy was the man to make my love blossom. He just never had the time. Instead of feeling sorry, I felt peaceful. Like I finally knew who I be. Freddy sacrificed more than he knew. Freddy who knew so much, who could debate, read all the pages in a book, didn't know me. Didn't know I be an ocean.

I heard a carriage pull up in front of the house. My heart raced, thinking maybe Rosetta came to support her old Mam. Or maybe, just maybe, it be Freddy coming to tell me I didn't need to leave for Cedar Hill. *Love be true.*

I breathed deep, smoothed my dress and hair. Morning sun made diamonds on the floor. I pressed a kiss to my wedding ring. "Freddy," I murmured.

But opening the front door, I didn't see the sweet brown of my husband. Saw instead Miz Assing, all white and shiny like a silk handkerchief freshly laundered and starched.

I folded myself up, wrapped my heart in lamb's wool and nearly cried.

Miz Assing had aged. Wrinkles were on her face just like mine. My hair had streaked white; her blond tresses had turned to silver. Funny, Freddy looked younger than us both. I hoped Miz Assing dried up like a prune. But she'd be a golden one. I couldn't deny that she was beautiful.

But I was beautiful, too. Just different. I remembered Pa saying, "Dark coffee be best." Mam saying, "Your inside-self be your glory."

Seeing Miz Assing made my stomach sick. Made me think Freddy done sent her to say good-bye. Did he lie? Was their room for her and not for me at Cedar Hill? I almost wailed.

I watched her eyes. She didn't flinch. For the first time, she and I be alone. Nobody else around, in my house. I could say and do whatever I pleased.

"Good morning, Anna," she said boldly. Her voice less harsh.

"Morning," I said, keeping my manners. No sense forsaking pride.

"You've been ill."

I stepped back. A colored woman would've been more polite, said I looked well even if it weren't true.

"May I speak with Douglass?"

My hand slapped the porch rail. "Freddy ain't here. He's speaking with President Lincoln. Making big plans."

"He is? Yes, of course, he is." There was no sass in her voice. Something else—a longing? Sorrow maybe?

"You've been ill. May I come in, Anna? Fix you tea?"

"I can get it." And I did. Turned around and walked through the front door. I could hear the soft patter of Miz Assing's slippers on the floor. My knees and knuckles ached. I'd wanted to take the tea to my bedroom, lay down and rest. But I didn't want Miz Assing to think she'd run me out of my own kitchen. Didn't want her to think I was afraid of her.

"Sugar?" Miz Assing took some and I was surprised. Thought she'd drink it strong. Black.

I sat and stared at Miz Assing's blue-vein hands, holding my best china cup. You could easily prick her vein, make her bleed. She sipped from the cup; on the rim, was pink. I was shocked. No man to lure here. But then she'd expected to find Freddy.

"Humpf." I shifted in my seat, glad to see Miz Assing's hands trembling.

We sat across from each other at my kitchen table. But we weren't facing each other. Not really. We were looking at my garden. Looking at the ball of sun, high up from the horizon. A bright, brand-new day. Looking at the birds perched on a tree. Looking everywhere 'cept in each other's eyes.

"You waiting for me to die?"

"No, Anna. I'm not. I wouldn't dream of such a thing."

"You telling me, if I was dead, you wouldn't marry him?" I glanced sideways, Miz Assing's mouth was buried in her lace collar. "Don't matter what I feel, then?"

"No, it does. But I can't help what I feel."

I wanted to smack her. Hit her across her mouth, breasts, and face.

"People ain't animals. You never learned anything that wasn't in books."

"What other learning is there?"

Her blue eyes stared straight into mine, something twisted inside me. I could tell she was ignorant. Ignorant, like Miz Baldwin, of a colored woman's feelings. But unlike Miz Baldwin, she was sincere. She really wanted to know.

"Passion. I think you've learned that."

"Yes."

I acted like I didn't hear. "Sharing Freddy's bed ain't in books. For a while, you climbed in the bed right with us. But I pushed you out. Each time I tried to love as best I knew how. Tried to take what I needed. Tried to give what I could. You understand?"

"Yes. I did the same. But Douglass, Anna, I mean Freddy—"

"—don't call him that."

"I'm sorry. But Douglass is a free man. Even as a slave, his heart was his own."

"Little things."

"What?"

"I was thinking of my Mam. She taught me love was 'little things.' Not big words or books of poetry but fresh-baked bread, a hand on your back. A kind word. A good laugh.

"Taught me the earth brimmed with learning. Soil that healed, nurtured food and flowers. But it was the sea, said my Mam, that brimmed with the spirit-bones, lost souls who never had a chance at life or love."

"Oluwand," Miz Assing whispered like a breeze.

I didn't answer. *I was seeing Mam sitting in my garden, snapping green beans for supper. Crabs, swimming in a bucket, were beside her.* "Lost souls living in the ocean's cold bottom. Lost souls who gloried in colored people living their lives full and complete."

"Lost souls who gloried in *all* people? Do you think, Anna? Lost souls who gloried in all people living their lives full and complete?"

"You've seen the bones?"

"Maybe. I don't know. I saw Oluwand, a slave girl, drown herself. It's been a long, long time since I've seen her. She used to haunt me. No, that's not quite right. She used to live, be with me, appearing at

the oddest times. I haven't seen her in a long while. Not since I left
Rosetta at school. Strange, sometimes I saw Oluwand and you."

"What you think she wanted?"

Miz Assing didn't answer. She went to the window, pressed her
hands and brow against the pane. Like she was looking for something,
yet trapped behind strong glass.

"See," I said. "All this time, you never learned."

"My mother tried to teach me things beyond books. Tried to
explain that mutual love was the highest love. Divine."

"Does Freddy love you?"

Miz Assing paled and her hands trembled like they'd a will of their
own.

"You don't know, do you?"

She shook her head.

I laughed. I didn't mean to but I did, loud and clear. Insulted, poor
Miz Assing who brushed past me, eager to go.

"Please." I caught her hand. "I'm not laughing at you. But at the
two of us."

"I don't understand."

"Sit down." I leaned forward, poured more tea like it was the most
normal thing in the world. "I never knew if Freddy loved me, either. He
never said, never did little things. Not truly. Not from his heart. Maybe
he felt he had to marry me. But didn't really want to. You, he wanted.
That's what hurt. I thought he choose you over me. I thought he must
love you, but now I see Freddy never really learned to love."

"Oh," she breathed. Miz Assing. German woman. Smart. Unloved.

She bobbed her head down like a baby bird. "I haven't heard from
Douglass in over a year. My letters are returned." She started weeping.
No sound. Tears just welled and fell. Slid down her face. She didn't
bother to wipe them away. Didn't seem to mind I was seeing them.

"Poor Miz Assing."

"Ottilie, please."

I said as gently as I could: "But we ain't friends."

"No," she said, mournful, "and never will be."

Miz Assing, with all her book-learning, was worse off than me. I was
free. She be chained by love. Locked in a jail, not knowing whether
Freddy'd ever let her out. Worse, she came to America to free the slaves

and became herself enslaved. By a great man. The great abolitionist. But he just a man. Mam and Pa had taught me when to lay it all down, let it go. Time came to walk on. To turn heartache into strength.

Miz Assing be hanging on to the bitter end. Hanging on until my death. Hanging on for Freddy to prove his love with marriage.

"Drink your tea," I said. "Forget Freddy."

For a long while, we sat in silence. The sun rose higher and higher, showering us with light, rainbows on the floor. Of all the rooms, the kitchen soothed me best. Even when clouds graced the sky, light still poured in. Light to cook by, think by. Light to make my garden grow.

"I'm sorry Annie died."

"Thank you." But she ain't gone. *Maybe tonight, Annie will come running up the stairs and sit in the rocker by my bed. She'll sit beside me all night while I sleep.*

"I must go now."

Miz Assing stood, face pinched tight, lips dry, her dignity cloaked about her. "Look, Anna. Do you see her?" She moved quick, opening the screen door. Her mouth open, shaped into an O. She stood riveted like a wood plank on the porch. "Do you see her?"

A young black woman, smiling, was standing beside my Mam. "Bones-woman," I sighed.

Miz Assing hesitated. "Anna, do you know what she wants?"

"She telling you to get on with it. Live your life. Find happiness where and while you can."

"You think so?"

I smiled. "I know so. Mam don't keep company with just anybody."

"Thank you."

"Good luck to you," I said. And I meant it.

On the other side of the screen door, she paused. "I'm glad Freddy wasn't here. I'm pleased to have met you, Anna."

I didn't follow. I stayed on the back porch, staring through the screen, watching her silver head bob, her white gown sway until I couldn't see her no more. I heard the front door open, then shut. She was leaving the house where she'd spent over a dozen summers. Her home, too, in a way. I wondered after she climbed into the carriage whether she looked back. Or forward. I heard the the "hi-yah" of the driver. Imagined the horses' hooves kicking up dust.

• • •

I turned back to my garden. Mam was beckoning me down from the porch. All day, we worked, side by side, weeding, harvesting the tenderest greens. The sweetest peas. The bones-woman, Oluwand, had the biggest smile. Sometimes she plucked plants; other times, she just swirled, her dress snapping at her ankles and knees. When twilight come, Mam shook her bucket. Blue crabs snapped, clicked, crawled atop one another. Oluwand took a stick and dug a hole. Shallow and wide. She laid twigs on it, dry grass, and clean branches. The setting sun lit the fire.

Annie would visit soon. Probably when Mam was ready to boil them crabs.

Ottilie

"*I don't believe in an afterlife.*"

—OTTILIE ASSING,
1882

"*When I die, bury me in water.*"

—ANNA DOUGLASS,
1882

August 21, 1884
Paris

*Ŧ*hough I've asked the hotel maids to build the fire, I still feel cold. As though my heart has already stopped pulsing blood. My scribbling is almost ended.

"Tell it all. Tell it true." Such was Douglass' advice.

Like Rip Van Winkle, I feel as though I'm waking from a dream. But no daughter or grandchild welcomes me. No neighbors cry, "We've missed you." Even my cat has died. Time has blurred, fallen by the wayside.

Like love . . . drifting away.

Lincoln never wished for a colored regiment. He even turned a blind eye when Union soldiers returned slaves to their owners. Oh, how he frustrated Douglass!

But I was there to bear witness to the truth. I wrote, furiously and feverishly, day and night, for *Morgenblatt:*

> *"As with the French peasantry, slaves will throw off their chains and rise up. Lincoln cannot stop a swelling tide of justice and enlightenment."*

Ottilie," Douglass said, reading my work, "You're remarkable."

I loved the sound of that word: *"remarkable."* But not remarkable enough.

His hair grew white. Distinguished. I stopped looking into the mirror. Whereas Douglass never failed to attract silly, young admirers, patience was my only armor. But it didn't end loneliness.

I embarrassed the abolitionists. Even Garrison pretended not to know me.

The suffragettes disowned me. My dislike of Julia Griffiths had lost me friends. Fine for Julia to be a whore. But my fidelity was meaningless.

Only Anna's children eased my loneliness.

An odd circumstance. Yet, not so odd considering the dozen summers I stayed in Rochester, watching them grow. My apartment became a haven for them to air complaints, to discuss war strategy, to buoy their spirits and ease the burden of being Douglass' children. There was no need for posturing or perfection in my small apartment. Freddy Junior could chew tobacco—a habit his father loathed. Lewis, always serious, dignified, could practice his magic tricks with abandon. (Oh, how he loved to make coins appear, then disappear!) And Charles Redmond, the liveliest and most mischievous, could roll back the rug and dance.

They brought guests from the most accomplished to the most lowly. They knew such distinctions mattered little to me. They honored me when they brought Lucius—a runaway slave eager to join the Union Army. One word from me, a white woman, and I could've claimed a reward.

Lucius was so quiet: "Yes, ma'am." "No, ma'am."

He had the sincerest demeanor. Faithful, trusting eyes. And I watched his expression change when he first saw Rosetta. His gaze nearly took my breath away. It was as if he'd seen heaven, paradise, utopia, all rolled into one. My heart lurched.

If William had looked at me that way—if anyone—I think I would've married him. Would've thrown off my years of waiting for Douglass.

Rosetta didn't yield at once. The girl who'd admonished herself: *"Don't embarrass Father,"* had grown to become an accomplished teacher, a graduate of Oberlin. Lucius could neither read nor write. But his loyalty and love were clear. He accepted Rosetta's instructions with the best grace: "A fork is held this way"; *"Isn't,* Lucius, not *ain't"*; "Stand tall"; "Shake

Father's hand firmly." Within a span of months, she tutored him in the fine arts: painting, literature, and especially music. "Liszt's *Consolations* were inspired by a Princess," she said. (Indeed, a German princess married to another!) She played *Consolation No. 3* while her brothers stomped and hooted for more popular, raucous tunes. Lucius never took sides. He faded into the woodwork while the Douglass siblings argued and debated.

Lewis teased, "You're henpecked." Rosetta blushed furiously. Lucius only smiled.

Later, when the boys had settled down to tea, Lucius went to Rosetta, sitting rigid on the window seat. He placed his hand on her shoulder, his thumb gently stroking, ever so gently, the slope of her neck. Exhaling, Rosetta closed her eyes.

I was transported too. A woman ages but her body still feels. Even at a distance, I could sense Lucius' passion. I could see, too, Rosetta returned his fire. A slight inclination of the body, a parting of lips. Yet everything banked down. Everything proper. It made me wonder: *Is that the secret? To be proper?*

But if I'd been proper, I would've run from Douglass. What glories I would've missed!

For months, Rosetta kept Lucius from meeting Douglass. One day, Lucius and I found ourselves alone. I'd offered to sketch him as a gift for Rosetta. He posed quietly, as still as a statue. Light draining, shadows deepening beneath his eyes, he spoke unexpectedly, "Rosetta has her mother's strength."

I didn't know what to say. "Tea, Lucius?"

His face grew plain and dull again. "That be fine, ma'am." And without quite understanding why, I felt irritable. Felt I failed him as well as myself.

When Lincoln approved the colored regiments, I planned a grand cele-bration. Rosetta asked if Lucius could come: "He's got false freedom papers. He'll enlist."

How could I not have said, "Yes"?

Douglass grunted, said nary a word through the soup serving, the roasted lamb, the creamed rice. Even my meringue pie couldn't tempt his manners. Never mind that I'd spent a month's income. Hired a cook. Scoured the city for the freshest food.

Freddy Junior, Lewis, and Charles Redmond spoke of mauling and killing as though such gore was proper table talk. Rosetta was on the verge of tears.

For Douglass, it'd been a night of revelation. Over dinner, he'd seen Lucius' love and Rosetta's tacit acceptance.

"I have work to do," he said, rising without a "thank you" or "good night," his napkin slipping to the floor. The boys quieted. Lucius stared at his taut hands. Rosetta rushed toward the hall.

"Not everyone can lead," I heard her protesting, "Father, please. He's a good man."

"I raised you for better than this. Better than him," he answered, struggling with his coat, not caring if he was overheard. "Ottilie, I'd appreciate it if you denied Lucius your home."

I looked at him. Such a big man squeezed into my entrance hall.

"I can't, Douglass. I've welcomed all your children's friends."

How furious he was. But he turned his ire toward Rosetta, shaking her, shouting fiercely, "I'm married to an old black log. Would you repeat my mistake?"

Rosetta stumbled back, trembling.

Douglass glared; his grief, naked, raw. The hallway narrowed, depleting air. Intensifying heat. I murmured, "As you well know, Douglass, not all passions can be controlled."

He stepped close, examining my face as if I were a stranger. Some odd creature he'd encountered. "We're at war, Ottilie. Fighting for racial uplift. Not degradation."

"Class prejudice. How bourgeois, Douglass." I thought perhaps he might strike me.

"For the love I bear you, Douglass, remember life's poetry."

"For the friendship I bear you, I'll overlook your interference with my children." Then, he was gone. Shutting the door on two women who'd displeased him.

Rosetta turned, her face as solemn as I'd ever seen her. "Shall we return to your guests, Miss Assing?"

"Indeed, my dear," I said. "Indeed."

We shooed the men into the parlor. Whiskey and a game of whist should lift their spirits.

Clearing the dishes, discarding the cold food, the spilled wine, I asked: "What does Anna say?"

"Mam says, 'Follow your heart.'"

Then Rosetta gripped my hands like she was eight again and I'd something meaningful to teach her. "What do *you* say?" she asked, intent. "Do you agree with Father?"

I stroked her cheek. "I agree with your mother."

We worked silently, then Douglass' sons burst in, wanting to attend another party. One far less respectable, I sensed. "Farewell, farewell," voices chimed and I hoped the boys would survive the war safe, sound in body and mind.

"I'll see you home, Miz Rosetta."

"Meet me downstairs, Lucius. I'll follow shortly." He left with no complaint.

I waited. Rosetta was truly lovely. As brown as caramel, as strong as steel.

Her voice was bitter. "I'm beyond the age of consent. Father doesn't realize no one has asked me to marry. Either they're afraid of him or afraid of my intelligence and education. Father expects the world to be color-blind and it isn't."

"I understand. I do." And when she left, I poured a large glass of port. Wrapped myself in my furs and tried to warm myself before the fire.

"Life isn't poetry, Ottilie."

At least I didn't go mad like Mary Todd.

Mid-July, 1883, Rosetta wrote that Anna had had a paralyzing stroke. Rosetta had nursed Anna, aided by Douglass and the three sons. On August 4, 1882, with her family gathered around, Anna died.

Why hadn't Douglass written to me?

Every fiber in my being urged me to rush to his side. With Anna gone, there would be no barrier between us. I thought it best, however, to continue my travels for a time. As with Annie's death, I knew Douglass would feel guilt. Knew for a time he would mourn and wish fiercely he could undo our illicit love.

I wrote Douglass, telling him he'd need only ask and I'd fly to his side. Then I waited. Firm in the belief that love would conquer all.

I traveled to Germany to settle my sister's estate. Only to discover Ludmilla had disinherited me. Her diaries were filled with malice. Shaken, I thought to depart at once. But the police forestalled me. I was taken to headquarters and humiliated. To them, I was only a Jew. A supporter of Socialist Democrats. They tried to make me small—I, Ottilie Assing, beloved of Frederick Douglass, writer, artist. I, who had crossed all boundaries of nationality, race, class, religion!

Perhaps it was too insensitive to have me arrive in America. So I wrote:

"Douglass. Please come. Meet me in the City of Light."

I didn't know then he'd hired Helen Pitts, a young woman, twenty years younger than I. A woman as white as porcelain; vibrant, fair-haired like Rapunzel; her lips, the color of Red Rose.

Douglass answered with a poem:

The Meeting of Two Friends after Long Separation

> Of trusted and truest friends,
> With pulses responsively beating
> > To noblest aims and ends.
> Could they live in light of each other,
> All trouble would pass as a dream.
> More they, than sister or brother
> > In friendship, love and esteem.
> Hard fate has decreed separation
> As fate has decreed such before
> But the sacred cords of affection
> > Are bonds that live evermore.

I thought surely this was my sign.

But still he didn't come. I wandered Europe like a vagabond. Venice with its canals charmed me. The Alps uplifted me for a time. I crossed into southern France, toured vineyards, studied the art of perspective, of recording impressions rather than reality. I painted Douglass, his skin infused with sunlight, moonlight, breaking into infinite shades.

I thought Douglass couldn't leave his grieving children. He'd send for me.

In Paris, a malaise stole over me. I'd difficulty keeping food down. Trouble sleeping. I'd wake, drenched in sweat. Twisted in sheets I'd mistaken for Douglass' arms.

In Paris, my cycle stopped. I felt pains in my chest. A constant upset in my abdomen. I thought the miracle had happened. A child. My breasts were hardening with milk. My womb was expanding.

I went to Paris's best physician. I felt amazingly excited, shy to have a man, other than Douglass, touch me so intimately.

"Mademoiselle, vous êtes trop âgée."

You are too old.

Old. Without a home. Family. A disbeliever in both my father's and mother's gods.

Spring, the cafés set tables outside. On Sundays, I took hot chocolate and a croissant at Rue de Mer and lingered for hours over the *New York Times.* The issues were always months old, since they made slow progress across the ocean and the social rounds of Americans living in Paris. I was always the last to receive them. Coffee spilled on them, wrinkled, ink-smudged, I didn't mind. Reading the papers connected me to my spiritual home. America—the land of dreams.

And there I saw:

24 JANUARY 1884

FREDERICK BAILEY DOUGLASS MARRIES HELEN PITTS. REVEREND FRANCIS GRIMKE OFFICIATES AT FIFTEENTH STREET PRESBYTERIAN CHURCH.

Douglass, two months married! And I'd heard nothing. No letter. No word from Rosetta.

Anna dead only eighteen months! To marry a woman he'd known for only a year.

"Mad'moiselle, Mad'moiselle." The waiter ran after me, carrying the papers.

"Non, non," I cried, hurrying to my hotel.

Breathless, I rushed upstairs to my room, to my desk. I wrote: *How could you?*

Then, the pains in my body returned.

I lay in bed and dreamt of Oluwand. Or was I awake?

Pitch-black night. A leg thrown over the rail. Her gaze pierced my soul. Do not pity me, her look said. She spoke her name, "Oluwand."

"Ottilie," I answered.

She threw her hands wide and graceful as a swooping seagull, fell backward, letting herself fall and fall and fall.

I woke up, shivering. My heart frozen.

I remembered Anna laughing. "I don't know if Freddy loved me, either." How could she have laughed? Yet, I remembered admiring her. She had gotten on with her life. Oluwand semed more romantic. If love was denied, what price living? Wasn't that what mother and father taught me?

I rang the bell service and asked for champagne.

Rootless. Homeless. Childless.

Still, I'd accomplished a great deal. Lived my American dream.

From my desk, I pulled an issue of *Douglass' Monthly*. Douglass had sent it to me years ago, a sign that our work was well done. My sacrifice hadn't been in vain:

PRESIDENT LINCOLN SIGNS EMANCIPATION PROCLAMATION

THE 13TH AMENDMENT WAS RATIFIED, DECEMBER 18, 1865.
SECTION 1. NEITHER SLAVERY NOR INVOLUNTARY SERVITUDE,
EXCEPT AS A PUNISHMENT FOR CRIME WHEREOF THE PARTY
SHALL HAVE BEEN DULY CONVICTED, SHALL EXIST WITHIN THE
UNITED STATES, OR ANY PLACE SUBJECT TO THEIR
JURISDICTION.

These words were precious to me. Few would know my heroism. My part in America's salvation. But I knew. Douglass knew.

Still, not to write, Douglass must pity me. For twenty years, the slaves had been freed. I'd fulfilled my näive boast to Jean Baptiste. While I longed to know, "Douglass, did you ever love me?"

I was a physician's daughter.

The vial was wrapped in a piece of satin, hidden in the secret drawer of my jewelry box. I'd had few precious gems. Those I'd had, I'd sold.

I couldn't remember buying the vial. Was it a year ago? Two? After my conversation with Anna? I didn't remember. Seems like it had always been deep within the box. Within my mind.

When the champagne bottle was empty, I pulled the bellrope and waited for the maid. "A bath, please."

It took almost an hour for her to heat the water, pour it in, bucket by bucket, into the claw-footed tub. As she worked, I finished my story.

Perhaps I would've been better off if I'd never met Douglass. But love knows no order, no sense of appropriateness. I mustn't regret.

I swallowed the poison. No false sleep like Juliet's. I was following Oluwand's lead. Papa's too.

Anna was wrong. For Oluwand, death, not life, was the more heroic choice.

The cobblestone streets glowed purple. Day was done. Notre Dame's spirals pierced the clouds. The River Seine flowed sluggishly.

Au revoir, Douglass, mon amour. I leave my estate to you. My letters and diaries to Rosetta.

I shed my clothes. Stepped one foot into the bath. Steam rose. I wondered if I'd melt? I immersed myself. No ghosts. No phantoms. No Douglass. No one in the room but me.

I blew bubbles and waited and waited and waited until I sank.

Author's Note

*F*rederick Douglass transformed himself from a runaway slave into an abolitionist and author, becoming one of the most famous men—certainly the most famous black man—of his century.

I had long admired Douglass' writings but, one day, I stumbled upon two quotes attributed to him: "I am married to an old black log," and "My first wife was the color of my mother, my second wife was the color of my father."

I'd never known Douglass had two wives: one black, one white. I felt great umbrage that he would refer to his first wife as a "black log." It also seemed odd for a man in love to categorize his wives only by race. My interest was piqued.

While Douglass' private and public life were often at odds, he did believe that an ideal world was "color-blind," and he tried to live his life accordingly. Without question, Douglass was an extraordinary man. But as in the case of all men (and women), Douglass was human, embodying complexities and contradictions of mind, personality, and the human heart.

My intent as an artist was not to diminish Douglass but, rather, to "lift the veil," to "reimagine" the emotional truth of two women loving Douglass in an era of sweeping social change.

What would it have felt like emotionally, psychologically, and spiritually to love, support, and cherish such a great man? What were the costs? The pleasures? The pains? Why does a lover continue to love, continue to "hold on," despite years of heartache and infidelity?

In this novel, I tried to convey the emotional truth of two brave women who lived vastly different lives. While inspired by history, the women's characters were spun in my imagination.

Anna, in her domesticity and in her refusal to read, was possibly trying to make Douglass and her world recognize that societies are built upon many people's differing strengths.

It is also questionable whether Douglass would've made it to freedom without Anna Murray's help. It is certainly true that she kept house and home while Douglass traveled extensively.

Ottilie Assing was a surprise to me. I had expected to write about Helen Pitts, Douglass' second wife. Yet Ottilie appeared, brash and bold, with steadfast loyalty to abolition and to Douglass.

Ottilie Assing did indeed commit suicide and leave her estate to Douglass. I consider it a tragedy that she could never merge love and intellectualism into a healthy union.

This is true: Frederick Douglass had a huge burial ceremony for Anna. Her casket was strewn with flowers, pulled in a wagon by white-plumed, black horses. She was lowered six feet into the ground.

In my fictional world, I dream Anna was buried in water.

For those interested in more history, I'd suggest the following wonderful sources: *Frederick Douglass* by William S. McFeely (W. W. Norton, 1991), *Love Across Color Lines* by Maria Diedrich (Hill and Wang, 1999), and *The Oxford Frederick Douglass Reader,* edited by William L. Andrews (Oxford University Press, 1996). There are numerous editions of Douglass' major writings: *Narrative of the Life of Frederick Douglass, an American Slave, Written by Himself; My Bondage and My Freedom;* and *Life and Times of Frederick Douglass.*

The PBS Video, "When the Lion Wrote History," is excellent.

Citations

For background, insight, and inspiration on Frederick Douglass' life, relationships, and speeches, I drew upon several key sources: *Narrative of the Life of Frederick Douglass, an American Slave*, edited by Houston A. Baker, Jr. (Penguin American Library, 1982); *Life and Times of Frederick Douglass*, edited by Rayford Logan (Crowell-Collier Publishing, 1962); *My Bondage and My Freedom*, edited by William Andrews (University of Illinois Press, 1987); *The Oxford Frederick Douglass Reader*, edited by William Andrews (Oxford University Press, 1996); *Frederick Douglass* by William S. McFeely (W. W. Norton, 1991); and *Love Across Color Lines* by Maria Diedrich (Hill and Wang, 1999).

While my story is fictional, there are lines that can be attributed to the actual historical figures:

Page 85: Ottilie's mother, Rosa Maria, did indeed write the poetry attributed to her. (See Diedrich's book, *Love Across Color Lines*, p. 38.)

Page 99: The italicized paragraphs about Mr. Gore's murder of Demby are excerpted from *Narrative of the Life of Frederick Douglass* (Penguin American Library edition cited above, p. 67).

Page 150: The stanza from "A Parody" was written by Douglass. The poem appears in *Narrative of the Life of Frederick Douglass* (Penguin American Library, p. 157).

Page 150: The italicized lines are from Christopher Marlowe's poem "The Passionate Shepherd to His Love."

Page 180: This speech is an excerpt from Douglass' "Letter to His Old Master." *The Oxford Frederick Douglass Reader* (Oxford edition cited above, pp. 103–104).

Pages 285–88: The italicized passages are excerpts from *Life and Times of Frederick Douglass* (Crowell-Collier edition cited above, pp. 466–74).

Page 302: Douglass did send this brief invitation to John Brown. (See McFeely's *Frederick Douglass*, p. 198.)

Page 350: The stanzas are from Douglass' poem, "The Meeting of Two Friends after Long Separation." (See Diedrich's book *Love Across Color Lines*, p. 360.)